As always, for Keira

I would like to acknowledge the following for their assistance, help, inspiration, and patience during the writing of The Reluctant Jesus: Robert Peel, Gissell and Ashley Pozna, Keira Whitehead, and LJ Anderson.

© 2014 Duncan Whitehead
All Rights Reserved.

No part of this publication may be reproduced, stored in a retrieval system, or transmitted, in any form or by any means, electronic, mechanical, photocopying, recording, or otherwise, without the written permission of the author.

First published by Dog Ear Publishing
4010 W. 86th Street, Ste H
Indianapolis, IN 46268
www.dogearpublishing.net

ISBN: 978-1-4575-2704-3

This book is printed on acid-free paper.

This book is a work of fiction. Places, events, and situations in this book are purely fictional and any resemblance to actual persons, living or dead, is coincidental.

Printed in the United States of America

THE RELUCTANT JESUS

by
Duncan Whitehead

CHAPTER 1

I FEEL IT IS IMPORTANT, just to make sure that there are no misunderstandings, especially at this initial stage of our acquaintanceship that I point out that I was, and still am, an ordinary guy. I blend into a crowd; I am one of life's extras, never destined to be a major protagonist in any scene, drama, or act. You see people like me every day, but you do not notice. I was just, well, to put it bluntly, there. If I ever committed a crime, which, to the best of my knowledge, I never have, and a witness was requested to describe me, I am sure the word boring would be used, probably more than once.

I do not ever recall doing anything that could be described as remarkable. I kept to myself, and not only did I like it that way, but I am sure that others did also. I went about and minded my own business; I went through the motions of a boring and uncomplicated life: I came, and I went, I worked as hard as the next man, but I did not over assert myself. I got along just fine. My ambitions were healthy and realistic, and I knew my limitations. To my recollection, I had never performed any act of bravery, kindness, or selflessness that would stand me out from any other rational human being, nor, by the same notion, had I ever performed any act of cowardice, unkindness, or selfishness. I was not overly generous, but I was by no stretch of the imagination mean. I always tipped the required fifteen percent in restaurants and bars and on occasion had been known to go as high as twenty, for the exceptional waiter, server, or bartender. I had in the past donated to charity, and I am sure clothing I once wore is now clad upon a deserving recipient delegated by the Salvation Army; however I have not given to beggars on the sidewalk, nor do I tip for fast food.

According to friends I was a stereotypical confirmed bachelor with no emotional responsibilities or ties. I did not have any other human being reliant on my income, my goodwill, my moods, the contents of my fridge, my apartment, or my television remote control. I was able to come and go as I pleased. No one questioned me, and in turn, I did not question others. I lived and let lived and considered myself a free spirit. I had no sexual hang-ups, and the stack of Playboy and Hustler magazines under my bed, not really hidden, were a clear indication that I insisted that my partners always be of the female variety.

I worked for money, and that money provided me with an apartment in New York City and all the trappings of a bachelor life that revolved around my love of sports—primarily baseball and the New York Yankees—TV, drinking beer, and enjoying myself. I shared my one-bedroom, but extremely desirable and comfortable apartment in Greenwich Village, Manhattan, with a house-trained and totally undemanding ginger tomcat named Walter, who used the litter box provided, shed minimal hair, and was an extremely good companion as he never said a word. Walter, who let me come and go when I pleased, was, I am told, probably the most low-maintenance feline known to man.

My name is Seth Miller, and though my surname does not suggest it, I am Jewish by birth though I cannot recall the last time I attended temple. When it came to religion, I could take it or leave it, so I left it. I enjoyed my rather unremarkable but happy and contented life. I did not consider that life was passing me by, but that I was merely pacing myself, and if I equated my life as it was to a marathon, then I was comfortable in the pack, with my eye on the pacemaker, but do not fear, if you are betting on me, for I am not letting the pacemaker out of my sight, and when the time comes I will change gear and break away from the pack, but only when I am good and ready.

The New York City summer of 1999 was not an unusually hot one. However, that particular Wednesday seemed hotter than usual. The Manhattan Streets were flooded with secretaries and

THE RELUCTANT JESUS

(female) office workers in short skirts and skimpy tops which contained less cotton than a Tylenol bottle. Delivery men and couriers were wearing shorts and T-shirts; the street vendors were selling ice-cold cans of Coke and Pepsi by the dozen. All welcomed the cool breezes that emitted from shop doorways, office blocks, and apartment complexes as air conditioning met nature. It was indeed a hot day—the day Mother called and changed my life forever.

I had a breakfast meeting with Henry Peel, my boss and senior partner of the well-respected construction firm that I worked for in my capacity as senior architect in residence. My field of expertise was office blocks, those towering skyscrapers you see that complete the panoramic view of every major city in the world. I designed them, drew up the proposed plans, and located and researched potential sites. It was a responsible and highly-paid career that I enjoyed, mainly because I was good at it, and it provided me with little stress. I had arranged to meet with Henry to discuss a potential contract and proposals by a Japanese consortium that wanted to create office space on the Upper East Side. I was excited and very happy to be alive. I loved to start new projects, and this was going to be an exciting and adventurous structure which would not only help my own reputation but also the firm's.

That Wednesday I rose earlier than normal; I allowed Walter to sit on my lap for a few minutes, or was it Walter who allowed me to have the pleasure of him sitting on my lap? I never knew with Walter. I fixed some coffee and drank it, maybe a little too quickly, before grabbing my briefcase.

Harvey, my apartment building's doorman with whom I had a unique relationship (more of Harvey later), hailed me a cab, and if I recall correctly I arrived promptly at The Barking Dog Diner on 3rd Avenue for my breakfast meeting with Henry and the Japanese consortium's representative, Mr. Hyomoko, who had flown in from Tokyo the previous evening. That meeting, I am pleased to say, was successful, and hands were shaken and a deal proposed. I felt I had ascertained a good idea of what was required, and I agreed to meet Mr. Hyomoko later that week at the proposed site, which his consortium had recently purchased, in close proximity to the Guggenheim Museum on East 87th and 5th. Once we had eaten breakfast Mr. Hyomoko left to relay the details of our meeting to whomever he had to report to, leaving Henry and I to grab another coffee, congratulate ourselves on a deal well done, and to stroll leisurely back to the offices of Peel and Associates situated on 93rd and Lexington, a ten-minute walk from the diner.

Henry and I arrived at the office at eleven or thereabouts. I answered a few e-mails; I drank coffee; I chitchatted with some of my co-workers about nothing in particular. There was a general feeling of excitement in the office that morning as news of the deal secured by Henry and I had already filtered back to my colleagues, which meant the mood was good. I wasn't too busy, so I decided that I might as well begin work on what was now known as 'Project Hyomoko.'

I called Bob Nancy, my best friend, whom you will meet later, to tell him about the lucrative contract I secured that morning and to invite him for a celebratory drinking session on Friday night. Life was easy, simple, and good, and I had the perfect life, of course, that was before Mother called......

CHAPTER

2

"SETH, I HAVE YOUR MOTHER on line one," announced the voice of the firm's receptionist, Jennifer, who, as my mind was on the subject, would have been an ideal candidate for my next sexual encounter. She was definitely my type, but then again, they were all my type.

"Thank you, please put her through, Jennifer," I instructed. Usually I flirted with Jennifer; in fact, I flirted with every unmarried woman in the office, but it did not seem appropriate to flirt while Mother waited on the other end of the line. God forbid she ever heard me flirting!

"Hello, Mother, how are you?" I inquired once I heard the click indicating Jennifer had put Mother's call through to my phone.

"Hello, dear, is this a good time? I hope I am not disturbing you." Mother always said that. It did not matter whether she was disturbing me or not; the fact of the matter was that even if she were, she would not have cared. If I was a stereotypical bachelor, then she was the stereotypical Jewish mother, and as an only child to a Jewish mother, living the lifestyle I had, you can imagine I had to make allowances when dealing with her.

"No, Mother, I am not that busy. How's Dad? How are you? Is everything ok?" Looking back, my reply was totally false. The call would definitely disturb me, and I was busy. In retrospect, I should not have said that. I should have told Mother I was extremely busy and that she should not call me at the office anymore, but I craved a quiet life, and for a quiet life, I had to sometimes tell a little white lie or three to my mother.

"Yes, dear, everything is fine," she replied, and that was the second lie of the conversation, because everything was not fine. Not by any long stretch of anyone's overactive imagination was everything fine. Without any exaggeration, this one call from my mother was the catalyst that would change my life forever. Yes sir. This was *the call*, and everything was certainly not "fine!"

Before *the call*, I have to say I had a strained relationship with my parents, Ely and Irma Miller of Borough Park, Brooklyn, New York. Since the call and as time has passed, we have become closer, but that day, that Wednesday in June now fourteen years ago, it certainly redefined our relationship and how I viewed both of them. My parents have been described by other relatives and friends of the family as, amongst other things, slightly "quirky." Slightly "quirky" is a good descriptive, because they certainly are not your typical parents. "Strange" would be a better analysis of their personalities, but they were my parents, and to me, they were just Mom and Dad. I never referred to Mother as Mom to her face; she was always Mother.

My dad, Ely Miller, was born and raised in Brooklyn, the younger of two sons born to immigrant parents who fled Ireland after Hitler took power in Germany. Why my grandparents fled a neutral country still remains a family mystery. What isn't a mystery, however, is that my dad was a great car mechanic. He ran a neighborhood garage, which became mildly successful, and though he did not have an academic or great business brain, with the help of Mother, they grew the venture into one of the most successful car repair facilities in Borough Park, eventually employing six mechanics and office staff.

My dad was an amiable old guy who people always liked. I remember as a kid he would take me to play softball; it seemed as if he knew everybody on the way to the park and everybody when we arrived. Dad was popular with the other kids' dads, and he would always be greeted with a warm handshake and a smile. Like me, Dad was a Yankee's fan, and he and his brother, my uncle Jacob, would take me to games at Yankee Stadium when I was boy. Those trips to the Bronx are among my favorite memories of my childhood.

Nowadays, Dad was known as "Mr. Pipe and Cardigan" due to the fact that he would tend the front yard dressed in his cardigan, wearing his house slippers, and smoking his pipe. Mother had deemed their home a smoke-free zone, so the only time Dad could enjoy his pipe was in the garden. Dad was a few years older than Mother, and he did look it. Dad did not speak much, which was understandable, living with my Mother for thirty years. He followed her; by that, I mean, he was always a few steps behind her, lagging behind, or pulling up the rear, to use a military phrase. It seemed these days Dad no longer walked; instead, he seemed to shuffle. I presumed it was a combination of old age and years of living in the shadow of a strong-willed woman that had reduced my father to a shuffler; it was as if he hadn't the energy to raise his feet to walk anymore. Either that or he was extremely lazy. It wasn't that my dad was slow, though he was a little slower than the average person; it was more that my mother was quick, always in a hurry, and that was apparent whenever they went anywhere.

On the odd occasion they went out for dinner, she was usually seated and ordering her entree before my father had taken off his jacket. His slowness and her quickness defined their whole relationship, such as a few years ago when Dad traded in his old station wagon for a Lexus.

He had driven them to the dealership in Bensonhurst. It was a Sunday, and the dealership's customer parking lot was full. Poor Dad could not find anywhere to park, not even on any of the adjacent side streets, so he dropped Mother off at the entrance to the dealership and asked her to wait a few minutes while he scooted around searching for a parking space. It must have taken him not longer than ten minutes to find a suitable spot, but by the time he had locked up the car and shuffled the short distance to the dealership, Mother had not only picked out a car for him, but she had also negotiated a deal, organized the finance, arranged delivery, and was waiting on Dad to sign the papers. Thus was the basis of Dad's role in the relationship. He certainly could not be described as the mouthpiece or spokesperson of the operation. She spoke, and he did.

I have to say, though, I never once heard my father complain. He seemed to accept that Mother was Mother, and she was the boss. I guess he put up with her dominance because he loved her, though as time passed, and especially after I had left home, I could see that maybe he wasn't as happy as he could be. I felt sorry for him, and maybe seeing the state of my father was the reason I did not want a committed relationship. Maybe Mother had put me off marriage. Of course, I dared not ever say that to her. Just as my dad, where Mother was concerned, I felt it best to toe the party line and accept how she was. I kept my mouth shut.

My mother, Irma Miller (née Crystal), was a dynamic woman whom I adored and respected as much as I did my father, though she infuriated me more than anyone else on this planet. She was a larger-than-life woman. I don't mean she was a big woman, though as the years progressed she lost her swimsuit figure and had put on a few pounds, which meant she was like me: "slightly" overweight. But neither I, nor anyone with any sense, would ever tell her that to her face. That face was still attractive despite the fact that she was well into her sixties. She had always been an attractive woman with a pretty smile and big brown eyes. It was very rare as a child that I would ever see Mother not in full makeup, and even today, she will not leave the house without lipstick, blush, her hair perfectly arranged and set, and all ten fingernails manicured and polished. Even at sixty, despite her slightly expanded waistline, she could still turn heads. Mother always seemed to dress impeccably and with a hint of sexiness about her. Please don't get the wrong idea: I do not have any thought of motherly infatuation. I am merely being honest in my description of her. She was classy, and at family gatherings she would be the center of attention, women complimenting her hair, makeup, and clothes, whilst men would congratulate Dad on snaring such a fox.

Unfortunately, they did not know that beneath the surface, my mother was a strong-willed control freak who ran my father's life for him and attempted to control mine as much as she could. Behind the glitzy frontage of a pretty face, elegant clothes, and an abundance of jewelry, she was a no-nonsense woman who knew what she wanted and knew what she wanted for her family, even if we didn't know what we wanted ourselves.

When dad's business began to take off, and he grew successful, Mother stepped in and took over. Even though she had no experience, she initially took over his bookkeeping to allow him to concentrate on the mechanical side of things. Then as business grew and more staff was hired, she appointed herself managing director and ran the office—taking bookings, ordering the spare parts, and putting herself in charge, reducing my dad to nothing more than an extra mechanic.

It became so you would have never known it was Dad's business. She hijacked it from under him. The only relief for Dad came after I was born and she acquired a new focus for her controlling persona. She hired her older sister, Marla, to run things whilst she stayed at home and raised me. Mother would still issue orders, using Marla as her mouthpiece, and though she was equally as unqualified as my mother, Father accepted Marla as his new boss with carte blanche responsibility, as he was directed by Mother to deal with the hiring and firing and general running of the business. Mother didn't care what she did or said as long as it suited her and her plans. She was the boss, there was no doubt about that, and she ruled all the roosts.

Where I was concerned, though, I was the golden child, and I could do no wrong. I was her pride and joy, her little miracle, as she would call me, which thankfully subsided when I got to high school. I admit quite freely that not just Mother spoiled me as a child, though she was the main culprit and chief spoiler, but my dad, my uncle Jacob, and my aunt Marla spoiled me. Only the best was good enough for me: private tutors, trips to baseball games, toys; you name it, I got it, and I readily admit I enjoyed being number one. My bar mitzvah, as my father likes to remind me, cost him well over five thousand dollars, which, in 1980, was a lot of money. It was quite a party though.

Mother saw to that. Like everything else, she hijacked it, and to her circle of friends and cronies, Seth's bar mitzvah was remembered and referred to as "Irma's most fabulous party ever; wasn't the boy there too?" I suppose it is understandable that my parents spoiled me. All Jewish mothers love to spoil their kids, and when you are the only child and a son, well, it was inevitable. A direct result of my mother's affection to me was that I didn't have many friends growing up. Mother would vet any potential playmates, and it seemed no one was good enough. I did have my buddies from little league, though I was never allowed to bring them home. School was the same. I was a bright kid and not unpopular, but after school, friends were not permitted, so I spent my summers and weekends with Mother and Dad and on the odd occasion, my uncle Jacob.

It was always a treat to spend time with my uncle Jacob, because he doted on me. He was in the Navy, some sort of officer who dealt with the ship's radars, and I would anticipate his visits with excitement when he had shore leave. I spent a lot of time with Uncle Jacob. He looked like a movie star, and we would always get free Cokes from waitresses who would often flirt with him. I was devastated when he died a few weeks after my bar mitzvah, as were my mother and my dad. I remember hearing Mother cry for the first time at his funeral, and I still remember her sobbing for days after his funeral. When Dad was busy with the repair shop, Uncle Jacob would sometimes take me to my little league games. I recall it was a great feeling, having him and Mother cheer me from the bleachers and hugging every time I hit or caught the ball.

Another relative who spent a lot of time with me when I was a kid was Aunt Marla. She was the total opposite of her sister. Though she was blessed with the same pretty features, she did not possess the hard-nosed attitude of her younger sibling. In the same way my mother bullied my father, I suspected that my mother bullied Aunt Marla. I always got the feeling that she felt uncomfortable around Mother, and there always seemed to be an underlying tension. When I would spend time at the garage with Dad, I would inevitably end up playing with Aunt Marla. All three of us would sometimes go for Coca-Cola or even to a diner for secret lunches and ice cream sundaes. It was strange, and maybe even a little sad, that my best and fun childhood memories of my parents when I was growing up were not of them together.

When I graduated from high school with excellent grades, it was time for me to escape from Mother's smothering and flee the nest, or so I thought.

Leaving home turned out to be extremely difficult and traumatic—not for me, but for her. I was offered places at several colleges. My preference was Yale and their School of Architecture, and it was their scholarship I took.

Of course, I realize it was my private tutoring, which Mother had insisted on, that enabled me to graduate from high school top of every class and with across the board straight As, and I am grateful that, thanks to her and the extra education she pushed me to take, I was able to follow my chosen career.

To my surprise, Mother offered no resistance to me finding a college two hours and ninety miles away. I felt it was a good compromise. I could travel home on weekends, and in an emergency, Yale was in easy reach of Borough Park. I had a plan, and that plan was to return home every weekend I was able for the first month I was at college, and then gradually reduce my returning to every two weeks, until eventually, I would only return home once or twice every semester. It therefore came as a horrendous surprise—no, scratch that, a horrendous and abominable shock—when Mother announced she had rented us, meaning her and me, an apartment in downtown New Haven.

I had hoped Dad would talk her out of this ridiculous idea, but my pleading to him was to no avail, and looking back, I realized why. As long as she was with me at Yale, then she was not with him in Borough Park. It gave him peace and a break from her. In a way, he sacrificed me and my fun-filled college years so he could smoke his pipe in peace, watch sports on TV, and enjoy life without Mother, and though initially I resented Dad for it, I understood why he allowed it. I would have done exactly the same if I had been married to Irma Miller.

This horrific and sorry situation was as bad as it sounded. While other kids were able to party and enjoy their first sexual fumbling, I spent my weekday nights with Mother. Some weekends we would drive home to Father, much to his dismay; many was the time we would return on a Friday afternoon, unannounced, to catch Dad smoking his pipe in the den. I missed so much of college life. I was a laughing stock and the butt of many jokes. I never dated; I never had the chance to join a fraternity; I never experienced the joys of spring break, and once again, I found it almost impossible to make friends out of class thanks to Mother's continual insistence on being with me twenty-four hours a day, seven days a week.

Again, though, like high school, thanks to Mother's ensuring that I kept out of trouble and concentrated on studying, I did graduate with full honors and top of my course. On graduating, I was headhunted by all the big firms. When Henry Peel offered me a position with his firm the day I graduated, I jumped at the opportunity, and I have never looked back.

Fortunately, Mother also knew it was time for her to let me go. It was she who helped me find my first apartment, not the one I am in now, but a smaller place in Turtle Bay. In a way, I supposed that was why I am the man I am today. I missed so much at college that I guess I was making up for it, but with money in my pocket. My relationship with Mother had definitely put me off commitment and marriage, and her championing of me as the great prodigy was why I insisted on being so run-of-the-mill and bland. Maybe what she did for me and the way she treated me as a kid was why, as a man, I had such a great time and why I loved my life. Who would not be enjoying life after spending their first twenty-four years living in close proximity to their mother and then suddenly becoming free of her?

I kept Mother at a distance. I did occasionally visit my parents on a Sunday, but only on special occasions. When I did, she overfed me and asked the same question a million times: "When are you going to find a nice girl and settle down?" and the obligatory "When you going to make me a grandmother?" and the inevitable "Why don't you visit more, call more, and invite us into the city for lunch sometime?" Anyway, she had her space, and I had mine, and Dad plodded along, trying to keep her happy—which, I suspected, he did to a certain degree. Therefore, I tried to limit my contact with Mother to phone calls. Usually once a week was more than sufficient, so it wasn't a shock that she had called. No, it was the events after the call that shocked me.

"Hello, Mother, how are you?"

"Hello, dear, is this a good time? I hope I am not disturbing you."

"No, Mom, I am really not that busy. How's Dad? How are you? Is everything ok?"

"Yes, dear, everything is fine."

"Well, that's good to know," I replied whilst reading an incoming e-mail. "You don't usually call me at the office; are you sure everything is ok?" I inquired, trying to sound at least a little concerned, when in truth, I suspected she was calling to berate me for not calling more often.

"Well, you could call more often. It's not like it's long distance," she said in her most whiny voice. But something was different. She sounded different; kind of subdued, and I suppose a little muted.

THE RELUCTANT JESUS

"Listen, honey, I, well, I mean, we, your father and I, need to discuss something with you, something rather delicate and personal."

She often called me "honey," and I hated it. "Honey" was a term men in the sixties called their wives. I always felt there was something horrifically incestuous about Mother calling me "honey." When I was at Yale, she would sometimes go grocery shopping without me to allow me the opportunity to study quietly on my own, and on her return from the store, laden with a bag of groceries, she would yell, "Honey, I'm home!" when entering the apartment. It made me cringe just thinking about it. It was like a perverted, incestuous episode of *I Love Lucy*, her favorite show, which she always insisted I sat through and watch with her, despite the fact that I found it not the least bit amusing. She would refer to me as Ricky and call herself Lucy as she laughed aloud at the crazy antics of the Cuban bandleader and his daffy wife. Believe me, it was the closest thing to Hell I had ever encountered.

"Well, that's fine, go ahead; I am all ears," I said with the phone tucked under my chin whilst I inspected a set of plans and drawings sprawled on my desk.

"Not over the phone dear. I, I mean, we, think it would be better if you came over to the house this evening after work, and we could all sit down and discuss it. I don't like talking on the phone, you know that," replied Mother, and again her voice sounded muted almost subdued. There was something obviously not right. I could tell. Mother was never this way; she was demanding, obnoxious, loud, and brash.

I must point out that I did not know my mother did not like to talk on the phone. She seemed to be an expert at talking on the phone. Indeed, I had always considered talking on the phone was one of her hobbies, as she did it often, and her comment about not liking to talk on the phone was a veiled attempt to try and cajole me into something we both knew I wouldn't want to do. Secondly, the mere thought of traveling across the city to visit my parents that evening was out of the question. I was a man of routine, and whilst I did not wish to sound callous, I did have more important things planned, mostly revolving around an evening of watching television, probably having a quick drink at Milligan's, my local neighborhood bar, and maybe doing some late work at the office.

Anything would be better than visiting my parents' midweek. It was unheard of and quite out of the question. She continued to speak before I had chance to rebuke her.

"...and anyway, we haven't seen you in such a long while; it's been nearly two weeks, and that's too long, Seth, you know that."

I didn't.

"You don't want to spend any time with your old Mother and Father now that you live in the big city? You don't have the time for us? You know, I should be a grandmother by now, don't you? When are you going to meet a nice girl and bring her over to meet me?" Before I could even muster a response or deliver my objections, she resumed speaking "Good, then that's settled. I, I mean, we, will expect you at seven," and with that, she hung up.

I tried calling her back immediately, but she didn't answer. That was the power she had. I did not want to go to Brooklyn, and she knew it. I should have been strong enough not to show up, but I knew if I didn't, I wouldn't hear the last of it. There was also something bothering me. Whilst the ending of the conversation with the rapid-fire questions leaving no pauses for me to reply to any of them was vintage Mother, her whole demeanor seemed different. I felt compelled to go, against my better judgment, to satisfy my curiosity.

So that was *the call* that changed my whole life. Not because it was an inconvenience for me to take a cab out to Brooklyn and rearrange my evening, even though I had nothing to rearrange. Not because the last thing I wanted to do on a pleasant Wednesday evening in June was break bread and eat chicken adobo, kosher style with my parents. No, that call changed my life because of what was to occur that evening. Oh boy, *THAT* evening!

CHAPTER 3

FOR ME TO ARRIVE AT my parents' home by seven o'clock that evening would mean traveling in peak hour New York traffic. A journey which should, in any normal dimension, take about twenty minutes. However, at that time of day, it would probably take at least an hour. I suppose to some people an hour is not a long time, especially if visiting loved ones or relatives, especially elderly parents. But an hour stuck in slow-moving traffic to spend an evening with Mother was simply a disaster. I was not neurotic, as I hope I have already established, however the mere fact that she had compromised my usual weekday routine made me feel nauseas. My day was ruined.

Repeated attempts to call Mother and postpone my visit were all futile. She was not answering the phone and rather conveniently for her, the answering machine was either broken or not switched on. Therefore, I could not even leave a message explaining my feigned disappointed that something entirely bogus had come up, preventing me from making the trip. I knew she was probably sitting, watching the phone ring, well aware it was I trying to cancel or come up with an excuse as to why I could not travel the twelve miles and one hour to Brooklyn. I gave up after the eighth attempt. My concentration broken and my earlier enthusiasm for work tainted, I decided I would stop work and leave early.

Before departing my office, I checked in with Henry and handed him the costing figures I had managed to complete for Project

Hyomoko, Henry was good like that; he didn't demand that his senior architects be chained to their desks nine to five, and, as the senior and probably the best architect he had, I had a lot of leeway when it came to my working practices. Not that I took advantage of Henry's trust and flexible attitude. I worked just as hard as the rest of his employees, but I rarely over exerted myself.

A visit to my parents' warranted a change of clothing. There was no way I was going to spend the rest of the day in a tie, and there was equally no way I was prepared to sit in a cab in the heat of the day dressed that way either. I needed to return to my apartment, shower, and change into my usual attire: the far more relaxed uniform of jeans and a T-shirt.

I arrived at my apartment just before four, leaving plenty of time to change and prepare for the hour-long journey to Brooklyn. Harvey, the apartment building's doorman, greeted me in the lobby.

"The man is back in the crib," said Harvey, a wide smile spread on his face. He looked at his watch. "And the man is early." He slapped my hand, which was his usual greeting. I often messed up our greetings by moving my hand too quickly, but today I got it just right.

"I know. I've got dinner in Brooklyn," I said as I removed my tie in an attempt to look casual and to confirm, probably symbolically, that my working day was over.

"Oh shit, man," said Harvey concerned. "Your momma? Hell no!"

Harvey and I had a unique relationship. We were near enough the same age, and we had the same interests: sport, mainly baseball, though he was a Braves fan, watching women, and generally, we talked about the same things. Harvey was originally from Atlanta, and he arrived in New York around the same time I did. He took up his position in the apartment block the same day I moved in. As newcomers, we hit it off immediately, kindred spirits in our early battles with the residents association, who weren't initially too happy to have a single guy in the building. As the majority of the residents were elderly and retired, I was privileged to have secured my apartment. I suspected, though, that the arrival of Harvey coinciding with my arrival might have also played a part. I had a feeling that many of the residents in my apartment building were not too comfortable with Harvey's appearance. Unfortunately for them, they had no say in who the building's owners could hire or not hire. Not that there was anything wrong with Harvey, he just looked, well, like a rapper.

The elderly and staid members of the residents association probably wanted me to keep an eye on Harvey for them. That maybe by having me around, I could watch out for them. Being young, they probably thought I could be a friend to Harvey and maybe be their spokesperson in any dealings with him. It was possible that swayed the vote to secure my apartment. Of course, I had no evidence of this; it was my own take on the situation, especially as I rarely saw Harvey converse with any of my neighbors.

Harvey was probably the only African American some of my neighbors ever spoke to, and I suppose to them he may have looked intimidating, but the truth was that he was studying to be an actor. Harvey had never told anyone apart from me. He rented a small apartment in Harlem with his sister, and his job at the apartment building was just a stopgap, temporary, until he got the part that would catapult him to fame.

Though I had no real social dealings with Harvey, we did talk constantly whenever I was in the lobby. Admittedly, Harvey did seem to take a little too close an interest in my comings and goings, so much so that I once joked he should become my personal assistant, as he knew more about me than I did. He would pass knowing glances each time I brought home a girl, which I tried to hide from my dates. It must have been quite discerning for my dates to have a doorman wink at them knowingly and flash a gold-tooth-encrusted smile when they entered my apartment block for the first time. Of course, I never said anything to Harvey. I knew he had my best interests at heart, and I liked him. If I needed a cab, Harvey would be there at the ready with his whistle. I could put up with Harvey and his familiarity because I liked him.

"Yes, my Mother," I confirmed.

Harvey's smile seemed to cover his whole face. I often pondered how much his mouth was worth. I wasn't even sure Mother had as much gold as Harvey did in place of teeth. The man was a walking safety deposited box. I was sure if the Federal Reserve knew there was another Fort Knox walking around Manhattan, then maybe we would all get some tax relief. Gold and diamond-encrusted rings adorned every one of Harvey's fingers, and I was sure the gold chain he wore around his neck weighed half a ton.

"Man, that lady sure knows how to jack your day," laughed Harvey as he sucked his teeth. Harvey called the elevator for me and returned to his desk, chuckling and muttering to himself. I was sure dinner with my parents was not that funny, but I supposed if you spent your whole day whistling for cabs, opening and closing doors, and calling elevators, then he probably pounced upon and milked any slight deviation to the day's normal events for all it was worth. As I was probably the only resident that likely passed any sort of time of day with Harvey, I supposed my life was the highlight of his day.

Walter greeted me when I entered the apartment with a faint meow as he looked up from the chair where he snoozed. I guessed he had probably been on the same chair all day and may not have moved since I had left that morning. I threw my keys onto the coffee table and nodded at Walter, who looked away in apparent disgust, as he always did.

I took an extended and luxurious shower. One of the many benefits of living alone was that I did not have to worry about anyone else wishing to use my bathroom. I shaved, dried, and inspected my wardrobe, as I had already decided it would be a T-shirt and jeans type of evening, it didn't take long to dress. I had time to watch a bit of cable TV, so I grabbed a Bud Lite from the refrigerator and lay out on the couch in front of some syndicated sitcom. At five to six, before locking up, I attended to Walter's litter tray and ensured he had food and water. Not that he cared; the whole time I had been in the apartment he had hardly moved.

Harvey hailed me a cab after pointing out I had shaving foam behind my ear. He was indeed a great unofficial personal assistant, and I reminded myself that I would increase last year's Christmas tip. One thing about Harvey that continually impressed me was his ability to hail down a cab. In all my years of knowing Harvey, he had never failed to hail a cab for me in less than twenty seconds. It was unbelievable; even at night, it was as if he had a sixth sense. The guy was truly a cab-hailing wizard.

The cab ride to my parents was the expected hour duration. The main bottleneck of traffic materialized on the Queen's Expressway, where I had joined the throng of commuters filing out of the city and back to their Brooklyn homes. My parents' home in Borough Park was the same house I had grown up in. It was, of course, now far too big for the both of them, but they would never move, and I, for one, was not going to suggest it. One of my biggest fears was that Mother would move to the city. God forbid she ever moved into my building. So it was good in a way that they had never moved, and had no intention of doing so. I suddenly had a horrific thought. Maybe that was why they had summoned me? Maybe they were selling up and moving to the city. I pushed the thought from my mind as the cab entered their neighborhood.

The neighborhood, though not exclusive, was affluent, which was apparent by the manicured lawns, the tree lined streets, and the top-end cars parked in driveways and along the sidewalk. Borough Park was a traditionally Jewish area, and as the cab approached my parents' house, it seemed every second person I saw wore either a skullcap or a felt-rimmed hat. My father tended his lawn religiously, mainly because it was the only place he could smoke his pipe. I had to agree with Mother when she claimed they had the best lawn in the neighborhood. I instructed my driver to stop when Dad's impressive lawn came into view. I saw no "for sale" or any "sold" signs, and I breathed a sigh of temporary relief. I paid the cab, took a deep breath, and walked to the front door. With a hint of trepidation and not a little dread, I rang the doorbell.

Father opened the door, dressed in his cardigan, his unlit pipe hanging from his mouth. He greeted me with a smile, and then he did something very odd: he shook my hand. I could only recall my father shaking my hand on special occasions; one time being my bar mitzvah, another when I graduated from Yale, and the other time that sprang immediately to mind was when I secured my first job. Dad never usually shook my hand. There was something afoot. I could sense it.

Dad led me into the living room where Mother waited. She was resplendently dressed in her temple-best clothes, adorned with her jewelry, and her hair and makeup immaculate. I could see her nails had been freshly manicured and polished. I guessed she had spent the whole afternoon preparing for my visit. This confirmed my suspicions that there was definitely something not quite right.

In public and out of the house I could accept her fully made up and bejeweled appearance, but just Dad and me? Come on.

Mother grabbed my hand with both hers and kissed my cheek. I could smell wine on her breath; I had noticed my Dad had also smelled as if he had been on the sauce too. While they were by no means teetotalers, my parents rarely drank at home, and if they did, it was never during the week. I noticed Mother was definitely acting out of character. She appeared unnervingly normal. There was none of the usual repetitive questions that usually accompanied my visits and the first half of the evening went well.

We all advanced into the dining room and sat down to dinner, making general chitchat. The food was excellent. Despite her other flaws, Mother was a great cook. I decided against bringing up the "delicate and personal issue" my parents needed to discuss with me. I thought it best to leave it up to them. I suspected that maybe there was no issue to discuss anyway. It was possible it had been a ruse, a smokescreen to get me over for dinner. After homemade apple pie for dessert and more casual conversation, Dad cleared the table, and we retreated back into the living room. I took the big easy chair in the corner and Mother and Father sat facing me on the sectional sofa. I glanced at my watch. It was eight thirty. I estimated that at this time of night, it would take me no more than twenty minutes to get back into the city. I smiled at my parents. They smiled back. It was odd, both of them staring at me, smiling, holding hands. It felt like a job interview, and it became obvious they had something to say. It was an uneasy feeling, and I felt uncomfortable with them staring and smiling. Granted, I was staring and smiling back, but they started it. In front of my parents, on the coffee table, that acted as a type of barrier between us in the center of the room, sat two mugs. I suspected those mugs contained alcohol. As none was offered at dinner, I guessed they were secretly drinking, unwittingly unaware that I had already rumbled their veiled attempts to disguise their clandestine wine. I decided I would play along.

"Good coffee?" I asked, gesturing toward the two mugs. They both nodded, still smiling, still staring. Once again, I looked at my watch and sighed. It was my attempt to show them it was late. Unfortunately, even though I would had loved to stay and have them stare at me some more, I really had to be going. I was about to rise and explain all that when at last, Dad spoke.

"That was a lovely dinner, Irma," he said to Mother. "Wasn't that a lovely dinner, Seth?" he repeated, smiling at me. Before either Mother or I could respond, he spoke again. "It was one of the best I've ever had."

I doubted it was one of the best he ever had, and it was obvious my Dad was trying to make small talk. Mother and I could play the staring, smiling game all night, but Dad, it seemed, was cracking. Mother ignored my father's compliment and continued to smile at me pleasantly. For a fleeting second, it looked like she was about to break her silence. Though her mouth began to open, she did not speak; it was as if she was thinking of the right words to use, a first for her. I felt I needed to take control of the situation, not just to ease the tension. Though I was slightly perturbed, I was not overly concerned at their behavior; it was more that I wanted to get back to my apartment so I could watch TV.

"Well, I need to be going if I want my beauty sleep. I have a busy day tomorrow, and Walter needs to be fed." That was a lie. Walter was extremely self-sufficient, but it was the only excuse I could muster, considering the unnerving sight of my parents' manic staring and smiling, which was very off-putting. I felt it was good enough. "So if there's something you want to tell me, now would be a good time." I hoped that this prompt would help Mother regain her vocal powers. In retrospect, I wished I had kept my mouth shut.

"I am a virgin," said Mother. It was more an announcement than an actual statement. It was the last thing I expected to come from her mouth. She continued to smile as I shuffled uneasily in my chair. I noticed this announcement had not changed my father's expression either. Now it was my turn to smile.

"I beg your pardon?" I said, hoping Mother would say it again. I had never seen her joke like this before.

CHAPTER 4

"I AM A VIRGIN," MOTHER repeated. This time her smile was not as strong as before. "I am a virgin, and so is your father." My father nodded as if showing he concurred with the rather bold and bizarre statement his wife had made. I grinned. They were playing a silly joke on me. They were testing me. Why they were testing me, I did not know, but I thought I would play along. I decided not to respond. Mother continued to speak as she fiddled with the mug of wine clasped in her hand. She spoke quickly but deliberately.

"Oh, Seth, we should have told you years ago, but the time never seemed right. I hope you understand, but, well, what with school, and the business, and then the golf club, and then Yale, and all the other things, we simply kept putting it off and putting it off." She paused for breath before continuing. "It's not as if we were trying to hide anything from you, and well, you know how sometimes things get forgotten, and as time passed, I thought it could have been a mistake." I had absolutely no idea what she was talking about, and my perplexed expression obviously relayed that, but I did not interrupt.

"Anyway, the thing is, but, well, you see, your dad really isn't your real father." I stopped smiling and looked at my father. What was this? I had no chance to ask as Mother was still speaking, and no one interrupted her when she was in full flow. "I am a virgin. In fact, we both are virgins. It's why we were chosen. I have always been a virgin, and I'm proud to be a virgin; so is your father." My dad nodded his agreement.

I still had no idea what she was talking about, and I put the bizarre announcement she had just made down to drink or hormones or possibly a combination of both. Why my father was playing along with this, I had no idea. Of course, it was a preposterous thing to say.

"So you're telling me I'm adopted?" I said. Not that I believed I was. I was merely going along with their little joke, for now. They looked at each other, and for a second, I thought they were going to laugh aloud, but all they did was smile knowingly at each other and then look at me.

"No, dear, you're not adopted. I thought you'd think that," said Mother knowingly.

"So what is this, what's the punch line?" I asked.

"Honey, this isn't a joke," replied Mother. I cringed at "honey" and a sudden feeling of despair washed over me. I could tell by her tone that this was not a joke. They actually believed what they were saying. I came to the immediate conclusion that my parents were mentally ill. The connotations of this were awful. I would have to have them institutionalized. I would have to care for them. I would have to visit them on weekends. This could be a disaster for my social life. My father interrupted my thoughts of weekend visits, drooling straightjacketed parents, padded cells, teeth removal, and other images and visions of caring for mad parents.

"What your mother is trying to say is that, well, it is difficult to grasp, and probably hard to understand, but it is no joke, and despite what you probably think, we are neither mad nor drunk." He looked down at his mug. "Well, maybe we are a little tipsy, but we needed some Dutch courage. This is a big thing, Seth." He sounded sincere. I was intrigued. Mother patted my dad's hand as reassurance, and that act of affection alone was enough to convince me that she too, in her mind at least, was being sincere.

Once again Mother spoke, again deliberately, but a little slower than before. "What we are trying to say, and really, we should have done this years ago, but like I said, it completely slipped our minds, and I don't think too much harm has been done. Well, not that you'd notice; it could have been a lot worse, but, well, oh dear, how can I say this.... Seth, you are the Son of God."

It was official. My parents were crazy. They had gone mad. The images of loony-filled wards and a social life revolving around hospital visiting hours returned. Or maybe it was even worse. Somehow, this old Jewish couple was suddenly evangelistic or Mormon, or maybe they had been brainwashed by Jehovah's witnesses or a cult. I wondered who had kidnapped my parents and replaced them with these two crazy look-alikes.

"Well, that's nice to know," I said, half-smiling. Once again, I glanced at my watch as if indicating the lateness of the hour. "I really need to be getting home now. When you return my parents, please have them call me. By the way, it was a lovely dinner. The chicken was perfect, not as good as my real mother would make, but I suppose being an imposter you couldn't get it all quite right, but it really was a good attempt." I began to rise, but mother spoke before I could completely free myself from the easy chair.

"Maybe we are not being clear enough, dear. Listen, what we are trying to tell you is that I am really a virgin, a holy virgin, like the Mary woman from the Bible. I always have been and always will be. Your Father, not this Father," she indicated to Dad, who raised his hand as if to remind me he was the "father" being discussed, "is actually God. Your real father," once again Dad raised his hand, "is not your real father. You are, well, sort of the Messiah, the second coming, Jesus's brother, the Christ child, the chosen one, the savior, or whatever those people call you."

By "those people" I presumed she meant Christians.

That's when I laughed. I laughed so loud that I thought I was going have to use the bathroom. I don't think I had ever laughed that hard before. I let rip. I felt bad, laughing at my parents, but it was hilarious. I had not expected this; it was highly original, and I was very amused. As I laughed, they stared at me, but they were no longer smiling. Their faces were deadpan which only made me laugh harder and louder. I had to grab my side; I laughed so hard it hurt. They continued to stare, their faces more stern than deadpan. It was a joke, their best joke ever—in fact their only joke ever—I had never known my parents joke. They never joked. Oh, shit. My parents do not joke. My laughter curtailed slightly, long enough for me to speak.

"Come on," I pleaded, my arms outstretched. "What is this?" They sat stony faced. I felt slightly guilty at laughing so hard. I could tell they were not pleased by my outburst of laughter. I felt I needed to speak and ease the tension that had suddenly emerged.

"For a start, we are Jewish. We don't go for all that Christ stuff. Come on, be real. If you are going to play a joke on me, you cannot expect me not to laugh. What is this? You guys started this. How was I meant to react? Have you two been drinking too much? Is there a hidden camera somewhere? Come on. Mother? Dad? What's this all about?" Their expressions had not changed, and if I were eight years old, I would have thought I was in trouble.

"It's the truth, son," said Dad, more somber and serious than I had ever seen him before in my life.

And that's when I realized they were not kidding around. That's when I realized that they believed every word they said was the truth.

CHAPTER 5

NOW OBVIOUSLY, THE EVENING DID not end there. It did not end with me casually calling a cab, kissing my mother on the cheek, shaking Dad's hand, and returning to my contended and uncomplicated life. It is important that I fill you in on my parents a little more. They did not joke around. I had never known them joke around. For them to joke around was unheard of. Oh no, to say my parents were jokers would not be true. They did not joke, I hope that is clear. Jokes were not on the Miller list of things to do.

"You are not joking, are you?" I said. I no longer smiled. I sank back into the easy chair.

"No, dear, we are not," replied my mother, no longer stony-faced, which was a relief because when she got that face on...let's just say you didn't want to be around for *that* face, or the words that came from the mouth of *that* face.

"You actually believe what you are saying, don't you?" I said, as more of a statement than a question; I already knew the answer.

"It's not that we believe or do not believe what we are saying, quite simply it's the truth; it's the truth, dear, it's the truth." I had never heard my Mother speak so sincerely. "I am a virgin; you were a miracle child. Your father," Dad raised his hand again, "and I were chosen by God to carry his second son—that's you, Seth—and to bring you up as our son like Mary and Joseph did." She seemed as if she actually believed that. It was not a joke. It must have been something else; maybe they had been hypnotized, or terrorists had put something in the Borough Park water supply, or maybe my earlier brainwashing theory was true. Or much worse, they could actually be mad. My parents could really be crazy. I wasn't sure whether to reason with them or try and bring them to their senses.

I decided I would highlight the total absurdity of it all. I spoke softly and quietly "Mother, we are Jewish. Why would God choose a Jewish couple to raise his son? Surely he would choose a Christian family?" I felt that was a good start.

"Well, it was all a bit of a mistake, that bit anyway. He did originally think we were Christians. I think our surname must have confused him. I did point this out at the time, but it was too late, and anyway, he said it wasn't important." Mother sounded convincing. It was ridiculous, but I knew she believed what she said. I felt, though, that God would realize Miller was the third most common surname for Jews in the United States. I thought everybody knew that.

"Anyway," said Dad. "He chose Jews last time. Mary and Joseph were both from Israel." I looked at him and shook my head.

"I suppose God pointed that out to you?" I asked, not really expecting an answer.

"Yes, I think he did, actually," answered Dad, rubbing his chin as if trying to recall something from his memory bank. Again, I shook my head in disbelief.

"Ok, ok, I will go along with your little game for now. If I am the Son of God, why are you telling me now? I am thirty-two, very nearly thirty-three. Surely by now I would have had some inclination as to who I am? Surely I would have performed some sort of miracle or at least some sort of trick?" I gave my parents no chance to reply as I continued to speak. "Why, if what you two say is correct, have I not turned water into wine, risen the dead, stopped war, won the lotto, married a supermodel, all that stuff? Why haven't I spoken to God? Answer that? If I am the son of God, why has he not spoken to me? Got an answer for that one? But more importantly, why was I circumcised? Why that, why at least didn't you stop that? It was extremely painful. I don't recall it, but I guarantee I wasn't smiling afterward."

"He said you would react like this," said Mother. "Didn't he, Ely?" Dad nodded. I shook my head once again. This was frustrating. Dad rose from the sofa, stretched, and yawned. I couldn't believe it; he was going to bed!

"Well, I'm beat. It's time for me to go to bed, and I get the feeling you're going to take some convincing. I will leave that to your mother." And with that, he was gone. It was as if the last twenty minutes had never happened. It was typical of my dad. As far as he was concerned, the truth was out, despite the ridiculousness of it all; it was time for bed, and nothing would stop him from sleeping. It was a trait I had never much liked in Dad. He never argued or became embroiled in controversy; once he made his statement, it was finished. It was why Mother found him so easy to manipulate. Unfortunately, this reinforced my theory that they actually believed what they were saying. I looked at Mother in the hope that she would stop my dad from leaving, but she just shrugged. She knew it would be pointless, and I got the feeling that maybe she had even orchestrated my dad's departure. It dawned on me she probably had more to say and didn't want Dad to hear it. Either that, or she wanted alone time with me. I bet myself she had instructed Dad to make himself scarce at an allotted point in the evening and that allotted point was now. Dad bid me goodnight, kissed Mother on the forehead, and with that, he was gone.

"Really, there isn't much he can add anyway. God came to me more, in any case. He chose me, not him. He sort of just went along with it; you know what he's like. I think God spoke to him once or twice but it wasn't anything important. He didn't much like the 'virgin all my life' business, but you know your father—well, that father anyway—he kind of likes an easy life." Could she hear herself? An easy life? The guy, according to both of them if this whole thing were true, which I assure you I did not believe it was, had never had sexual intercourse! He had brought up another man's child and got nothing for it. No miracles, nothing. He had spent his whole adult life succumbing to Mother and her overbearing methods.

I was becoming annoyed, and despite my deep-rooted fear of the consequences of confrontation with Mother, enough was enough. "Oh, come on, Mother," I said, my tone aggressive, which was a first for me when talking with Mother. "This is totally ridiculous. If any of this is true, why didn't you tell me before? Why wait until now? Why not tell me when I was thirteen? After I left high school, college? Not that for one minute I think any of this ridiculous and tiresome story is true anyway." I waited for the reaction. The eruption. I had never spoken to my mother like that before.

"To be honest, your father really wanted to tell you. I mean, Ely your father, not God your father, but I felt it would interfere with your schoolwork, and then you headed to college. You were doing so well, and you seemed so happy. It didn't seem fair to burden you with all this Messiah and second coming business. Then one thing led to another, and it slipped our minds. We brushed it to one side. Kind of hoped it would go away, and that maybe your real Father, God, had forgotten about you. You see, he is like that. He is very forgetful." It was a relief that her reaction was not volcanic; however her answer was beyond ridiculous, as was the whole evening. I could not believe it; she talked about God as if she had actually spoken to him. She was very convincing; she had obviously already convinced herself. What was more bizarre, though, was that she was talking about God, the creator of the Universe, as if he were some sort of forgetful, old uncle who had a reputation for mislaying his spectacles! A different approach was required. I felt if I placated her for a while, she might come to her senses.

"So let's just say, for arguments sake, that I actually believe you. Let us assume, for the time being at least, that what you have told me is true. Run it all by me from the beginning and in chronological order. Dates, times, everything." So she did. My mother proceeded to tell me the whole story from the moment of my alleged 'Immaculate Conception' right up to the phone call she made that afternoon to me at my office. I will not bore you by reciting what she said word for word. She was far too dramatic and went into far too much detail. To be honest, it would take much too long to recite word-for-word her version of events. I will give you a condensed and briefer summary of what she said, but in my own words, and with a little added family history so you can keep on track.

CHAPTER

6

IRMA CRYSTAL FIRST MET ELY Miller in 1965 when Ely was thirty-five and Irma was thirty-two. They met through their parents, with whom they both lived with. Their respective siblings, whom I have already mentioned, my father's brother Jacob and my mother's sister Marla, had already flown the family nest. Irma and Ely had never been successful daters. Boys found Irma extremely pretty but far too pushy and overbearing. After one date it would become apparent that, despite her angelic appearance, the girl was hard work. Any potential suitors could forget carnal relations; Irma was not giving it up for any man unless it was her husband to be. Even if one of her dates was prepared to wait, she would soon extinguish any budding romance with her ability to totally alienate and upset all who came in contact with her. Basically, she was too much hard work. So as one by one all her peers married, Irma remained single, waiting for Mr. Right to come along. But Mr. Right would come and go, unable to cope with her personality or the lack of physical contact, so to her, all Mr. Rights became Mr. Wrongs.

As for Ely, girls found him too much of a pushover. Inevitably, the girls he dated usually wanted to get to know his much better-looking older brother, Jacob. Some girls even used poor Ely as a route to meet Jacob, which did nothing for his confidence or self-esteem. Yes, there were a few movie dates and some holding hands but nothing serious. Ely was too nice. He never tried to push the issue of sex, and it seemed this put off the girls he dated. They felt he was too lethargic and uninterested. That was, of course, not true. Ely was industrious, and his car repair garage business boomed.

When he met Irma at the bar mitzvah of a friend of both families, Ely had fallen head-over-heels in love. He didn't seem to notice, or maybe he chose to ignore, her overbearing and persuasive persona. He didn't mind Irma bossing him around and telling him what to do, and he seemed quite happy to let her take the lead in their relationship.

By the same token, Irma was impressed by Ely's restraint regarding sexual relations. He didn't badger her like the other boys for sex or a quick fumble under her skirt. What impressed her most was Ely's acceptance that she was the boss. He would do anything for her and never answered back. She had found a man she could control, who was relatively wealthy and already successful. They were indeed well suited.

They married the following year after they met, in 1966. It was a traditional Jewish ceremony, and understandably, both sets of parents were relieved that their mature offspring had finally married and would now vacate the family home. It was on their wedding night when Ely was ready to consummate not only his marriage but also his relationship with Mother, that Irma had her first visitation from God. The visitation came in the form of a dream, just as God had come to Mary two thousand or so years before. She recalled that the dream was extremely vivid, and it occurred whilst my Father, Ely, showered before bed. The dream involved a lot of harp-like music, references to lambs, strict instructions, and the odd joke.

God, she claimed, had a pompous-sounding English accent, which she found initially odd, but he explained that if had he a Yonkers accent, it would be even more preposterous. Mother agreed. He told her she had been chosen to carry the Nazarene, the son of God, the second coming, Jesus Christ part two, into the world. Just as it had occurred two thousand years before, a virgin would carry the child. Only a true virgin could deliver God's only begotten son; well, second begotten son. As God had been reliably advised, Irma was indeed a virgin, and he was under pressure to get it done. (Apparently, he had gotten his timings wrong, and he had thought it wasn't until the following year that he should be doing all this virgin hunting stuff.) Luckily, some wise old Saint had pointed out that if all the prophecies of the Bible were to be fulfilled by the end of the millennium, then God needed to act immediately.

Being under pressure, he had found a virgin who fitted the bill. She met the required profile and, well, apparently that was the way it worked. She was the chosen one. She herself had pointed out in the dream that she was Jewish and that surely God had made a mistake. God indeed had made a mistake. Confused by the surname Miller, God and his team mistakenly assumed Irma and Ely were good Christians. More thorough research wouldn't have gone a miss. After some deliberation, God decided my parents' religion was of secondary importance. It was the virgin thing that really mattered. As he pointed out, the last ones were Jewish, and it didn't seem to affect anything. And that was that.

When she awoke from the dream, which apparently had lasted the time it took for my father to shower and shave, she immediately told her new husband of the visitation from God and the contents therein. After returning to the bathroom for approximately three minutes, for what, my mother did not know, Ely returned, slightly out of breath and a little flushed, and declared it fine with him. If that was what God had said, then that's what God had said. He would wait to consummate his marriage after the birth of God's son. He had already waited his whole life, so a little longer wouldn't matter.

That night turned into a month, and eventually, according to Mother, they never did consummate the marriage, and she remained a virgin, as she felt that it was what God meant by Virgin Mother. So when she went to visit the doctor for a regular health check seven days after her wedding night, it was indeed a miracle when her physician announced she was pregnant.

Luckily, it would seem God had taken the precaution of visiting my father in a separate dream. I reminded myself to verify that with him later. God assured Ely that the child was indeed God's, and that despite the awkwardness of the situation, he was grateful to Ely for allowing him the use of his wife's womb, and he apologized for any inconvenience the event may have caused.

Nine months later in January, 1967, yours truly, Seth Miller, was born. Not in a stable, but at King's County Hospital in Brooklyn,

New York. Apparently, I weighed in at nine pounds and eight ounces and was nineteen inches long. There were no complications, and no wise men bearing gifts bothered to show up or offer my dad a cigar. It also seemed there was no shining light directing shepherds or other well-wishers to my birth either.

After my birth, my mother and father waited for another sign from God. Since my mother had discovered she was pregnant with God's son, God had been conspicuous in his absence; no visitations, no dreams, and no signs for either Irma or Ely. They assumed now that his son was born, God would once again enter their lives, but I came with no instructions or directions.

For the first few months of my life, my parents were at a loss. They did not know what to expect. They felt that sooner or later, God would come and claim me. But he never did. They tried praying, they visited churches and temples, and they consulted the yellow pages, but nothing. It was as if God had simply forgotten about them and his son. As they watched me grow up into a normal and well-adjusted child who showed no signs of miracle-doing and who was not overtly kind to others, nor showed any natural inclination to any religion, they soon forgot, or chose to forget, that I was a miracle birth and the Son of God.

Time passed, and when I reached thirteen, it seemed to Irma and Ely Miller that maybe God had made a mistake. When no disciples came a-knocking, no miracles occurred, nor words of profound wisdom emitted from my lips, they presumed it had all been a misunderstanding, and that maybe God had found a good Christian family to bring up another one of his sons. This other son, guessed Irma and Ely, would be the real Messiah, and I must have been a mistake. They put it down to the fact they were Jewish. It was good news, as it coincided with my bar mitzvah.

They read the papers every day, looking for news of miracles or revelations about the second coming, but in time, they stopped even doing that. They both agreed it was probably wise not to mention the circumstances of my birth to anyone, just in case word got out, and I became a religious freak show. So they never told a soul, not even me, and by the time I graduated from Yale, it didn't seem to matter. Even they themselves began to doubt the whole thing. For thirty-two years they dismissed the whole thing, shut it completely out of their minds, and pretended I was a normal child not born from an immaculate conception, and that suited them both. Mother told me she had remained a virgin, as she felt it was the right thing to do, and she convinced Dad that God, despite his total absence from the scene, might become enraged if she gave up her virginity. Dad, she claims, apparently agreed with her. I found that hard to believe, as I did the whole story, but I decided would go along with it until I had spoken to the man himself. Ely that was, not God.

All was well. Their secret, my secret, our secret, God's secret, was safe. My parents carried on with life and presumed that everything was fine, and even though he was the creator of the Universe, God was probably as susceptible to the odd mistake as we all were. All this changed, though, that morning.

God had apparently called. But this time, he hadn't appeared in a dream or a vision. No, this time God had called. On the telephone. Mother said he still had the English accent, and his voice was as deep and as pompous as she remembered. He made his apologies about not being in touch sooner. He explained he had been away, and he could see that he had let things slide. He had taken a longer than planned vacation and foray into the Universe to develop other planets (he didn't go into details,) and was extremely apologetic that he hadn't been around. He could see things on Earth had gotten into a bit of a mess since they had last spoke.

Apparently, he asked after me, and though he hadn't followed my progress on Earth, he was delighted to hear I had graduated top of my class at Yale. He was also extremely pleased I had secured such a highly paid and lucrative position with Henry, who he didn't know, but was sure there would be a file on him somewhere. He inquired if I was married and if he had any grandchildren, and was, Mother claimed, relieved that I had never married and had no children. Also, he was concerned that during his hiatus of "thirty something" years that his credibility had waned. Before he contacted me directly with instructions of how to proceed, he said it might be better if Irma and Ely broke the news to me gently to warm things up for his grand entrance.

He felt arriving unannounced and barging into my life would not be the best ploy to adopt. He had seen a recent episode of

Oprah about absentee fathers trying to establish relationships with their estranged children. Oprah had been harsh on the fathers and had given good advice on the right way to go about reestablishing broken relationships. Therefore, heeding the advice he had seen, he felt it better that Irma smooth the way for him. He felt it was time we "got this thing back on track" (God's words, not Mother's,) and that my parents should get me over that night and break the news to me gently, so that his call to me, when it came, would not come as too much as a shock.

He would have one of his assistants pencil in a call for the next day, and he would be in touch with me, disasters and other unscheduled events, such as unplanned acts of God or the sudden death of a Pope, permitting. Now, just in case you have missed anything here, let us not forget whom we are talking about. We are talking about God, the creator of the Universe, the creator of Man, and not, as it sounded to me, Donald Trump.

Before he hung up, God once again apologized for his tardiness. He told Mother she had done a great job and to pass on his regards to Ely. Apparently, he also told her she needn't have remained a virgin after I was born. The virgin thing only applied to my initial conception. It seemed quite a few people had made that same assumption before, and it was one of the things he needed to rectify. Anyway, no harm done, and like he said, he would call the next day.

Mother made me promise not to tell Dad that his years of abstinence had not been required. I did make her promise, though, to right that wrong as soon as she could. I wasn't sure if I was doing my father a favor or not, but I took the chance.

I looked at my watch and realized Mother's story had taken her over three hours to relay to me. It was tomorrow. The late evening had turned into early morning. Mother knew how to talk, hence my condensed version of the events leading up to her phone call. There was no way I would get a cab this time at night out in Borough Park. It wasn't like Manhattan. Unlike the city that never slept, Borough Park turned out the lights and put the cat out at ten thirty every night. In any case, I was exhausted. I was also concerned that both my parents could be lunatics, and I felt I should stay the night, or what remained of it. They were my parents after all, and if they were mad, they needed watching. Who knew what other craziness could happen? I felt it wise to remain in Borough Park whilst I planned my course of action.

Mother, when she had finished relaying her story, put her hands in the air, exclaiming I had all the facts. All I could do now was wait further instructions. She didn't mind at all that I didn't believe her. All would soon be revealed. And that was that.

"Well, there you have it; it all crept up on us, really. I think between me and your dad, we did a good job. You are still my boy, though no matter what, Ely your father still loves you and sees you as his flesh and blood. Who knows if God will call or not; he didn't leave us a number, and his track record at keeping in touch isn't the best, but he said he had your number." Mother yawned and stretched her arms above her head. "I'm beat; it's been a long day," she said as she kissed me on the forehead and left me where I sat. She explained she was tired and needed to sleep, and she had said all she could say, and it was now up to God. I felt sorry for her. I never thought my Mother would lose it as she had.

The easy chair was comfortable, and even though there was a bed for me in the house, I decided I would sit, relax, and ponder the best way to obtain some psychiatric care for my parents. I was genuinely concerned for their mental health. Before long, I had a plan of action formatted in my mind, and I dozed off.

Luckily, my father was an early riser, and he woke me from my impromptu slumber with a cup of coffee and a smile. He told me it was seven in the morning, and he would call me a cab. Once again, I was going to sit in rush hour traffic for an hour to complete the twelve-mile journey into the city. Also, I was going to be late for work. By the time I would return back to my apartment, shower, and shave, the morning would be all but over. Great. The perfect end to the perfect evening. My parents were certifiable, and the first thing I planned to do when I got home was to call their doctor and get him over there.

Please do not think for one minute I believed any of the previous evening's revelations, because I assure you, I did not. As far as I was concerned, my parents were totally mad, especially Mother. Now that my dad was up, I could hopefully get some sense of this whole thing and maybe between us, we could convince Mother to seek some much-needed help. I was positive Mother had put him up to the whole thing. I guessed he was going along with it and her crazy biblical illusion for the sake of a quiet life. Now was my chance to get at the truth. Unfortunately, I was wrong.

My father repeated the exact same story my mother had. He even confirmed God's telephone call the previous day. Apparently, Mother had put God on speakerphone so Ely could listen in. He claimed he had actually said "hi" when God mentioned him, but he thought God didn't quite catch it. Yep, my dad was adamant that I was God's son too. I made a mental note to definitely call their doctor as soon as I got back to the city. They had obviously turned crazy, or senile, or both. I could hear that the cab dad had called waited outside, so I finished the coffee Dad had made me and prepared to depart.

"Now son, remember your mother and I did the best job we could, so don't hold it against us if we didn't fill you in on things until now," said Dad as he showed me to the front door.

"Dad, do you seriously think that I believe any of this?"

My father shook his head. "I know, son, it is a lot to take in, but I assure you, it is all true." He paused and put his hands into his dressing gown pockets. I got the feeling there was something else he wanted to tell me. I always knew when he had something he wanted to say but didn't know how to say it by the way he fumbled in his pockets.

"What is it, Dad? You're not telling me something, I can tell," I said as I stood in the open doorway. Dad rubbed his hand on his chin and sighed. My dad was no good at keeping a secret; well, not from me anyway. I could read him like a book.

"Well, son," he began, "promise me you won't tell your mother this." He looked around him as to check that Mother was not in earshot. She wasn't. She slept, and knowing her, she would sleep until the afternoon. I agreed that anything he told me would be in confidence. "Well, the thing is, this whole virgin thing never sat right with me," he explained. "Your Mother may well be a virgin, but I promise you, son, I am not." Once again, I felt a wave of dread loom over me. Where was this leading? "You know your aunt Marla?" whispered my father. I nodded. I guessed where this was going. I did not like it, but I sadly now knew where this led. "Well, we kind of had a thing. It's over now, has been for a while. I didn't think I needed to stay a virgin, but your mother was adamant that she had to. Well, you know what I am saying. We all have needs." Dad was obviously looking for my approval or my forgiveness, I was not sure which. What I did know was that my dad was confessing to his son an affair with his wife's sister on his doorstep at seven in the morning. All of this coming after telling me I was the son of God. I was in the *Twilight Zone*. I didn't know what to say. It was incomprehensible that my parents would think I would go along with this whole fantasy, and now this!

"Well," I said, "let's hope God doesn't find out." I was joking, being ironic, and attempting a little humor.

"Hope he doesn't find out?" said my dad, closing the front door and waving away the cab. The cab driver shrugged and switched on his engine. I watched as my escape from Borough Park shifted into gear. I thought about waving him back, but Dad put his arm around me as I saw my passport to sanity speed away, and he led me back into the living room. Dad faced me, and he smiled. It seemed there was more to hear, and I wouldn't be making it home just yet. "I am not worried about God finding out anything," said Dad. "It was all his idea!"

CHAPTER 7

THERE WAS MUCH FOR ME to ponder as I sat in the back of the second cab my father had called to collect me from Borough Park and return me to the relative sanity of Manhattan. The most pressing concern I had was, of course, the state of my parents' mental health. My second concern was my father's recent confession. At no stage during my one hour cab ride back to Greenwich Village was I concerned that maybe, just maybe, my parents were not mad, and I was indeed the Messiah and the Son of God. Not for one fleeting moment did I consider it, nor did I dwell on it. I did not suppose on consequences, nor did I play out any scenario in my head that would entertain the possibility that what my parents had told me was true. I dismissed the notion totally from my thought processes and allowed my mind to concentrate on the best course of action to resolve the dilemmas introduced by my crazed parents.

My father had felt he needed to explain his relationship with Marla before I left Brooklyn. I, in turn, tried to explain that it wasn't necessary for him to do so. He felt that in my new capacity as savior of all men, that maybe I should take the time to listen to him. I tried to assure him there was no need, and as far as I was concerned, consenting adults could do what they wanted whether I was the "savior" or not. It wasn't that I was not bothered. The situation was not great, granted, but I felt I had spent enough time with my whacko parents for one day. In the end, though, my father persuaded me to stay in Brooklyn a few hours longer and listen to his version of events regarding God, virginity, and Aunty Marla. As Mother slept, oblivious to her husband's adulterous affair, Ely relayed his story. Once again, I shall not bore you with a word-for-word rendition of my father's adulterous antics; I shall, in my own words, describe what he told me.

He confirmed most of what I already knew, and according to him, he was never confident when it came to the opposite sex. It was as much a surprise to him as it was to others when he began dating the attractive and nubile Irma Crystal. As time progressed, it became apparent to my dad why such a good-looking woman such as Irma was still on the marital shelf; she was, by all intents and purposes, almost impossible to live with. This did not bother Ely. He was prepared to put up her with controlling ways and intimidating character as long as he would not be alone for the rest of his life and, to put it bluntly, get laid.

Unfortunately for Ely, it didn't work out that way. When Irma told him of her visitation from God and his informing her that she was imminently going to be carrying his child as she was now the appointed "virgin to God," Ely initially thought it was a test, so he went along with it. He did not believe for one minute that God had chosen him and Irma to bring up God's second child. He was convinced Irma was either playing a game or testing him to see how long she could control their sexual relationship. And why not? She controlled everything else. Ely was convinced that sooner or later she would crack and it would only be a matter of days before he bedded his new bride. Until, that was, God came to *him* in a dream.

God confirmed every detail of Irma's story. Ely was devastated. All his life he had been waiting for the opportunity to sow his wild and now desperate oats. God was understanding and apologized to my father for "the terrible and ghastly inconvenience." However, there was a bright side. Irma was only required to remain a virgin until after my birth. The virgin bit only applied to the birth of God's child. Once this child was born, Irma could do what she wanted sexually, finally lose her virginity, and consummate her marriage with her real husband. Once again, though, things did not go poor Ely's way. It seemed my Mother enjoyed the notion of remaining a virgin. Why? Only she could answer that, but Dad felt it was just one more weapon in her armory of control. Perplexed by this situation and unable to get his wife to part with her virginity, he called on God for advice.

Unbeknownst to Mother, God did visit my father a second time (according to him that was; remember, I am relaying what he told me; I did not believe any of this outrageous and ridiculous story.) Just before my birth and after numerous previously unanswered prayers, God once more came to my father in a dream. God explained he had no idea where Irma had gotten the idea that she needed to remain a virgin for life. God himself had told Father that it was ridiculous, and what sense did it make? Apparently, according to God, a lot of other people had got this wrong before, and he had absolutely no idea where that theory had come from. It certainly hadn't come from him. God gave my Father a solution. God explained he understood my poor father's unenviable position, and though God accepted no responsibility for Mother's actions, he did feel that maybe his involvement had not helped the situation. God began dropping hints to Ely. He mentioned that Marla, who Mother had recently appointed in control of the car repair business, was not a bad-looking woman. Indeed, she was quite "hot" (God's words apparently, not my father's.) Throughout this alleged visitation, God continued to drop innuendos about Marla, how she was a little older than Mother and nearer to Ely's age, how she was more fun, how if only God were fifty-five thousand years younger, you know, that sort of thing. My father, whilst not slow, hadn't caught on to what God was implying. God, who could sense this, eventually came out and suggested my father take up with Marla on the sly. According to my father, his exact words were, "For Heaven's sake, don't you get it? I am telling you Marla wants it, I guarantee it, and you have my word. I have influence. I also promise you that no one will catch you. Irma will never know unless you confess, and as I am not a great advocate of confessing, I can't see that being a problem, as I am my own witness. I promise you undetected extramarital sex with Marla for as long as you like."

So thanks to God's suggestion, Father propositioned Marla, and just as God had promised, Marla was receptive to his advances. They embarked on a sexual and romantic relationship that lasted over twenty years. I could not believe he had pulled of an affair with his own wife's sister for over twenty years, especially considering that his wife was my mother. If what my father had told me was true, and I did not doubt that the affair part was true, it was all the references to God that I did not believe, I suppose Mother had brought it on herself. She had systemically denied my father his conjugal rights, she had been the one who had introduced an attractive woman into my father's life, and she was the one who had spent the best part of four years ruining her own son's chances of any sex by moving out of the family home and accompanying me to college. It didn't make it right, but father had a good case.

According to my father, the relationship with Marla was over. Not because he wanted it to be, but because she had moved to Miami and was now, in fact, married to a dentist I had never met named Joshua Zip. He went on to say he had no regrets from cheating on Mother and was very grateful to God for setting the whole thing up.

I took Dad's confession, and I instructed him not, on any account, to tell Mother of the affair with her sister. The consequences of her finding out would not bear thinking about. I left Dad as he lit his pipe and waved me farewell from his immaculate garden. The poor man, I thought as the cab pulled away, totally and utterly mad.

As my cab crossed into Manhattan, I sighed with relief. It was good to be back in the city and back to normality. There was something, though, that puzzled me. Madness and craziness was not contagious. It could not be passed through the air. If a mad man sneezed in the grocery store, his mad germs would not fly through the sky up and down aisles infecting his fellow shoppers. Nor would germs he had left on his shopping cart infect the next user of said shopping cart. How then could both my parents have turned completely crazy at the same time?

The cab neared my apartment complex. After much deliberation, the only logical answer to the whole crazy issue was that they must have been on drugs. That was it. My parents were high on some mind-altering, hallucinogenic drug that had poisoned their brains. I would call Doctor Hienenberger, their physician, as soon as I returned to my apartment. I had taken the precaution of calling Henry from my parents' home to let him know I would be taking the day off. Henry had offered no resistant. He knew that if I needed a day off, it was for a good reason. I did not go into details as to why I would not be in the office that day; I told him it was Mother trouble. Henry had met my mother, and he said he understood. Harvey was on hand to greet me as I entered my building.

"Yo, bro," he shouted. He always seemed to shout. I wasn't sure if he knew he was shouting or not, but there was no need for him to shout, especially as he was less than two feet away from me. I often wondered if Harvey had the capability of speaking in any other volume other than shouting volume.

"Yo, bro, check out your fro, man," he cried. I had no idea what this meant. "Your fro, man, check it out. Man, you look like shit," he said again, pointing to my head. I was tired, and I had important things on my mind; I was not in the mood to decipher whatever Harvey was trying to tell me. I stopped and took a look at my reflection in the mirrored walls that adorned the far side of the lobby.

Harvey was right. I looked like shit. I had slept in my clothes, I was unshaven, and my hair, which had attracted Harvey's attention, looked as though I had just had two thousand volts shot through my body.

"What happened to you, man? I've never seen you like this before. What the hell happened out there?" Harvey said pointing outside the lobby door. I assumed he was pointing toward Brooklyn. It was touching that Harvey was concerned for my welfare, but it was a little over the top.

"Oh, just a rough night with my parents," I answered shrugging to show I was not overly concerned that I looked like a tramp. I decided I would take that opportunity to ask Harvey's opinion on a couple of things. As it was only Harvey and I in the lobby, I felt no inhibition in asking him questions that normally a resident wouldn't ask his doorman.

"Harvey," I began, "I have a question for you."

"Go, bro," said Harvey, who was still examining my disheveled appearance with a screwed up face.

"In what circumstances do you think two previously sane people could possibly turn crazy at exactly the same time?"

"It doesn't happen, man," confirmed Harvey.

"Ok, next question," I said, satisfied that Harvey was on the same wavelength as me on that one.

"Do you believe in God?"

"Hell yeah," screeched Harvey.

"Ok. If God, hypothetically, spoke to you, how do you think he would do it?" I asked the now confused doorman.

"In a dream, I guess," was Harvey's reply.

"Would you expect him to call you on the phone?" I was confident that another "hell no" was on its way.

"Only if he had my number," was Harvey's unexpected reply.

"What?" I asked. "You think God would call you up on the phone if he knew your number?"

"Hell yeah. Why not?" said Harvey, bemused.

"Never mind, forget it," I said as I walked into the elevator. I was going to ask Harvey if he knew about mind-altering drugs that could make previously sane persons crazy, but I thought better of it. Harvey waved as the elevator door slid closed. What a morning. No doubt Harvey would have believed every word my parents had said if he were me. I shook my disheveled head. I would call Doctor Hienenberger. He would prescribe some medicine, everything would be fine, and I'd save some for Harvey. Dad's little secret would be safe, and Mother would admit she was not "God's Virgin." She would also apologize for the ridiculous events of the previous evening and feel utterly remorseful at ruining my Wednesday evening, and then she would return to the acid-tongued woman we all knew and feared, and we could all get back to normal. I laughed to myself. What a crazy day. But things were about to get even crazier.

CHAPTER

8

THE TELEPHONE RANG THE MOMENT I stepped into my apartment. I decided I would let my answering machine catch it. As I threw down my keys onto the coffee table, Walter ran from the bedroom to greet me. I say "greet," but what he really did was look me up and down and immediately return to the bedroom where I guessed he had taken full advantage of my night away in Brooklyn by sleeping on my bed. I always got the feeling Walter was somewhat disappointed when he realized it was me entering the apartment. I wasn't sure whom he expected; maybe he thought someone better would come and rescue him from his hellish life of luxury. I checked his food and water, and he had ample. Walter seemed to survive on sleep and evil stares. I noted that whoever the caller was, they had declined to leave a message, as when the ringing stopped, my machine did not click in. I presumed it meant the call was not important.

My first priority was locating Doctor Hienenberger's telephone number. I knew I had it stored somewhere. More than likely it was on one of the numerous business cards I had in the drawer of my bedside table. I had no doubt thrown it in with the rest of cards I had collected but had seldom or never used; I remembered my Mother gave it to me "in case of an emergency." Well, this was an emergency of the highest magnitude, an emergency that the doctor would soon rectify with pills, and maybe even a couple of afternoons on a psychiatrist's couch. I was about to retrieve the card and return my life to normal when the phone rang again.

Normally, I would not have answered. Normally, I would have let it ring to the machine. If the caller, who I presumed was the same caller who had called two minutes earlier, felt that a message was warranted, then the caller had the opportunity to leave one. That's how it worked, as I am sure you know. If the caller knew me, he or she would have my cell phone number. All my friends, colleagues, even my parents knew that if I didn't answer my home number, they should call my cell phone number. I assumed then that the caller did not know me personally. At this hour of morning it was probably a cold-calling salesman trying to cajole me into buying something I did not either need nor want. So why then, you may wonder, did I answer? I wish I knew.

"Yes." I was annoyed, not just with the unidentified caller, but at myself for answering. I had grabbed the phone on instinct; something I was sure most people had done from time to time. My tone was purposely aggressive, and I was sure whoever was on the other end of the phone would pick up on that. I hoped my initial abruptness would be enough for them to hang up, as well as be a sufficient deterrent to make them think twice about calling back.

"Seth?" said the voice on the line. I detected an accent, but I could not place it. Australian maybe, possibly New Zealand?

"Yes, who is this?" I replied, my voice was still aggressive. I hoped the caller would sense my annoyance, Australian or not.

"Seth Miller?" No. Not Australian. Definitely British.

"Yes, *again*, who is this?" I was becoming impatient. I had things to do. One of those things was not converse with a pompous-sounding limey.

"Yes, of course. I am so sorry to disturb you, especially unannounced and at this time of the day. I really do not make a habit out of calling out of the blue. I do apologize; it is frightfully rude of me," the still-yet-to-be-identified caller said. He sounded sincere, and his smooth, well-spoken voice helped in easing my initial aggressiveness. He did, however, sound slightly 'uppity,' and maybe there was even a sardonic undertone to the voice. In a split second, I surmised the owner of the voice was full of self-importance.

"I'm sorry, but who is this?" I said, annoyed at the pace of the conversation. Time was of the essence, and the sooner I got Lord Snooty Pants off the phone, the better.

"Ah yes, well, ahem, son. Wow, been a while since I said that. Anyway, well, it's me, God. Didn't your mother tell you I was going to call? Oh dear, I was very specific that she should give you the heads up, so to speak. It's not the first time people haven't followed specific instructions. Oh dear, this is a little awkward and a tad embarrassing. I wish people would take these things a little bit more seriously...."

Whoever this idiot was, he could talk. He hardly seemed to pause for a breath. I felt I needed to interject, but he continued to speak.

"Maybe if people listened a bit more instead of presuming, then things wouldn't be in the state that they are. I am so sorry if this is out of the blue, but I thought I should call straightaway, the moment you got home. I was hoping to get you sooner, but you know how it is when you check your diary and things don't really fall into place...." Ok, this guy *really* needed to take a breath. I waited for at least a pause for oxygen so I could talk.

"I wanted to catch you as early as possible this morning, so this is perfect timing for me. Perfect. When you are as busy as I am, it is important that your day is structured. I have a team of assistants and secretaries, but my motto is, well, not my only motto, I do have a few, but one of them is 'never rely on others when it comes to family.' I had wanted to do this whole thing last week, but some underling managed to screw up my diary, and, well, to be perfectly honest, when you're as busy as I am, things just seem to get on top of you, and one erroneous diary entry can have far-reaching repercussions. I said to Saint Peter the other day that we really needed to update our office organizational software and that we needed to get someone on board with some new ideas and some savvy, modern-day technical know-how. I wasn't proposing to bring someone up early; it was more a general comment. I do hope he didn't think I needed 'an accident' arranged. Oh dear, I had better double check that one. We do seem to be behind, though, when it comes to software packages. I really—" Enough was enough.

"Stop!" I shouted into the receiver. There was silence for only a couple of seconds, but that silence was deafening.

"Pardon?" said the voice at the other end. The voice now sounded severe. It was the sort of "pardon" my mother would have said; it was the sort of "pardon" my old high school principal would say if you ever talked back to him.

"Stop, just please stop. I have no idea who you are or what you want. What I need to know is what the hell have you done to my parents, and how much do you want to stop all this?" It was obvious to me that this idiot was somehow involved in the attempt to either brainwash my parents or ply them with the drugs that had sent them crazy. It was ridiculous for him, whoever he was, to think that for one minute I would believe the voice on the other end of the line belonged to God. It was original; the concept of God being some highly stressed, pompous-sounding CEO surrounded by assistants with all the trappings of a modern day office. Software? Oh, please. If anyone were to impersonate God or pretend to be God then that person should not treat me like an idiot. Be original, yes, but don't go over the top!

There was nothing but silence coming from the other end of the phone. Obviously, this joker had realized I was not as susceptible as my parents were to his silly little ruse. If this biblical imposter had thought I would be playing along with his ridiculous charade, I guessed I had burst his bubble. I imagined my unidentified caller squirmed in his seat. I had probably derailed him from his prepared script.

Nothing. For at least ten seconds, no sound came from the other end. I was going to hang up, call Doctor Hienenberger, then call the police and have the call traced and my caller charged with a variety offenses. Those offenses, I was sure, would include either illegal use of hypnotic powers, the distribution of mind-altering and hallucinogenic drugs, or the impersonation of a celestial being. Maybe all three.

But then a sound came over the line. It was laughter. It was quiet at first, and then rose to a crescendo. I was tempted to slam down the phone, but once again, for some inexplicable reason, I didn't. Finally, once the laughter subsided, my caller resumed speaking.

"My dear boy," said the voice. "I must apologize once again. There's me rambling on about Saint Peter and how we should get Bill Gates up here sooner rather than later when I really should be getting straight to the point. That's typical of me, it really is, going off on a tangent, and starting something I can't finish. Reminds me of the Great Plague of London in 1665. Now that was really meant to escalate. It should have gone on for years and done a lot more damage. Not that it was malicious or anything, it was that we needed to clear things up, and I wanted to try some new things without too many people getting alarmed. Unfortunately, cheese, of all things sidetracked us. Now, of course—"

"Shut up!" I cried. This guy was driving me mad. Cheese? "Shut up and tell me what you want and what it will take for you to stop bothering my parents and to never call me again. By the way, where did you get my number?" I asked the lunatic on the other end of the phone.

"You're in the book."

"I am not in the book."

"You are listed."

"I am not listed."

"You're not?"

"No. I am not."

"Are you sure?"

"I am sure. Now where did you get my number? Did you threaten my parents to obtain it? Did you hypnotize them?" I was becoming increasingly angry with every breath.

"I assure you I did no such thing," my caller replied. "It must have been something else, then. I have it here on a post-it note. They must have gotten your number, you know, 'my team.' I don't ask where they get these things; I'm much too busy to search for telephone numbers. That's why I have a team entirely devoted to that sort of thing. The truth is I really need more help. Getting that one past the committee though won't be easy, what with budgets and cut backs and all that other boring stuff. Ideally, I should have four PAs, six secretaries, and a bigger section to help with prayers. It's not as bad as it used to be, the prayers, I mean. A few years ago, it was in the billions; now there's not as many, but that doesn't mean it's any easier. Not at all, actually. People seem to want a lot more these days, and the amount of 'lucky dippers' we get is, to be brutally honest, becoming frightfully boring.

Oh sorry, 'lucky dippers' is a term we use to describe the lottery jackpot request prayers. They really do pray a lot, and with so many people doing it, the more prayers we get, and it is, well, I hate to use the word, impossible to listen to them all. How they think I can help them, I have no idea. If I had any influence, don't they think I would be playing a few numbers myself? They clog up the system. Saint Simon calls it 'spam,' but I thought that was a type of meat. We are trying to introduce a prayer filter so we can sidetrack them, but the problem with that is they slip something else into their prayers. You know something like, 'and, oh please watch over Uncle Harry,' or 'forgive me, Lord, for I have sinned.'

I said to Peter, 'look, what we need is structure, some sort of organizational tree.' Where I can delegate some of the prayers? Did he listen? Did he take my suggestion to the committee? No. He sat on it, just as he sat on the whole New World discovery back in 1492. Tell me, I said, the moment they find it. What did he do? Left it for a few days, that is what he did. If I had known about those poor Native Americans, then I would have scrapped the whole thing. I swear I hadn't realized they were already there, but no, 'the big guy doesn't need to know, he's too busy.' Well, let me tell you, son, it's not all it's cracked up to be. Too much dead wood holding up progress, that's the crux of it. Too many people thinking they know best, too many thinkers and not enough doers. Too much red tape and too many regulations; we are getting tied up in knots up there. I sometimes yearn for the good old days of stone tablets, when I could do my own thing; now it's all got to go through a committee, think tanks, and advisors. They're talking about speechwriters, you know? Can you believe that? I invented the speech."

Once again, I felt the urgent need to interrupt, this man was mentally ill, and I had two other mentally ill people to deal with who happened to be my parents. I had no time for this, and as most people do when confronted by madness, I thought the best thing to do was ignore it.

"Listen. That's enough. Just stop there right now. I am putting down the phone. This conversation is over. Get help. You need it. You are crazy, a nut, a crazy man." And then I hung up.

That was when Walter spoke.

CHAPTER 9

"IT'S NOT ONLY THE RED tape; it's the restrictions on 'Acts of God' that gets me. I wouldn't mind, but this is all my own doing. Thank heavens, no pun intended, that today the 'committee on the second coming' gave me veto power and carte blanche authority to do what I needed to get through to you."

Walter was speaking. Walter—my cat, my lethargic, maintenance-free, obsessively self-cleaning, dried food and tuna-eating cat—was speaking. Walter, the same cat who I had inherited five years before, the exact same cat who slept all day and all night, the same cat who had never before uttered a solitary word, sat facing me on his haunches, talking to me in an English accent about red tape, acts of God, and committees.

I stared opened mouthed at my previously mute feline companion. Was I hallucinating? Was the voice coming from Walter? It was impossible. How could this be? I challenge any man, woman, or child, if faced with the same scenario, to act any more logically than I did. The damn cat was talking, for Pete's sake! Walter was speaking, even though I knew that cats did not possess voice boxes. I knew that never before in the history of cats has one ever talked, and I knew if Walter was able to talk, it would certainly not be with an English accent. He was from Greenwich Village. As far as I was aware, he had never left New York. I knew it sounded preposterous. I knew if someone asked me to believe that a cat spoke to them, I would call them crazy too. I knew it sounded ridiculous, but with God as my witness, which ironically, he was, Walter was talking.

"Ah, I see I've finally gotten your attention at last. That one always works. Don't be alarmed for poor Walter here, he hasn't a clue what's going on. I'm just speaking through him. I've done it a few times in the past, but never with a cat. Sometimes it works, other times...well, I'm afraid sometimes people completely freak out. Never mind those times, that's all in the past now. Anyway, Walter will be fine. He has no idea what's going on. He can't hear me, despite me using him as a vessel. It's quite safe. Now, Seth, listen. I suppose you're wondering what in God's name is happening here, and quite rightly so. I totally understand your aggression and your earlier attitude, but it's not often I get told to 'shut up.'"

I remained stood and opened mouthed, staring at my cat. Walter proceeded to jump down from the sofa and walk toward me. Initially, I wasn't sure whether or not to run. He rubbed against my legs, weaving in between them as he did when he wanted food.

"Are you hungry?" I asked Walter. "You need feeding?"

"I beg your pardon?" replied Walter. "Oh, heck no. No, I am so sorry. This isn't me; it's an involuntary reaction. I can only control his voice, not his actions. I do apologize; I hope I'm not getting hair on your rather soft trousers. Just ignore it if you can. But I have to say, it does feel good. Maybe you should sit down, Seth."

I did as Walter suggested. I sat down.

By then, of course, I realized it was not Walter speaking. Whilst the words were definitely coming out of his mouth, it was the same voice that had spoken to me on the phone. Please believe me when I tell you I had no choice. I had no choice but to accept that it was indeed God speaking to me. I am sorry if you may feel that I accepted it too readily and far too quickly. I assure you, I am a practical man who explores every logical explanation when dealing with problems or occurrences. But I plead with you to understand, the voice came from Walter! He sounded convincing, and coupled with the events of the previous evening, I had no doubt I was conversing with God! Believe me, please, when I say I was still searching for a logical explanation. I waited for any evidence that would disprove that I was talking to God. I looked for wires, hidden microphones, and cameras. Please do not think I did not try my best to find some sort of more earthly and logical explanation.

"Now, let me explain, Seth," began God, still talking through Walter. "All this is my fault. I should have been in touch a lot sooner. A lot, lot sooner, like, maybe twenty-nine years ago. Unfortunately, I had another project on the go, a big one, actually, which I can explain later if you require, and I haven't been around that much lately, as you could probably tell by the state of things down here. To be honest, in 'God' years, as we call them up there, thirty-two years isn't that long at all in the grand scheme of things. I know that's a lame excuse, but it's the only one I have. I sincerely hope you realize that none of this is your mother's fault; well, not all of it, at least. I let things slide, and to be brutally frank, I forgot about you."

I sat, now with my mouth now closed. While I listened to what God said, I was not exactly taking it all in. It was only later, when I went through the day's events in my head, that I dissected and analyzed the conversation, which up until that point had been virtually one sided.

"You forgot? You forgot what?" I asked. Forgot about me, did he say? Why would he even care about me? What was special about me? Unless what my parents had told me was true. While I gradually accepted that I was conversing with God, I had not accepted that I was his son. Surely he wasn't saying the same thing. Confirming Mother's claim of her virgin birth? Surely he was here to explain that there had been a mistake, an error by one of his underlings. *Oh please, tell me this is not what he is saying.*

"What are you telling me?" I asked, looking Walter directly in the eyes. Walter's eyes squinted. I have heard that is a sign of affection, but I am no cat expert.

"I am telling you I am sorry for abandoning you as a child, for being an absent father, for not being there to guide you and help you develop. I should have organized a training package, but I didn't," said God.

"Are you," I began, "trying to tell me that what my mother told me is true? That I am your son? That my father is not my real father? That I am Jesus?"

"No," said God. "You are not Jesus." That was a relief. Though I was still tense, I felt a little better. I wasn't Jesus; phew, that was something.

"What I mean by that," said God, "is that technically you are not Jesus." Oh no. The tension was back. My relief was short lived. "Jesus is his own man. In fact, he is up in Heaven; he is a member of the committee. No, you are not Jesus. However, you are Christ. You are my son, as he is, but you are Seth, not Jesus. Jesus was my vessel, who did an excellent job; I hasten to add, but he you are not. You are the Messiah, though, if that helps." Helps? Oh yeah, that helped.

"So you forgot about your son?" I asked, sounding incredulous.

"I know, I know, I know. It sounds awful, I agree, but it was so quick. The whole thing was rushed. I was in a hurry, and like I say, my so-called *staff* is not the best, I assure you. I am not passing blame or shifting responsibility, but I rely on these people, you know? Anyway, the long and short of it is that the Universe is a big place. This planet is not my only venture. There is a lot of undeveloped real estate out there, and it takes time and planning to build a civilization. There are certain conditions that have to be met, and quite frankly, I can't trust anyone up there to help me with that. That is my responsibility. I do not delegate creation. Anyway, this place I was 'prospecting,' in your terms, is five hundred million light years away, which even for me is a hike, so you can imagine I was not readily available to come back at a moment's notice. I had it all planned, booked, and organized. I really couldn't cancel. Anyway, I had people watching you. I asked Saint Peter to watch over you, and apparently he didn't get my memo, and blah, blah, blah, you get the picture; a total mess. A cock-up from start to finish."

"Anyway," God continued. "No real harm done. Well, nothing we can't sort out between us. All you need to do now is to listen and learn. You're a bright man; I am sure you will pick it up as we go. I am sorry for my tardiness, but I am here now, and I have never been one to dwell in the past or to pass blame, so I am happy to proceed and move forward. Even I can't change the past. I have been a bad father, and I can understand any resentment, but you need to get over that. You have done well without me; I read your file, and though you're obviously not there yet—far from it— we have something to play with. Something to mold. My boy, I'll make a Messiah out of you yet! Never fear! Now, there were a few things I needed to mention straight away, and I am sorry to do this, but please believe me when I tell you time is at the premium. Hold on, let me think; that's right, you're masturbating a little too much I'm afraid. You'll have to watch that. It's a little more than the committee would like. It's draining your energy apparently, and there is no need for the excessive amount of time you waste. Just an observation, but the committee felt it important that we get that one nailed down immediately."

First of all, I feel I need to point out that I do not consider myself an excessive masturbator. Whilst I am unaware of any guidance notes or recommended daily dosages, I am pretty confident that my personal habits are not outside the norm. Where God was getting his information from, I did not know, but I would have liked to have taken a peek at my file. I was naturally horrified to learn that "the committee" felt it necessary to make this their first priority in their dealings with me. Furthermore, it was inconceivable to me that my natural father, who had been had been away for thirty-two years and had practically abandoned me, critiqued me almost immediately! He had a file on me! A file! I felt the need to vent some of my views on this whole subject.

"Hold on a minute. Walter, Dad, God, or whatever I am meant to call you."

"'God' is fine; 'Dad' is fine too, though I prefer 'Dad' or 'Father,' even."

"Ok, '*Dad*,' I have a question." I wasn't sure if he caught the sarcasm.

"Shoot," said God.

"Did you really tell my father to sleep with Marla?" It was playing on my mind. I felt he needed to answer that one. I realized I had the opportunity to ask God any question I liked, but the masturbating thing had gotten my hackles up. I felt I needed to make a point that he also had some traits that were, should I say, a little questionable.

"I'm your Father," said God. He was stalling; he knew what I meant.

"Ely," I said.

"Ah, well, that, erm, well, I may have implied it was probably an option. Look, I felt sorry for the man. You know how your mother is once she gets an idea in her head. Listen, I did him a favor. I can't believe you've even brought that up. Why have you? Has he said something?" God sounded annoyed.

"He has mentioned it," I replied.

"Well, he was a willing participant; you can't put it all on me. Ely is his own man. I hope he wasn't complaining. I am sure he wasn't complaining at the time. He didn't need to tell you. I told him he was safe." God was becoming defensive. "I am a bit disappointed Ely told you that." Not wishing to incur God's wrath onto Ely, I dropped it. What was done was done; however it gave me an inclination into what I could be dealing with. I felt I had had made my point. The man had abandoned not only his son, me, but by his own admission, he had abandoned the rest of mankind for the last thirty years as well. On top of it all, he had at best aided and abbeted my father in an affair, or at worst, organized and orchestrated the whole thing! I pondered for a few seconds.

"Ok, I'm letting that one go. I am not happy about it, but I am letting it go. I won't mention it again." However, I did have another question that ate at me. "Why us? Why me? Why Ely and Irma? I really don't get it. Why a Jewish couple? Why not Christians? Surely Christians would have been better."

"Good questions," said God. Hopefully, I would get a good answer.

"And?" I prompted God for a reply.

"You have to remember, things up here were not as organized as I would have liked them to have been. We have a large turnover of administrative and support staff, and sometimes things get left to the last minute. I assure you that things have improved lately. I am sure I mentioned new innovations, and it is definitely not as bad as it was. But back then? Wow, those were chaotic times! It was a bit rushed; sometimes you mean to do something but keep putting it off and putting it off until the next thing you know, a deadline is looming. To be honest, we all got our years mixed up. I thought we had another year to plan this, but it was Saint Eligius who pointed it out; ironic, really as he is the patron saint of clock makers. Anyway, it was Eligius who made us aware we were out a year. So, as you can see, we were rather rushed to get you consummated." I didn't see. But I didn't interrupt.

"Eventually, we found ourselves in a bit of a pickle," continued God.

"A pickle?" I asked.

"A jam," said God.

"A jam?" I asked. Why God felt the need to refer to food stuffs I was not sure. I knew what he meant, I was merely trying to point out that "jam" and "pickle" were not really the terms I would have used when describing the most important event of the last two thousand years. I wasn't sure if he got it.

"You know what I mean; we ran out of time: double-booked, diaries crossed, missed communication, mistaken timings. The truth is I had this great couple from Wisconsin lined up. Great couple, absolutely fantastic couple, they were ideal, would have been wonderful. Christians, one hundred percent devout, total believers, honest, hard workers, full of faith. They were perfect, absolutely perfect." God sounded teary-eyed as he reminisced about the couple from Wisconsin. I took a good look at Walter, who remained sitting on his haunches. I checked, but I could see no tears coming from Walters oval-shaped peepers.

"What happened to them?" I asked, somewhat intrigued as to why such perfect candidates didn't get the job and why my parents appeared to be the on-field substitutes.

"What happened? What happened?" replied God, sounding perplexed. "Clerical and administrative error, that's what happened. You've guessed it. Lost memo. Some idiot messed up the paperwork. Once again, it boils down to bad and shoddy admin," God tutted. I wasn't surprised; it seemed there was a big problem involving paperwork wherever God was based, which I presumed was Heaven, but I was learning that assumption, when dealing with God, was not a wise pastime. God continued: "Anyway, I missed *it*; I know for definite that Saint Peter missed *it*, and obviously Gabriel and the other on-watch angels missed *it*."

"Missed what?" I asked.

"Missed the fact that she wasn't actually a virgin," replied God "Textbook error, really. Bad research and bad background work. It transpired that Dave—Dave was the husband," God clarified for my behalf, "well, Dave had indeed already consummated the relationship, and it seemed that Samantha, the wife, failed to mention this. I don't blame her; they were delighted to get the job.

Gabriel initially did the background check, and it was some of his team who I put on 'sex watch.'"

"Sex watch?" I asked.

"Sex watch is where I have angels on a twenty-four hour watch ensuring that virginity stays intact. It seems there was a novice angel on watch who missed the 'dirty deed.' I had been grooming this couple for years. It was a disaster, I assure you. Gabriel took full responsibility and did offer his resignation. Of course, I did not accept, but it left me with a major problem. I needed to find a virgin couple quickly. So I got my *best* man on to the job of finding one."

Believe it or not, I was still listening.

"Your *best* man?" I asked, intrigued as to who that would be.

"Ah yes, at first he was a bit reluctant. He felt I was going about it the wrong way, and he did voice his concerns. You see, he wanted to come back. He felt, as he had done such a great job the first time, he should be the one down there. He pointed out that a lot of people 'down there' believed he would be the one returning and not some newcomer. I was surprised that he agreed to get involved, but I think when he saw what a mess we were in, he decided to help. It was Jesus, your sort of half-brother, who found Irma and Ely."

"Jesus?"

"Yes, Jesus. I know I was surprised he even agreed to help, but he came through in the end. He spent hours researching Ely and Irma and then a couple of months on 'sex watch.' We really needed to avoid a 'Code Dave,' what we had named a virginity snatch, and if I couldn't rely and trust my own son, who could I trust?" asked God. The question was rhetorical, and in any case, I had no answer.

"But they're Jewish. They don't even believe in the whole 'Christ the Son of God' story," I pointed out.

"That is a good point," said God. "But so were Mary and Joseph, the original virgin couple. Both were Jews, good Jews, so it didn't seem to me that it would be a problem. Turns out, it really wasn't."

I nodded my head, indicating I understood that what he told me actually made sense. It didn't, and neither did I understand. I just felt the explanation sufficed. I was sure there would have been better and more suitable candidates than my parents, but I decided not to force the issue. What was done was done.

"Well, I suppose you do move in mysterious ways," I said, half-joking.

"No, son, that's actually a limp. There's nothing mysterious about it at all," replied God.

CHAPTER
10

I FEEL I SHOULD TAKE this opportunity to explain what was occurring in certain places around the world at the exact same moment as I was talking to God. God, it would seem, had decided to coincide his call to me with "setting the wheels in the motion" (his words, not mine.) As we spoke, he introduced the world to the new Messiah using old and trusted methods. Unfortunately, this didn't go as well as he would have liked.

These "old and trusted methods" included an image of my face miraculously appearing on a slice of toast in Sydney, Australia. Unfortunately, the recipient of this miracle toast, "Little" Timmy Grayson, aged seven, told his mom that, "there was a scary face of the Frankenstein monster on his toast" and that, "it freaked him out and he hated it." Without even looking up from the morning television show she was watching, his mother had told young Timmy to, "just eat it and shut up, you whining little git, it's the way the bread was made, just eat it," which young Timmy duly did.

Similarly, an apple cut open that morning in Johannesburg, South Africa by a Margaret Deveraux while she prepared ingredients for an apple strudel she had promised to bake her sister, Dorothy, had somehow ripened inside to produce a startlingly realistic image of my face. This apple was subsequently tossed into a bin for being "funny looking" and mistakenly presumed to be rotten. Jasper, the Deveraux's German shepherd then proceeded to rummage through the trash and devoured the Holy Apple.

THE RELUCTANT JESUS

Other attempts at these image miracles had also failed miserably. The one that I heard of later that most offended me was the image that manifested itself inside a recently felled tree in Sweden. Apparently the cut of the tree had revealed the face of "Oliver Hardy—but without the moustache" on the stump that remained. Crowds flocked to see the image of the "chubby and rotund comic" from all over Europe and indeed, the Sons of the Desert, the global Laurel and Hardy fan club, had declared that this occurrence was proof that God himself was a fan of the black and white movie greats. Especially the fat one. Actually, God did find their antics amusing but had never considered them worthy enough of an image miracle.

Like all first meetings between children and previously absentee fathers, after thirty years or so of abandonment and neglect, there was bound to be a bit of negativity and animosity on my behalf. However, I believe I handled it well, and I tried to be as understanding as was possible despite the circumstances surrounding the events of my birth and subsequent lack of preparation for the role I had to fulfill. It wasn't as if God and I would have been able to have spent quality time together anyway; I am sure he wasn't the sort of father who would have taken me to little league, taught me to ride a bike, spent time taking me on fishing trips, or even attended Parents' Evening at school. Ely had been an ideal stand-in, so I had no reason to feel animosity toward him for that.

Please don't assume that I did not like the guy. Granted, he talked to me through a cat, which was slightly off putting and a little bit strange. However, he had annoyed me, and his attitude continued to annoy me. I was annoyed primarily because I found it arrogant on his behalf that he felt he could walk straight back into my life as if nothing had happened. I was annoyed that he seemed to readily blame others for my lack of training and lack of preparation. It seemed to me that God thought he had a divine right to walk back into my life and presume I would welcome him with open arms and agree to be the Messiah. He didn't seem to fathom or even consider for one minute that maybe I was not interested in being the Messiah. Granted, I was pissed, pissed beyond belief, but the truth was that it wasn't just his pompous attitude and his unwillingness to accept responsibility that annoyed me; it was the fact that I was quite happy with my life as it was, and to be perfectly honest, the whole God and Messiah business was his business, and thanks, but no thanks. I didn't want it. I had got on for thirty-two years just fine, thank you. Thanks for calling, but unfortunately, I was not interested in what he was selling. That was how I felt, and that was when my conversation with God that morning turned a little nasty.

Walter had curled up into a ball, and it appeared he was planning on going to sleep.

"Ignore this," said God. "I am still here, I am still listening, it's just that Walter is taking a probably well-deserved catnap," explained God. Walter was now talking in this sleep, and though his eyes were closed, his mouth still twitched open and close whenever God spoke. It was a most unnerving sight. I decided now would be a good time to thank God for his visit, but to let him know I was not interested in being the Messiah or second coming of Christ.

"So, God, Dad, it has been great meeting you and everything," I said politely and pleasantly, "but what is it you actually want from me?" I asked, still unsure of God's plan.

"Want from you?" asked God, sounding a little surprised that I did not already know.

"Yes, want, need, require. There must be a reason you picked today to call? It's not like you were in the neighborhood passing through, or you are on your deathbed and wanted to make peace with those who you did wrong, trying to amend for the years you forgot about me." I paused. "You're not on your deathbed, are you?" I asked, suddenly concerned with the implications if God suddenly died.

"No, I am fine, never felt better, actually. I do not possess a deathbed, nor any other type of bed, come to think of it," God reassured me. That was a relief. The implication of no God was worse than a forgetful, pompous, responsibility shirking, and absent God.

"Well, then," I continued, "what is it that brought you here? Why now? Why today? I am a little confused as to the urgency of all this." Walter's ear twitched involuntarily as he slept. It often did this, and I used to mistake it as a sign that he had fleas. Many were the times I would transport Walter to the vet's office for unnecessary de-flea treatments and tick removal. The fact that Walter, to my best knowledge, had never ventured outdoors unless to visit the vet's office for these flea treatments made the whole flea issue a non-issue, but it was best to be safe rather than sorry.

"Armageddon," said God.

"Come again?" I asked, trying not to be overly distracted by the twitching ear and the fact that Walter appeared to be sleeping. It wasn't that I hadn't heard what God had said; I felt the need to hear it again, for clarification.

"Armageddon, the Apocalypse, the end of days, Revolution chapter whatever, you know, end of the world, the battle for souls, the final conflict, fire and brimstone, good versus evil, and all that," said God as if describing nothing of real significance. I felt the need to find out more. Actually, I felt it imperative and highly necessary that I gleaned some more information from my nonchalant father.

"What about it? What about Armageddon? How does that affect me, exactly?" I asked. I hoped the underlying tone of panic that accompanied my voice was not overly apparent.

"Well, it's time, you know, as foretold in the Bible, chapter whatever, verse something or other, book of Revolution. Surely you've heard of it?"

I scratched my head as Walter's ear continued to flick. For some inexplicable reason, I had a sudden urge to swipe Walter. It wasn't that his ear flickered and moved manically as he snoozed; it was something else. Ah, yes, it was my frustration at God. I had the feeling this Armageddon thing was a big issue, and if I hadn't asked, I wondered when he was going to bring up the subject. I had the underlying and sinking feeling that God seemed to think I would be playing an important part in this "Armageddon" scenario.

"Have you actually ever read the Bible?" I asked.

Walter's ear stop flicking, and he raised his head and stared at me straight on before yawning.

"Sort of," said God.

"Sort of? What does that mean? Sort of? It's your book. It's about you! How can you quote the Bible when you have only 'sort of' read it? I've even read part of it, and I'm Jewish. For a start, it's not the book of 'Revolution,' it's the book of Revelation. How could you not know that?" Deep down I already knew the answer, and I did not expect a reply. Walter stood up and arched his back to stretch, which he always did after a nap. He yawned again, jumped down from the sofa, and made his way to where his food and water bowls lived inside the kitchen.

"I was meant to proofread it before they released it. I kind of glanced through it, you know, got the general gist of things. What I read seemed fine. A few spelling errors, the odd grammatical error, and some chapters were better than others, but overall, I thought it was a good effort, good plot, great characters, and I enjoyed the bits I read in detail. To be honest, we had a whole team working on it, proofreading, re-writing, editing; there wasn't much more I could add. And anyway, writing isn't my sort of thing. I leave that to the eggheads and scholars. I am a much more hands-on, give-me-a-screwdriver, give-me-a-hammer, give-me-a-Universe-to-create sort of fellow."

God paused to allow Walter to drink from his bowl of water before he spoke again. Walter licked his lips, and I was sure he was going to start on his fish-flavored dry food, but instead, he left the kitchen and returned to the sofa and sat, once again, on his haunches.

"With Armageddon just around the corner, I thought it was time you started to earn your keep."

"My keep?" I queried.

"Just a figure of speech. Sorry, I didn't mean to say that. Scratch that, there is no keep, bad term of phrase," apologized God, rather too readily, I hasten to add, and it didn't go unnoticed. In any case, I had more pressing concerns.

"What do you mean by 'just around the corner?' What do you mean by Armageddon?" Once again, I hoped the nervousness in my voice was not as apparent to God as it was to me. God seemed to ignore my questions and continued to speak in his unnervingly jolly and pompous-sounding voice.

"Anyway, we really need to get cracking; we have no time to lose. We need to get you out there on the streets, collecting the lambs for saving, and all that, getting everyone prepared."

"No," I said.

"Sorry," said God, "for a minute there I thought you said 'no.'" Walter had jumped down form the sofa and flicked one of his toy balls with bells in it along the floor. The jingle jangling was slightly distracting.

"I did say 'no.' No, I am not interested. I don't want the job. Thanks, but no thanks. Great meeting you, no hard feelings and all that, but I am not interested in your offer. I get the feeling that Armageddon is probably not a good thing, and if my memory is correct, I am sure it involves violence and destruction and hassle. I do not need hassle in my life. The fact that you said 'around the corner' is also not a good indication. I don't think this is the job for me. I think you should go to plan B."

Walter stopped flicking the ball and rolled over onto his back.

"No plan B," said God, "and anyway why ever not?" He sounded a little upset. "It's a great job."

"Because I am quite happy with my life as it is, thank you very much. For a start, I already have a great job. I am happy, and I don't need this right now. Not now, not ever. I am sure it won't be too difficult for you to find somebody else. Surely there is another virgin birth out there or at least someone whose parents just did it once. Is it really that important, this whole virgin thing? I know I am your son, and I know this is obviously a family commitment, but couldn't you maybe adopt? Why not adopt some super priest who knows karate or something? Surely there is a better candidate out there than me." I hoped I didn't sound too desperate.

Walter stretched his claws on my sofa. He had never done that before, and I suspected it was God's influence. I thought about smacking him on the head but reconsidered.

"I would appreciate it if you would stop that. This sofa is new," I said. Walter stopped clawing at the sofa and returned to sit on his haunches. I inspected my furniture and saw the damage was minimal.

"I am sorry," said God. At first I thought he was going to apologize for scratching my sofa. "I am afraid the job *is* yours. There is no one else, and you are it. The *one*. *El numero uno*. Do you think there is another virgin-born child out there? You think I have a ready stock of virgins just hanging about, hoping they miraculously become pregnant? What, I need to place an advert? 'Wanted, male, age 32, born to a virgin mother, prepared to save the world in upcoming battle against evil. Long hours, some traveling, and excellent benefits.

Training package provided.' Come on, son, be realistic. Adopt? A super priest? Karate? I have to say, I'm a little disappointed in your attitude."

I could tell from his tone he was getting annoyed. I got the feeling not too many people said 'no' to God. I also got the feeling that I should not push him too far. I was sure he probably had a temper. I think I had read that somewhere. His voice was getting louder, and I noticed Walter staring at me. Usually, I always won our little staring competitions. In fact, I always won. But Walter's gaze was not diverting. I felt even more unnerved. I broke away from Walter's gaze.

"You think I wanted it this way? You think this is how I planned it?" shouted God. "Did you not hear me when I told you about the couple from Wisconsin? They were ideal. It's not my fault we are in this forsaken predicament. I cannot believe any son of mine would be so uncompromising. I would have thought you would have jumped at the chance. I really do not understand your reluctance."

God's tone softened slightly, "Come on, Seth, be a sport; most people would jump at the chance of being the Messiah, and you know some people out there actually dream about things like this."

"I'm not most people," I answered.

"Please?" pleaded God.

This was ridiculous. Not only did he want me to take the job, he wanted me to take the job at probably the worst possible time: at the beginning of the end of the world. I hadn't read the Bible all the way through, and I was no expert, but I had seen the movies. Brimstone, fire, volcanoes, pestilence, plague, disease, famine, great special effects, maybe, but what a time to appear.

"Listen," said God, his tone hardening, "it's not negotiable anyway. You are doing it, and that's final. There is no one else; if you don't do it, then I am afraid that you are going to let a whole lot of people down. Millions are relying on you. If you do not step up to the plate, then the forces of darkness will win the day, and that will really put a bad spin on the whole Universe. The consequences would be, well, unimaginable. I do not think you fully realize the implications of you doing nothing. I don't remember it being as difficult as this last time." Walter paced the living room, his tail flicking from side to side, as it did when he was annoyed.

"Oh, do come along and say you'll at least give it a try. A volunteer is worth a thousand pressed men," pleaded God again.

"No," I said.

"You will do it," said God. The anger had once again returned to his voice, and I felt slightly intimated.

"I won't do it," I said. There was shakiness in my voice, and I knew he would pick up on it.

"You will!" shouted God. The outburst startled me, but I remained steadfast.

"I won't," I said calmly. I could not believe I was even having this conversation. Walter sat on the coffee table, his face inches from mine. I could smell the tuna on Walter's breath.

"Oh yes, son, oh yes, you will do it. This isn't the last you've heard of this," and then Walter meowed.

CHAPTER 11

I KNEW THAT GOD HAD left the moment Walter meowed. That meow signified that the conversation was over and God had left the building. Walter resumed his sleeping; he curled up in a ball in his favorite position on the sofa. I eyed him for a few moments, half expecting him to raise his head and for the discussion with God to start again. Once I was satisfied that this was not going to happen, I decided the one thing I needed was a drink. I poured myself a neat scotch and drank it quickly. While not unusual for me to take a drink alone at home, it was unusual for me to drink before noon. I felt the burn in my throat as the whiskey descended my throat. I sighed and took a deep breath. I needed that.

I made a mental note to call my parents. I supposed I owed them an apology. It seemed they were not as mad as I had first thought, however their failure to inform me of the full facts surrounding my birth until yesterday remained contentious. I held off calling them immediately. The encounter with God that morning had really taken it out of me. I had a lot to ponder and a few more questions for God. I was not happy that our conversation had ended so abruptly. I was usually not so confrontational, but he had rubbed me the wrong way. I felt his attitude, while maybe acceptable wherever he came from, was not going to work with me. Maybe I had gone too far, and maybe I hadn't shown the respect due to the creator of the Universe, but the fact that he felt he could waltz into my life and proclaim me his Messiah galled me slightly. He certainly had some nerve.

THE RELUCTANT JESUS

I wrote a list of questions in preparation for our next encounter. I felt if I had a direct line to the Almighty, I needed some important questions answered. Despite our conversation that morning ending abruptly, I was sure he would be back in touch once we had both calmed down. I supposed I might have hurt his feelings by turning down his job offer, but I could not see myself as the second coming. There were reasons, many reasons, as to why I was not a suitable candidate to be the Messiah. I imagined the looks of sheer horror on the faces of Christians the world over once they realized their savior was a podgy, Jewish architect from Greenwich Village. In any case, who would ever believe it? I was sure that history was full of pretenders, who claimed to be the second coming of Jesus Christ, and everyone laughed at them and they were incarcerated, or worse. I was sure I would be the least believable of them all despite the fact I actually was the Messiah.

I was intrigued, though, as to what Armageddon entailed. Did it actually mean the end of the world? Had God passed me crucial information as to the destiny of mankind? I wasn't sure what my next move should be. Should I call the Pentagon and warn them that the end of the world was nigh?

I took another mouthful of scotch and closed my eyes. I needed to share my burden. I also needed the views of a third party. In a situation like this, a man turns to one person for advice, the one person who could shed light and reason on all of life's tribulations, the one person a man can truly rely on—his drinking buddy; mine being Bob Nancy.

I had known Bob Nancy for five years, and I considered him to be my best friend. While on the surface, it seemed we didn't have a lot in common, but if one scratched away a little, you would find we shared a lot of common interests and had similar thought processes. Our main common interest was baseball and the Yankees. We were both season ticket holders and avid fans. Like me, Bob had been a fan since childhood, and as we were the same age and both originally from Brooklyn, I guessed our paths probably crossed on many occasions as children without either of us ever realizing.

We attended games together during the season, and when the Yankees were on the road, we would sit in bars together watching our team and partaking of our second common interest: drinking copious amounts of beer. In the history of my life, I have not had many friends, wholly due to my mother's interference during my college and high school years. However, I made up for my lack of fun growing up by drinking more beer than any college kid ever has with my good friend Bob Nancy. Our drunken nights were the highlight of his life and one of the highlights of mine. We would talk baseball, eat chicken wings, watch girls, and talk crap. Bob and I were soul mates when it came to sport, drinking beer, and talking crap.

Bob was a teacher of elementary kids at a school in Harlem, the name of which eludes me. Harlem was also where he lived with his wife, Nancy. Yes, you read that correctly, his wife Nancy—Nancy Nancy. Bob and I first met at a party hosted by a friend of Nancy's whom I was dating casually; we were both wearing Yankee pins, both against the wishes of our respective partners, and were both completely and utterly bored with the party. While my relationship with Nancy's friend eventually fizzled out, Bob's and my relationship blossomed, much to the annoyance of his wife.

Nancy didn't care for me much, and I guessed there were numerous reasons why she didn't. No doubt her friend whom I had dated and then dumped had blackened my name. I am sure tales were told of the way I had callously ended the relationship. Though Nancy had never confronted me, I got the feeling from her stares and the hostility I sensed from her that she thought I was "flaky." Maybe the hostility was also due to the fact that I was single, and I spent a lot of time with her husband. It was always my fault when Bob returned drunk or late from a game or bar. I was her nemesis, and Bob assured me that in any argument between the two of them, they would mention my name at least five times. I therefore only called Bob when I knew Nancy wouldn't be around. I had only visited Bob's home once, and my apartment had become a haven for him whenever he needed time away from Nancy.

Bob was, by all accounts, a good teacher, and if I had had kids, I would have been happy for a guy like Bob Nancy to be teaching them. I liked Bob because he listened, and he was objective. I liked Bob because he liked me and because Bob was the least judgmental person I had ever met.

Bob and Nancy had no children. Nancy was a cop, one of New York's finest. Being a cop meant that Nancy spent most of her time either sleeping or out of the house, which was good for Bob's and my relationship, as she hardly ever veered from her monthly scheduled roster, of which I had a copy, provided by Bob, so I knew when the coast was clear to call.

The Nancys were not a religious couple. I wasn't even sure what religion they were. Bob and I had never discussed religion, as it was something neither of us considered important in our lives. I knew they were married in a church, though; I had seen the photographs. Bob had shown them to me once when Nancy was working her shift. I think he was trying to show me that Nancy had once been an attractive woman, which I was sure she had been, maybe one hundred pounds ago.

The Nancy's were an odd-looking couple. Though she had a pleasant face, she was extremely heavy. When I say heavy, I mean obese. When I say obese, I mean morbidly obese. She is a big woman, and I am sure the mere sight of her strikes fear into the hearts of the city's criminal fraternity. I am sure New York City is a safer place thanks to Officer Nancy Nancy, and her equal dedication to both duty and doughnuts. In stark contrast, Bob was as skinny as a beanpole. I mean, really skinny. Despite our joint consumption of calorie-laden beer and fast food, Bob never put on weight. He was tall too, six feet three, and he had the face of a weasel, but even though he did look like a cunning mammal, he was the nicest guy you could ever wish to meet.

One thing was for sure, though; Bob Nancy was my best friend, and right now, I needed a best friend. I checked Nancy's duty roster, which I had placed on my refrigerator, secured by a Yankee's fridge magnet, and was satisfied to see the coast was clear for me to call. As it was summer break, I knew Bob would be home, so I hit the quick dial button that housed his number and took a deep breath.

"Hi, Bob," I said when the phone was answered, secure in the knowledge that only Bob would answer.

"Mr. Miller, how nice of you to call," replied Bob jovially. He had programmed my number as Mr. Miller rather than Seth into his phone. Nancy did not know my surname, and it was a devious plan of Bob's should she ever catch him talking to me. She inevitably always wanted to know who he was conversing with, and he would point to the display. She presumed Mr. Miller was just another school teacher. A cop she was, but a detective she wasn't.

"She's not there, is she?" I asked, double-checking in case he had brought the Mr. Miller ruse into play because Nancy was home.

"No, just kidding around, she's working, as per her schedule; no change there. In fact, she could be working more; there's some crazy stuff going on. Some guy's chained himself to the railings of some downtown church. He's been there all day, apparently. I've been watching it on the local news. It's causing chaos with the traffic," said my friend.

I could hear the TV in the background; I imagined Bob stood watching the TV while he talked with me with the remote control in one hand, the phone nestled under his chin, and probably a sandwich in his other hand. Bob had a lot of free time in the summer, and while I envied his hours and holidays, I didn't envy his paycheck.

"Never mind that," I said, relieved that Nancy was not there. "I've got something to tell you. And it's kind of crazy."

"Go ahead, I'm listening," said Bob. I told Bob to sit down and listen with an open mind. I felt I needed to prepare him fully for what I was about to tell him. If my fate was sealed and there was no getting out of this thing, then I had to start somewhere. Sooner or later the world would have to know who I was, so I started with Bob.

I threw caution to the wind and told Bob everything. I explained it all from the start. From Mother's phone call to the talk with Walter, the English accent, the other planets in the Universe, the apocalypse, Dad's affair with Marla, the whole thing, committees, clerical errors, computer programs, and post-it notes. I made sure I left out no detail. I relayed to him every event that had occurred in my life in the last twenty-four hours. Just talking about it helped. I felt a wave of relief pass over me. It was a cleansing feeling; it was as if by telling all to Bob, I had somehow shifted some of my burden on to him. When I had completed my story, I waited for Bob's response.

"Well, it seems as though you may have a problem." That was the understatement of the year. I was relieved, though, that Bob's first words hadn't been "you're nuts." At least that response indicated that he believed me. "If you ask me, this God character of yours is a real piece of work. At the very best, he seems to have no idea how to run a large organization. Sounds as if the whole thing is a pig's ear from the start." Like I said, Bob pulled no punches. He said it how it was, and I usually agreed with him. My initial fears that Bob would declare me mad, inform the nearest asylum, and have me carted away were totally abated. Luckily, Bob and I had shared many a strange drunken conversation, and I suppose he just accepted what I had to say. I mean, let's be honest, who would really invent such a crazy story?

"It seems to me you really need to get out of this thing. The Armageddon thing does not sound good. In fact, it sounds bad. It seems God is putting a heck of a lot of pressure on you. It's like going from the minors to the majors overnight and finding yourself in the middle of the World Series," surmised my friend in terms we could both relate to. I agreed with Bob. It was imperative I got out of being the Messiah. I hoped Bob had a plan.

"Unfortunately, I don't have a plan," said Bob, "and as I see it, there is one underlying and unequivocal problem. As God has clearly pointed out, there is no replacement. There is nobody else that can fill your shoes, and it seems to me that you have little choice for now but to go along with it." My heart sank. I knew Bob was right; he usually was. "The most pressing concern in my mind," continued Bob, "is that unless you take up the mantle, then the world is doomed. By the way, have you read Revelation the whole way through?"

I replied that I had not. Luckily, Bob had more knowledge of it than I did. "Well, basically, if memory serves me correctly, the whole return of the Christ and the second coming culminates in this big battle between Heaven and Hell, kind of like the *Return of the Jedi*, where Luke has to fight Darth Vader. Seems to me that if the Bible is correct, then you win; however, there seems to be some elements that don't quite fit. I mean the seven riders of the apocalypse and all the signs. It seems to me as though some bits are missing. The Bible was very specific on the events surrounding your manifestation."

I explained to Bob about God's tardy proofreading of the Bible, how it was possible that certain things may not be one hundred percent accurate, and that the Bible, while it might be a good reference point, was not reliable on its contents being completely gospel, so to speak.

"Well, that may be so, but one thing that must be considered is the possibility that your life is in danger," said Bob after a brief pause for thought. This was something I did not want to hear, and hadn't previously considered.

"In what way?" I asked.

"Well, on a number of fronts actually. I am sure there are nut jobs out there who would love to take out the son of God. God's not as popular as he thinks. He may have a lot of fans out there, but there's always the nut factor. Let's not forget the anti-Christ either, your arch enemy, your nemesis, your Darth Vader, the son of the devil, the beast, the serpent, you know—the bad guy. Let's not forget him. Sooner or later, you're going to have to face him."

Bob had a point. Even if I didn't take the job and went on with my everyday life, then all this "beast" character would need to do would be to knock me off, and the battle would be over. I was probably better off with God on my side, protecting me, than if I buried my head in the sand. Even if I didn't want to save the world—and really, apart from Bono, who actually did?—then I needed to at least save myself. Bob and I both agreed that the forces of darkness probably had a lot of resources, and that maybe I was better siding with God and obtaining some sort of protection, guidance, and training.

"So you think I should go along with this whole thing?" I asked Bob.

"After considering all the implications, you have no choice. I hate to say it, but yes, you should go along with it. Not totally, maybe long enough to defeat Satan and save the world, but more importantly, save you. Then you can forget it. Try and negotiate some sort of short-term contract; take it to Armageddon and reconsider your options. Maybe take the job on a trial basis." I wasn't sure how God would react to contract negotiations, but it was better than refusing point blank. At least it was a compromise, and considering the alternatives, I didn't have much choice.

The problem was I had no idea how I could contact God and put forward my proposal.

I had taken enough of Bob's time, and chances were that Nancy was on her way back home.

"Bob, thanks for listening, I will give you a call if there are any more developments. One more thing though; I wouldn't mention any of this to Nancy. You know what she's like when it comes to me. I think the less people who know about it at this stage, the better." Bob agreed that telling Nancy would be a disastrous move, while no doubt she would find it highly amusing at first, there was no telling what she would do. She could have me locked up as a madman for all I knew. I wouldn't have put it past her.

"Hey, listen, I just had a thought: you're going to need disciples, a team of helpers like Jesus had," said Bob just as I thought our conversation was over.

"Disciples?" It was something I hadn't had chance to consider, but it sounded a good idea. If they were good enough the first time around, I saw no reason why they shouldn't be good the second time.

"Yeah, disciples. Listen, I'm your man, count me in. I'll be your chief disciple, your number two. Hey, I've got six more weeks off school! Nancy's got no vacation time, and I am getting tired of watching Doctor Phil and Judge Judy," said Bob, who sounded excited at the prospect at joining me in my misery.

"God didn't mention disciples," I said. "He said a lot, but he didn't specifically mention disciples. I'm all for it, and I could use some help and support. I'll run it by him during contract negotiations," I promised my friend.

"Well, make sure you do, I'm very interested. Think about it, and don't forget to run it by him when you next talk. Hey, I'm with you man, I'm there for you. It could actually be fun, if you discount Armageddon and the end of the world." Unfortunately, "fun" was the last word that sprang to my mind as our conversation ended.

After concluding my call with Bob, I waited for God to either call back or talk through Walter. I watched Walter for any sign that would indicate he was about to speak, but none came. The scotch I had drunk earlier was beginning to take effect, and I decided a lie down was the best course of action. I hadn't slept well in the easy chair at my parents' home the night before, and it was no surprise that my eyelids felt heavy.

I slept well for four hours straight. No dreams or visions from God molested my thoughts, and when I awoke at five in the afternoon, I felt refreshed and revitalized. During those first initial seconds of awakening, I felt relaxed, calm, and contented. I stretched my arms and legs and smiled to myself; there was nothing quite like an afternoon nap. It was only when my brain shifted into gear and my senses were fully restored that I remembered. The events of the morning came flooding back, and my original feeling of contentment vanished, and my stomach knotted.

I rechecked that Walter was still Walter, and I satisfied myself that the ball of ginger fluff curled up on a sun-drenched patch of floor near a window was indeed my cat by whispering, "Are you there?" into his ear. When I received no response, it was clear to me that God was not here. The phone hadn't rung while I slept, and I had no messages. I grabbed the TV remote control and switched on the local evening news.

I wasn't paying much attention to the news, but when I saw a familiar figure pass onto my screen, I increased the volume and leaned toward the screen. Nancy, her frame unmistakable, was giving an interview to a reporter on the street. Nancy, who always looked ridiculous in her super-sized NYPD police uniform, was obviously the police spokesperson for whatever the news channel was covering.

It seemed that downtown traffic had been brought to a standstill all day. Nancy explained that while the situation was not yet over, it was contained. The reason for this chaotic traffic situation was due entirely to the events at Christ Church, located at the corner of Park Avenue and 60th Street. A man, previously unidentified but now known to be Ronnie Misfud, aged thirty-eight of Queens, New York, had chained and padlocked himself to the railings that surrounded the church. He had used extra strength chain and had super glued the twenty-five padlocks that fastened him to the railings, thus making it virtually impossible for the police locksmith to pry him from the railings. Various types of bolt cutters had also been called for, but none were strong enough to break the chains that entwined Ronnie's body with the railings.

THE RELUCTANT JESUS

The progress to remove Ronnie was slow, as he had chained himself to the church railings for well over nine hours. The police, represented by Nancy, were confident they would remove Ronnie within the hour; extra-strength bolt cutters had been called for. Meanwhile, traffic slowed to walking pace in the vicinity of the church as onlookers, television news crews, and emergency vehicles blocked the adjacent avenues.

Some suggested that all the police needed to do was merely saw through the railings, but the church had expressly forbidden any actions that could result in damage to their historic railings. Because of that, the process of freeing Ronnie was slow and laborious, and had taken up many police resources.

I found the whole thing quite amusing, and a smile spread across my face. Not because it seemed Nancy struggled with the reporter's questions and veiled implied remarks of police incompetence, but also because if I had gone to my office today, I would have been one of the tens of thousands stuck in traffic with a cab's meter ticking away. It was only when the reporter touched on the reason for Ronnie's actions that my smile disappeared.

It seemed, according to Ronnie himself, that he had had a vision from God earlier that morning. In this vision, God had informed Ronnie that he had been chosen to spread the good news that the Messiah was amongst us, and soon the new son of God would reveal himself to world. It also seemed that God had told Ronnie that the forces of darkness were readying themselves for what Ronnie described as the final conflict between good and evil, as prophesized by the book of Revelation.

Ronnie had told the assembled media that the only way he could think of gaining public attention was to chain himself to the church and cause as much disruption as possible. It seemed psychiatrists were on the scene, and an ambulance stood by to transport poor Ronnie to the nearest mental hospital for tests and treatment the moment Nancy and her colleagues freed him.

Naturally, I found this rather disturbing. Was Ronnie a deranged lunatic, hell-bent on causing disruption to the New York City traffic, or had he genuinely received a message from God? According to the reporter's research, Ronnie did not have a record of any mental health problems, and according to friends and family who had gathered at the scene and who were now giving interviews to the press, he was not an overly religious man, and none could explain why Ronnie had secured himself to the railings.

Usually, a news item like this would not keep me glued to the television, and even considering my current predicament, only so much footage of Ronnie chained to a railing could keep me enthralled. I was about to switch channels when the reporter said something that sent shivers down my spine. Apparently Ronnie was not the only one to receive word from God that morning.

Reports were coming in from around the globe of individuals causing disruption and attempting to gain media coverage while claiming they too had spoken to God, and just like Ronnie's story, it seemed the Messiah was amongst us, and preparations were afoot for Armageddon.

The reporter informed her viewers that an unidentified man had attached himself to the Sydney Harbor Bridge, causing disruptions to early morning commuters. In London, where it was approaching midnight, Big Ben would not be chiming, as another unidentified male had perched himself on the hour hand of the famous clock. In Los Angeles, the airport halted lunchtime flights while several airport police tried to coax a rather animated and naked young man from the main runway at LAX. While these events, according to the reporter, were not directly linked, it seemed every individual was proclaiming the same thing: that God had spoken to them and told them to spread the word that his son was on Earth, and to prepare the people for the battle for souls.

I was jolted from my thoughts by the telephone. It was Bob calling me to see if I was watching the news. I confirmed I was, and he whistled and hewed, which didn't help matters, but it confirmed what I thought: God was serious. I said I would call Bob back as I needed to keep the line free for God's call. I also woke Walter by throwing a cushion at his still-sleeping mass. He raised his head and stared at me indignantly. I urged him to speak but he appeared uninterested. Bob told me to call him immediately if there were any developments and not to worry about Nancy, as she had called home to say she would be working late. Apparently Ronnie was going to take longer to remove than the police were telling the assembled media. Before hanging up, Bob told me he thought Nancy looked great on TV and that maybe they would make her the department spokeswoman. I declined to comment and told him I would call him with news when it came.

A split second after I replaced the handset of the telephone onto the receiver, it rang again. I answered it quickly, hoping it was God. It wasn't him, but the second best thing: my mother. Like Bob, she asked me if I was watching the news, and I told her I was. I also told her I had spoken to God that morning. Luckily, Thursday nights were her bridge night, so we didn't stay on the line for long, and she cut the conversation short, which saved me from telling her to get off the line. I did not feel like going into my refusal to take the job or any of the other details of my morning's talk with God, so it was a relief that she was not on the line for long.

After I hung up the phone, I waited for it to ring. It didn't, so I resumed viewing the chronicles of Ronnie chained to the railings. Shots were now coming in from London where a crowd had gathered and spotlights had been erected to highlight the man perched on the minute hand of Big Ben. He had some sort of sheet he was using as a banner, which, when unfolded, proclaimed, "The Messiah is amongst us."

It was while pondering the fates of all the global announcers of my arrival that the phone rang. It was him, at last.

CHAPTER
12

"RATHER IMPRESSIVE DON'T YOU THINK?" said God, the voice no different from the last time he called.

"So you *are* responsible. You know these poor men will probably all be arrested, don't you? I think poor Ronnie could be heading to a psychiatric ward." I was genuinely concerned for the welfare of these individuals. I felt somehow responsible for their predicaments.

"That's my boy," said God, "compassionate and caring. Don't worry, I will see no harm comes to them, and I assure you that they will not be charged or detained in any institution." I was relieved to hear this; the last thing I wanted on my conscience was any of those modern-day prophets to fall to their death or incarcerated in mental wards.

"Good. That makes me feel a little better," I said. "Look, I'm glad you called. I felt bad about the way things went this morning. I feel I should apologize. Maybe I came across as being a little abrupt." It was, I suppose, an apology.

"Apology accepted," said God, "and I trust you don't need me to do the whole cat thing again, do you? I found it a little uncomfortable, and I am sure poor Walter wasn't pleased."

"I'm fine with this," I confirmed, convinced I was indeed talking to God, that God was indeed my father, and that I was indeed the Messiah.

"Maybe I am the one who owes you an apology," God said "I think maybe we did get off on the wrong foot, and it was probably down to me. I do that sometimes, come across all almighty and demanding. I should have considered your feelings. It's not every day you find out your whole life has been a lie." I felt that was a little dramatic, but it was a good feeling, hearing God apologize. It seemed we might have turned a corner in our relationship.

"It's been a busy day around here," continued God, "and the committee and I got together to discuss things. Well, you, really. The upshot of the meeting was that maybe I, we, them, rushed you into this, and that maybe we should have broken you in gradually." *That was good to hear,* I thought to myself. "Mind you, we still do not know for sure what the other side is planning. We need to get you trained and vested in my ways as soon as possible. While there is a set of rules pertaining to Armageddon, the final conflict, and indeed Satan, I have discussed the matter in the past, and I have learnt that we must approach dealings with him in caution. The committee and I all feel we must progress but at a slower pace than I had earlier anticipated. I take it you're in? I mean, you have reconsidered? You will do it, won't you?" I got the feeling God already knew the answer.

"Yes, I will do it, though I do have a few conditions—" God interrupted before I could outline my conditions.

"Not a problem, the committee has agreed to your conditions already." So God had been watching me. I wondered how closely he, his angels, or even one of the committee had been watching. I was sure I hadn't masturbated that afternoon, so that was a relief.

"Who actually sits in on this committee?" I asked, intrigued, and of course interested as to who might have had the job of watching me over the years, and who was responsible for compiling my file.

"Me, of course, as chairman, Saint Peter the apostle—he's kind of my right hand man—Saint Francis, who represents the patron saints; a couple of old Popes; John the Baptist—you'd like him, he's the voice of reason—Mother Teresa, she's relatively new, but it's good to have a woman's perspective; she's quiet and sometimes a little overly awed, but she spots things we would otherwise miss; Gandhi; and Gabriel—the angel Gabriel; as boss of the angels, he is pivotal in providing feedback on what is going on on Earth. He's a bit like an enforcer, does my dirty work and snooping around, plus a lot of the ground work for stuff on Earth."

"Wasn't Gandhi a Hindu?" I interrupted.

"Yes, but he had so much to offer, and we needed his perspective on things, so I made a couple of calls, pulled a few strings, and got him on the committee. He's very placid but extremely good when it comes to ideas. He's my idea man."

"Who else?" I asked.

"Let me see; it's not a permanent committee, it only convened when it was decided you would be doing my bidding. Let me see, Joan of Arc, she's a member but doesn't input too much," said God.

"What about Jesus?" I asked.

"Who?" said God. I was sure he had heard me, but I repeated myself for his benefit.

"Jesus, you know, you're eldest child. The original Son of God and my half-brother," I clarified so there could be no mistake as to whom I was referring. There was quiet on the line. It seemed, for the first time since I had met him that God was at a loss for words. Either that, or Jesus was a subject he didn't like to discuss. Had I hit a nerve?

Eventually God spoke.

"Yes, he's on the committee. As I mentioned earlier, I gave him the job of watching over your parents and helping with their selection. He's my adviser, my left hand guy as opposed to my right hand guy. Listen, don't be offended and don't take this the wrong way, but he doesn't care for you too much. In fact, he doesn't like you at all."

I was rather taken aback by this revelation; considering we had never met, I felt it slightly bold of Jesus to dislike me, especially considering who he was. I felt an explanation was in order. "Why not?" I asked, slightly hurt that my only sibling, albeit a half-brother, did not care for me. "Why doesn't Jesus like me?" I could tell God didn't want to get into this debate.

"It's not important. He's agreed to work with me on this, and that's that. He'll get over it; we have far more important things to discuss than Jesus's feelings toward you." Unfortunately for God, I was not about to let it drop. Despite God's attempts at fudging the issue, something I was beginning to realize he was rather good at, I felt I deserved more information.

"Ok," said God after I badgered a bit more. "There are several issues that Jesus has when it comes to you."

"Several?"

"Yes, several. First, he thinks you're the wrong man for the job. He says you're flaky, and he doesn't like your attitude. He's disappointed that you haven't taken the job on in the same vain he did. He thinks you lack commitment and that you are whiney."

"Flaky? Whiney?" I repeated.

"Yes, in modern day terms he refers to you as a 'loser.' He says you lack inspiration and leadership qualities. He thinks you are shallow and rather self-centered. He thinks you could possibly show him in a bad light and ruin the work he has already done."

If I was to be brutally honest, Jesus had some rather salient points, and if I were an outsider, I would probably concur with his appraisal of my character.

"Also," God continued, "I think he is still a tad annoyed that it isn't him back down there. I think he presumed I would send him back to finish the job he started two thousand years ago. I think he is a little jealous that you are the one who is going to be in the limelight, so to speak." Great. On top of everything else, I had sibling rivalry to deal with. "Don't get me wrong, though," continued God. "You have his support, and he is one hundred percent behind you. It's just that, well, give it time, and I am sure he'll come around." I wasn't sure how I felt about the Jesus issue.

"Is there anything else he has said that I should know about?" I asked. I felt I needed to know everything should we eventually meet.

"He has commented on your lack of disciples," admitted God. "You know, he could pull a crowd, and he was very, very popular with his own disciples. He has pointed out that he doubted you could find any." Aha, so God didn't know everything and neither did Jesus.

"Well, in that case, I have good news for the both of you," I said gleefully.

"Good news?" said God. "Please do tell."

"I have a disciple," I said a little boastfully.

"You do?" God sounded delighted "That is fantastic news, absolutely fantastic." I was glad God sounded delighted. "Splendid, excellent, that's a good start, that's an amazing start for just one day. How many do you have?"

"One," I answered.

"Oh," said God, not sounding as delighted as he was a second ago.

"Hey, it's a start; it's only been a day, for your sake!" I cried, sensing God's disappointment.

By reading between the lines, not only did Jesus dislike me, which God had already reliably informed me, but I also suspected that he was about as pleased as I was with the whole thing. Despite the fact that God had told me Jesus was behind me, I could not help thinking that if I were him, I would be a tad disappointed also. Let's face it, the guy did a pretty good job. Two thousand years later, and he is probably the most famous man on the planet. I doubt that even Elvis or the Beatles combined had as many portraits, statues, and shrines dedicated to them. He had a bigger fan base than all the NFL teams combined, he had more print devoted to him than all the U.S. presidents, and he was more recognizable than Mickey Mouse.

Considering he hadn't even been on the planet for two thousand years, that was some track record. I had to hand it to him; he was definitely popular. I wondered if Mel Gibson would ever make a movie about my life using authentic New York accents and dialect. I wondered if Andrew Lloyd Webber would write a musical about me, and I wondered if everyone would erect trees and decorations every year on my birthday.

Yes, Jesus must be pretty disappointed that an overweight, middle-aged Jewish guy with a penchant for baseball and beer had been handed the baton of man's savior. I also got the feeling that without a shadow of doubt, he was God's favorite, notwithstanding the fact that they had at least two thousand years to gel. No, despite that, I still felt that even if I united the world's religions and got God season tickets for the Yankees, Jesus would still be number one. God hadn't compared us, but I was sure it would only be a matter of time before he did. I had the feeling he was restraining himself from doing so as not to hurt my feelings.

I supposed that Jesus probably felt the same way Sean Connery felt when he gave up the role of James Bond. Despite his Oscar, (which, in my opinion, he didn't deserve,) I had never rated

Sean Connery as an actor, unless he played a gruff Scotsman. It never failed to amuse me how often Scotsmen appeared in the movies he starred in, be it in the Wild West or outer space. He had to be the second most overrated thespian the world had seen.

Apart from when he played Bond. He was good, damn good. I'd wager that when they gave the Bond role to Roger Moore, the most overrated thespian the world had seen, he must have been mortified. He was Bond! And now younger generations would see Bond as a wooden, poorly acted, and quite unbelievable buffoon. I guarantee that secretly Connery willed Moore to mess up. I bet that Connery would say to family and friends, "Look at him, he's awful. I got far better reviews." I bet he would laugh at the mess Moore made of Bond, yet at the same time, despair that his previous good work had been wrecked and the character he had so masterfully crafted into an ice cold super-agent had been reduced to an idiot playing for laughs.

Maybe that's how Jesus felt about me. Unfortunately for me, like Connery was and always will be the best and only James Bond to his legion of fans, Jesus will always be the best and only Messiah to his fans, which I guessed, numbered considerably more than Sean Connery's.

"All right," said God. I assumed putting on a brave face. "Who's this disciple?"

"Bob Nancy. You know him?" I replied, certain that God would have no idea who Bob Nancy was.

"The name sounds familiar," said God to my utter astonishment. In the history of God, there must have been at least one hundred billion names. I wouldn't have expected him to remember them all. "Hold on, I remember it from somewhere. It's on the tip of my tongue," said God who I imagined was rubbing his chin and scratching his head. "Hang on a minute, I think I've got it, Oh, good heavens," he chuckled. "I remember him." He laughed louder. "Oh yes, I remember him. Oh dear, what a small world, and I made it, how funny." God continued to laugh.

"What's so funny?" I asked, eager to get in on the joke.

"Well, you know I am extremely busy, as I explained, but when there is a church wedding, and my name is mentioned, such as, 'We are gathered here in the presence of God,' that sort of thing, well, anyway, when that happens, I have to either be present myself or delegate a proxy. It's one of the rules we made up years ago, and it has stuck. Anyway, I always send a proxy, inevitably an angel, a low-ranking one, but occasionally Gabriel goes, you know, just to keep his hand in." God chuckled to himself. "Anyway," he said, between spurts of laughter, "Gabriel did his wedding, your Bob Nancy's," he laughed again. "I remember now, he mentioned it when I was away in our weekly update call. He told me about the bride, Nancy. Nancy Nancy! How ridiculous. Did they not realize? What on earth were they thinking? It tickled me, all of us. Gabriel was in fits for days."

I must admit even, I found it a little ridiculous, and I was his best friend. I often wondered why she hadn't kept her maiden name.

"Why she didn't keep her maiden name, I will never know," laughed God.

"Have you finished?" I asked God.

"What?" said God innocently.

"Laughing at my disciple," I answered.

God apologized. He was pleased that I had at least one disciple despite the fact that his wife had a ridiculous name. "Ok, at least it's a start. I am sorry for laughing," he said, though I still detected an element of mirth in his voice.

"You were saying, earlier, about the committee? What have they decided?" I reminded God of the initial reason for his call. God explained how the committee had agreed we should take the whole thing slowly, that rushing it could prove to be counterproductive. They had come up with a strategy, and now that I had Bob as a disciple, it made things easier. They decided the public needed a miracle, something to grab their attention, and maybe even attract more disciples.

"What type of miracle?" I asked. Under no circumstances would I go near lepers, and nor would I raise the dead. I felt I needed to make that extremely clear from the outset. I had an aversion toward sick people, and death freaked me out. I gave thanks each day that Walter didn't leave the apartment so there was no way I could deal with the dead birds or mice that cats inevitably murdered.

As I had no idea of how to perform a miracle, I was intrigued as to what God's answer would be.

"Oh, I don't know nothing too big. Something simple to start off with, something that will get people talking around the water cooler but have them wanting more. You need credibility; even Jesus would tell you that. We were thinking of a food-based miracle, kind of like JC's feeding the five thousand with fish and loaves of bread."

I had of course heard of this miracle. Even being Jewish, I was familiar with the story, and I had often thought that had delis been around in Jesus's day, he wouldn't have been popular with them, stealing customers and hurting trade.

"JC?" I asked, unfamiliar with the term.

"Oh sorry, it's what I call him. Jesus, Jesus Christ, JC," replied God, as if I should have known.

"Have you a pet name for me?" I asked, conscious that the acronym SM had possible sexual deviant undertones.

"No," answered God.

"I see," I said.

"You see what?" said God.

"Oh nothing, just thinking out loud; forget it." My feelings were hurt. Why did Jesus have a nickname, and I didn't? I had always wanted a name with good initials, such as AJ, or TJ, or KC. I was slightly upset that God hadn't thought of a pet name for me.

God ignored my pouting. "Oh, well, anyway, as I was saying, it has been deemed we need a small miracle and the vote was unanimous. We were thinking maybe you could feed some hungry people." God sounded pleased with this announcement, though I myself had some concerns.

"Sounds great, fantastic, a brilliant idea," I said sarcastically, "but you seem to be forgetting that there isn't an abundance of starving people in New York City. Even the homeless get hot meals provided by the Salvation Army, and if you think for one minute I am going to surround myself with flea-ridden, dirty hobos, you are sorely mistaken."

The moment the words left my mouth, I felt bad. It was the least charitable thing I had ever said, and I guessed if Jesus was listening in, he would be nodding his head as if to say "I told you so." I spoke again quickly.

"That was wrong; what I meant is that I have no idea whatsoever how to perform a miracle. I haven't a clue where to start, and I think there must be a better way to go about this." I hoped God hadn't picked up on the homeless thing, and it seemed he hadn't.

"Not to worry, dear boy," said God. "I have a plan."

CHAPTER

13

BEFORE I EXPLAIN GOD'S PLAN and the subsequent events after his second call, I feel I ought to pass on a few snippets of information I managed to glean from God, which you may or may not find interesting. God, as you may have realized, relies heavily on angels to do his bidding, mainly due to the fact that he has other ventures spread across the Universe. Apparently, like any good CEO, he liked to delegate as much as he could. The angels, he told me, are led by Gabriel, who is an archangel.

While not all the angels have a direct link to God, or for that matter, to Gabriel, there is a structured chain of command not dissimilar to that of the military. While not astounding news, it was nevertheless interesting. What was astounding was the numbers of angels currently on Earth amongst us, doing God's bidding. According to God, angels make up twenty-five percent of the world's population, which meant one in four humans is actually an angel.

I was astonished at how many angels were on Earth, because I am pretty certain I have never encountered one. Apparently, we all had a guardian angel of varying levels of competency and ability. It is simply the luck of the draw as to which one is allocated to you. Each angel is guardian to at least four different souls; however, one cannot rely on the angel all the time, as he or she is spread so thinly, hence why, according to God, some people have accidents, and some do not.

The second and slightly more alarming fact I discovered was that God worked closely with Lucifer. While not what you might call friendly, they do have a cordial relationship. Their acquaintance, so God informed me, goes further than the recognized figureheads of good and evil.

As I had read elsewhere, Lucifer was a fallen angel, and he was also pivotal in all aspects of God's reign on Earth and indeed, the Universe. I was also shocked to discover that Lucifer had accompanied God on his foray out into the Universe for the last thirty years. Apparently, Lucifer and God got together on occasion and discussed topics related to each of their spheres, such as the allocation of souls, disasters, and other issues that God didn't have time to explain to me.

It would seem that God and Lucifer had discussed the forthcoming Armageddon and indeed, had agreed on the date before they ventured on their prolonged journey into the Universe. However, with the date approaching, it was not good form for them to be seen in cahoots. Therefore God had no idea what Lucifer and his team were planning in regards to the apocalypse.

The final piece of gossip I think you should be aware of is God's acknowledgement that he cannot control everything. Apparently, natural disasters have nothing to do with him. He has no control over earthquakes, tidal waves, volcanoes, or any other natural phenomena. He can, though, "whip up a storm" if required, but he tries not to mess with the weather too often. He usually does it only when he is annoyed and wants to make a point. Apparently, what we mistakenly call "an act of God," he refers to as "maintenance issues." As the earth is as not as young as it was, it has become difficult to maintain, and certain issues such as land faults, ozone layer holes, and melting icecaps are victims of expired warranties. Luckily, God was pleased to inform me he built his newer planets spread throughout the Universe to a much better design code. Therefore, he eliminated structural and natural damage and minimized the effects of weather. On some planets, he can even control the weather, in part due to the developments of new technologies and his expanded experience in the planet-building trade. While I know the news is relatively irrelevant to you and me, it is reassuring to know that other civilizations and planets, under God's wing, need not worry about global warming.

THE RELUCTANT JESUS

The next morning, I arranged to meet Bob at the Vandam Diner in West Village, a short walk for me, and a cab ride for him. The Vandam was a regular meeting place for Bob and I, and we considered ourselves regulars, even though I sometimes got the feeling the wait staff considered us a pair of assholes. I felt it important that I included Bob in all aspects that pertained to my new role as Messiah, and as such, it was important we met and talked about God's suggestion and the proposed miracle.

I was also pleased to report that Ronnie had eventually been pried from the Christ Church railings at around three thirty in the morning. According to Bob, Nancy had crawled into bed exhausted, and it was unlikely she would surface again until her next shift began at seven that evening. It was assured that Bob and I could converse and meet without any interference or objection from his wife. It had dawned on me that I hadn't eaten a thing the previous day, and I was famished. I ordered steak, eggs, and a coffee, and Bob ordered a Triple Crown omelet. Bob was in a buoyant mood, and I could not recall ever seeing him so animatedly happy; even after last year's World Series games he hadn't been this ecstatic. My call summoning Bob for breakfast had been rather cryptic. I had told him we needed to talk, and he was in. After the waitress had taken our food order, and Bob had, as usual, annoyed her by asking if the coffee was freshly brewed, to which she had replied yes as she always did, I relayed God's plan for my first miracle.

"This is the deal," I began, "first of all, he is happy for you to be a disciple, so officially you're on the books; you're in."

Bob was delighted with this news. "Yes!" he exclaimed, clenching his fist as if he had scored a home run. I was a bit taken aback by Bob's excitement. I wish I shared his enthusiasm; unfortunately, however I was still dubious of the whole thing. I choose not to comment on Bob's animated response, and I continued to speak.

"He wants me to feed some hungry people, a multitude, and he wants me to produce food from thin air and distribute it to a crowd. It's not a dissimilar miracle to the one performed by JC with the fishes and loaves and the five thousand."

"JC?" queried Bob.

"Jesus Christ," I clarified.

"Oh, I see," said Bob. "Nicknames, eh? You got one?"

"No," I replied quickly. "Anyway, he suggested I feed the multitude, find some hungry people and feed them, produce food from thin air, and he wants you to film it, as proof, so we can send it to the media." I knew Bob had a camera, and I knew he was a competent cameraman. God hadn't actually suggested Bob film it, I had, but I felt it sounded better if I said it was God's idea.

"What do you feed them with?" asked Bob. It was a good question, and I had asked God the same thing.

"Well, those were my exact words to God. I tried to explain that I had no idea how to produce food from thin air, and that thus far my miracle working skills were zero."

Bob jammed his omelet into his mouth eagerly. The man could eat, and I was sure he would order another; I could tell that he was listening intently, though; the same as when he ate hotdogs at Yankee Stadium at the same speed and never missed a play. A piece of onion fell from his fork onto his plate. He scooped it up with his finger and popped it into his mouth. "So, how do you do it? How do you make food appear from nowhere?" he asked between large mouthfuls.

"Well, he, God, my father, made a pretty good point. He asked me if I had ever attempted a miracle before. Obviously the answer was no. Why would I have? He told me all I have to do is will it to happen, and it will happen. Apparently, I have had this power all my life, but of course, I never knew I did. I can do most things, within reason, but as a novice, I can't expect to be on a par with JC; not yet anyway," I said as I chewed on a piece of steak. Bob nodded.

"That makes sense, I suppose," he said as he continued to eat.

"Well, I have already tried one. A miracle. Last night," I said proudly.

"You're kidding," said Bob as he wiped away melted cheese from his chin.

"No, I am not kidding. God talked me through it. It was, if I say so myself, pretty impressive," I boasted, genuinely pleased with what had occurred the previous evening. As Walter had been my only witness, it was good to include Bob in my moment of triumph.

The night before, while discussing the miracle idea with God, he had instructed that I pour tap water into a glass—just normal, New York City tap water, into a standard, normal, everyday glass. I did as instructed. With the phone pressed tightly to my ear so I would not miss any instruction and with God's encouragement, I concentrated hard. God had told me to concentrate on the glass of water. According to God, I needed to will it to happen and to have faith that it would happen. What "it" was, I wasn't sure. While I was the one who performed the miracle, I couldn't do it without God's help. He was the one actually performing the miracle, but he needed me to act as his vessel. Only his son could be the vessel, hence the fact that only Jesus and I could perform miracles.

At first, there was nothing. For at least fifteen minutes, I sat, staring at the glass of water, and nothing happened. God told me to be patient, which I naturally was. But to be honest, I thought I was wasting my time, which was another problem. I was missing the faith aspect of miracle working. God explained that I needed to believe the miracle would happen, and his gentle coaxing and encouragement enabled me to relax. And then it happened. The miracle. My first miracle. The first official miracle in more than two thousand years. Right in front of my eyes, the water in the glass began to stir. I could not believe it, and my eyes widened in wonderment.

The water seemed to effervesce, slowly at first, then, as if an Alka-Seltzer had been deposited into it, the color of the water began to change. It turned darker, slowly at first, then it picked up speed, and gradually it changed color completely. The water had changed. In front of me was no longer a glass of water. The liquid inside the glass was now a golden color. The liquid was familiar. It seemed to seduce me, to tempt me; it was a beautiful sight to behold. The gentle fizz sent bubbles climbing up the glass to disappear into the air. Gentle, frothy foam settled at the top of the miracle nectar. It was a wondrous and magical moment. God invited me to taste the golden liquid in front of me, and I didn't need to be asked twice. The miracle nectar. The liquid of God, the miracle brew. It was Bud Lite.

There was no mistaking the taste; it was genuine Budweiser Lite, my third favorite beer. I also drank Guinness and Sam Adams, but I suppose that they would have taken a little more effort. It tasted fine, better than fine; I had fancied a beer all evening and had none in the apartment, so when the Bud descended down my throat, I felt exhilarated. It was my first miracle. I had turned water into beer. It was confirmed. I was the Messiah.

"Far out," exclaimed Bob, who sat opened mouthed as I relayed the events surrounding my first miracle.

"I know," I said feeling rather proud of myself. "It blew my mind. I swear it wasn't a trick, and it tasted perfect. It was even cold!" I tried to contain my delight, aware other diners might overhear our conversation.

"The possibilities are limitless," said Bob "we could open up our own bar," Bob wiped away more melted cheese from his lips. "We never need to buy beer ever again. We shall never run dry. We could produce it in bulk, and take it to games. We can sit in a bar and order water for free, and hey presto, abracadabra, we have two brewskis!"

"No," I replied. "No, apparently I can't. God warned me that my miracles were only limited to the needy, and I needed his assistance to do them; therefore, I can't 'sneak one in.' I wouldn't be able to 'miracle for profit,' as he put it. Kind of makes sense, I suppose." I was as disappointed as I sounded. I had the same idea and thought as Bob, but God had curtailed my enthusiasm by listing a whole set of rules which meant it was extremely difficult for me to profit from my miracle doing.

Bob agreed that it made sense we shouldn't miracle for profit; however he did point out that we both knew people who needed beer every day, and maybe we could exploit a loophole regarding the "needy," should we be so inclined. I promised I would point that out to God the next time we spoke.

Unfortunately, we had more pressing matters to discuss. We needed to work out the best way to perform my first public miracle and plan a strategy that would not only work but would produce suitable camera footage we could distribute to the world's news networks.

"You see, when JC did this one, he had a crowd of five thousand, give or take, and word of his powers had already spread. At the time he performed his fish and loaf miracle, he was already an established attraction. People came from miles around to catch a glimpse of him. At the moment, I am a nobody; I have no following. What we need is a crowd, a hungry crowd at that, and maybe some publicity." Bob nodded that he concurred with my thoughts as he took a sip from his third cup of coffee.

"Finding hungry people in this city shouldn't be too hard," said Bob. "I mean, people are always hungry. How does God define hungry? Does he mean starving, or does he mean peckish, or does he mean famished? What's the play here?" It was a good question and a good point.

"Well, the homeless are not necessarily always hungry, and God didn't specify what level of hunger deemed a miracle," I replied. "The problem is location; we need a crowd, in a public place, suitably hungry and ready to accept a miracle. As it's not football season, we can't turn up at the Giant's Stadium and offer to get the hot dogs, and the Yankees are on the road this week, so Yankee Stadium is out too," I surmised.

It was Bob who came up with the idea, completely out of the blue. It was sheer inspiration. "Central Park," he said, matter-of-fact, "Central Park is where we should head. There are always crowds, and I bet you'd find a hungry crowd amongst the throngs of tourists, dog walkers, and joggers. All you need to do is stand up and shout 'free food.' Create a noise, a scene, and people will watch. They always do." Bob, as I thought he might, ordered a second omelet, and was busily chewing away. He was right, of course. If anyone shouted and waved their hands in Central Park in June, a crowd would flock, especially the Japanese tourists and out-of-towners.

Admittedly, I wasn't entirely happy about shouting out for free food in the middle of Central Park. There was probably some city code against giving out free food, though if this applied to miracles, I did not know, and I wasn't sure which department I should call to find out. Bob continued with the good ideas, which seemed to be flowing from his mouth that morning.

"Obviously, I will alert the media; call CNN, ABC, NBC, or Fox, maybe even all four, and tell them a miracle is about to occur in Central Park, and it is all related to the events around the world: the chaining to the church and everything happening in London and Australia. I will tell them to get their cameras down to the park. Once they set up, you produce the bread and fishes. Hey presto, the whole world sees your miracle. Then you then go on record, proclaiming yourself the son of God, the Messiah, the Christ, spread the word about the approaching apocalypse, and I guarantee, I guarantee, every loon and nut out there will be lining up to follow you." Bob had convinced himself this plan would work, and it sounded plausible.

The "every loon and nut out there" aspect of it perturbed me slightly, but I got the drift. I had to agree it was probably the best way forward. I really couldn't think of a better plan. Bob and I agreed to meet the following morning at Central Park. He would call the press and bring his camcorder as back up.

CHAPTER
14

YOU MAY BE WONDERING HOW I had managed to meet up with Bob and organize to meet him the following day without it encroaching on my work. Earlier that morning, I received a very odd phone call from Henry Peel, my boss. Henry began the call saying how pleased he was that I was associated with his company, and he thanked me for my years of loyal, exemplary, and dedicated work and how he would like to get on record that he would like to increase my salary by fifty percent, effective immediately.

He had also organized for a courier to drop off my new contract, which he urged I sign immediately and return just as quickly. He summarized the details of this improved contract, which was speeding its way to me as we spoke, the main details being the improved salary, a place on the board, and a partnership deal if I committed to a minimum of four more years with Henry.

In itself, receiving a call at seven in the morning from my boss offering me the deal of lifetime was strange; however what was stranger was the fact that it had come completely out of the blue. Henry had obviously drafted the contract, had it approved by the board, and organized the courier either the previous day or during the night. Of course, I was curious as to what had prompted this startling offer. As to the best of my knowledge, I had done nothing to warrant such a spectacular and unexpected revised contract.

"Henry, slow down for a second, take a deep breath, and please explain to me what this is all about," I asked as I sipped on a glass of orange juice.

"It's all about the contract you secured. It's excellent, absolutely fantastic, and the fact you did it all on your own is even more remarkable; we, the board and I, that is, are absolutely delighted. Well done. And the contract we are sending over for you is a token of our thanks and appreciation," gushed Henry. I had never heard the man so happy. Unfortunately, I had no idea what he was talking about.

"Remind me," I said, "what contract did I secure?" I was extremely confused. Henry proceeded to tell me about the call he received from the head Bishop of the Episcopal Church in the United States, whose offices were based in the city. Apparently, the bishop had informed Henry that the church wanted to build information centers in every major city in the country. The church would use the information centers to showcase the Episcopal religion to potential new members in an environment other than the confines of a church. These information centers would house office space, mini cinema facilities, and some would host conferences and visiting guests from out of town. The concept was previously unheard of, but the bishop had an epiphany, was convinced the idea would work, and had gained approval to begin the project.

While the bishop did not elaborate on how this idea had come to him, he had, according to Henry, suggested divine intervention, which Henry had found amusing, but had, like any good businessman, kept this amusement to him. The bishop's vision initially entailed twenty-five of these city-based information centers built on land already owned by the church, with the option for twenty-five more should they prove to be a success. They wanted blueprints, designs, and plans. They wanted contracts signed and sealed immediately. They wanted Henry's company to oversee all aspects, from design to build. It was a multi-million dollar contract, the biggest the company had ever procured, and one of the biggest contracts ever won by any building firm. However, the bishop had one stipulation. And it involved me.

Apparently the bishop was a big fan of mine. He had followed my career closely and enjoyed the concepts and designs I produced. He had often marveled at the architecture I had developed. I did ask Henry to specify which buildings the bishop enthused so much about, but Henry, in his excitement, had failed to ask. In any event, it was of secondary importance to Henry. What was important was that I agreed to do it, hence my contract offer and the need for my signature. It also seemed the bishop had recommended I abandon projects I was currently working on and hand them over to colleagues to prepare for the task ahead. The bishop suggested that Henry give me a well-deserved vacation so I could begin the church project refreshed and revitalized. Henry had agreed that this was a great idea and proposed I take four weeks off work immediately on full pay.

Only a buffoon would not realize this was more than a coincidence. I had no doubt this was the work of my Father, and though I had no idea how he had gotten into the bishop's head, it was obvious he had. I did not believe for one minute that the bishop was a big fan of my work. It was ridiculous; however, the contract was genuine, and our company accountant had already received a deposit. Just as genuine was the contract that arrived from Henry while he was still on the line. I duly signed it and sent it back with the courier to Henry. Henry said it was a miracle. I tended to agree.

I met Bob at ten o'clock sharp the following morning as arranged. We met at the Sherman Monument located at the main entrance to the Park. If you have never visited Central Park in the summer, then you have never lived. One of the great things about living in Manhattan and being a New Yorker is the park. For two guys like Bob and me, Central Park in the summer was a Shangri-La. We could spend hours ogling female tourists in skimpy outfits, lunching office workers in skimpy outfits, and to be honest, any female of the species in a skimpy outfit that happened to be enjoying the park. I hope you do not form the impression that Bob and I were perverts; it was that we appreciated the female form, and Central Park was a great place for the voyeur. So we ogled; what man doesn't? It doesn't make us perverts, despite what Nancy thought. Nancy had often cited our visits to Central Park as perverted. She had often claimed it was unhealthy for two men to visit the park in the summer for the sole reason of feasting their eyes on attractive women. Bob and I thought it perfectly normal. I assumed Nancy wasn't jealous, because though she chided Bob, she never stopped him from going. She just found it "disturbing."

Disturbing or not, our visit to the park that morning had nothing to do with ogling scantily clad females. Luckily though, Nancy had no idea what we were doing for as of yet, Bob had not informed her of his new role as disciple to the Messiah Seth. I was glad he hadn't. Bob had managed to sequester the Nancy family camcorder and depart the house that morning without disturbing his sleeping wife, who still worked the night shift. I was sure if she had risen from her slumber, then her natural curiosity and domineering and overbearing personality would have forced Bob to admit he was heading down to the park to film me, her nemesis, perform a miracle as ordered by God. The last thing I needed was Nancy's hulking frame looming over me as I attempted to feed the multitude. I doubted even with God behind me I could produce enough food to quell her appetite anyway. It was probably wise not to mention free food when around Nancy, even if you had unlimited powers. Feeding five thousand is one thing; feeding Nancy Nancy is another.

"Did you call them?" I asked Bob as we walked into the park, referring to media channels that Bob had promised to call.

"Indeed I did," said Bob as he looked around, as if waiting for someone.

"And are they coming?"

"I'm not sure, I can't see them," said Bob as he continued to look around, "I called all of them, and the local news channel and the newspapers. I can't see anyone yet though." Bob continued to look around. This I found slightly irritating, as I wasn't sure what he expected—hordes of reporters charging toward us, or a fleet of news choppers circling overhead? It wasn't that I didn't trust Bob or thought him incompetent, I just felt I probably needed to ascertain exactly what he had told the media.

"What did they say when you told them about me? In fact, how did you broach the whole subject?" I asked.

"Well," Bob began, "they didn't seem too enthusiastic. They all seemed to think I was some sort of nut job. I got a similar response from them all, really, but they said thanks and they would note it, and if they felt it was warranted, they would send a news crew." That didn't sound to promising. I could imagine the reaction of the media organizations quite easily. It would have been the same reaction I would have given forty-eight hours ago. We had to face facts; they weren't going to show.

"You can stop looking around, Bob," I said dejectedly. "You know they won't show up."

Bob stopped his searching and sighed. "Yep, I guess not. At least I've got the camcorder, and at least we will have some footage?"

"Of what though?" I said, still unsure how the miracle would manifest itself.

Deep down I was slightly relieved that the media had given us the cold shoulder, no doubt convinced Bob was some sort of weirdo jumping on the Ronnie bandwagon. I wasn't sure if I was ready to be catapulted into the spotlight just yet. For a start, I was skeptical of how the public would receive me; it occurred to me that I was probably not what people expected when they imagined the Messiah. I had toyed with the idea of growing a beard, but decided against it. What significance a beard had, I wasn't sure, but it seemed a "Jesus" thing to do. I could imagine outraged Christians the world over disappointed that a tubby Jew was their new figurehead. I could also imagine the vast majority of the world calling me a fake and hounding me until I confessed to it all being a giant hoax. So the fact the media wasn't going to be present came as a relief to me. Unfortunately, though, Bob felt otherwise. He was bitterly disappointed that we wouldn't be featuring on the six o'clock news. Not tonight, at least.

My stomach was in knots. Though I was confident my face wasn't going to be splashed around the world that night, it was still nerve-wracking that I would have to speak in public. I had read that just as many people feared public speaking as they did death. Unaccustomed as I was to public speaking, which in itself was daunting, performing a miracle at the same time, was even more so. I was about to be exposed as the Messiah, and I wasn't ready. To be honest, I was hesitant about the whole thing. Things were moving too quickly, and I didn't like it. Maybe it was nerves or maybe in the cold light of day in the middle of Central Park, I realized the enormity of what lay ahead.

"I can't do it," I said, stopping in my tracks and staring directly at Bob.

"You have to," said Bob, urging me to continue walking, "you know you have no choice." He was right of course, no matter how reluctant I was. God had made it very clear that there was no alternative, and despite my own trepidation, I was "it."

"Well, what now?" I asked Bob, thankful I had my friend to support and assist me at least.

"Gather a crowd," said Bob as he looked around him once more. We had stopped next to the Swedish Cottage. The Swedish Cottage was a former tool shed converted into a children's theater, and it was located on the west side of the park.

Gathering a crowd was a lot harder than it sounded. Initially, we were both reluctant to accost passersby, who were predominantly tourists. After thirty minutes of us both standing around like idiots and with no crowd gathered, Bob decided he would try enticing a crowd by shouting. For the following two hours Bob stood, shouting like a madman. For two hours in the middle of Central Park, people ignored Bob. They did not just ignore him, they avoided him. Those park users who did walk by tried not to make eye contact with him. The mere sight of Bob waving his hands and shouting was enough to disturb anyone.

A cop patrolling the park, eyed us suspiciously. Bob stopped shouting when he saw the officer approaching, and luckily, the cop continued his patrol, glancing back at us. I supposed we weren't breaking any law, and as it was a free country, Bob could shout what he wanted, but it was obvious our tactic wasn't working. However, Bob was adamant, and for another two hours, he continued to shout and try and draw attention, but to no avail. I tried to encourage Bob, and I also did my fair share of shouting. However, there came no crowd.

"This is hopeless," I said. "Where are the hungry? Where is the multitude? Where are the five thousand?" I looked upward and raised my hands. "Come on, Dad, show a little compassion. Help us out here, do something, anything," I pleaded jokingly. "Give me a sign." I yelled in mock desperation. I think Bob was not that amused by my antics. I noticed his expression was stern. "Come on," I said, "lighten up. Look, it's two thirty. I am starving, which I know is a bit ironic, but I am. Let me buy you lunch. Let's face it, it's not happening. I'm only kidding around; there is no need to look so stern."

But Bob seemed to be ignoring me; he wasn't staring at me, he was staring behind me. I turned to see what had grabbed his attention. As I turned, I saw Bob point, his mouth open. And then they came.

Bob had seen them first, hence his open mouth and dumbfounded look, which I had mistaken for sternness. He pointed for my benefit. At first I couldn't quite make them out. They seemed to appear from nowhere on the horizon. It was definitely a crowd, or a large group. Without any doubt, it was the most people at one time we had seen all day. They came from the east side of the park, and they were heading toward the Swedish Cottage, and therefore, us. It was... the crowd, a hungry crowd, the multitude. Well, sort of; there were at least twenty of them.

Troop twenty-three was a Boy Scout troop located in West Salem, Oregon. Each summer, eighteen members of the troop plus two adult supervisors embarked on a field trip. That year, they choose New York. Troop twenty-three was heading our way. Led from the front by a grown man dressed in full scouting uniform, which made him look ridiculous, and behind him in columns of two, came his troop, all eighteen of them, and brought up at the rear was another male adult, dressed as they all were, in their resplendent Boy Scout uniforms. I looked at Bob and Bob looked at me. We were thinking the same thing: could this be them? Was this a sign from God?

Eventually the man leading them, with his troop following close behind, reached the point where Bob and I stood.

"Excuse me," said the man, "you couldn't help us out here, could you? We're actually lost." I had always thought Scouts were expert navigators and could read maps and compasses. How lost could they be? They were in Central Park with signs everywhere. Only an idiot could be lost in Central Park.

The man spoke again, "We're troop twenty-three from West Salem, Oregon." I nodded that I understood. "I'm Lester Smith, Troop Leader." Ah, so that's why he was a grown man dressed as a boy. I shook his outstretched hand; they sure were a friendly bunch from Oregon. "The thing is, we are completely lost, and to top it off, we have forgotten our lunch," he said. "Jason here," a small, bespectacled scout appeared from the crowd of boys. I guessed he could not have been older than twelve. Troop Leader

Smith playfully ruffled Jason's hair, who did not seem too pleased at this. He shrugged, and for a second I thought he mouthed an obscenity. Oblivious to this, the troop leader continued to speak. "Jason, here, was meant to collect lunch this morning, but forgot." He once again playfully ruffled little Jason's hair, much to Jason's chagrin, as he again shrugged and grimaced. I was sure he mouthed a word that would make a sailor blush. "So we are kind of stuck, and we ran into a very friendly police officer back there," he pointed back into the direction they had just come, "and he told me that there were two guys giving out free food in this direction near the children's theater, so I put two and two together. Have you seen two men giving away food? We are starving."

Obviously two and two equaled five for Troop Leader Smith. I was amazed that any parent would entrust their child with this man. It must have been a sign. Surely God had done this. I knew it wasn't the multitude that my half-brother had catered for, but at least it was a start. Who knew why young, foul-mouthed Jason forgot to collect the lunch. From whom and what that lunch had been, I did not know, nor did I think to ask. I had been presented with a chance to perform my first miracle. So the media were not present; it didn't seem to matter. I instructed Bob to prepare the camcorder. This was it.

"Ok!" I shouted, my fear of public speaking somehow diminished and my confidence soaring. I felt that if God had produced a crowd, then he was behind me and with God behind me, I could do anything. Bob nodded, indicating the camcorder was filming. "Come on gather around," I shouted, and with the help of Troop Leader Smith, the Boy Scouts gathered around me, forming a semi-circle two deep. I closed my eyes and concentrated. I could hear groaning coming from the assembled throng, and I was sure I heard one of the scouts call me a name. I guessed it was probably Jason; however, I did not let the chiding distract me. And then I spoke. Why I said the words that I did, I did not know. They just came to me.

"Ok, listen, I want you all to reach into your left pocket of your pants and feel around." I heard Bob wince; maybe they were not the best words for addressing young boys, but I had no control. I had no idea why I had made the command or what it entailed. Something compelled me to say it; it was like before, with the water turning to beer; it just... happened.

As instructed, the Boy Scouts placed their hands into the pocket. I watched intently as one by one, they all removed their hands from their pockets. This was it; this was my first public miracle. I watched as the troop leader delved into his pocket, and I saw Jason delve into his. This was the first miracle in over two thousand years performed in public. This was an event. This was history. This was a defining moment in time. This was not what I had expected.

"Wow," said a voice from the crowd of Scouts.

"Great trick," said another.

"Cool," said another.

"I don't like them," said one more.

"How did he do that?" said another voice.

"I hate them. Can't we have something else?" said the detractor again.

I stood motionless as each Boy Scout removed his hand from his pocket and revealed what was there. Each Scout, including Troop Leader Smith, held in their hands a piece of paper. I squinted to get a better look. They looked like coupons.

"Great stunt," exclaimed Troop Leader Smith as he showed me what he had pulled from his trouser pocket, "how did you do that? You some sort of magician or illusionist or something? Fantastic trick, utterly amazing. I take it they put you up to it? The restaurant that is. Great idea. I suppose we have to buy the fries and drink though, that's the catch, I bet, but so what, eh? A free meal is a free meal!"

Catch? What was he talking about? It was a miracle, not a trick, and who were "they?" Where was the food? Where were the loaves and where was the fish? I took a closer look at the voucher that the scout leader handed to me. *"McHUNGRY'S FREE FOOD VOUCHER, FILLET OF COD SANDWICH, DOES NOT INCLUDE FRIES OR DRINK,"* proclaimed the slip of paper. Accompanying the text was a photograph of a fried fish sandwich. It looked genuine; in fact, it was genuine, McHungry's issued those vouchers to customers who called their hotline to complain about the service in one of their thousands of restaurants based all over the world. They were tokens of McHungry's concern that someone had not enjoyed their meal. They were genuine all right; I had seen them before.

I flipped the voucher over. I handed it back to Troop Leader Smith. So that was it? Feeding the hungry scouts with free fast food, courtesy of compensation vouchers, was the miracle? While the fish and bread were a miracle, they had to purchase fries and a drink?

"Wow man. That was great. Thanks a lot," said Smith, who despite, being an idiot had assumed what any other rational human being would have assumed, that they had witnessed an elaborate publicity stunt performed by an illusionist. I was no more a miracle worker in the eyes of my dispersing crowd than a Las Vegas conjurer was. I watched in silence as Smith assembled his troop and led them back the way they had come. I heard Jason say that he had seen a McHungry's earlier, and he knew the way. Off they went to claim their free sandwich.

For those of you who do not care for fast food or have never heard of McHungry's, please allow me to enlighten you. Let me take this opportunity to describe and tell you what exactly a fillet of cod sandwich is. If I may, I would like to quote McHungry's own website, where, on my return home, I found the description of the McHungry's Cod Sandwich: *A McHungry's fillet of cod sandwich is a golden, crispy fish filet, topped with American cheese and special tartar sauce on a toasted bun. It makes a perfect snack, or with fries and a drink, a perfect meal.*

If I may, I would now like to quote the Bible:

"*Then, taking the five loaves and the two fish and looking up to Heaven, he said the blessing, broke the loaves, and gave them to (his) disciples to set before the people; he also divided the two fish among them all. They all ate and were satisfied. And they picked up twelve wicker baskets full of fragments and what was left of the fish. Those who ate (of the loaves) were five thousand men.*"

As you can see, it is not too dissimilar. What had occurred in Central Park mirrored exactly what had occurred in the Middle East two thousand years ago. The similarities were astounding. It was as if history had repeated itself. And if you believed that, then you are as mad as a hatter!

"What was that?" asked Bob as he lowered the camcorder. "Was that it? Was that the miracle? Please tell me that wasn't the miracle."

"It would seem so," I answered as the last scout disappeared from view.

"I don't get it," said Bob, "fast food vouchers? That's what you gave them?"

"Did you get it on tape?" I asked Bob, not exactly sure what "it" was.

"Well, yeah, sort of, but it's not much. It's basically a group of scouts putting their hands in their pockets, acting all surprised, and then walking off. To be brutally frank, it looks crap."

Bob was right. I needed another talk with God.

CHAPTER 15

"WELL TECHNICALLY I *DO* THE miracles. I thought I had explained that," God had called the moment Bob and I entered my apartment.

"If that's the case then why didn't you do something a little more dramatic?" I asked.

"Well, let me see. When I say I do the miracles, what I mean is we do the miracles; it's my power channeled through you, and it's more a joint effort, but you are as responsible as I am for the success of these things. Obviously we were not ready for anything too dramatic, but it is 1999. I suppose it was the modern day equivalent. Not ideal, but it was a start. I managed to find the Scouts for you, didn't I? On the whole, I would say it was good day." God sounded pleased with the day's events. Unfortunately, I was not as pleased.

"Listen, I have Bob with me. Can I put you on speaker phone?" I asked.

"Sure, why not?" replied God.

I proceeded to explain to God that despite his enthusiasm, the day hadn't gone as well as he had presumed. For a start, the Boy Scouts hadn't acknowledged the miracle. By that I meant none of the witnesses to the miracle understood that it was indeed a miracle. Troop Leader Smith and his troop of Scouts believed they had met an illusionist who was in the employ of a fast food chain. Being from out of town, they assumed that this was the sort of thing that happened in the Big Apple. They thought we had treated them to a free magic show and complimentary vouchers to entice them into McHungry's. There had been no opportunity to explain to the assembled throng of Scouts that what they had witnessed was divine intervention to cure their hunger. As I tried to explain to God, the human race was far more skeptical than they were two thousand years ago.

"Well, at least you got it on film," said God, conceding that it was highly unlikely Scout Troop Leader Smith realized he had witnessed the first miracle in two thousand years. But, there was even more bad news for God. Bob and I had watched the recording made on Bob's camcorder whilst we had God on speakerphone through my television and video system. It wasn't exactly Stephen Spielberg. The first problem was the sound, or lack of it. Bob had failed to mention that his camcorder's microphone was malfunctioning so there would be no sound. Therefore, all the footage we had was of a group of Scouts, led by a grown man dressed as a Scout, placing their hands into their pockets and pulling out paper. You could clearly see Troop Leader Smith and a few other Scouts smiling and disappearing into the horizon. It was hardly the sort of footage the news media outlets would be clamoring to air. I was not visible in any shot. It was, by Bob's admittance, an unmitigated disaster.

"Well," began God, his tone sharp and his voice filled with disappointment,

"JC certainly didn't have this trouble. It went very smoothly when JC did it; in fact, they talked about it for years afterward. When he did it, there were no snags, no 'technical problems;' there was no doubt it was a miracle. It was a highly successful miracle. It is a proven miracle, it works; hence why I thought a re-run would work." I got the feeling God was annoyed, but luckily, his tone softened slightly. "I know you must be a tad disappointed, but it was only your first try. Half the secret in these things is the crowd. The audience needs to be just right. The mass hysteria, the chanting, and the expectation, sometimes screaming, sometimes fainting: that's what makes these things memorable. You need a good audience. Maybe I am to blame a little; I should have thought harder about what type of crowd to pull in."

Bob cleared his throat.

"Excuse me, sir... your highness... your Lordship," he said, his voice filled with nervousness.

"'God' is fine," said God.

"Ok, Sir, God, I have a suggestion," said Bob. I would have been happier if Bob had run his suggestion through me first. I felt uneasy when Bob had ideas. He seemed to be far more enthusiastic than I was in revealing myself to the world.

"Yes, Bob, please feel free to add any input into this forum. I like to run an open house. Any suggestion would be welcomed. By the way, how is Nancy?" God's welcoming tone belied the fact that I couldn't help but think he was probably sniggering at the thought of Mrs. Nancy Nancy and her ridiculous name. In fact, I was sure I could hear stifled laughter emitting from the phone speaker. Bob didn't seem to notice; he was too busy grinning from ear to ear.

"Wow, you know me? You know Nancy? Wow, we're both fine, thanks; you really do watch over us all. I have to say, it is an honor to speak to you. By the way, how is Mrs. God?" I shook my head in disbelief. God did not answer Bob's question. He was too busy trying to curtail the muffled laughter from others who were obviously in the same vicinity as him, and I could definitely hear sniggering in the background.

"Excuse me," I interrupted, "are we on speaker phone too?" I asked, annoyed that God had us on his speaker phone without informing me. I was also curious as to who else was listening in.

"No," said God, but I knew he was lying. I let it drop, but he hadn't fooled me.

"Well, Bob," said God eventually after the muffled giggles had subsided, "what is your suggestion?"

For all the time I had known him, Bob Nancy had never had a good idea. And things weren't about to change. Unfortunately, God didn't seem to see it that way. God thought Bob's idea was great, ingenious, fantastic, and inspirational. God was so pleased with Bob I thought he was going to make him a Saint there and then! However, I doubted even God would make a Saint Bob. Bob's idea basically consisted of me walking across the Hudson River. I am serious. I couldn't believe my best friend would propose such a ridiculous stunt either!

It transpired that Bob had been doing some research into the Bible and miracles. As I had already made clear, I would not be going near dead or people close to death—all resurrecting and healing miracles were out. Bob, by his own inclination and quite independent of me, had spent the previous evening not only unsuccessfully attempting to repair the ability to record sound on his camcorder, but had taken the time to research Jesus and his miracles. He had come to the conclusion that the best way to grab attention, ensure media coverage, and get tongues wagging was not to get the media to come to us, but to go to them.

Through the night, Bob, thanks to the wonders of the internet and information gleaned from Nancy, had discovered that tomorrow, New York City would be hosting the Ambassador of Peru. During the visit of the Peruvian Ambassador, the Mayor of New York had organized a tour of New York Harbor in his private Yacht. Though no one anticipated large crowds for such a minor diplomat, the city expected a small gathering to demonstrate against the Peruvian Government's alleged intention to start the farming of llamas, exporting their meat as a delicacy. Bob assured me that at least one news crew would be present at the Mayor's Harbor Launch pier, which was located south side of pier sixty and West 23rd Street.

This information was all courtesy of Nancy, who would also be present along with several other New York Police Department colleagues should the demonstrators become unruly. I personally had not heard of neither the Ambassador's proposed visit nor the llama meat debate. It had also come as a shock to me that the Mayor had his own yacht!

Bob's idea was, if it hadn't involved me, quite clever. Unfortunately, as the main protagonist, it did involve me. The idea was for me to walk toward the launch atop of the water. Yes, that's right, atop the water and approach the yacht. As there was likely to be a demonstrating crowd and several NYPD officers present, we would have our reliable witnesses, the news crew would divert their cameras from the demonstrators onto me, and to top off the whole thing, we would have not only the Ambassador of Peru as a witness, but Mayor Giuliani himself! I could reveal myself and prepare the world for whatever lay ahead. I was still unsure of what did lay ahead. God had been playing that one close to his chest.

I wasn't entirely satisfied the plan would work. There were a number of reasons for my reluctance, the prime reason and most overbearing was that I did not relish the opportunity of walking on water. It sounded extremely difficult, and though God reassured me that I could do it, the thought of sinking to the bottom of one of the most polluted rivers in the world did not endear itself to me. Also prevalent in my mind was the reception I would get from a hostile crowd of llama-loving fanatics. The attention I would grab would detract from their protesting; millions of llamas could die because of Bob's "great" idea. Finally, there would be no escaping the fact that I would be propelled into the media spotlight. If Bob's plan worked, then there would be definitely no getting out of it or turning back. Regrettably for me, God was in a buoyant mood and loved the idea. I reminded myself to thank Bob for his great idea; I also made a mental note of not including Bob in anymore family meetings.

The Mayor and his party, including the Ambassador, would be arriving at the pier at around ten the following morning. God encouraged me to have a good rest, and before ending the call, once again thanked Bob for his ingenious idea.

"What an absolutely charming man," gushed Bob after I hung up the phone. "He is not half as bad as you said. In fact, I would have loved to have had a Father like that." I looked at Bob, shook my head, and sighed. He had no idea the pressure that came with being the Son of God. "And what a fantastic memory the man has," continued Bob, "and he is so charming, him remembering that I'm married to Nancy. It just shows you he really is watching and does care. He is one heck of a guy!" Don't worry; I didn't have the heart to tell Bob what God had said about his nuptials!

I have to admit I did not sleep easy that night. After Bob left my apartment, still gushing on about how great God was, I made some hot chocolate—from a packet, not miraculously—and surfed through the news channels looking for any discussion on llama meat, which I did not find. I actually wondered what llama meat would taste like. I supposed it would taste like chicken. I decided a bath would be in order. Luckily, I didn't lie atop the water, but I fully submerged myself into the warm water and bubbles. I did try to practice floating, but I merely sank into the tub. I had hoped a bath would help me relax; I was tense, and once again, the knots in my stomach twisted and turned. The mere feel of the water on my skin, though, was a constant reminder that the next day I could be kicking and flailing in front of the world's media, swallowing polluted water.

It didn't help that every time I pictured myself drowning, I also pictured Nancy's bulking frame rolling with laughter as I gasped for breath. I went to bed early but I lay awake, running over the likely events of the next morning. It was only nine thirty. It was a Friday night. I fleetingly thought about masturbating, but the thought of Mother Theresa watching my every move doused my enthusiasm for private pleasure. I looked at Walter who sat watching as he sat on the chair in my bedroom. "Walter?" I asked, making sure it was Walter in there. No reply. Good. God wasn't around. I dressed and locked up the apartment, heading out into the night.

CHAPTER
16

BEFORE I WAS ABLE TO head into the night, I first had to navigate around Harvey who was manning his post at the entrance to the building.

"Why, Mr. Miller," said Harvey playfully as I appeared from the elevator. He raised his hand so I could slap it.

"Good Evening, Harvey," I said politely as I slapped his palm.

"All right! And where are you heading this fine evening?" asked Harvey, not that it was really any of his business, but as I said, Harvey was unique.

"Just going for a stroll," I answered, and for some reason, I felt I needed to justify my actions, so I added, "I can't sleep," and smiled at Harvey, who stared at me without emotion.

"Uh huh," said Harvey in a tone that indicated to me he disapproved, "I see your skinny-ass friend been 'round today." Harvey was referring to Bob. "Man, he is one ugly mo-fo," continued Harvey. "He's a teacher, ain't he?" I confirmed that Bob was indeed a teacher. "Man, I wouldn't let no child of mine near that brother; man, they'd be having nightmares and all other scary shit from him and his rat face. Ain't he married to the fat-ass lady cop? Man, does that woman not know how to ask for the check? She one lardy-ass bitch." Harvey sucked on his teeth. "Man, that crazy-assed bitch sure does enjoy a pie." Harvey shook his head and stared into the distance as if imagining Nancy scarfing down a family-sized apple pie, a look of disgust covering his face. "Well then, Mr. Miller, you be careful out there," Harvey pointed onto the street, "don't be getting all drunk and wild and getting yourself mugged by some brothers." Harvey winked at me. I acknowledged Harvey's concern and for a split second debated whether to invite Harvey for a beer after his shift had ended but decided against it.

Milligan's was a great neighborhood bar and only two blocks away. It was one of those long bars that seemed always to be in semi-darkness no matter what the time of day, so days and nights always seemed to merge into one. It was never crowded, but you always knew you wouldn't be a lone drinker. It didn't open until late and only seemed to close when the last customer decided they could leave. Even though I wasn't a regular, by that, I mean an every night patron, the barman always recognized me and greeted me by name.

"Hi there, Jackie," greeted Sean, the usual barman. Like I said, he always greeted me by name. Just not my name.

"Hi, how's it going? I'll have my usual, please," I replied. Sean nodded. I decided against calling Sean, Steven, in retaliation. My usual drink at Milligan's was a Sam Adams. They had it on draft, one of the few bars that did, and it was all I ever drank in there. Sean returned with a pint of Guinness. I thanked Sean and sat at the bar with my beer. It was by all accounts, a quiet night for a Friday. The regular crowd seemed to have taken their seats either at the bar or around tables that were secluded in booths and the atmosphere was muted. Soft music played in the background. Actually, I felt a little miffed, as really, technically, I could have quite easily have made my own drink. What I should have done was order a glass of water and changed it into a Guinness, Sam Adams, or whatever. I could have done it, had I been inclined.

How Sean would have reacted would have been a different matter. No doubt the story of "Jackie" turning his water into a Sam Adams would become the stuff of bar legends, I imagined, because "Jackie Boy" always drank Guinness. Now, Guinness is not my usual beer, and to be honest, it is a little strong for me; not that I can't drink, but for some reason, Guinness gets me tipsy quicker than Budweiser or even Sam Adams, but that didn't stop me ordering another, and then another, and then another. Usually four Sam Adams were enough for me, and then I would hit the weaker Budweiser. Maybe I just wanted to drink, or maybe I didn't want to upset Sean, who kept refilling my glass. It dawned on me that I was actually on the verge of getting drunk, and I realized that if I didn't puke then, it would be my second miracle of the day. I hadn't eaten all day and for some reason, I felt a compulsion toward a fast-food fish sandwich. I debated whether to produce one, but once again, I thought better of it. Anyway, I wasn't sure if Sean would be too happy with me bringing in outside food, miracle or not.

I had become the barfly, the drunk at the bar who talked drivel. Luckily, no one ever listens to drunken men in Irish bars in the middle of summer in New York City. In Milligan's, people sometimes punched them, but they hardly ever listened to what was coming from their mouths, which in my case, was a good thing. I had proceeded to tell Sean the whole story. He had been a good listener, and in between serving other customers and drying glasses, he nodded and shook his head at all the appropriate times, whistled when he felt it warranted it. He agreed with me that the whole thing was crazy, and what was God thinking? Luckily, he hadn't believed, understood, or maybe even listened to a word I said. It was the trick of the seasoned barman, to pretend to listen and be interested in your customers' woes whilst plying them with more alcohol to compound their problems even more.

Unfortunately, even though Sean hadn't been listening, SHE had heard it all, and for some bizarre reason, SHE had believed every word. I hadn't noticed her sidle up next to me at the bar. She must have arrived at either Guinness number three or Guinness number four. She could have arrived when I bought Sean and I a chaser shot of whiskey. I had been in full flow, recalling my story to the attentive Sean. Maybe I hadn't noticed her slide up next to me because Sean had pressed the secret button behind the bar that made the bar spin around; it was only slightly, but I could definitely feel the room spinning. I wondered why he did that. It was very annoying.

I thought I could smell something, though, a sickly sweet smell that seemed to drift up my nostrils that I found irritating. The smell was familiar initially, and in my intoxicated state, I had thought it was the smell of English cider, but then realized it was perfume. A nice perfume, though whose fragrance, after the initial introduction, seemed to settle nicely in the air.

"Far out," *she* said. "Great story, no, fantastic story, amazing story, kind of neat. Hey, being the Son of God and all, sounds fun," she nudged me and winked. I was startled. I hadn't realized she was even there. I turned to face my new and uninvited audience.

To be totally honest, I did find her attractive almost immediately. I was in no fit state to say that, because, let's face it, after five pints of Guinness, I would have found Seabiscuit attractive. She had kind eyes, whatever that meant; how eyes can be kind, I did not know. I had never heard of eyes helping old ladies across the street, nor had I heard of eyes donating to charity. I suppose what I meant by kind eyes was that they seemed to sense my pain. It was as if her eyes were a beacon for the angst and tension that encompassed me. Her eyes drew me in; they were large and brown and full of life. Her hair was short, almost boyish, and her features I would describe as elfin. I don't mean she had pointed ears, I mean she looked cheeky, kind of sexy, but boyish, friendly. Not that I liked boys, friendly or otherwise, nor was I confused as to think that this was not a woman next to me, when in fact, it was a hobbit. She was definitely a woman. She was petite too. And had great tits.

She wasn't large or hefty, more tiny and petite, and she was properly proportioned. In food terms, I would say she was like a capon, a smaller version of a chicken, yet an adult, evenly proportioned, yet tinier. She wasn't, though, I hasten to add, a little person, despite the description I just gave.

"I'm sorry," I slurred, "but what did you just say?"

"I said, it must be neat," she placed a cigarette in her mouth and lit it with a Zippo lighter she produced from her jacket pocket, "you know, being the Son of God and here to save the world." She inhaled on her cigarette and blew the residual smoke into my face. "He sounds kind of cool, too. It must be great."

"Are you crazy?" I asked in disbelief, not because of what she had said, but because she had believed what I had spurted out to Sean. Despite the fact it was all true, it was so crazy that even an uninvited eavesdropper with an ounce of sense could see it was a farcical tale.

"No," she replied. "Why?" She once again blew smoke into my face. I waved my hands to disperse the smoke and to highlight that I did not appreciate her actions. Why Sean was allowing her to smoke in the bar was a mystery in itself. It violated the city codes, and had I been sober, I would have told her.

"Two reasons spring immediately to mind. Number one, why would you believe such a wild story, for Christ's sake?" I looked upward and said jokingly, "Sorry, 'JC,' didn't mean to bring you into this." I stared at her with an incredulous expression on my face. "You are listening to a drunken man in a bar on his own on a Friday night! How can anything I say be reliable? You are either drunk yourself, or you are crazy. I go for crazy," I chuckled at my comment, though it wasn't amusing, but in my drunken state, I thought it hilarious. I continued to speak. I became more animated. For some reason, I pointed at my half-full glass of beer as if it could back me up.

"And B—"

"You mean 'two,'" interrupted my uninvited companion.

"What?" I said.

"You said 'one, why would you believe such a wild story?' and then you mumbled something I didn't hear, and then you said 'B.' Your second point should have been 'two.' If you had said, 'A, why would you believe such a wild story?' and then said 'B,' that would have been correct," once again, she blew smoke into my face. Technically and grammatically, she was correct, but really, who gave a shit? I shifted in my seat to face her head on.

"Who are you?" I asked, still slightly slurring my words. Despite her uninvited intrusion, the blowing of smoke into my face and her obvious insanity, I liked her.

"Maggie," said my new friend as she offered me her hand to shake. "Maggie De Lynne."

CHAPTER

17

"YOUR NAME IS MAGGIE DE Lynne?" I asked. It wasn't really a question. I laughed out loud as I took another swig of Guinness. I shook my head. "Mag De Lynne" I said again.

"Yeah, freaky eh?" said Maggie.

"Your parents certainly had a good sense of humor." I turned to face her once more and once again, I found her eyes and face appealing.

"Yeah, I get that a lot. I suppose it is funny. I'm not sure they realized the connotations, though—my parents, that is." She inhaled once more on her cigarette, but this time, she blew the residual smoke over the bar and not into my face. She then took a sip of her drink, which I guessed was either vodka or gin.

It wasn't that funny; it was an amusing name, given my current circumstances, but funny? Not really.

"Yeah, it's pretty funny," I said.

"Bit of coincidence, though, don't you think?" said Maggie as she lit another cigarette and blew the smoke behind her. "Given your circumstances," she added once she faced me.

Didn't I just think the same thing? It was a very odd coincidence; however, that didn't concern me. What did was the fact that this woman actually believed I was the Messiah. I guessed her name was probably Jane or Sarah and that she was playing around with me. I decided not to play, though.

"Yeah, what is?" I said, pretending I wasn't paying attention.

"You being the Son of God, the second coming, the resurrection of the spirit, and the Messiah, and me being named after the one woman who some say could have been at very best his wife, or at worst, his whore." So that was it. Maggie was a hooker touting for business, and this was her ploy to get me to pay her for sex. Maggie didn't look like a whore, though.

"Are you a prostitute, Maggie?" I asked directly. The last thing I needed right now was to be seen with a hooker, especially as tomorrow I would be expected to save souls. I could imagine Sean telling the press how the Son of God picked up a hooker the night before he walked across the Hudson River. I am sure Mother Theresa would be horrified, not to mention Mother Irma, at the potential headlines.

"No, I'm a lawyer," she said as she faced me dead on, her kind eyes looking deep into my suspicious ones. It seemed she hadn't found my question offensive, which begged the question, why not? She certainly dressed like a lawyer, and I had never seen her in Milligan's before.

"You come here regularly?" I asked, slowly beginning to sober up. Maggie shook her head.

"No, first time."

I looked around the bar. We were the last customers. Sean was at the other end of the bar facing a stack of dirty glasses he had collected from the empty tables.

"Maggie, I have a question," I said as I slowly began to merge into sobriety. A thought which had entered my head a millisecond before began to grow. "Do you have any animals at home?" Maggie shook her pretty, elfin-like head.

"No, none." She lit another cigarette.

"In that case, did you get a telephone call tonight from a guy with an English accent claiming to be God, telling you to come here tonight and find me?" This time Maggie nodded and once again reverted to blowing smoke into my face.

"I sure did," she replied.

It seemed my mother and I were not the only ones who received telephone calls from God. Maggie De Lynne, it transpired, had been conversing with God for the past two days. Initially, God had come to her in dream, informing her she been selected for a very important task; to assist his son in his preparation for the final conflict on

Earth between good and evil. She would provide guidance and a female perspective and would become a disciple of the new Messiah. Maggie told me she had totally disregarded the dream as a by-product of a late night cheese snack, despite its vividness. God, though, persevered, and appeared in a further dream while she took an afternoon nap in her office. This time, God told her he would call her on the phone, as he did with my mother and I, and not to be perturbed by it. When she awoke, she was unsure of the validity of the dream; it was only after he called that she realized God had a mission for her.

Initially suspicious that the voice on the phone claiming to be God was either a nut or a joke-playing colleague or friend, she gave him a few tests. First, she hid objects around her office and instructed God to tell her what she had hidden and where. He was correct each time. Though semi-convinced it was indeed God on the phone, she set one final task. Should the owner of the voice on the phone be watching her through a telescope or a hidden camera with the caller watching her every move on CCTV, Maggie decided on a foolproof test. Maggie thought of a number and asked God to guess what it was. When God immediately replied two million, three thousand, and seventy-two, Maggie was convinced. He then told her she was going to ask him to think of a color, and that color would be lilac. Maggie told him to stop. She didn't need any more convincing. God re-explained what he had told her in the dreams—that she was on a mission for God to assist the Messiah and to wait for a call with further instructions.

That was yesterday. Maggie, obvious curious as to why God chose her for the mission, wondered if it was anything to do with her name. God admitted that her name fitted the role he chose her for, but it was mere coincidence that the name Maggie De Lynne resembled Magdalene. God chose her for her determination and open mindedness.

Maggie's latest call from God had come an hour ago. He had called her at home and told her she was coming into play sooner than had been anticipated, and she would find the Messiah at Milligan's Bar in Greenwich Village. She had arrived midway through my drunken talk with Sean, and it didn't take a genius to realize who amongst the bar folk the Messiah was. He would be the one at the bar confessing all to a bored barman.

Maggie De Lynne was indeed a lawyer. Her chosen field was property law, which meant we did have something in common professionally. I would come to learn that she was aged twenty-eight and lived alone in a plush apartment in the TriBeCa district. She was born and raised a Roman Catholic in Hackensack, New Jersey. She was not overtly religious, and indeed her religion had lapsed, which made God's calling even more puzzling to her. She had no siblings, and both her parents were dead. Her father had died several years before, and her mother had passed away recently. The dying wish of her highly religious and devout Catholic mother had been that Maggie return to the Catholic faith and re-find God. I guessed that maybe her mother had probably nominated her for the role she was to play. Her father had left her a reasonable sum of money on his death, which paid for her plush apartment in TriBeCa and meant that Maggie lived a comfortable life.

Maggie was therefore a good catch, as she was wealthy, professional, and attractive. It was a surprise to me that she was single, but then again, this was New York. Maggie had enjoyed various relationships, but like me, found it difficult to commit long term. She had once been engaged to a fellow lawyer, a colleague at the firm she practiced. Unfortunately, she had caught him in the photocopying room with a paralegal in a compromising position, and that was the end of that. It didn't help that the paralegal was called Phillip. Losing her fiancé to another man, especially when all her co-workers knew of the affair and she didn't, had left Maggie somewhat scarred. She dated as I did, and though open-minded, she was not what you call promiscuous. She spent her evenings reading and planning vacations, and I would have suggested, if I had known her better, that she was lonely. I guessed that was another reason God had selected Maggie; she needed a purpose in her life. And now she had one. I had sobered up enough to assimilate the information Maggie had passed. I had to admit, I liked her.

"You weren't hard to convince," I said as we left the bar area and found a table secluded in a booth. Two new customers had entered the bar, and Sean was chatting away, pouring drinks, and wiping glasses. Maggie smiled.

"I think the number did it; he is very convincing." She didn't have to tell me that. God had managed to convince me to walk on water. He was very convincing.

"Did God expand on your role? What are you actually meant to do? I mean, did he give you a game plan? You know everything I presume, as much as I do, at least. What's your take on this?" I asked, now completely sober.

"Well," she said, as she stubbed out her cigarette, "I presume I am going to have to sleep with you, for a start."

At last, a perk. God was obviously making up for lost ground. He was trying to make up for my childhood abandonment. Unlike most fathers and sons, we hadn't been fishing together, camping, or even been out for a beer. Maggie was obviously a gift. He had found a lonely, attractive woman with a similar sounding name as Jesus's alleged wife who would sleep with me and not want commitment. That was Maggie's role, and the reason God had selected her as my disciple. What a great guy. I was beginning to like him more. I knew of dads who had paid for their college-aged son's first sexual experience, but this was better than that. For one thing, no money had changed hands.

But Maggie wasn't a gift, and God's plan hadn't included free sex for me. As soon as Maggie said she was going to sleep with me, I paid for our drinks and tipped Sean. It took us less than eight minutes to reach my apartment. Admittedly, I walked faster than I usually did, but who could blame me for wanting to get home quickly? I hoped Harvey's shift had finished and that I wouldn't have to parade Maggie past him. Unfortunately, I had no such luck.

"Well, what do you know?" said Harvey, "You been a busy boy, dog." I smiled at Harvey pleadingly. I hoped he was going to be nice to Maggie.

"This is Maggie, an old friend of mine," I lied. Harvey nodded and sucked on his teeth.

"Oh really," he said. "Isn't that nice?" he added, nodding his head and looking Maggie up and down as if inspecting a second-hand car. "It's a great feeling when you unexpectedly bump into an old friend, ain't it?"

We both nodded and agreed it was a great feeling. Luckily, the elevator arrived before Harvey could say anything else. It was obvious he knew I was lying, but I had no idea why I felt so guilty. As we entered the elevator, Harvey leaned and tilted his head so all Maggie and I could see was his face covered with a beaming, gold-and-white smile.

"You two old friends have a good evening, you hear?" The elevator door slid shut, and I thought I heard Harvey call me an "asshole," though I wasn't sure.

"Is he your doorman?" asked Maggie.

I nodded. "Sure is," I said, as if it were normal doorman behavior for him to act like my mother.

"Why did you lie to him?" asked Maggie.

"Uh?" I answered, pretending that I did not know what she meant.

"Your doorman, Harvey, why did you tell him we were old friends?" she asked again. The truth was I wasn't sure. I felt kind of guilty, like Harvey would be disappointed in me for what I was about to do. I couldn't explain it, so I didn't. I shrugged. The moment we entered my apartment, the telephone rang, and there are no points for guessing who it was.

"Don't answer it," I cried as I hurriedly undid my shirt buttons.

"Why not?" Maggie asked as she pulled one leg from her trousers and hopped on the other.

"It will be him. My Father, God, I'm sure of it," I replied as I too hopped on one leg.

"So answer it," said Maggie as she removed her sweater.

"No way," I said as I removed my T-shirt and threw it onto the chair where Walter sat watching.

"Typical," said Walter as he dodged the T-shirt and jumped from the chair onto the floor to stare up at the half-naked Maggie and the totally naked me. "That's just typical of you humans, that is," said God through Walter. "Sex over everything, typical." He sounded pissed. I should have known God would get our attention somehow.

"Is that God?" asked Maggie "It sounds like God." She bent down to stroke Walter.

"Yes, Maggie, it is me," said God, as Walter stood and bent his head to one side to allow Maggie to stroke his face. "Maggie," said God, "I would be grateful if you desisted from that; it is extremely off-putting, despite how nice it feels."

Maggie stopped stroking Walter, who returned to sit on his haunches.

"Oh, sorry," she said and flashed an apologetic smile at both Walter and myself.

"Thank you," said God. "Now, Maggie, really," God sounded like an English headmaster, "you do realize this isn't necessary." Walter seemed to be staring directly at me. "You know you don't have to sleep with him. It isn't part of my plan, you do know that?" I closed my eyes and shook my head. "If you did, it would be a big mistake," continued God as Walter rose and stretched. Walter stared at the half-naked Maggie. I was relieved that he had averted his gaze from me, and I quickly put my pants back on. I made a mental note to thank God for this; his timing was impeccable.

"You really don't have to," reiterated God, "so why don't you get dressed? I am sure Seth will call you a cab." I was about to reach for the phone when Maggie spoke.

"I know," said Maggie. "I know I don't have to, but I kind of like him."

Yes! You tell him girl. I moved my hand away from the phone, and Walter turned his gaze once more to me.

"Are you sure?" said God, as if the mere thought that Maggie found me attractive was ludicrous. "Well, in that case, there is not really much more I can say," said God. "You're both adults." Phew. That was close. For a minute, I thought God had blown it for me. "Well, do me one favor, Maggie: sleep on it. Think about this, you know he gets around."

What was he doing? This guy was determined to make sure I would not be having sex that night. He was doing his best to dampen the ardor that still remained, which wasn't much, considering we were both half-dressed and talking to a cat when we were thirty seconds away from getting laid.

"Ok," said Maggie. "I will sleep on the couch." My heart sank.

"Good," said God, "then that's settled." And then Walter meowed.

"Has he gone?" said Maggie as she turned to face me.

"Yes, he's gone." I had a sudden urge to kick Walter, but decided he wasn't to blame. "Look, you take the bed," I said. "I'll grab a blanket, and I will take the couch."

Maggie thanked me and kissed me on the cheek. When I returned with a blanket, Maggie had already found my bed and was sleeping soundly. I closed the door and made a bed on the couch. Now fully sober, I was annoyed that God had ruined my night of passion. I considered the situation for a minute and, being extremely frustrated at being so close to getting laid, I thought, to Hell with Mother Teresa and my file, this one is an emergency. I was asleep three minutes later.

CHAPTER

18

I AWOKE, AND, FOR A split second I was confused as to why I was curled up on my sofa. I was also confused as to why I could smell coffee and breakfast being prepared. Then I remembered Maggie, and I remembered that today I was due to perform my second miracle. My heart sank, and I pulled the duvet over my head.

"Good morning," said Maggie, as I tried to forget about the events ahead of me.

I peered up from under the duvet. "What time is it?" I said as Maggie handed me a cup filled with coffee.

"Six thirty," she said. I noticed she was dressed, and I could tell by the towels strewn on the bedroom floor, which I could see through the open door, that she had also showered.

"Six thirty?" I cried and rubbed my eyes. "It's the middle of the night!" My usual Saturday morning entailed a lie-in, a leisurely stroll to a diner for a late breakfast, and a read of the weekend newspaper.

"It's a busy day," said Maggie. "You need to get ready." And with that, Maggie snatched the duvet away from the couch, exposing my naked body. "Oops," she said. "I didn't realize you slept naked." I usually didn't, but my pajamas were in my bedroom, and so as not to disturb the already-sleeping Maggie, who had been curled up in my bed, I had decided to forgo pajamas.

"Well," said Maggie as she stared at my nakedness. "Seeing as though you are ready, we might as well get this over with."

Maggie grabbed my hand and led me into the bedroom. Walter sat curled up in a ball on the bed "Is that you?" asked Maggie to Walter. Walter didn't move.

"Good!" we both said in unison.

Thus my relationship with Maggie began. I won't go into details, but let me say, it was well worth the wait. An hour later, I showered, dressed, and called Bob to confirm our meeting point. I didn't mention I would be bringing Maggie with me; I thought I would wait until I saw him. I switched on the television and checked the news channels; there was no mention of the mayor, the Peruvian ambassador, or of any potential demonstrations. Maybe Nancy had got it wrong. I hoped so.

Harvey was not on duty that morning, so we were able to leave the apartment without any interruption or hold up. I wasn't in the mood for Harvey's comments this morning. He would want details, and even though Maggie would have been in earshot, it wouldn't have stopped him asking. I felt I needed to review my relationship with Harvey; it was beginning to feel like he was trying to monitor my life. Maybe it was just me, but he was becoming as bad as my mother. We eventually found a cab after a twenty minute wait, one disadvantage of no Harvey on duty, and I called up Bob on my cell phone to let him know we were on our way. He had questioned the "we," and I told I would explain when we arrived at the harbor.

Bob was waiting for us as we pulled up to pier fifty-eight, two piers from where the mayor's yacht was berthed. I could see as we exited the cab that a small crowd had formed around the pier. The demonstrator's had arrived. I could see a few blue uniforms of the NYPD, one in particular that I suspected had taken a whole cotton field to make. It was Nancy. I also spied a local news channel vehicle, so the media was here. All that was missing was the mayor and the ambassadorial party. I paid the cab as Bob approached.

"Bob, meet Maggie. Maggie, meet Bob." Bob looked surprised as Maggie offered her hand.

"Hi," she said, smiling.

"Hi," said Bob, looking confused as he weakly took her hand. He looked at me for an explanation.

"It's a long story," I said. "We will explain later."

We all walked along our pier to get a better view of the adjourning pier. Bob seemed to accept this, shrugged his shoulders, and led Maggie and I along the pier. "We need to keep out of view," he said, referring to him and Maggie. "The last thing I need is for Nancy," he turned to Maggie, "that's my wife, to see me with you," He looked over at the crowded pier sixty.

The mayor and the ambassador had arrived as we had proceeded along the pier, and we could hear the llama-loving demonstrators' whistles and boos.

"Once they get on board, you should start walking toward them," said Bob. "I have worked it out. The cameras will still be rolling, and the crowd and the press will all be focused on the boat and the water. They will see you appear from the distance, and hey presto, the Messiah is with us. I can see the headlines now." I was not totally convinced that Bob's plan would work, but I did not have a better one. I looked at Maggie and she nodded, confirming she saw no problem with Bob's plan.

"Okay," I said. "I'm ready."

I crept down the pier ladder pensively and onto the water. Yes, onto it, not into it. I felt as light as a feather; it was a strange sensation. I thought at any time I would sink like a stone, but I didn't. I closed my eyes and then opened them to look down at my feet. I was definitely stood on top of the water. I clung to the pier ladder.

"Let go," encouraged Maggie. I didn't want to, though; I knew the railing was not preventing me from sinking. It was a psychological thing. I wasn't ready to let go.

"Yes, let go," shouted Bob. I couldn't, despite the fact I was not sinking; I froze with fear and trepidation.

"I can't," I hissed back. Maggie lent over and grabbed the hand that clutched the ladder rail. She pried my fingers open and loosened my grip. "Don't do that!" I shouted, afraid I was going to plummet into the murky water.

"Oh, be quiet," ordered Maggie as she twisted the final finger that clung to the rail.

"Hey!" I cried, "That hurt." I looked at my hand and checked that my finger wasn't broken. It wasn't. Then I realized I was no longer holding the ladder rail. I stood, unsupported, atop the water. I hadn't sunk. I couldn't believe it.

"Try walking," shouted Bob. I looked up and saw Maggie and Bob both peering down.

"Okay," I said, and I took a small step forward, then another, and another. I was walking. I was walking on water, and it was easy! I was concentrating hard initially, but after six or seven steps, the nerves disappeared, and my confidence grew. Maggie and Bob whooped and cheered behind me.

"Go on," shouted Bob, "they have arrived." He motioned toward the adjacent pier. I looked toward pier sixty, which was about five hundred feet away, and the mayor's yacht; I could see that all eyes faced the water. I headed toward the crowd.

No one seemed to notice me at first as I walked the first two hundred feet. As I approached closer, I could see hands pointing, and heads turning from the yacht toward me. I could hear people gasping, and I could see the flash of camera lights. There was a commotion at pier sixty. The crowds were trying to surge forward for a better view of the approaching Messiah. The people aboard the yacht were all staring too. I wondered what the mayor thought of this. There was no doubting it, it was a miracle; I was walking on the water, heading directly toward the yacht and cordoned of crowd of pro-llama demonstrators. I couldn't make out her face, but I could see Nancy's bulky frame, and her head was turned, facing me, as her outstretched hands blocked the crowd from rushing the pier. Ha! What a surprise for her this would be! Just as I thought I had cracked it, just as I thought that being the Messiah might not be as bad as I had thought, just as I mentally prepared myself for what lay ahead, just when I thought being the Son of God could actually be fun…disaster struck.

"Stop! I repeat, stop! Do not approach any further!" I looked around to see where the voice projected by the megaphone was coming from, and to whom it was directed at. "I repeat, stop. This is an order." It was the coast guard; they were in a little rubber speedboat, and they were headed my way. I hadn't seen them earlier, and they had appeared out of nowhere. I could see a gun trained on me. Obviously, I did what anyone else would do. I turned back in the direction I had come, and ran. Luckily, I had about three hundred feet on the coast guard patrol, and running on water was like running on land. I ran as fast as I could back toward pier fifty-eight and my disciples.

At first, Bob and Maggie looked confused as to why I was running so quickly to where they stood, but then they also spotted the rubber boat and the weapon trained on me. Maggie and Bob both urged me to run faster. The coastguard was gaining, but I had the edge on them. There was no way they would reach me before I got to safety, but that didn't stop them from chasing or shooting. Luckily, or miraculously, their bullets fell short, and I reached the pier steps well ahead of them. Bob and Maggie gave me a hand up the ladder.

"Let's get the heck out of here, now!" I yelled as my feet touched solid ground. Bob and Maggie didn't argue, and we bolted along the pier. Just as we hit the sidewalk, a taxi appeared. We hailed it and sped off just as the coastguard vessel reached the end of our pier. I looked behind me out of the cab window and could see the police hadn't seen our escape, and they were too busy escorting the mayor and ambassador to safety. We all slid down in the cab as a cavalcade of police cars sped past on its way to the pier. All three of us looked at each other. We instructed our driver to take us to Milligan's where we needed to regroup and discuss the events that had just transpired. We were all in shock, not least of all me.

Luckily, our cab driver seemed totally unfazed by all the commotion at the pier and the speeding police cars headed in the direction we had just come from. In fact, he never said a word the whole journey. I thought his silence odd and his sudden arrival on the scene extremely convenient. It seemed God was watching over us, maybe.

Milligan's was quiet. It was a Saturday morning, and only the hardened drinkers ventured there before noon. We found a booth, which ensured us the privacy we needed. I looked around the bar and saw only one other customer. A blind man with his guide dog sat at the furthest table from us. I felt safe that no one would recognize us. Sean took our orders and called me John, which suited me fine; Sean's bad memory meant he couldn't place us should the need arise. None of us spoke until Sean returned with our drinks: three straight up double scotches.

"Okay, then," Bob was the first to speak. "Out of ten, how do you think that went?" The question was directed at both Maggie and I. I shook my head.

"How did it go?" I asked. "Bob, I was just shot at!" I couldn't believe Bob was even contemplating it had gone remotely well. "It was a disaster! The whole thing. Did you not see what happened? I thought I was going to die." I was shaking, and I took a swig of scotch to calm my nerves.

"I thought it was a success," said Maggie. I nearly choked as the whiskey hit my throat.

"You are joking," I spluttered. "How on earth can you construe what just happened as a success?" I remembered now why I had thought her crazy in the first place; maybe she was.

"I agree with Maggie," said Bob. "We have to put that down as successful." Maggie nodded as Bob continued to speak. "First of all, you walked on water. I saw it, Maggie saw it, and so did everyone else, including the cameras. Secondly, there is no doubt we will have publicity; not only was there a TV crew on the pier, I am sure I heard a helicopter overhead. They will have gotten shots also." I wasn't sure what type of shots Bob was referring to; gunshots or filmed shots.

"So, what, the cops spoilt the party?" said Maggie. "The thing is, people will see that on TV and make up their own minds." Bob and Maggie seemed to be in total agreement, despite my animated objections, that the miracle had been a success. Granted, it had caused more of a stir than the fish sandwich fiasco, but really? Were they serious? The coast guard shot at me, for Dad's sake! I was too nervous to argue, and maybe they were right. Maybe this would create the attention we needed, but the circumstances were not ideal.

I took the opportunity to explain to Bob Maggie's presence. Bob seemed quite pleased to have Maggie on board, and though I hadn't told him we had slept together, I knew he was dying to ask me if we had. Luckily, Maggie never left the table, so he couldn't ask, but I knew he would want to as soon as he got the opportunity.

I took a deep breath and sat back in my chair. I was happy it was over. If indeed it had been a success, then I wondered what our next move should be. Once the TV stations broadcasted the images across the world, people would see that a miracle had occurred, and that the only other known "walker on water" was Jesus himself. Therefore, we all presumed the multitude would rightly assume that only a Messiah could walk on water and would demand I reveal myself, thus beginning the process of saving the world.

Milligan's did a great breakfast: Irish sausage, bacon, eggs—the works. Feeling a little better, I ordered us all breakfast, and we reverted to coffee now that our nerves, well predominantly mine, had settled. We discussed what we should do next, and the unified answer was to wait for the press and people to demand I reveal myself.

"Hey," exclaimed Maggie as she shoveled a fork full of Irish sausage into her mouth, "we should really check the TV news to see what they are saying." She was right. If we had made any impact, then we would be on the news. I had no doubts there would be some mention of the morning's events. It wasn't every day that the coastguard in New York City fired shots, even if they were just warning shots, Bob proposed whilst chewing on a piece of a toast. Nor was it every day that the mayor and a visiting ambassador were driven away from a scheduled event at high speed under police escort. I however, did not share my companion's enthusiasm in seeing what the media was saying about the morning's events.

I asked Sean if he would switch on the TV perched above the bar, which he did before returning to his newspaper. It seemed we were the only ones interested in watching television in the bar, as Sean was engrossed in the sport pages, and I doubted the blind drinker and his dog would be viewing.

Sean handed me the remote control so I could select channels. I found our local news channel. The picture was a little grainy, and you could not make out my face, which was a relief. However, it was definitely me, unless someone else had been walking on water at the same location and at the same time. The helicopter Bob had heard must have indeed been a news crew, as there were shots from above, which clearly showed me walking atop the water. Bob and Maggie sat with smug smiles on their faces. They were right. It seemed the cameras had caught the miracle, and my walk across the water had indeed been filmed. The footage shifted to a view of me walking toward pier sixty and the mayor's yacht. Again, you could not make out my features in the footage, which was another relief, and I relaxed. It was impossible to identify the mystery man walking atop the Hudson River. The images repeated over and over again, obviously in some sort of loop. Maggie shrieked with delight, and Bob shook my hand. We had done it. We had shown the world that the Messiah was amongst them.

"Not too loud, guys," I said. "Let's try not to attract too much attention. I think we should keep as low a profile as possible until we work out our next move." I looked around the empty bar as if to reiterate the need for a little decorum, but neither Sean nor the blind man and his dog paid us any attention.

"This is fantastic," said Bob. "We pulled it off." He took a drink from his coffee cup.

"Oh shit," said Maggie.

"What next do you think? Call a press conference, contact a publicist?" I said to Bob. Maggie stood up and walked toward the bar, leaving Bob and I in the booth.

"Oh shit," said Maggie again as she walked toward the television set above the bar.

"It was a brilliant plan, if I do say so myself," boasted Bob. "Hey Maggie, get me another scotch; get us all a scotch—it's time to celebrate!"

I turned to watch her as she walked toward the bar. "Yeah, Maggie, get some champagne or something," I added.

"Shit, shit, shit," said Maggie. This time Bob and I heard her.

"What is it?" I asked

"That," said Maggie, pointing at the TV screen. Bob and I followed her finger toward the screen. The images on the news hadn't altered, and the loop still played, the overhead shot followed by the shot from the shore, and then back to the overhead shot and so on. What was different, though, was the ticker of text that accompanied the pictures.

"We need to turn the sound up. We need to turn the sound up!" I said pleadingly, searching for the remote control. It was Maggie who grabbed the television remote from the bar where I had left it. Sean glanced up, as we had all risen, but when he saw we didn't require refills, he returned to his newspaper, which he was fully engrossed in. The reporter's voice that accompanied the ticker and the looped pictures sounded serious and earnest. He described the pictures and the events that occurred that morning for the benefit of the channel's viewers.

"....here we are again, with pictures from earlier today of the attempted attack on the Mayor of New York and the Peruvian Ambassador by what is believed to be a lone terrorist, who authorities now believe is a member of The LFG, an acronym for the Llama Freedom Group, who is attempting to stop the exportation of Peruvian llama meat. Unconfirmed reports are now suggesting that the terrorist was attempting to approach the vessel in a possible attempt to sink the Mayor's yacht." The accompanying ticker tape was also as dramatic: COASTGUARD THWART ATTEMPT TO SINK NY MAYOR GIULIANI'S YACHT. ONE TERRORIST SOUGHT. The Reporter continued his commentary.

"As you can see from these exclusive pictures, the terrorist appears to have approached the vessel with the intention of detonating explosives that were apparently strapped to his body."

We all stood open mouthed at the scene on the television screen. What explosives? Where were they getting this from? It was unbelievable. Surely they realized they had made a huge mistake? There was no mention of the fact I was actually walking on water; it was as if that was irrelevant. Could they not see? Were they idiots? I looked harder at the images. Though it was not easy to make out, it seemed obvious to me that I walked on water. Surely they could see it. Did they think I was atop of some sort of motorized surfboard? Straight out of a James Bond movie? The reporter continued his dramatic description of the morning's events.

"It would seem the terrorist used a motorized surfboard to approach the yacht, like something from a James Bond movie. Though you can't actually see it in these images, eyewitness claim that he was definitely on top of the water. It is being suggested, by unconfirmed sources, that the LFG had acquired several surfboards, and had been experimenting in motorizing them for an attack such as this."

Who were these sources? This was crazy! The media was making this up!

"I don't believe it," said Bob as he cupped his head into his hands.

"How could this be?" said Maggie in disbelief as the pictures continued to loop on the screen at which we stared. "Explosives? Terrorists? Motorized surfboards? Are they crazy?" Maggie exclaimed as she too cupped her head in her hands. I watched the screen for several minutes more while there was silence amongst us. None of us felt like speaking. Maggie and Bob continued to sit with their heads in their hands the whole time as I stared transfixed at the screen, not believing what I saw or heard.

"It's just a minor setback." The voice was unmistakable. All three of us jolted from our personal thoughts and turned collectively to the voice we all recognized. Bern was a Labrador. A seeing-eye dog for the blind, more specifically for the blind man who sat at the table farthest from us, who it seemed hadn't noticed that his guide dog was not at his side as he continued to sit engrossed in his Braille book. It was also apparent that Sean hadn't noticed Bern make his way to our table, let alone notice that the dog was speaking, as his head was still down, reading his newspaper.

"It really is a minor setback, team," said God. "It's not a big deal. Tomorrow's always another day, and I am sure we will think of something else." Bern sat staring up at us, his tail wagging.

"You call that a minor setback?" I asked. For me, the novelty of God talking through animals had worn off. I was used to conversing with them now. Bob, however, had yet to witness this phenomena, and for a minute, I thought he was going to faint. He sat opened mouthed, staring at Bern. "I'm probably on the FBI Most Wanted list" I said, pointing at the TV screen. Bern didn't turn to look but simply continued to wag his tail.

"Oh, poppycock. Don't be so over-dramatic. They have no idea who you are. Anyway, I'll make sure this is all cleared up quickly. I do have some influence," said God, "and you can't even see your face. Anyway, I will pull a few strings, and tomorrow this will be yesterday's news. Don't worry about it."

It wasn't entirely clear to me if God had cracked a joke about yesterday's news or if he had said it without realizing. If it was a joke, I hadn't found it funny.

"Don't worry about it?" I asked. "Don't worry? They shot at me. They think I am a terrorist. I am no closer to convincing the world I am the Messiah than I was yesterday. This whole thing is failure after failure and one disaster after another. Surely there is a better way; to be honest, this is playing havoc with my nervous system." That was no exaggeration. I was trembling, and I had lost at least three pounds in weight in the three days since I had discovered I was the Messiah. The final straw for me would be if my hair started falling out; there was no way I was prepared to lose my hair, not for the savior of mankind, not for anyone.

Bern sat on his hind legs and then stood up to scratch his ear with his back left leg. It looked like an uncomfortable maneuver, and I was surprised he kept his balance. Maggie and Bob remained silent. Bob had closed his mouth; I assumed he realized I was talking to God.

"Do you two feel that way also?" God asked. Maggie and Bob didn't reply. Maggie shrugged, indicating she didn't see a problem with moving forward, and Bob gulped loudly before he spoke.

"No. I'm with you, God. I think it was unfortunate, but I think we are improving with each miracle." What a pair of cowards. I couldn't believe they were not admitting the whole thing was going down the pan.

"See," said God triumphantly, "a man and a woman with faith. That's what's missing, your faith. Faith in your own ability, and faith in my ability." Bern stopped scratching his ear, and instead tried to scratch his back.

"Faith isn't the problem," I said, "it's just not working. It's too much. I am a nervous wreck. Look at my hand." I pushed my hand toward Bern's nose so God could get a better look at my shaking, which Bern licked.

"Oh come on," said God, "pull yourself together, man. It's not that hard. I can't believe any son of mine would give in so easily. You know, JC went through a lot more than you ever will. When he was on that cross, I never heard him once say 'I can't do it,' or 'I'm hurting,' or 'I'm a nervous wreck, I need to lie down.'" God emphasized the comments by exaggerating in a whining voice. "You never heard him complain once. Not once!" God was getting angry; I could tell by his tone. The guy certainly had some issues and, indeed, a bit of a temper. However, he did not intimidate me.

"Oh, that is so typical" I said. "JC, this. JC, that. I am so sorry I am not living up to big brother's standards, but there are one or two differences. He had a lot more breaks than I did. Three wise men bearing gifts for a start, thirty years of preparation, and he had twelve disciples, he had a following. I would like to see how he would have got on with the US Coastguard shooting at him." I said, pointing at the television screen. God ignored my outburst.

"Well, you'd better shape up," said God, "and quickly. I have some rather disturbing news!"

All three of us stared at Bern. Not because he was licking his private parts, but because of God's last sentence.

"Well, I see I have your attention," said God once Bern had finished what men could only dream of doing. "The committee held an emergency meeting earlier today, and the vote was unanimous. The committee has voted that we begin our preparations for the final conflict. We need to out the anti-Christ and bring him to the fore. You must issue your challenge and prepare for the battle," said God. "We need to show the other side that we are ready and strong."

"But I am not ready, and I am not strong" I said. I was conscious that my bottom lip trembled as it always did when I became scared. I hoped God hadn't seen it and thought that I was crying.

"Are you crying?" God asked.

"No. If you knew me a bit better you would know it's a nervous twitch. It happens when I become scared."

"How off-putting," said God indignantly, referring to my quivering lip, as Bern once more licked his balls. "Anyway, it doesn't matter that you think you are not ready, because I think that you are, and as I am in charge here—that's what counts. I will be in touch shortly with details of where we go from here, and as for miracles, no more, not for now, not until you hear from me." Maggie, Bob and I all exchanged glances. "Oh," said God as Bern stood up and headed in the direction of his blind owner, "one more thing."

"Yes?" I replied.

"Are you going to eat the rest of that sausage?" I looked at my plate, on which sat a piece of uneaten sausage. I threw it at Bern, who caught it in his mouth, then barked.

We decided it was time we left. Bern's bark had stirred Sean from his newspaper, and he came over to take our money. Maggie quickly switched channels; not that it mattered, as he didn't once glance up at the television. I hoped Maggie and I would resume where we had left off that morning. I enjoyed her company, and I didn't feel like being alone. I was to be disappointed, as she had to prepare for a case and would be working all night, so I could forget any hopes of sex. Bob was going to be as equally occupied, not that I wanted sex with him, I hasten to add. Nancy had planned a dinner for them both that would involve several courses and much belching. Tonight was her first night at home not working the late shift, and she expected Bob to be there and to be ready and willing to perform whatever conjugal activity she so desired. I pitied the man. As we left Milligan's, we walked past Bern who now sat at the feet of his blind master. He had just finished consuming the sausage I had thrown him. Bob bent down to pet him and Bern growled and flashed his teeth. Bob quickly pulled his hand away.

CHAPTER 19

MAGGIE HOPPED IN A CAB and disappeared into traffic toward TriBeCa. She promised me she would call later. Bob walked off toward the subway station. He too would call later, he promised. Maybe it was good that they had left. I had a lot to think about. God's final words rang in my ears. Not the request for sausage, but the need to prepare for the final conflict. I wasn't a fighter and never had been. This whole thing was getting out of hand, and things were suddenly going faster than I had ever anticipated. Why couldn't I be oblivious to the whole thing? Why did I have be the one who confronted the army of Lucifer and the beast? I was a natural coward; of all the people to choose to defend the existence of Earth, I was not that person. I dreaded to think what the anti-Christ would do to me. He would pulverize me and beat the crap out of me. It was me who needed defending. I was the meek, and one of my greatest fears had always been what if the meek inherited the earth, and then the Martians invaded? Who would protect us? Me? Are you kidding?

The walk from Milligan's to my apartment usually took me ten minutes, and as thoughts of impending destruction and disasters and possible beatings by a giant of a man known simply as 'the beast' developed in my head, I was not paying attention to anything going on around me, least of all the fact

I was being followed. I did, though, get the feeling that something was not quite right despite my state of mind and the amount of thoughts that occupied it. I first realized something felt odd as I passed the Gap which I often shopped at for jeans and T-shirts. It was handily located and very reasonably priced, but I guess that isn't important right now.

I spun around quickly and without warning, attempting to surprise whoever, if anyone, was following me. I didn't notice anything suspicious or untoward, though my fellow pedestrians seemed slightly perturbed by my sudden spin. I carried on walking, but the feeling was still there. I decided to alter my route home. I took a left where I usually took a right and then a right where I usually took a left. The ten-minute journey home increased as I circled a block and crossed and re-crossed avenues unnecessarily. Periodically, I would spin around but saw nothing or anyone that seemed untoward. Maybe I was going crazy; it was highly probable, considering the events of the past three days. Or maybe I was becoming paranoid, thanks to God's warning that the battle with the anti-Christ, who I knew would be at least eight feet tall, was looming, but the feeling still persisted. I turned right and then a left and double backed once more, and again I did a quick spin and saw no one that I recognized from my previous spins. I was back en-route for my apartment building, and I did a final spin. Again the only thing it achieved was more curious glances from my fellow pedestrians, but though I felt uneasy, I was satisfied that I hadn't been followed. Or so I thought.

Harvey, who had arrived for his shift an hour earlier, greeted me. It was good to see him, and for some reason, I felt safe in his presence. At over six feet tall and looking as he did, Harvey was a good person to have on your side, should the need arise. The news that day had been completely dominated by the terrorist attempt to sink the Mayor's yacht, and Harvey was eager to hear my opinion on the matter.

"I really don't have an opinion," I said, knowing the truth made it impossible for me to have an opinion.

"Don't have an opinion? Man, that's lame," cried Harvey. "Those poor llamas, man. I dig on meat, ribs, and fried chicken, but llama? What sort of sick mother wants to chow down on a llama? They are like goat, man, and I have eaten goat. It is chewy and tastes like shit. I say leave them be and don't mess with no llama. Now, I don't think sinking the Mayor's yacht is the way to go about it. No, sir," said Harvey. It seemed as though the whole issue of llama meat had become the topic of the day throughout the country, and the debate was in full swing. At least some good had come out of the morning's miracle doing. Mounting pressure and the public outcry toward the plight of the poor llama had resulted in an immediate suspension of the exporting of llama meat. It appeared the Peruvian government had underestimated the strength and determination of the LFG.

"Have you ever tasted llama?" Harvey asked as I glanced out onto the street.

"No, I can't say I have" I said.

"How about your lady friend from last night, she ever tasted llama?" asked Harvey, once again prying into my private life, and I guessed trying to work out who Maggie was.

"If you mean Maggie, that's her name, then no, I am sure she hasn't."

Harvey nodded, indicating to me that he approved that neither Maggie nor myself were devourers of llama meat. "By the way," said Harvey, "who's your other new friend?" I didn't know what Harvey was talking about, and my expression must have shown that.

"What other new friend?" I asked.

"The Woody Allen type dude who was looking for you," replied Harvey. "Skinny, short guy, glasses, dressed liked his momma picked out his clothes. He was around here asking if you were home. I told him to either try the diner, the Gap, or Milligan's. I thought he was a friend of yours; he looked freaky enough to be a friend of yours, all small and frightened looking cracker ass honky fool." Despite Harvey's assumptions of what my friends looked like, I knew no one fitting that description.

"Hey," said Harvey "that's him there." I followed Harvey's finger to where he pointed. Harvey's ring-laden finger led to a small, bespectacled man who seemed to be talking to himself. He was no more than five feet and five inches, and thin. He wore a pair of large, obviously very strong prescription horn-rimmed spectacles that made his head look tiny. If I were to compare to him an animal, which I often did when describing people, I would have to say he had the features and characteristics of a frightened mouse wearing spectacles. He was, as Harvey had described him, dressed in an outfit that my mother, if she were able to, would have bought for me. He wore a blue and white striped cardigan over a white shirt which hosted a bowtie at the collar. He wore baggy black slacks and sneakers, and a dirty, knee-length raincoat finished off the whole outfit.

I guessed he was of similar age to me. Harvey was also correct when he said the guy looked like Woody Allen. He could have been his brother. He was a pathetic sight. There was no doubt that this man was one of life's losers. He saw me looking at him, and I hoped he didn't see the look of pity on my face. He stopped whispering to himself and raised his hand slowly and timidly as if to wave.

"Uh huh," grunted Harvey "that's him. He was here earlier, asking what time you'd be home and where he could find you. Look at him, man, that is some sorry-ass fool." I had never seen the man before in my life. I looked at Harvey and shrugged.

"I don't know him." Harvey shrugged also. The man entered the building and cowered as he passed Harvey, who eyed him suspiciously. It was a ridiculous sight, as the six-foot-tall Harvey leered at the poor man. The nerd approached me.

"Excuse me, but are you Seth Miller?" he asked timidly. His voice was nasally, and I guessed by his accent that he was probably from the Bronx.

"Yes," I answered politely. I felt instantly sorry for the little man. "I hear you've been looking for me," I indicated Harvey, who leered at my visitor, "and you are?" I asked politely.

He was quite harmless looking, and to be honest, he looked like he could burst into tears at any moment. I had never met anyone so timid, and I wondered what he wanted from me. "My name is William Lee Zachariah Bubb, a mouthful, I know." He laughed nervously. "Most people call me Bill." I shook his outstretched hand. His handshake was, like him, weak. I thought I was going to crush his hand.

"Well, Bill," I said, "how can I help you?"

Bill looked around nervously to check that no one was listening, and of course, Harvey was. In fact, Harvey had stood next to us the whole time as if poor Bill had come to speak to him as well.

He eavesdropped so obviously that he didn't even disguise it. I half-expected him to introduce himself. "Maybe somewhere a little more private," said Bill, jerking his head toward Harvey, indicating to me that he didn't want Harvey hearing what he had to say.

"Uh huh," Harvey said rudely as he sucked on his teeth. "Like that is it, little man?" I wasn't sure if Harvey thought he was my secretary, personal assistant, or even my bodyguard, but Bill had obviously upset him. I thought Bill was going to collapse as Harvey once more leered at him. I thought the best move was to take Bill up to my apartment where Harvey could not intimidate him.

"Let's go up to my apartment," I said to Bill. I nodded at Harvey as if indicating I could handle things from here. Harvey nodded back, indicating that if I needed him, he would be ready. Needed him for what, I had no idea. Bill didn't seem like the sort of person I would need assistance in kicking the crap out of if I were inclined to do so, which I wasn't.

Walter looked up nonchalantly from the sofa as we entered my apartment and returned to sleep when he saw it was me and no one else interesting. I offered Bill a coffee, but he refused on account of his stomach ulcer. A Coke would keep him awake, and as he was lactose intolerant, a glass of milk wouldn't work either. His IBS precluded any fruit juices, and alcohol was totally out of the question, as he was a teetotaler. Carbonated drinks made him gassy, and herbal tea caused him to vomit. He eventually settled on water, and then recanted when I informed him I only had distilled. Apparently, distilled water could contain parasites, and he could only drink natural spring water. I had never heard of parasites in distilled water and made a mental note to look it up on the internet when I had chance.

I considered myself a patient man, but Bill, as nice as he was and as pathetic as he was, annoyed me. He was allergic to cats, so he asked if I could place and secure Walter in another room, which I did, despite Walter's indignant look. Bill was also extremely susceptible to air-based germs and therefore requested if I would be so kind as to open a window so any germs that omitted from me could circulate outdoors. Once again, I did as he asked. He then asked if I could remove the cushions from the easy chair I had offered him to be seated on, as the feathers inside the cushions could spill out, and that would cause a rash if they were goose feathers. I told him they weren't goose feathers, that they were actually duck feathers, but unfortunately, they too caused a reaction. For at least fifteen minutes, Bill recounted to me his ailments and allergies.

"Bill," I said putting up a hand to show that I needed him to stop dithering and get to the reason he had sought me out, "if you could please get to the point. What can I do for you?"

Bill shuffled uneasily in his chair and didn't speak for at least twenty seconds. "I know who you are," he said finally.

"I know you do," I replied calmly, "I'm Seth Miller."

"No. I mean I know *who* you are." This time Bill winked as if we shared a secret.

"Bill, please, I don't want to sound rude, but I am not following you," I said, genuinely unsure of what Bill was trying to get at.

"Am I annoying you?' asked Bill, and I did think he was definitely going to burst into tears there and then. "I do this. I always do this. I always upset people. People hate me; now you hate me." I was astounded. I had never encountered such neurosis before. It was indeed like having Woody Allen on my couch. I patted him on the hand.

"Don't cry, Bill. You haven't upset or annoyed me," I said in the softest and most reassuring voice I could muster. Bill looked at me with his pleading, watery eyes. "Really?"

"Really" I said reassuringly. This seemed to cheer Bill, and he wiped his eyes with a handkerchief he produced from the pocket of his raincoat. I urged him to come to the point and say what he had to.

"I know you are the Son of God," said Bill as he dabbed a tear from his cheek. I was initially shocked by Bill's words, but not surprised. Obviously, he had been a recipient of one of God's dreams, and Bill was going to be one of my little helpers, my third disciple.

I smiled and nodded. "He sounds very pompous, doesn't he?" I said knowingly.

"Who does?" asked Bill, looking a little confused.

"Him," I said pointing upward.

"Your upstairs neighbor?" asked Bill looking even more confused.

"No, him, the big cheese, Dad," I said again pointing upward, "God."

"I don't know," said Bill; "I've never spoken to him."

"You haven't spoken to God? Then how do you know who I am?" I asked, now I was the one who was confused. And that's when Bill L. Z. Bubb told me his story.

CHAPTER

20

WILLIAM L. Z. BUBB, OR Bill as he liked people to call him, was born on the exact same day I was. I was right about his accent. He was Bronx born and bred but resided in Manhattan where he also worked. I would like to think that was all we had in common. Unfortunately, there was one minor detail which bonded us further.

Bill was a journalist of sorts; he was a columnist for the computer magazine, *Bytes*. Everyone had probably seen *Bytes* on the newsstand with a free CD with every purchase stuck to it. Many probably picked up a copy and browsed through it, then discarded it without even remembering what it was at their doctor's or dentist's office whilst waiting for their appointment.

Unless you are a computer nut and need to know all about the updated virus checkers, the new games, megabytes, gigabytes, and how to correctly handle your joystick, I very much doubt you would have ever purchased a copy.

Bill had two weekly columns in *Bytes*; they were not the highlight of the magazine but not the lowlights either. Each week, in his first column, Bill would appraise his readers on the newest anti-virus software currently available on the market, which games were worth downloading, or what other computer "geek" items were available for purchase. He would rate each piece of software and advise his readers on whether or not it was worth spending their hard-earned cash on updating or protecting their laptops or computers with products such as "Firegate Version 3.4," "Lock

Out Version 18.9," or my personal favorite, "Scum Blocker Version 1.2."

Bill's knowledge on those subjects, I later discovered, was undisputed amongst the computer communities of the world, and he was indeed an expert in his field. Bill's second column was the more widely read of the two. It dealt with all aspects of retro arcade games, where to buy them, where to have them repaired, and where to buy updated software for them. Bill had a claim to fame that revolved around computer games. Bill was the 1983, 1984, and 1986 World Space Invader Champion, a game I had never played as a kid but had seen. He was, without doubt, the best player of video arcade games that the United States had ever produced, and he still receives fan mail, mainly from Japan, but also from Europe and Australia. He was an expert in the workings of those machines and many considered him the guru on all subjects relating to them. Bill was also extremely deft at other computer-related games and was a source of endless information about their workings and programs.

I personally had never read computer magazines, and if I did, I would doubt I would read either of Bill's columns, but each to his own. I doubted Bill would ever look at one of the buildings I designed and comment on its angles, natural light consumption, or its parking facilities.

Bill and I were both white collar, single, and relatively successful New Yorkers. We both lived alone, but due to his allergies, Bill did not share his home with a pet. His apartment was like mine, but was located mid-town, without any animals. Unlike me though, Bill was not a fan of sports; he did not like baseball and detested football, both games far too physical and violent for him. Apart from his computers and his interest in Space Invaders, Bill's only other hobby was a thing I had never heard of called "cosplay."

Apparently, this pastime was extremely popular in Japan, but also had a very large following in the US. It revolved around the dressing up in costumes worn by superheroes, computer game characters, cartoon characters, and other fictional beings. The idea was that an individual would design and make the garments to enter into competitions judged by revered members of the fantasy and science fiction communities. Bill was well known on the cosplay circuit, and on average once a month, Bill would join other individuals and parade around conference centers, hotels, and other suitable venues dressed as Darth Vader, Batman, Pokeman, or some other fictional character. To be honest, it was hard to imagine Bill as Darth Vader or Batman; however I would later learn that Bill made a very convincing Bilbo Baggins, and other elfin-like characters were his forte. I would have found the whole thing laughable and ridiculous until I realized how many hot chicks Bill knew through this hobby. I did later verify that women outnumbered men two to one at those events, and Bill, despite his looks and appearance, often had propositions from scantily clad women looking for an elf. Bill was far too shy to ever to take up those offers, so the only tights he ever got into were his own.

So that was Bill, really; he had a lot of friends scattered about the country, all members of the various costuming groups he belonged to, but he avoided close friends due to his painful shyness. His colleagues all respected him, as he was indeed a fountain of knowledge, but even his fellow geeks found him hard to socialize with. His endless complaints and allergies made being with Bill extremely tiresome even for a guy he worked with, who had changed his surname to Spock.

It seemed the things Bill and I had in common were cancelled out by the extreme differences we had in our respective professional and social lives, which, after spending two hours with Bill, was a relief. There would be no way I would ever dress as an elf and parade in front of thousands of other people, even if it did mean there was a chance I was going to get screwed by Catwoman later. However, despite those differences, I found myself liking Bill. He was extremely genuine, and I felt he was the sort of guy who would not or could not harm a fly. He was timid and gentle, and despite his ailments and lack of social prowess, I was enjoying his company. If I thought I was one of the meek, which I had, then I was wrong. Bill was without doubt the meekest and most humble individual I had ever encountered. So it came as a bit of shock, I have to say, when Bill revealed to me that he was actually the anti-Christ.

CHAPTER 21

AT PRECISELY THE SAME TIME that Bill had revealed to me he was "the Beast," I had, rather unfortunately, been drinking a beer. I was not sure how much hit my poor guest, but the amount that sprayed from my mouth was vast. For one fleeting second, I thought I was going to choke. I coughed and spluttered for at least five minutes before I regained any normality of breath. I apologized profusely to Bill and was extremely pleased that I had laid clean sheets over my furniture at the request of Bill so none of Walter's hairs would assist in provoking any reaction to Bill's numerous animal allergies.

"I know I seem like an odd choice," said Bill. He wiped away my spit and beer from his face with a new handkerchief he produced from his raincoat that he still wore, and considering the unexpected shower he had received, his decision not to remove it had proven highly fortuitous. "I only found out four days ago."

I offered him some tissues to soak up the beer that had landed in his lap, giving the unfortunate illusion that he had urinated himself. "Four days ago?" I said trying to ignore Bill's jerking hand movements in the vicinity of his crotch as he attempted to soak up beer with the tissues I handed him. It was a good job Mother Teresa was not around. "You mean you only discovered this four days ago? That for the last thirty-two years you had no idea you were the son of Lucifer?" Bill nodded. It had to have been more than a coincidence. How could Satan and God both have abandoned their offspring for the same amount of time?

"Apparently Satan had been away for a while," said Bill. "Said he'd been out in the Universe, helping to create planets and new civilizations, and apparently he got waylaid." Once again, I felt the need to interrupt.

"Bill, did Satan, by any chance, mention that God accompanied him on this journey around the Universe?"

"Yes," replied Bill "Satan, Lucifer, the Devil, or however you want to address him—he prefers Satan, though," confirmed Bill.

"Then Satan's fine with me," I interrupted.

"Well, Satan sent me an e-mail explaining everything—the whole thing, my birth, his absence—everything. At first, I thought it was a prank, but the email contained so many details only I would know that I decided to investigate its source. I know about tracing e-mails and viruses and all that stuff, so I did a track on my reply e-mail. It hadn't originated from any computer or server I could fathom. I used all my expertise and the expertise of others—I mean people who *know* computers—in trying to find out where this e-mail had originated from, but no matter which program I used or tracing method I adopted, the results were always the same; it came back as unknown." Bill spoke quickly, and I urged him to take a breath. Bill reached into his coat pocket and produced an asthma inhaler and sucked on it hard. Was there no medical condition this man did not have? Bill wheezed, and I asked him if he needed water. He waved his hand indicating to me he didn't. Bill waited until his wheezing had subsided and then continued his story.

"Eventually, I found a program that would allow me to successfully trace the e-mail address, so I sent an e-mail to the address that Satan's e-mail had originated from. It returned to me with a message stating the e-mail originated from no computer on Earth, which was impossible, but I couldn't argue with it, as my knowledge of computers told me it was true."

I knew exactly what Bill was trying to say. I had been through it myself. When faced with the illogical and what normally would be the impossible or bizarre, your brain tells you it is unacceptable to believe, but you start believing it anyway. I was amazed how quickly I believed I talked to God. Yes, I know my talking cat had helped, but I understood why Bill had accepted that the e-mail he had received was from Satan. He did not need to convince me. I already believed him.

"What exactly did the e-mail say?" I asked Bill.

Bill once more delved into the pockets of his raincoat and removed a folded piece of paper. "I printed it out for you," said Bill as he handed the e-mail over to me, "please read it for yourself." I unfolded the e-mail and began to read:

From: <u>*D.evil_BC232@Hell.org*</u>
To: <u>*Billlzbubb@bytes.com*</u>
<u>SUBJECT: HI THERE AND AN APOLOGY</u>
    Dear Son,

This e-mail may come as a bit of a shock to you, and I would not blame you for thinking that it is a hoax or a prank from one of your friends, but son, you do not have any friends who would be bothered to play such a prank on you. I urge you to take what action you want in ascertaining the validity of this mail. You will though discover that it is genuine, and so am I. I know you have the capability to trace the origin of this mail, and I would not expect anything less of you to try and prove this is a fake, but I assure you, your efforts shall be in vain.

First of all, I owe you a rather large apology. I have been a very bad father to you, but I never intended for things to be this way between us. I promise you, son. I deeply, deeply regret the missed years and missed opportunities, and I realize this is all my fault. I accept full responsibility for all my wanton and selfish actions. I have no excuse, and I feel nothing but remorse for the way I abandoned you and your mother. I am ashamed. I feel I am not fit to be called your father, but son, that is what I am—your father—and a prouder man than I I challenge you to find.

As you are fully aware, your mother always told you she did not know who your father was, and even up until her death last year, she continued to tell you she did not know the identity of your true biological father. Well, son, I am your father. Your mother was only trying to protect you from the truth, and who could blame her? I have always had a somewhat tarnished reputation, and I suppose that when the years passed and I never showed up, she must have thought I never would, so she felt no need to burden you. For this, I am also ashamed. I promise you it was never my intention or plan to not return and be there for you and your mother.

 I met your mother in 1966 at a costume party in Queens. Your mother loved to dress up, and she loved masquerading, and I understand you have inherited the same quirky hobby. Your mother was an excellent costume maker and I am sure, if she were alive today, she would be extremely proud of the little dwarf costumes you wear. Your mother dressed as Catwoman, not the modern day Halle Berry or Michelle Pfeiffer version of Catwoman, but the sixties version as worn by Eartha Kitt, Julie Newmar, and Lee Merryweather in the TV show, the one with Adam West as Batman and Burt Ward (was it?) as Robin.

 Well, your mother and I got chatting, and she said she simply adored my costume. I tried to explain that it wasn't a costume, but she laughed and said she didn't believe me. She said it was the best devil impersonation she had ever seen. She especially liked my tripod, and I recall she thought I had done an excellent job with the papier-mâché. Anyway, the drinks were flowing, one thing led to another, and we fell in love that very night.

 You see, son, you are a love child. Unlike other celestial and underworld myths, not all births have to be from a virgin. That whole virgin thing has been very misinterpreted, by the way. And your mother was no virgin, believe me. Nor was she a jackal, which is another myth, due in no part to some bad proofreading of the Bible before the so called "experts" released it. No, son, your mother was quite the "goer" back in the day. Boy, could that lady party. She could even turn me red, or redder! A virgin she was not. Oh no.

 Anyway, we began a relationship, and as the months passed, she gradually began to believe that I was indeed who I said I was. I suppose the fact that I was never out of costume, my refusal to ever meet with her friends or family, and my hesitancy to ever be seen out in public helped in her realization. Other clues helped, I guess, such as my insistence on the heating to always be as hot as Hell (which it could never be), my penchant for raw meat, my inability to enter a church, my horns, and the fact that I would only ever call after she had recited the Lord's Prayer backward whilst looking in a mirror. Despite your Mother discovering after three months that her boyfriend, who appeared to be permanently painted red, was really the Devil, she had fallen head-over-heels in love with me, just as I had fallen head-over-hoof for her.

When I found out your mother was pregnant, I was the happiest man in Hell. We planned you; you were not an accident. We had discussed my need to produce a child, and your mother agreed. It was all I had ever wanted, and I had waited such a long time for the opportunity to be a father. It was a bonus that you were conceived out of love.

Unfortunately, business and other duties involved with my capacity as the Lord of Darkness took me away before you were born. A "colleague" of mine, who shall remain nameless, but we could refer to him as 'God', just for convenience's sake, convinced me to join him on a trip into the Universe. He told me he had found a great planet that we could work on and maybe even develop. I remonstrated with him that I had responsibilities on Earth, that I was about to become a father, and I needed to be with my child to help with his upbringing and watch him grow up, not to mention my need to support your mother and help her with her pregnancy. I had responsibilities, and I swear I did not want to shirk them. My colleague, whom we are calling 'God', just for convenience's sake, assured me that we would be gone for only a few months. He convinced me that he was in a similar position, and that he would never allow me to miss you birth.

I have no excuse, and I am not trying to apportion blame, but he lied to me. Despite my protestations, I could not be released from my commitments elsewhere in the Universe. Each time I tried to curtail my absence from Earth, a situation would arise or another excuse was levied at me to pressure me into staying. Now I realize that my traveling companion was enjoying his time away from the pressures of his job and did not want to return. Unfortunately, due to certain rules and regulations, I was obligated to accompany him and not return to Earth on my own without him. It seems no one trusted me not to cause mayhem, chaos, and havoc. Believe me, son, when I tell you that was the farthest thought from my mind. My only desire was to return to be with you and your mother. The trip turned into a year, then a year turned into two, and then five and then, well, I suppose I lost track of time. I admit, I enjoyed my extended vacation, and the old adage "out of sight, out of mind" is true. I disregarded my responsibilities on Earth, including you and your mother, and I indulged myself. The place where we were was indeed beautiful, and we had got into developing the project a lot deeper than we had thought. Maybe one day I will take you to visit it and, who knows, hopefully we could rule the place one day. It depends on how things go.

This brings me to the real point of my e-mail, dear son. I am Satan, the Devil, the Angel and the Prince of Darkness, the fallen angel, king of Hell, Lucifer, Old Nick –call me what you will, but I assure you, I am who I say I am. I do prefer Satan, though, should anyone ask. I know this has come as a shock to you, but it is the truth. I swear it. As my son, this makes you, by default, the anti-Christ, or as you are known in some quarters, "the Beast." Personally, I hate that term because you are anything but a beast to me, son; you are my precious son whom I have missed so very much, and whom I love dearly.

I returned to my home—a place you call Hell, but for me, it's my sanctuary—a week ago to find that your mother had passed on and, unfortunately for me but fortunately for her, she had made it to the other place. I immediately looked you up, son, and I am so proud of your achievements. I admire your informative and well-written columns, your great costumes, and of course, your video-gaming skills are legendary. I am sorry about the allergies. I am afraid you may have inherited those from me. I have a problem with eider, and the only animals I seem to be able to tolerate are jackals and serpents. All other creatures bring me out in a rash.

I feel so bad that we have not spent any time together, and when I think of the things we have missed doing as Father and Son, it breaks my heart (well, it would if I had one). I know money isn't everything, but I want to make up for being such a bad father to you somehow. Therefore, I have deposited today, into your bank account, a little something to say sorry and make up for my years of absence. I know money is not enough to make up for what I have done, but it is the root of all evil, and well, it was the least I could do. I have accumulated all the allowances and pocket money that I should have paid you, plus a little extra to make up for birthdays, and though I do not celebrate it myself, Christmas. I have also taken the liberty of compounding the interest and have adjusted for cost-of-living rises, so please do not be shocked when *you receive your next statement, and do not worry about the IRS; I have many, many followers there.*

I love you, son, and I am so sorry for the way I have neglected you. Trust me when I tell you my former aloofness stops right now.

Son, we have many things to discuss, pressing matters that will affect you and the world as you know it, but I will call you and discuss with you man-to-demon the responsibilities that come with being my son. Once again, I will not blame you for tracing this e-mail or disbelieving these startling revelations. In the meantime, son, you do what you have to do.

All my love,
Satan (Dad)
XXXXXXX

    I read it and then-re read it. And then I read it again. I got the feeling the author of the e-mail had put a lot of thought into its content, and I sensed the remorse expressed in it was genuine. Bill's father had poured emotion and honesty into the e-mail, and I found it hard to believe the writer of such a humble and soul-searching document was the Prince of Darkness. I looked at Bill, and for some inexplicable reason, I felt a connection with him unlike I had ever felt with anyone else before. Like me, he had been abandoned by his father, and like me, he had been thrust into the family business, untrained, unprepared, and reluctantly.

    One thing that was apparent from the e-mail was Satan's bitterness toward my father. Despite their apparent "working relationship," I got the feeling Satan was not best pleased with being an absent father, and he put the blame for the lack of relationship with his son squarely at Dad's door. For God to cast him out of Heaven was one thing, but to be then be unable to be with your family due to God's apparent selfishness and "need for a break" was another. I suspected Satan was annoyed. I refolded the e-mail and handed it back to Bill.

    "He sounds like a very nice guy. He seems very remorseful," I said as Bill took the e-mail and placed it back into his raincoat pocket. Bill nodded.

"Generous, too. He deposited over two million dollars into my bank account."

My eyes widened "Wow, now that is generous!" I calculated in my head how much I was due in missed allowances and pocket money, then realized that for any amount to be deposited into my bank account, it would have to be approved by one of God's committees. Then there would be paperwork to be completed and ledgers to adjust. I doubted I would be as lucky. Then again, I had gotten my raise and partnership thanks to God, but I did note that the money was not coming from his own coffers, but from Henry's and his partners. I let the matter rest in my head but filed it for later use.

"So, what happened next?" I asked Bill. "What did you do when you realized the e-mail was genuine?" I was eager to know exactly how Satan had dealt with the same situation as God. Already I felt that of the two, Satan was coming out on top.

"Well, I tried to trace the e-mail like I said, and I couldn't." Bill took a deep breath, and I thought his asthma was going to set off again, but luckily, it didn't. "Then he called me at home." Aha, so it seemed Hell also had a telephone network.

"What did he say? What did he sound like?" I asked eagerly.

"Texan," said Bill. "He sounded like he could have been from Texas." My expression did not hide my surprise. For some reason, I expected an Eastern European accent, kind of like Dracula's voice in those old movies. "He wasn't brash or loud; very pleasant, actually. He explained what was expected of me, as his son, and re-explained his absence of thirty-two years." I found myself nodding, picturing the telephone call between father and son. "I thanked him for the money, and then we got on to you. He told me all about Armageddon, and he told me to read the Bible and specifically the Book of Revelation. He then told me to forget it, because that was not how he saw it."

"Saw what?" I asked.

"Saw the ending. In the Bible, God wins, but Satan says he isn't going to take a dive just to fulfill a prophecy. He wants to win, and badly. That's why I am here, you see, I don't want to be responsible for the end of the world, nor do I want to send mankind to Hell." I saw Bill was shaking.

"He told you this over the phone?" I asked. Bill shook his head and pulled another e-mail from his pocket, handing it to me.

From: *D.evil_BC232@Hell.org*
To: *Billlzbubb@bytes.com*
SUBJECT: ARMEGEDDON/APOCLYPSE/FINAL CON-
FLICT–CHANGE OF PLAN

Hi, son,
It was great talking with you earlier today.
Don't be alarmed by the title of the e-mail! As I mentioned in my previous e-mail, being my son means you have some responsibilities. As I have already explained, you are the anti-Christ, or as described in the Bible, the beast (argh! I hate that!). As such, you need to prepare for the final conflict, or apocalypse, as referred to in the New Testament book of Revelation. I know you may think you are not ready yet, but I think you are; in fact, I know you are. You do not have to fear the Lamb of God. My intelligence is good, and I assure you have nothing to fear. He is weak and will be no match for you. We are going to cream them!

I know the book of Revelation indicates that in the end, God will prevail, but, after careful and thorough consideration, and due in no small part to the way I feel I have been treated by some so-called 'colleagues,' I have decided not to go along with what is written and prophesized, bowing down to let God win this one. Not after what he did.

I have consulted lawyers—believe me, I have many down here—and it seems I signed no contract that binds me to the contents of the Bible. I have also discovered that it was not correctly edited nor proofread before it was released, and therefore whoever deemed I was to be eventually defeated had no right in saying so without my consent, which I did not give.

So, dear son, disregard what is written. We are not going to throw this one; we are going for it! God's son is called Seth Miller, but keep that under your hat. He actually seems like a nice guy, but remember that nice guys finish second in our business. When the time is due, he will reveal himself, and then the battle shall begin. Do not fear—you are definitely the stronger. Well, looking forward to seeing you on Saturday. I will meet you near the main hall, and don't worry, you'll recognize me.

Dad

I handed the e-mail back to Bill.

"You are meeting him today?" I asked.

"Yes" replied Bill, "I need to go soon and get ready." Bill checked his wrist watch. "We are meeting at the New York Comic Con this afternoon, at the Jacob Javits Center on 11th Avenue. I need to change and get into costume if I am going to make it."

"You mean Satan is going to be in New York? Today? But how?" I asked, amazed that the Devil could think he could simply blend into a crowd. "Won't he be recognized? Doesn't he have horns, and isn't he red?" I asked incredulously.

Bill smiled for the first time since we met. "It's a costuming convention; no one will even bat an eyelid. You should come."

I declined Bill's offer. I wasn't sure how Satan would react when he realized that his son's new buddy was the son of the man he hated. "What are you going to tell him about me? Are you going to tell him you sought me out?"

Bill shook his head. "No, I am trying to stall for time until I can figure a way to resolve this. We must keep this meeting between us quiet from our fathers," Bill said earnestly. I agreed. I doubted God would be none too pleased either if he knew I had been fraternizing with the enemy.

Before Bill left, he confided in me that he felt bad betraying his father in this way, but the responsibility was just too much; his irritable bowel syndrome had flared up, and he felt that condemning the human race to Hell and taking over the world was not something he could see himself doing. Between us, we agreed we would find a solution to our problem, and as two, logical and sane-thinking adults, we felt we could avert Armageddon and the looming battle for souls. I wished Bill luck at the costume convention and shook his hand vigorously before he left. We exchange telephone numbers and agreed to meet up soon.

I breathed a heavy sigh of relief once Bill left. It was a double sigh, for I was doubly relieved. For one, it seemed as though this whole Armageddon thing was not going to happen. Bill and I would avert the final conflict and sanity would prevail. God could go back to doing whatever it was he did, Satan could hire more lawyers, and I could return to being just plain old Seth Miller. Secondly, should Bill and I fail to avert Armageddon, and should they force us to go through with it, I had no doubt that I could kick

Bill's ass if I needed to. Like I mentioned earlier, I am not a fighter, I never had been, but, really, even Professor Stephen Hawkins could probably whoop Bill's ass. What was Satan thinking in his e-mail? Did he really think Bill could beat me in any physical contest? I supposed it was a case of a father trying to live through his son. Unfortunately though, like most things when it came to God, things were a little more complicated than they appeared.

CHAPTER

22

WHILE I HAD AGREED NOT to mention my encounter with Bill to God, I had made no such promise when it came to my disciples. I decided I needed to contact Bob and inform him of the meeting between myself and the anti-Christ. Notwithstanding the fact that I knew tonight was Bob and Nancy's 'intimate' night, I felt the circumstances warranted a call. However, plucking up the courage to call knowing there was a fifty percent chance Nancy would answer, was a different matter.

    I hadn't spoken to Nancy in several months, not since the pizza incident. The pizza incident occurred at Sonny's Pizza Parlor on 37th around Easter time. I had agreed to join Bob and Nancy for dinner; it was Bob's attempt to ease the tension that existed between his wife and his best friend. He had hoped that by us all breaking bread together, we could iron out our differences and maybe even become friends, and what better way to do that than over pizza and beer. To be honest, it hadn't been a bad idea; I felt that if I could charm Nancy into liking me—and I was sure that over a drink she would realize I was a likeable guy who posed no threat to her relationship with her husband—then it would pave the way for a smoother baseball season without the added worry of Nancy jeopardizing our fun. Initially, I had been reluctant to go through with the evening, but Bob had convinced me otherwise, and by the time the evening of the dinner rolled around, I was confident that our "Nancy problem" would soon be a thing of the past.

The evening had started well enough; there was the issue of the booth of course, which Nancy could not fit into due to the proximity of the fixed seating to the table, and of course, her size. We eventually settled on a table, which Sonny quickly set for us. Bob and I were semi-regulars at the restaurant, and Sonny explained to me that the booths were standard size; even the largest American could slide into them usually, and that Bob's wife must be expecting an extremely large baby.

I advised him not to mention that to either Bob or Nancy, as they were trying to keep her pregnancy a secret. Pleased that I had defused a potentially horrifically embarrassing incident, not to mention probably having saved Sonny's life, I felt the evening was going to be an undoubted success. I made small talk with Nancy, who initially was hesitant to become embroiled in a prolonged conversation with me, but I persevered; the old Seth charm was working. After a few beers, Nancy loosened up a little, and Bob flashed me a grin that said that things were going well. Indeed, at one stage I had Nancy laughing at a joke I had heard that day in the office. All was going well until the food arrived. We had decided to order the largest pizza they had, and in the spirit of the evening, we thought it apt that we shared it amongst us. I was not too particular as to what flavor our pizza should be, and I suggested that Nancy choose the toppings.

When I heard Nancy mention the word "anchovies" to the waitress taking our order, I froze. I hated anchovies; I detested them; the only thing more vile-smelling than an anchovy was an anchovy with a body odor problem or bad breath. What the hell was an anchovy anyway, and who had decided they made a good pizza topping? Of all the pizza toppings available, why did she have to choose anchovies? Conscious of the fact that I had given Nancy carte blanche authority over ordering the pizza, I found myself in a rather delicate position. Not wishing to spoil Nancy's evening or her pizza, I made a rather noble and logical suggestion. I politely pointed out to Nancy and Bob that I was unable to eat any pizza that contained anchovies, but, in the spirit of the evening, why not leave one slice anchovy-free, as I really was not overly hungry and really, in all honesty, my evening was complete thanks to the great company I was with. It was not a big deal. Bob asked why I couldn't take them off the slices I ate; I informed him that was totally unacceptable, and that by just touching an anchovy, it would ruin my evening of fine dining.

Surprisingly, it was Nancy who asked the waitress that she inform the chef to make sure that one slice of pizza be devoid of anchovy, and therefore reserved for my exclusive consumption. I thanked Nancy for her understanding, and she smiled nicely as we cheered each other.

Once again, I felt my diplomacy and actions would only endear Nancy toward me. I was, in fact, extremely hungry, and I could have easily suggested that they make more than one slice anchovy-free; however, my sacrifice of a full meal was worth it if it meant baseball season would run smoothly. The pizza duly arrived, and Nancy and Bob both took a slice. I excused myself to use the bathroom and wash my hands. I was gone no longer than five minutes, but when I returned to the table to rejoin my dining companions, I was shocked to see that only one slice of pizza remained. Bob and Nancy, though I suspected Nancy, must have eaten seven large slices of pizza in what one could only describe as superhuman time. I estimated they had consumed seven slices in five minutes, which equated to more than one slice per minute. The remaining slice sat on my plate and naturally, I assumed it would be the anchovy-free slice. Without checking the pizza—and why would I?—I took a bite. At first, I wondered why Nancy smiled at me; her grin was disturbing, and she had a mischievous glint in her eye, but I presumed she had begun to warm to me and this was her natural look when smiling. Bob, oblivious it seemed to Nancy's moronic grinning, was busy quaffing his latest beer.

It hit me after about five seconds, the taste provoking what I can only describe as a knee-jerk reaction. I vomited. It wasn't normal vomit, but projectile vomit, which hit Nancy directly in the face. To this day, I am sure Nancy deliberately exchanged my anchovy-free slice with an anchovy-laden one; her motive, to watch my discomfort. Unfortunately, the chain reaction of events that was set in motion was horrific. My vomiting caused Bob to vomit. Unfortunately, though, for Nancy, he had turned his head to face her after my initial vomiting began. Nancy was therefore covered not only in my vomit, but in Bob's. Tragically, and by what I can only describe as a macabre twist of fate, our waitress was passing at the exact same time Bob and I vomited in relevant unison. The sight of our vomit led the poor girl to throw up herself; unfortunately, she happened to be standing directly behind Nancy.

Nancy was covered from head to toe, front and back, in three separate bouts of vomiting. How she lasted as long as she did, I do not know, but eventually, the inevitable happened, and she herself vomited into her own lap. It was at this moment that Sonny appeared and explained, at the top of his voice to the full and packed restaurant, that Nancy was pregnant, and with a baby the size she was carrying it had to be expected that the poor woman would have delayed morning sickness. Nancy and I had not spoken since that night.

I took a deep breath and called Bob's number.

"Hello?" It was Bob, thank God.

"Bob, it's me, Seth; we need to talk" I said quickly, and for some inexplicable reason, I was whispering.

"No, thank you, we already have cable," said Bob cheerfully. "Thanks for your call; we will certainly bear you in mind should we decide to change providers. Goodbye." Bob hung up. I looked at the receiver, puzzled. I considered calling him back, but the odds of Nancy answering had just increased. I was about to grab another beer when the phone rang. It was Bob.

"Are you crazy?" he whispered. "Are you out of your freaking mind? You do know what night it is, don't you? You do know she is here?" Bob sounded perplexed. As soon as the opportunity had presented itself, Bob had called me back. Nancy needed to use the bathroom, and it sometimes took her as long as twenty minutes, depending on what she had eaten earlier.

"Sorry," I said "but it is an emergency." I told Bob about my visit from Bill, the anti-Christ. Bob listened without interrupting. Once I relayed the full details, Bob spoke.

"It sounds as though we have nothing to worry about. I presume you are going to go through with it now? You know, take him down." The way Bob said it suddenly made me aware that I couldn't do it. How could I hurt poor Bill?

No, no matter what, I was not going to get physical with Bill. There had to be some other way. I told Bob that meeting Bill had changed things, and I explained there was no way I was going to hurt him. Bob, after some persuading, agreed that it would be wrong, especially after Bill had been the one to offer the olive branch of peace. Bob thought that it would be good if all four of us—Bob, Bill, Maggie and I—to get together on Sunday to formulate a plan that would somehow prevent Bill and I from "getting it on."

I thought I should include Maggie in the day's events also, so after completing my call with Bob, I called her. I could have waited until the morning, but the truth was, I missed her company. I hadn't been able to get her out of my mind, and I didn't need an excuse to call her. It was a feeling I had never had before. Maggie answered after the third ring, and I explained all about Bill. She agreed that we shouldn't harm Bill and that we should all work through this together as suggested by Bob, and that she would be available tomorrow.

"So what are you doing now? You still working on your case?" I asked. I pretended it was passing conversation, but the truth was I wanted to see her.

"No, I've finished. I'm relaxing. Why?"

I wondered why she was asking why I was asking. Did she want me to invite her over? Could she tell from my voice that I missed her? "Oh, no reason," I lied.

"Is there anything else?" asked Maggie. There was; I wanted to invite her over, not just for sex but because I, well, I just wanted to.

"No," I said, immediately regretting what I was about to say, "nothing else. I will see you tomorrow." As soon as I hung up, I kicked myself. I thought about calling her back, but I couldn't muster the courage. Anyway, if she wanted to see me, she would come over, right? Was I not the Messiah? Surely I shouldn't be doing the chasing; or should I? I looked at Walter, hoping for some divine inspiration, but none came. Was I falling in love with Maggie? I was a confirmed bachelor. There was no way this could be happening to me. But much had happened to me over the last few days, and I could feel it; I was changing.

I snapped out of my thoughts of Maggie and decided I had better call Bill to organize tomorrow's meeting. I dialed the number he had given me, but there was no reply. I checked my watch. It was approaching eight. Maybe he was still at his costume convention. I decided to try again later. I got the feeling Bill was not a night owl, and that his bedtime on a Saturday night was probably before ten. I called again at nine, ten, and eleven, and still no Bill. I left him a message with my cell phone number and told him to call me when he got in. I thought Milligan's would be a good place for us to meet on Sunday, and my message included this suggestion.

Maybe Bill's convention went on longer than I had thought. Still, I would have expected him to be home. Usually on a Saturday evening, I would be having fun in the city, but I was tucked up in bed with thoughts of Maggie by eleven thirty. I drifted off to sleep, and I slept well, very well; it was good to be back in my bed after the previous night on the sofa, but I wished Maggie had been with me.

I awoke suddenly; something was making a noise, something that didn't make a noise usually at six am on a Sunday morning. I could hear a humming noise, and I could feel vibrations. Confused, I fumbled in my bed until I found the reason for the disturbance. My cell phone, which was set to vibrate, buzzed and shook. I had a call.

"Hello?" I said groggily as I answered the cell phone, ending its incessant jig.

"Seth, it's me Bill. I just got your message."

I rubbed my eyes; it was indeed six in the morning. "You just got it?" I asked still a little groggy.

"Yes," exclaimed Bill, "I just made it home."

I found myself becoming more alert. There was something different about Bill's voice, and I couldn't quite put my finger on it.

"You have been out all night?" I asked. Bill didn't strike me as someone to stay out all night.

"Yes, kind of had a heavy one." I heard laughter in the background, female laughter.

"Have you got someone there with you?" I asked. Once again, I heard laughter and possibly the clinking of glasses.

"Oh them." Bill, I presumed, cupped the receiver at his end before shouting, "You two, keep it down will you? I am trying to make a call." Bill returned to me, "Sorry about that, it's the twins." The twins? Bill had a pair of female twins at his place? The laughter became louder, and then I heard different sounds, disturbing sounds, like zippers being undone, moaning, and more laughter.

THE RELUCTANT JESUS

"Bill, are you still there? Are you all right?" I asked, images appearing in my head that really should not have included Bill.

"Yes," replied Bill as if he was being pulled around. "Look, I will meet you at Milligan's—I know it; I saw it yesterday. I will be there at noon." I heard female cries of disappointed in the background. "Ok, one. I will see you at one, but come alone." Either Bill hung up or one of the twins yanked the phone from him, because I got the impression they dragged him off as the line went dead. As I was awake, I got up and showered, made coffee, fed Walter, popped outdoors for the Sunday paper, made some eggs, and relaxed.

I wondered why Bill wanted me to come alone. It was a disappointment, as I wanted to see Maggie, and now I had no idea when I would see her again. I waited until the hour was more reasonable and called her. I explained Bill's phone call and how it seemed totally out of character; he hadn't sounded nervous or even remotely timid. I mentioned the twins and what I had heard in the background. Maggie said Bill sounded like a party animal, and I had to agree that it did seem I may have underestimated the man. But how? How could the timid, shy, nervous, allergy-ridden nerd whom I had met less than twenty-four hours ago have suddenly transformed into Hugh Heffner on acid?

I checked Nancy's schedule magnetized to my fridge and saw her shift had started an hour ago, so the coast was clear for me to call Bob. I knew he would be exhausted after his night of passion with his mammoth wife, but I woke him anyway to tell him about Bill. He agreed with Maggie that Bill sounded like the proverbial party animal and agreed with me that it was a strange metamorphism for Bill to go from Woody Allen into Woody Harelson overnight.

At 12:45 I made my way to Milligan's for my rendezvous with Bill. Harvey, who had just started his afternoon shift, accosted me as usual, as I attempted to leave my building.

"Hey, man," he said, "how's it hanging, homey?" He raised his hand for me to slap it, which I did, despite thinking it was a ridiculous thing to do. "Where you headed, dog?" asked Harvey, moving from side to side as if dancing to some imaginary beat only he could hear. Harvey made drum machine noises as he moved; it was slightly distracting and a little annoying.

"Just going for lunch, meeting a friend." I replied, unsure why I continually answered Harvey's question about my movements and private life. Harvey nodded and carried on moving his body.

An elderly couple who also lived in the building walked through the lobby on the way, it seemed, to church.

"Good Morning, Dr. Lovett, Mrs. Lovett," said Harvey who immediately curtailed his dancing the moment he saw them. "What a beautiful morning it is, sir and madam; the sun is shining, the birds are singing. It is a delightful day. I do so hope you enjoy it." Dr. Lovett and Mrs. Lovett thanked Harvey and wished him a good day too. The couple nodded to me politely, probably wondering why I stood with my mouth wide open. What the hell was that? And his voice? He practically sounded like an English poet! So this was how Harvey spoke to the other residents. It was only me who got the gangsta-rapping act. He looked at me, dancing again and smiling.

"What, dog?" he asked, once more sounding like a gangsta rapper as he resumed spitting out his drum machine noises. I shook my head and made my way to Milligan's.

I have always done my best thinking whilst walking, so I took the opportunity, en-route to Milligan's to mull a few things over in my head. I felt that God owed me an explanation; it seemed that Bill's father was far more remorseful than he had been, and that upset me. I was also a little hurt to discover that God had deliberately continued his absence from Earth despite Satan's protestations that they both had parental responsibilities here. Out of the two, I had to say Satan seemed the better father. I was also a little miffed that it seemed Jesus was by far my Father's favorite. The constant comparisons he made were getting to me, and whilst I accepted that he and Jesus had been a through a lot together, I felt it was unfair that he constantly compared us.

No sibling liked to play second fiddle and of course, Jesus did a great job when he did his stint on Earth, so I could understand some of his animosity toward me. Despite God telling me I had my brother's support, I couldn't help but think that maybe Jesus was secretly enjoying my constant failures. I got the impression he harbored a grudge against me, and even God had admitted that Jesus didn't like my attitude. I knew Jesus didn't think I was the right man for the job. Maybe I was being paranoid, but I imagined Jesus sitting with his former disciples, ridiculing and belittling my efforts as they shared an afternoon beer.

I also mulled over my feelings for Maggie. I did not believe in love at first sight, but it did feel as though I was falling for her. I had only known her two days, but I could not get her out of my thoughts. I was pining for her, and I was worried that maybe, once this was all over, she would disappear from my life just as quickly as she had appeared. I didn't want that. I wanted her in my life, and I had to admit, the way I felt, I wanted her there permanently. I decided the best course of action to take would be to throw caution to the wind and tell her exactly how I felt. It was a gamble; maybe she was only looking for a quick fling and nothing serious; if so, then I would ruin even that. For a man who had previously shied away from commitment, I suddenly craved it. I was startled from my thoughts by the ringing of my cell phone. It was God.

"Hi, son," greeted my father in a somewhat cheerful way.

"Shouldn't you busy?" I asked "Isn't today your busiest day?" I was referring to the fact that it was Sunday. God laughed. I think he thought I was joking around. I didn't feel like joking around. I was still a little bitter, and his call had come just as I was debating how to handle his attitude toward me.

"In a way, yes" he replied, "but that can wait. Where are you?" he asked. So he wasn't watching me, which was good.

"On my way to Milligan's for lunch," I replied truthfully.

It was a strange feeling. How many times have you seen people talking on their cell phones as they walk along the street? Sometimes you overhear snippets of conversation, and you sometimes wonder who is on the other end of the phone. I know I do. Anyone eavesdropping or listening to my conversation with God that Sunday would have probably assumed it was a normal conversation between a son and father, catching up with each other's week. I fleetingly imagined the reactions of passersby and my fellow pedestrians if they knew I had God on the line. I wondered what questions they would ask him and how they would handle the situation. I felt like handing the phone over to a random fellow New Yorker and saying "It's for you, it's God; he wants a word," and watching their reaction. I supposed God's reaction would be equally as interesting.

"How are you feeling?" asked God. I was impressed that he had called to chat, and I was especially impressed that he was asking after my welfare. "How are you getting on with Maggie? She's a cutie, isn't she?"

I agreed that she was, and I very nearly told him that I was hopelessly in love with her, but I refrained from doing so. "Fine, I think we gel," I said, understating what I really thought.

"Well, don't rush things, son," said God. It was the first time I had ever detected a hint of concern from him. Maybe I had underestimated his perception. Could he see what was happening? Could he gauge my feelings? Instead of thanking him and confiding in him, I replied as if I didn't need his advice or guidance.

"I'm thirty-two; I know how to handle women." I regretted my hostility but did not apologize. God's toned changed. I had upset him. His show of concern and interest in me had been rebuked.

"All I am saying is, don't rush things, and don't let it interfere with business." I said I wouldn't.

"The word on the street is that Lucifer and his son are building a cozy little relationship. Seems he's not too bad at doing the Devil's work," said God. I didn't mention my initial meeting with Bill or my imminent lunch date with him.

"Oh, really?" I said. I hoped I hadn't sounded too unconcerned.

"Yes, really," said God, he sounded annoyed by my nonchalance. What God didn't know was that I wasn't concerned about Bill. Even in the worst case scenario where we would have to come to blows, I really did fancy my chances. God changed the subject slightly.

"I have been thinking about miracles. Have you any idea of how you would like to proceed? Up here the consensus is raising someone from the dead, but I know you had your reservations about that." At least he had listened and was consulting me. I cut him some slack, and I softened my tone toward him.

"I hadn't thought about it, to be honest," I said. "I am open to suggestions, and if you feel raising from the dead is the way forward, then I will consider it." Of course, anyone eavesdropping then our conversation would be thinking that this father/son relationship was a little, well, odd.

"Let me think about that one. One thing is for sure, you need to get you powers together. You need to be able to counter anything the anti-Christ throws at you. Heaven only knows—which I know it doesn't—what they could throw at us. Knowing Lucifer the way I do, he will have something nasty up his sleeve."

I felt like telling God that he shouldn't be overly concerned at what Satan had up his sleeve, but I had promised Bill I wouldn't mention our meetings. It seemed God expected, as I had, a big guy, a bruiser, a "beast" of a man. I could imagine his relief when he discovered that my foe weighed in at one hundred and ten pounds and had never thrown a punch in his life! As the conversation was going well, I asked God about my allowance and if he had ever considered, as Satan had, on making good my pocket money.

"By the way, while you are on the line, I have a question," I said casually.

"Go ahead. Shoot," said God, "but make it snappy."

"My allowance."

"Your allowance?" God sounded confused.

"Yes, my allowance. Did you ever consider that maybe you should have given me an allowance, or at least made up for the allowances you never paid when I was growing up?"

"Well," said God, "it did cross my mind, and I took it to the committee." So he had considered it, which made me feel a little better. "There was a vote. It was tied, actually, but your brother, Jesus that is, who had the casting vote, brought up a very good point." I was listening; somehow I knew Jesus would have been involved.

"Which was?" I asked, eager to learn what pearls of wisdom my half-brother had come up with to void my allowance.

"Jesus suggested we gamble the money I had earmarked for your allowance on lottery tickets. We thought it was worth the risk, and with two million lottery tickets, you'd have thought we would have at least broke even. We played every lottery on the planet, and bought multiple tickets, via angels of course, but you'd never believed it...." That's where God was wrong, because I would believe it. Jesus had gambled away my allowance. Fantastic. I made a mental note to thank him, should we ever meet. I had stopped listening to God, as I knew the outcome. He waffled on about the numbers Gandhi had selected coming close but falling short of a jackpot.

I reached Milligan's with God still talking in my ear about how bad they all felt about losing my money.

"Well, I need to go," said God "I will be in touch," and my phone went dead. I had arrived at Milligan's with two minutes to spare, and I half-expected Bill to be waiting for me in a booth. I was about to enter the bar when I heard the roaring sound of a sports car. I turned to see a red, convertible Ferrari pull up to the sidewalk. The car itself was impressive, but the driver was even more so. She had legs that seemed never-ending and her skirt might as well have been a belt. She was, without a doubt, the sexiest woman I had ever seen in my life. I would have guessed she had to have been a model, but more was to come. Next to her, in the passenger seat, was an equally as attractive woman. I say equally because they looked identical. I guessed they must have been…twins…and that was when I noticed their rear-seated passenger. At first, I didn't recognize him as he skipped out of the car, kissed both girls on the lips, and waved them off. He wore sunglasses and an expensive suit, and walked with the confident swagger of a man who had it all. Bill, it seemed, had received a makeover.

CHAPTER

23

NOT FOR THE FIRST TIME that day, I stood open mouthed, as Bill approached.

"I'm not late am I?" he said, checking his watch. "I told them I needed to go, but you know how chicks are, if they want it, they want it!" Bill nudged me, then lifted up his shades and winked. I couldn't believe this was the same guy who had sat in my apartment the previous day.

"Bill," I stammered, "what's happened to you?"

Bill smiled and took my arm. "Let me get you a drink, and I will explain everything," he said as he led me into Milligan's.

It turned out Bill had met his father as arranged at the costuming convention. Bill had arrived at the convention dressed as his fantasy alter ego, Bilbo Baggins the hobbit. Satan, whom he had recognized immediately due to his red skin, horns, and hooves had been punctual and was waiting for Bill when he arrived. On any other day, Satan, if he had appeared in public, no doubt would have attracted a lot of attention, and maybe even widespread panic and pandemonium would have ensued. However, he barely received a second glance as he mingled freely with the costume-clad attendees of the convention. The only attention he did receive was the odd compliment for his excellent costume. Apparently a few costumers were unsure who he was meant to be, but they thought his makeup was excellent regardless. After mingling for a while with the crowd, Bill and his Father had found the bar. Bill tried to explain that alcohol did not agree with him, but Satan told him not to worry, and that his physical ailments were all in the mind. Bill, not quite convinced, but not wanting to offend his Father, threw caution to the wind and tried a beer.

One beer led to another, and before long, Bill had lost count of how many empty beer bottles sat on their table. More importantly, he had no adverse reaction. It seemed Satan might have had a point, and maybe Bill's allergies and ailments were all in his mind. Father and son discussed many wide-ranging topics. Bill, interested mainly in the existence of UFOs, quizzed his father on the Universe and his role in it. Satan, it seemed, was more interested in talking about the women, who outnumbered the men at the convention two to one. Each time a scantily-clad warrior woman or kung fu girl walked by, Satan nudged Bill, who acknowledged that it was a rather fortunate ratio. It would appear that Satan and son had bonded quickly. Bill, who unlike me had never had a father figure in his life to guide him, listened as Satan told him the facts of life according to him.

After an hour, Bill was a changed man. Satan was very convincing, and for the first time in his life, Bill decided to have fun. Satan and Bill proceeded to party, and party big. After several beers and several shots of vodka, Bill and Satan joined the crowds of costume-clad beauties. Bill was amazed how easy it was to pick up girls. They seemed to flock around him and his father, admiring their costumes. His confidence growing, Bill found himself flirting for the first time in his life. The convention ended at seven in the evening, and just before they left, the convention awarded Satan second prize in the "supernatural" category for his "imaginative and traditional" costume. He was just one vote short of the first prize, won by a costumer dressed as Death. Satan pointed out in a whispered comment to Bill that Death would be mortified; he looked nothing like the costumer's portrayal of him.

Bill and his father found themselves invited to a costume party after the convention and tagged along with a hundred other revelers to a grand apartment on Fifth Avenue owned by two famous modeling twins. At some time during the evening, Satan made his apologies and bid his son farewell. He had pressing business to attend to. Bill thanked his father for the best night of his life and instead of returning home, carried on partying. He eventually arrived back at his apartment, accompanied by Tori and

Kelly, the twins who had dropped him off at Milligan's earlier, at around six, when he collected my message. Bill informed me that the suit he wore was a gift from his Father, and he delivered it that morning. Bill, as well as looking different, acted different. He was more confident, and he had a twinkle in his eye. I didn't ask him what had transpired between him and the twins, but I could guess.

My main concern was that maybe Bill's bonding with his Father had changed the way he felt about our upcoming conflict.

"Not completely," said Bill as he poured himself another glass of champagne. I was surprised that Milligan's even had chilled bottles of Cristal but not half as surprised as I was that Bill ordered a bottle for us. "I have to say I feel a little guilty. My father has really opened my eyes to some things, and I have never felt better." That didn't sound good. "I was thinking maybe we could play for a draw," said Bill as he raised his glass, gesturing a cheers.

"A draw?" I said, rubbing my chin. It was a good idea. Between us, we could fight to a stalemate without either of us getting hurt. "Do you think that would work?" I asked.

"Why not?" said Bill. "At least we wouldn't be disappointing our fathers, and by ensuring a draw, I figure neither can claim Earth, and hopefully it could get them talking again." I had to admit, I went along with Bill's train of thought. I agreed with Bill that we would fight to a draw, and he ordered another bottle of champagne.

Milligan's had quite a crowd for a Sunday afternoon. They were serving food, and Bill and I had lunch together. Bill was disappointment that llama meat wasn't on the menu, as he had heard so much about it lately, so he settled for meatloaf. I attracted the attention of a waitress, who arrived at our table to take our order. Throughout the ordering process, Bill flirted unashamedly with our waitress, and by the time we had finished our meal, he had secured her telephone number; it was impressive. Bill got the check, and I thanked him for my meal and champagne. Bill had burned the midnight oil and was tired. He arranged for the twins to collect him, and we planned to meet up later in the week. He expressed his desire to meet Maggie and Bob, and for some reason, I felt a little wary of introducing him to Maggie.

I returned to my apartment and called both Maggie and Bob, telling them we needed to meet. We arranged to meet at my apartment at six that evening. I took the opportunity to use the time I had to read the paper. The first headline that grabbed my attention was "MAYOR IN TERRORIST DRAMA," the second was "BOYSCOUTS IN FOOD POISONING SCARE." I set the paper down and sighed. I wondered how God would react when the final conflict ended in a tie and what he would do if he ever discovered that Bill and I had conspired together. For some reason, I was far more afraid of God than I was Satan.

"And so you should be," said Walter.

"Did you really think I wouldn't know?" said God as Walter jumped onto the headrest of my chair. God's voice was directly in my ear as Walter perched himself behind my head. "Let me tell you, Seth; I am a tad disappointed in you." He didn't sound too mad, but I could sense the disappointed that he had expressed in his voice. "Let me let you into a little secret," he continued, "I am everywhere; don't forget it!" he roared into my ear. Now he sounded mad. God told me that, as we were speaking, Satan was chastising Bill for his part in our conspiracy.

There would be no draw, and there would be no conspiracy. Bill and I were not to meet again, despite what we might have thought we were going to do. Bill and I would be the protagonists in the ultimate battle. God was very clear on that. If I even attempted to contact Bill before Armageddon, and vice versa, the consequences would be severe. God left me no doubt that I had crossed the line, and I was treading on very, very thin ice.

"I hope I have made myself clear," said God once he finished explaining the consequences of my failure to win the final conflict. Apparently the loser would be condemned to the "pit."

God made what the "pit" consisted of abundantly clear to me, and I imagined the "pit" was not a place where I wanted to spend eternity. Should Bill and my conflict somehow end in a tie, we would both end up in the "pit." Walter jumped down from the chair and curled himself into a ball and slept. I was tempted to call Bill, but I knew God was not bluffing; no doubt Lucifer had already paid his son a visit and told him of the "pit" and the consequences should we fight to a tie or contact each other again. It seemed I had no choice; I was going to have kick Bill's ass.

CHAPTER 24

MAGGIE AND BOB WERE IN total agreement with God. They had both arrived at my apartment promptly at six, and I relayed the day's events from my lunch with Bill to God's visit.

"Do you think he is watching us now?" asked Maggie, looking around the room. I had taken the precaution of locking Walter into the bathroom, much to his disgust, so I felt pretty confident our discussion was private.

"No, I think we are fine," I said.

"Well, there is not much to debate," said Bob. "Quite simply, you are going to have to win. I am sure Bill is thinking exactly the same thing, I guarantee he is going to put up a fight, and I am sure the thought of spending eternity languishing in the 'pit' appeals to him as much as it does to you." Bob was right, of course. It looked as if I had no choice. "Are you confident that you can kick this guy's ass?" asked Bob.

There was no doubt in my mind I could, but as a precaution, Maggie recommended martial arts training and a couple of sessions at a boxing gym.

"Just in case," she said. "Better to be safe than sorry," she added, unsure whether she had hurt my feelings. She hadn't. I understood their concern, but I was sure if they saw Bill, they would realize that they needn't be worried. I agreed that I would take some exercise courses and condition myself. I did, however, refuse martial arts training, but promised I would maybe do some punch bag work.

"What's next?" asked Maggie. "Do we just sit around and wait?"

I wasn't sure of the answer, but I couldn't see what else we could do. "I suppose so. There was talk of another miracle. But when? I don't know."

Bob looked at his watch. "Nancy's shift finishes in an hour. I have to leave." I looked at Maggie, hoping she also didn't have an excuse to leave. If meeting Maggie was a result of me being the Messiah, then I supposed it wasn't such a bad thing. She stayed over that night, and we both realized that our relationship was becoming more than a casual fling.

An uneventful week passed. I did not hear from God at all, despite encouraging Walter to speak. Nor did I hear from Bill. I was tempted to call him, but each time the thought entered my head, it was accompanied by an image of the "pit" and God's description of it. Whilst God chastised me, he had elaborately described the location, reserved exclusively for those who incurred not only the wrath of God, but had also displeased Lucifer. I won't go into current residents of the pit, but I was assured that several former dictators and a couple of lawyers were currently spending eternity in a place that I was assured was worse than Hell.

Apparently, residents of the pit were in continual pain that never abated, mainly due to the scorching flames and heat that was several hundred degrees hotter than Hell. They were subjected to what can only be described as constant torture that was unimaginable, but it did include reruns of *I Love Lucy, The Golden Girls,* and *Mork and Mindy* continuously played on giant TV screens while Icelandic whale music was piped in twenty-four hours a day.

While I had assumed Lucifer administered the pit, I was surprised to discover it was a joint venture and that my Father and Lucifer had equal shares in it. I knew for certain I wanted to avoid the pit, but felt guilty that I was going to have to condemn poor Bill to it. God, I had also discovered, was well aware of Lucifer's intention not to go by the script and his desire to win, and despite consulting his legal team for advice, the ruling, it seemed, due to God's failure to proofread the Bible, made what was written in the book of Revelation null and void. Therefore, I had to expect that Bill was going to come at me as hard as he could. I tried to imagine Bill fighting, but it was inconceivable that for one minute Bill could muster enough strength to win our confrontation. As promised, I had attended a gym and had also thrown a few punches at a punch bag, encouraged by Maggie, who had become my constant companion throughout the week.

Maggie had practically moved into my apartment. Each day, she would arrive with more clothes. Her toothbrush stood next to mine in my bathroom, and the place seemed empty when she was not there when she needed to attend to work during the day.

I did make a visit to my office, where I was met by applause from my colleagues, exuberant from the contract I had secured, thus ensuring inflated bonuses for them. I was their hero. Henry insisted I continue my vacation, leave, and relax. I picked up a copy of *Bytes* to read Bill's columns. It seemed he hadn't the luxury of not working as I did, though with two million in the bank, I supposed if he wanted to, he could have taken a vacation. His column was quite good, and his Space Invader column was quite informative and interesting. I wondered how poor Bill was preparing for Armageddon. I doubted he had joined a gym, and there was no way, not even with Lucifer's help, that I could see him suddenly becoming an expert in any type of fighting style. I guessed Bill was probably partying every night with the twins, and enjoying his life while he could before he was banished to the pit. It pained me every time I thought about poor Bill, sweating as they forced him to watch the annoying antics of Lucille and Desi, The Golden Girls, and Robin Williams day in, day out, for all eternity, as whale music played in the background.

Bob had taken advantage of Nancy's profession to find out how the Giuliani terrorist investigation was going. Nancy had told him they had assigned her to the case, as she had been an attending officer at the scene. The case, though, was cold. The authorities had no leads, and the descriptions of the man aboard the motorized surfboard, obtained from various witnesses, had produced some bizarre artist impressions and photo fits. Not one resembled yours truly. I was a little upset to discover that one or two witnesses had described the terrorist as rotund and portly.

The other major event of the week was the news story that a group of Boy Scouts were suing McHungry's. Twenty or so visiting Scouts from out of town had contracted mild food poisoning after eating fish sandwiches from a McHungry's located near to

Central Park. While a McHungry's spokesman declined to elaborate, the press had discovered that McHungry's was looking into a batch of fish that might have been stored incorrectly next to contaminated anchovies at one of their distribution facilities. The scouts probably had a good case, especially as the meals they had eaten had been free, courtesy of promotional vouchers.

Also in the news that week was a fascinating story from Peru. Llamas had been put on the protected species list, and their culling for meat production purposes had been banned. This was due entirely to the publicity and the subsequent public outcry the llama's cause had gained after the Giuliani incident.

It was exactly two weeks from when I had first spoken to him that I heard from God again. Maggie and I had ventured to Milligan's for a nightcap, and it was there that once again, God managed to ruin my day. Maggie and I, now established as a bona fide couple found our usual booth, and Sean, who at last called me Seth, had already poured and served our drinks as I collected them from the bar. He asked me if I had seen my friend in the snappy suit lately; a certain waitress was keen to meet up with him. I told Sean I hadn't, but as soon as I saw him, I would let him know. Unfortunately for Bill, it was highly probable that the next time I saw him, the last thing on his mind would be a date with a waitress. Once I had our drinks, I returned to Maggie and placed them on our table.

"I am just popping to the bathroom," I said as Maggie took a sip of her drink. It was whilst I was on my way to the bathroom that I was intercepted by God.

"You are not taking this very seriously, are you?" I was startled. I recognized the voice, but could not see from where it was coming. I looked around the bar. There were no animals present, and I was definitely alone. Maggie saw me looking around and waved. I waved back as I continued to scan the bar. It was quiet; in fact, apart from Maggie, Sean, and I there were only two other customers and they were at the far end of the bar, well out of earshot.

"Down here, you idiot," said God. I looked down toward the floor and saw something crawling along the ground. It was a cockroach.

"You can't be serious," I said. "Why didn't you just call?" I asked. The cockroach appeared to be circling around my feet.

"I would have, but since Maggie moved in, your phone is continually busy or off the hook. What are you two doing up there?" God asked. The answer was obvious, but I didn't reply. "I also see you have been keeping Walter in the bathroom. Let me tell you, he is not at all pleased with it." What God had said was true. So God wouldn't interrupt our lovemaking, I had begun to lock Walter in the bathroom. Walter, I had thought, was becoming accustomed to this new routine, but obviously God had more insight into his moods than I had.

"A cockroach, urrgh," I said, "could you not think of anything better?"

"Hey," said God, sounding offended "this is still one of my creations. I will have you know that these little guys come in for a lot of undue stick; you know they are very resilient." I had heard in the event of nuclear holocaust, cockroaches would very likely be the only surviving species. I wondered if God did indeed have a bigger plan for them. All the same, it was a little disconcerting talking to a bug, even if they were resilient and likely to one day rule the planet. I dismissed the thought from my head. What was more pressing was God's sudden reappearance into my life. God sounded annoyed.

"You sound annoyed" I said.

"I am."

"Oh."

"Oh indeed," said God as he continued to crawl in a circle around my feet.

"What's the problem?" I asked, looking around to ensure that no one, not even Maggie, could see me conversing with the insect at my feet.

"The problem is," said God "is that you are not taking this seriously enough. You don't seem to have even attempted to prepare for Armageddon and the conflict ahead. I thought that maybe I was being too hard on you. That's why I have laid low for the past few days. I was hoping you would be a little proactive. It seems I was mistaken in thinking you could be. My spies tell me you are too busy wooing Maggie, who, I have to say, is looking delightful this evening. But that isn't the point. You should be training, getting in some practice. Do you want to spend eternity in the pit?" I didn't but I thought God was being paranoid. I had been preparing—I had joined a gym, and I had lost even more weight.

"I appreciate that," I said, "the fact you have left me to my own devices and are letting me prepare my way."

"Really?" said God "Is that so?" There was a hint of sarcasm in his voice.

"Yes really," I said upset that God was taking this tone. I didn't see what the big deal was. He must have seen Bill, or at least his spies must have. He must have realized that even I would have no trouble in dispatching Bill and thus winning the final conflict and saving the earth, ensuring God's continued rule. I could not understand his concern.

"Then why, pray tell, have you been spending your free time reading magazines, philandering, and basically not in preparation?" he blustered.

"I have joined a gym," I said "and learnt how to throw a punch," I added defensively. The roach stop circling for a second, and I was positive it looked skyward toward me before continuing its circumnavigation of my feet.

"You know they want to win, don't you?" said God. He sounded perplexed. "Lucifer and his son, you do know that, don't you?" he reiterated.

"Yes, I am sure they do, but don't you think you maybe overreacting?" I replied.

"Overreacting? Overreacting? We are talking about Armageddon. Do you not realize the responsibility you have? Do you not know what we are facing? I can't help thinking that somehow Lucifer has gotten one over on me. How, I don't know, because he was with me for the last thirty years. Let me tell you this: they are not messing about. They are serious about this." He sounded exasperated.

"Just relax," I said. "It won't be a problem. You know I wrestled in high school some?" That was true; I had been a good wrestler. My uncle Jacob had been Navy champion, and he had taught me several moves. Even if I couldn't knock Bill out, I would surely out wrestle him.

"Wrestle? What good will that do you?" said God. It seemed he was genuinely concerned that there was a possibility I could lose.

"You know, if I get him on the ground, I know some good moves." I replied, trying to explain that I had thought about my fight with Bill.

"Never mind wrestling, I can't believe you haven't started any preparation. It's beyond me," said God. Was he not listening? I felt I needed to reiterate a few things.

"Well, despite what you may think or have heard, I am preparing. I am fitter than I was last week. I know how to throw a punch, and I know for a fact that I can wrestle the ass out of Bill. Have you seen him? I can't believe you could even consider he would be able to beat me in a fight. Have a little faith in me; I am not going to lose this for you."

God didn't reply straight away. No doubt he realized he was being over cautious and was calming down. I expected an apology was on its way. When he did eventually speak, he spoke clearly, slowly, and deliberately.

"What fight?" he asked.

The roach on the floor stopped circling and seemed once again to be staring directly at me.

"The fight, the final conflict, the battle between the anti-Christ and yours truly. Armageddon, you know; the main event." I was surprised I needed to remind God of this.

"What on earth are you talking about?" said God. "What fight?"

"*The* fight. *In the red corner, representing the forces of darkness, Bill. In the blue, corner representing goodness and light me. The* fight!" I stressed, becoming annoyed at God's slowness to catch on. Maybe the cockroach hadn't been such a good idea; he didn't seem as sharp as he usually was.

"Where on earth did you get the idea you would be physically fighting the anti-Christ?" asked God. "A fist fight? A wrestling match? Are you completely mad?" This didn't sound good. "Do you think Lucifer and I would agree that the future of mankind and the resulting fallout to be decided by a fight? Do you think we would pin everything on something as barbaric and unseemly an event as a fight between our sons? A fight? Whatever gave you that idea?"

I didn't have an answer. I had presumed. I mean, what other way was there?

"I- I- I- " I stuttered.

"Come on, spit it out, boy," chided God.

"I assumed" I said.

"Well, you shouldn't have," said God.

"So there is no fight?" I asked.

"Of course not, you stupid man. Did you really think a fight would decide the end of the world? Don't be ridiculous." I felt stupid.

"Then how will it be decided?" I asked, intrigued as to how Armageddon could be pulled off in a civilized and cordial way. And that's when God gave me the bad news.

CHAPTER 25

"SPACE INVADERS?" I SAID TO the cockroach at my feet.

"Yes, Space Invaders, best out of three. We agreed on it years ago," said God.

"Why didn't you tell me?" I hissed.

"I thought I had," said God. He hadn't, of course. Once again, his forgetfulness had potentially devastating consequences.

"Well, you didn't. Space Invaders? Whatever possessed you to agree to that? You mean to tell me that Armageddon is going to be decided by two grown men playing Space Invaders? An arcade game? It's the most ridiculous thing I have ever heard." It was my turn to be annoyed.

"At the time we agreed on how we do this, that video game was the in thing. It seemed the best way of keeping things civilized. We didn't want anyone to get hurt through this. It's a game of skill that involves the saving of a planet; it just seemed to fit. Lucifer and I thought it was an excellent way of doing things. A war would have just caused too much damage and destruction. The last thing we wanted was a big mess to clean up afterward."

I couldn't believe my ears. I had initially thought the idea of Bill and me wrestling for the world ridiculous, but I had come around to the idea. I had no inkling that my Father and Lucifer would have come up with an idea as crazy as this.

"You do know he is good," I said to God. "And that I have hardly ever played the game. Not since I was a kid, anyway."

"I know. I can't help but think that somehow Lucifer planned this. I assure you, I have had everyone working on this, such as lawyers and judges. There is uproar, but we can't prove anything. The consensus is that it is nothing more than a freakish coincidence that the son of Lucifer happens to be one of the best Space Invader players the world has ever known. It is rather unfortunate. Despite what the legal eagles say, I am convinced that somehow he must have snuck back here whilst we were out in the Universe and got this Bill chap interested in the game." Unfortunately, I disagreed with God's theory.

"I think you are wrong. I read the e-mail Lucifer sent Bill. He didn't come back when you were away; he wanted to, but he didn't. I think we are the victims of a hideous twist of fate!" I sighed. This was a disaster.

"Well, there is only one thing for it. You had better get practicing, and quickly." I was going to reply, but I noticed that Sean approached. I presumed the conversation was over, in any case, as the cockroach ended its circling around my feet and headed of toward the bar.

He didn't get too far, as seconds later Sean crushed him underfoot.

"Sorry about that," said Sean, "disgusting things; we have the place treated, but one or two always seem to get in." Sean had already returned to his spot behind the bar before I could tell him he had been three seconds away from crushing God. I looked at the crushed cockroach and thought to myself that he was not that resilient; they may be able to survive a nuclear bomb, but Sean's size ten? Not a hope.

I returned to our table and grabbed Maggie by the hand.

"We have to go." I said as I drank my beer in one swift movement.

"Already?" said Maggie. "We've only just got here." Maggie downed her drink just as quickly I did.

"I know, but there has been a development. I've made a huge mistake." Maggie collected her things, and we both made a hasty exit from Milligan's, heading back to my apartment. Harvey gave me a knowing wink as I hurried Maggie into the elevator.

"Yo, dog...." he began. I put my hand up, indicating that . needed him to stop speaking.

"Not now, Harvey," I said, "not now." The elevator door slid shut, leaving Harvey open mouthed and at last, silenced. Once we were inside the apartment, I told Maggie what I had learned from God.

"I'm screwed," I said as I paced the apartment. "There is no way I am ever going to beat Bill. The guy's a professional; he's been World Champion. I am not sure if I was any good when I was kid." I took a deep breath and looked at Maggie for reassurance. She was laughing. "What's so funny?" I asked.

"This is," she replied "the whole thing, it is totally ridiculous; I can't believe they even contemplated it, let alone agreed on it." She was right, but it wasn't the only thing that was ridiculous. If I wasn't involved, I would no doubt have found the whole thing highly amusing. Unfortunately, I was involved, and it was no joke.

I spent the rest of the day contemplating eternity in the pit. Maggie tried to distract me from my thoughts, but the idea of constant pain coupled with Lucille Ball ensured that I wasn't good company. Maggie suggested that maybe she needed to return to her own apartment to leave me to contemplate my next move. I managed to convince her to stay the night. I was glad I did. Maybe it was the thought that I made love for one of the last times in my life, or maybe it was because I made love to a woman whom I had fallen head-and-over-heels in love with. Whatever it was, Maggie and I made love all night. It was, I have to say, the best night of my life, and when I awoke, I felt happy and contented despite the predicament that loomed over me like a hulking dark shadow.

It turned out Maggie needed to go into her office that morning, so after coffee and breakfast, she left me alone in the apartment. Once again, I found myself tempted to call Bill. Indeed at one stage, I lifted the receiver and dialed his number, only to slam the phone down. God had made it quite clear the consequences should my dalliance with the opposition continue. I switched on the television and found a news channel. A strike involving garbage disposal collections loomed, and New York City could soon be finding itself with heaps of uncollected refuse and garbage piling up on the streets. The potential turmoil had city officials on the back foot, and it seemed that the dissatisfied garbage collector's demands would be met before the industrial action began. The news report informed me that the city had initially threatened to fire any strikers, but thanks to the intervention of lawyers on behalf of the garbage workers union, it seemed that firing the striking workers would have been illegal. It gave me an idea. I checked Nancy's schedule and, once satisfied, that the coast was clear, I called Bob.

"I have an idea," I said after updating Bob on the previous day's developments. "Why don't I see a lawyer, maybe even Maggie, and go on strike? I think I may have a good case." Bob didn't reply at first as he considered my suggestion.

"Do you think God would accept that? Do you think he would fear legal action?" I wasn't totally sure.

"Think of the bad publicity," I said. "He wouldn't want that."

"What are your grounds for striking, if you did strike?" asked Bob. I had considered it in great depth. There were numerous grounds I felt that justified strike action. "Insufficient training, no pay, lack of health plan, unsociable hours, hazardous working conditions; the list is endless. Any decent lawyer would rip God's lawyers apart. My strike would be legal and therefore, as I see things, I couldn't be condemned to the pit until my demands were met."

"And what exactly are your demands?" asked Bob, sounding a little dubious that my suggestion would work.

"I need more time to prepare, and to get to Bill's standard of video game playing. I guess I need at least an extra two years and back pay, which I know I wouldn't get, but it would mean a stalemate and years of legal wrangling. My idea is to tie this up in the courts for years until God tires of it and finds someone else." I knew I was clutching at straws, but I knew that when all else failed, hire a lawyer.

"I'm not convinced your plan is totally foolproof," said Bob. "Wouldn't you be better of spending your time trying to learn how to play Space Invaders and at least attempting to put up a fight? I could get over there, and we could search for a machine you could practice on. Don't you think you are antagonizing God? And anyway, didn't he say there was no going back on any of this?" Bob had a point, but even if we did find a machine, which according to Bill's column, were very hard to find, how could I ever get up to

Bill's standard of play? I explained this to Bob, who rather reluctantly agreed that maybe striking and hiring the services of an employment lawyer was my only option.

Walter, who had been sitting on the sofa the whole time I had been conversing with Bob, raised his head.

"I'll feed you in a minute" I said as I cupped the telephone receiver. Walter rose and stretched.

"That really won't be necessary," he said. I told Bob I would call him back and hung up the phone.

"How long have you been listening?" I asked God as Walter jumped down from the sofa and walked toward my feet.

"Long enough," replied God. It won't work, your little idea. Do you know who I've got up there?" Walter looked up to the ceiling. "I have some of the greatest lawyers who ever lived up there, that's who, and I assure you I would fight you vigorously in any court. A strike? Oh please." I wasn't sure if he was bluffing or not.

"Well, I am sorry you feel that way, but do you want your name dragged through the courts?" I was sure he wouldn't.

"It is every day, my dear boy," explained God. "Have you never taken an oath? Have you not seen Court TV?" He had a point; his name was always being dragged through the courts. "I will give you your back pay, if it means so much to you," said God indignantly. He knew that was not the reason I wanted to strike, but his implication that I was only after money was designed to provoke me into feeling guilty. It didn't work.

"Thanks, that's a start," I said not falling into his trap. "I do have other grounds for striking, though."

"Which are?" said God. I was getting to him. He was bluffing, I could tell.

"Lack of training," I answered.

"Is that it? Is that all you've got?" mocked God. "It won't hold up. The courts won't entertain that. I have provided training, on-the-job training," He countered. He had a point.

"Ok then," I said as I felt my confidence waning, "not enough vacation days." I was clutching at straws.

"You work from home," said God. He was right, of course. What chance did I have negotiating with God? What lawyer would take my case? What court would listen? Despite everything, despite all the avenues that existed for the rest of the population when faced with unscrupulous employers, he was God, and there was no loophole, no basis for striking, no legal way out, and with no way of ever beating Bill at Space Invaders, I was doomed and so were the souls of millions. What I needed was a miracle. And that miracle came from a most unlikely source just in the nick of time.

CHAPTER 26

I HAD TO CONCEDE THAT I had no case for legally striking. Therefore if I did strike, then God was entitled to condemn me to the pit. I had no choice; I would have to go up against Bill at Space Invaders, and I would lose and be condemned to the pit. No matter which way I looked at it, I was headed for the pit.

Before Walter had returned to purring and meowing, God had given me one final piece of bad news. The final conflict would be taking place earlier than I had expected. Not that it made much difference, as no matter when it was to occur, I was going to get creamed. All it meant to me was that my centuries of turmoil would begin earlier. God, despite my obvious belief that I was going to lose him the earth, appeared unconcerned. I hoped he wasn't relying on the prophecy of the Bible, especially as we both knew Satan had no intention of complying with what it had foretold. I suspected God had other planets spread amongst the vastness of the Universe which needed his attention; maybe he thought he could start again, and maybe he secretly hoped he could abandon the earth and the headaches it gave him and simply move on. It turned out it was neither. God had faith in me; he genuinely thought I could do it. He was convinced I would prevail. He told me if David could slay Goliath, then I could beat Bill. I was his son, I came from good stock, and he believed in me. I was touched by his faith in me, but it was totally misguided. Bill would pulverize me, and now I had the added guilt of letting down my father, who believed in me.

And then the miracle occurred. I would not usually call an unannounced visit, especially from her, a miracle, more a hindrance, and when I first heard her banging manically at my door, my heart sank. The last thing I needed was her further ruining an already-ruined day. I was tempted to hide, turn down the television, and pretend I wasn't home, but, then again, she was my mother.

It was quite apt, I felt, that she should arrive uninvited and unannounced, especially as I felt all my woes and problems were due in no small part to her failure to tell me the truth and full facts about my birth. It would be a final opportunity for me to thank her, for not only condemning me to the pit, but to tell her that, thanks to her years of mollycoddling whilst I was at college, and during my high school years, I should have been playing video games in bars or arcades with my peers, not studying twenty-four-seven. Maybe, just maybe I would have stood a chance in saving not only the world, but myself from a fate that was actually worse than death. On top of all this, I considered mentioning the fact that for the first time in my life, I had met a woman who I could consider spending the rest of my life with, but once again, thanks to Mother's little secret, that life was likely not to last the week. I opened the door to let the whirlwind that was my mother enter.

"That bastard!" she screamed as she barged past me into the apartment, the door swinging against its hinges such was the speed of her entry. I had never heard Mother swear before, and I hastily reconsidered the verbal onslaught I had prepared for her. "That no good, two-timing, back-stabbing...." She seemed lost for words, which was a first for her. "Philanderer!" she finally spluttered.

I closed my apartment door and watched as she paced around my living room. Walter, who had been snoozing quite contently, jumped from the sofa and headed into the kitchen where I caught a glimpse of him jumping on top of the refrigerator, where I presumed he felt safe. I wished I could have joined him.

"All these years, all these years!" raged Mother. To say she was annoyed would have been an understatement. I had never seen her so mad. "And that whore! How could she, how could she? My own flesh and blood, my own damn sister!" I wasn't sure if that was a question for me or a general question that didn't need answering.

THE RELUCTANT JESUS

"Oh shit," I said under my breath. What had my father—Ely my father—gone and done?

"Years, apparently," continued Mother, "years! Right under my very nose! The betrayal! The lies!" She sobbed into her handkerchief as she continued to pace the apartment. I considered comforting her, but the sobbing stopped, and the venom and anger in her voice returned. "I gave that man the best years of my life. He will pay; he isn't going to get away with this, the... the... fornicator!" She shouted the word fornicator, and I dreaded to think what my neighbors could hear. I closed the kitchen door as not to upset poor Walter, who had scrambled to the highest vantage point, which was on the shelves above the fridge. He was perched precariously, his eyes scared, shifting from Mother to the main door. No doubt, he was considering making a bolt for it at the first opportunity. I thought if he did, I would be close behind him.

"He was nothing, nothing without me!" Mother's tirade continued. "I could have done so much better than him," she said, the sobbing once again taking over from her rage. Her last sentence was, of course, untrue, but I decided not to point that out to her. In fact, I hadn't said a word.

"Your father is a lousy rat!" she screamed, this time directly at me. I decided to play dumb; the pit would be a piece of cake compared to the wrath of Mother if she found out I already knew about my father's infidelities.

"That's a bit strong. He did create the Universe, so he can't be that bad," I said, implying that I thought she was talking about God.

"Not him," said my mother, "Ely, the bastard!" Once again she felt the need to scream the word "bastard." "The lying weasel!" she added.

"Dad? Why? What's he done?" I asked, knowing full well what he had done. I hoped my act was fooling her; I attempted to sound surprised and shocked.

"Is he ok?" I added, just for luck. Actually, I was concerned for his well-being; I dreaded to think what Mother could have done. At any time I was expecting her to produce my father's severed penis from her handbag and place it on my coffee table. Not only would I have to reconsider the further usage of said coffee table, the sight of another man's penis, severed or not, is not something I was looking forward to, least of all my dad's. I shook the image from my mind.

"Ok? Ok?" she shouted. "Of course he is ok; I left him in the garden with that damn pipe in his mouth!" I hoped she didn't mean underneath the garden, but a quick check of her hands and clothes indicated that she had done no digging that afternoon. "Oh, he's ok, but he won't be, believe me, he won't be." The old adage about a woman scorned took on a new meaning when applied to my mother; I wondered what she had in store for poor Ely.

"You haven't told me what has happened, what's he done?" I asked again, continuing my act of ignorance.

"What's he done? What's he done?" for some reason Mother was feeling the need today to repeat everything I said twice. Once again, I didn't think there would be an appropriate juncture for me to mention this so I let it drop.

"He's only been sleeping with your aunt Marla, the evil whore!" Mother was obviously not holding back, "He's been at it for years, the two-timing, lousy, no good, philandering fool." According to Dad, his tryst with Marla had ended years ago. I guessed Mother was adding her own dramatic vibe to story.

"He told you this?" I asked, suddenly aware that if he had admitted his affair with Marla, he could have also added the line, "and Seth knows all about it," which would mean I needed to prepare myself for Mother's rage to turn on me once the rage directed at Ely had subsided.

"Yes, he told me all matter-of-fact like, as if he didn't care, as if he was getting something of his chest, as if he was telling me he had just got a parking ticket!"

I presumed that Ely had admitted all to Mother because he assumed that by confessing to me it would be easier. I wished he had consulted me first; the last thing I needed was Mother's dramatics. It was then I noticed something that made my heart miss a beat. I had missed it at first, when she had barged into my apartment screaming and shouting, but it sat by the door. Obviously, she had dropped it as she entered. It was a suitcase! Mother looked me straight in the eye.

"You didn't know, did you? About your dad and Marla?" She walked toward me. Despite the coming onslaught in the Space

Invader arena of death and the ensuing pit, nothing filled with me more dread than my mother in a rage.

"No!" I shouted. I had never lied to my mother directly to her face before, but the circumstances warranted drastic action. Mother seemed to relax, albeit temporarily, obviously pleased that I was in no way involved in the conspiracy. Her calmness didn't last long.

"That bastard has been screwing her for years!" she screamed once more. "He even told me God said it was ok!" She stood with her hands on her hips, shaking her head. "Can you believe he would say such a thing? As if God would condone such an act of... betrayal!" Once again, she screamed the last word of the sentence. If only she knew that God had indeed not only condoned it, but had suggested it. Lucifer would be the least of his problems. The ringing of the telephone interrupted Mother's tirade. I grabbed it quickly before she had the opportunity to tell me not to answer it. As I raised the receiver to my ear, she whispered:

"If that's him, tell I am not here."

"Hello?" I said.

"Yo, dog, your Momma is in da house, and she is pissed, jacked up on crack or something. I tried to stop her, man; well, at least stall the bitch, but she is one fiery hoe." It was Harvey, warning me that Mother was on her way. I appreciated his call, but a few minutes earlier would have been better. Normally, referring to my Mother as a bitch and a hoe would provoke a reaction, but bearing in mind the circumstances, I let it drop. I thanked him and replaced the receiver.

"Was that him?" said Mother, pointing at the phone.

"Who?" I asked.

"Ely!" she screamed "Was it Ely, looking for me?"

I told her it wasn't, which brought me to the subject of her suitcase. "Where does he think you are?" I asked, nodding at the suitcase by the door.

"Newark," replied Mother, "at my friend Denise's house."

"Is that where you're headed then, after you leave here? Do you need me to call a cab, organize a car?" I hoped I was not being too obvious. Despite her being my mother, there was no way she was going to be staying with me, not during my last week on Earth, oh no.

"I am staying here dear," said Mother, "with you. At least until the divorce." This was totally unacceptable, and I needed to think fast.

"But wouldn't this be the first place he would look?" I asked. "Once he realizes his mistake, and he wants to work it out?" I said, hoping Mother would take the hint.

"I doubt it," said Mother, "he never comes into the city alone." Actually, Ely did venture into the city on his own; this would be the first place he would look for Mother, and she knew it. That's why she was here. She was bluffing. There was no way she was going to divorce Ely. She would want to make his life a complete misery, and divorcing him would be the easy way out for him. No, I knew what she was doing. She wanted him to come look for her, grovel for forgiveness, and then she could make his life even more miserable than she had for the last thirty or so years. I decided to play the double bluff.

"Maybe your right," I said coyly, "and he would never come here. He would never think of coming here to look for you. To make sure he doesn't, I could call him, pretending I had no idea of all this, and ask for you. That would make him think you were at Denise's." I watched for Mother's reaction. She contemplated what I had said. I went for the deal breaker. "You are dead right, Denise's is the first place he would look, and when he realizes you are not there, he'll probably stop looking; you know how he is. You never know, he might even start the divorce proceedings himself." Actually, I wasn't exaggerating; if Ely did look for my Mother (if he had any sense, he would take this opportunity to get the hell out of Dodge,) he would probably stop looking after his first failure. I could see that Mother hastily rethought her course of action. She needed one final push.

"You know, he believes everything you tell him. Look how he was about God and the virgin thing. He trusts every word you say. If you told him Newark, he is going to think Newark is where you are going to be." I said, then smiled pleasantly at my mother and put on my "yes, you are right, you are always right" face.

"Well, maybe he shouldn't trust me. Maybe he shouldn't believe every word I say," said Mother. "Maybe I have a little secret that he doesn't know about." I had no idea what she was talking about, and I blamed it on her emotional state.

"He isn't your father anyway," said Mother as if this was meant to be a shock to me.

"I know," I said. "We've been through all that. I know who my real Father is." I said, my eyes fixed firmly on her suitcase that still remained by the door.

"You do?" she said, sounding surprised.

"Yes, remember? God?" I said, my arms outstretched. Had she forgotten that I was the Son of God? Had she already forgotten that she was talking to the Messiah? "Virgin? Immaculate Conception? Ring any bells?" I said, nodding, waving my hands, and pointing at my chest. Mother put her hand to her mouth as if she had just realized she had left the oven on and was miles from home.

"You believed all that?" she asked. She sounded surprised.

"Not at first, but a lot has happened since I saw you last. We've been in contact. My Father and I—God—things have gone a little faster with him than I would have hoped, but of course, I believe you now." I was little dumbfounded, I had to say, that Mother had asked me if I had believed her. I would have thought that had been obvious. Mother sat down onto my sofa and forced a smile.

"Oh dear," she said, "oh dear." Once again, she was repeating herself. She looked at me, and then shifted her gaze to the floor, titling her head to one side. "Oh dear," she said again.

CHAPTER 27

"I DIDN'T THINK IT WOULD go this far," said Mother rather meekly. She was no longer ranting or shouting; in fact, she was rather subdued. She raised her handkerchief to her mouth as if she were worried. I had never seen my mother act this way. Something was definitely wrong.

She beckoned me to join her on the sofa by patting the seat next to her. I was inclined to bolt; the last thing I wanted to do was get close to Mother. She was liable to turn back into the raging monster she had been not five minutes ago.

"I think I will stand thanks," I said, still shifting the odd glance toward Mother's suitcase that remained by the door.

"I think you may want to sit," said Mother gently. I compromised and took the easy chair that faced her. "I think there might have been a little mix-up," said Mother once I was seated. I stared at my Mother, urging her to elaborate.

"To be honest, I am very, very surprised God let this go this far." She blew her nose on her handkerchief. I found it odd that with all her sobbing, none of Mother's makeup had run; in fact, on closer inspection, I noticed her mascara was fully intact. As I had suspected, her sobs had been crocodile tears, though I did not doubt the authenticity of her rage. I had a feeling that she was not heartbroken by Ely's confession of adultery. I pulled myself from inspecting Mother's makeup and returned to the conversation.

"Let what go too far?" I said, referring to her previous comment.

"The Messiah thing. I would have thought he would have realized by now," said Mother.

"Who would have realized what?" I asked.

"God, realized about you," she answered.

"Realized what?" I was becoming annoyed. Why this woman could never get straight to the point, I did not know.

"Realized you weren't his son," said Mother as she returned her handkerchief to her purse from where it had originated. I had no idea what she was talking about. We had been through all this before. Maybe she was confusing things.

"We are talking about God, not Ely," I said "I do know that Ely is not my Father. I know my Father is God," I said, hoping that she realized what she was saying.

"But that's just it, dear; neither of them is your father." It took a couple of seconds for this announcement to sink in. "That's what I meant by your father—Ely your father—being foolish, believing everything I told him. You see, I didn't want him to find out." I noticed now that her mascara was running. It was a hideous sight, watching my Mother's makeup dissolve before my eyes; it was like having a deranged clown with a half-melted face sitting opposite me.

I shuddered as she delved back into her handbag and reproduced her handkerchief. Those were genuine tears, I knew; there was no way she would have let me see her looking like a member of the rock group Kiss if her tears hadn't been real. I was still confused but gave her a moment to compose herself. I was conscious that her dripping makeup might stain my sofa and my carpet, and I did consider collecting some old sheets to cover my furniture.

"You didn't want Ely to find out what?" I asked my Mother once her tears had stopped.

"About the truth," she answered; she looked up at me, her face caked in dripping makeup which now gave her the appearance of a melted waxwork. I had to do something to help her, so I left my seat and collected a towel for her, which she used to wipe her face. Once I returned to my seat, I spoke.

"What is the truth, then? If neither God nor Ely is my father, then who is?" I asked. My Mother smiled to herself, as if reminiscing about another time and place. I should have known what she was going to say. I really should have guessed.

"Jacob, your Uncle Jacob."

CHAPTER
28

IT SEEMED THAT WHILE MY father was fooling around with my mother's sister, Aunt Marla, my mother was fooling around with my father's brother, Uncle Jacob, and neither one had any idea that the other was cheating. It seemed that Uncle Jacob had always had a soft spot for my mother, and their affair started before Ely and Irma even married. In fact, it turned out that Jacob had been the first to spot my mother, but his naval duties had meant he was unable to start a romance. When he returned home on leave one summer, he discovered that his younger brother had snagged the woman he secretly yearned for. He confessed his love for my mother two nights before her marriage. Overcome with lust and guided by a far more sexually experienced man than Ely, Irma succumbed to his advances. Of the two brothers, Jacob was considered by far the most handsome. He looked like a movie star and many likened him to a young Charlton Heston. It was really no surprise that a young and naïve woman, despite her self-assurance and hard-nosed exterior, would fall for his charm, especially if he was wearing his naval uniform.

Unable to break his younger brother's heart, Jacob urged Irma not to cancel her wedding to Ely despite his own desires for her. So, after one night of passion, they put their relationship on hold. God came to Mother on her wedding night, and, unable to deny that she was a virgin, especially as Ely would discover she had been unfaithful, she became the willing carrier of God's child. But there was one problem, one secret that only she knew: she wasn't a virgin, and, according to her, she was already pregnant before God's seed entered her womb.

All along, it would seem Irma had never been convinced that she was ever carrying the son of God inside her, and she managed to avoid any sexual encounter with Ely by maintaining the virgin ploy. He never knew his wife had had sex with another man. When God didn't claim me after my birth, my Mother presumed that he had discovered her dalliance with Jacob, and, knowing the child was not his, God had simply moved on.

When God called her a few weeks ago with the news that he was back on the scene and that it was time I found out who my real my father was, it was too late to tell the truth. For one thing, Ely would have discovered the affair between his wife and his late brother, and Irma was sure that God would be none too pleased either, so she had said nothing and hoped God would realize that I was not his son by my total inability to perform any of the tasks that were likely to be set for me.

It explained why when I was a child Uncle Jacob had such a great affinity toward me. The affair between Jacob and Mother continued until his death and was in full swing whilst Ely and Marla enjoyed their illicit affair. One thing confused me after Mother finished explaining the complexities of her adulterous life. How did God not know? How could God not realize that the son he thought his own, me, was, in fact, the bastard son of a naval commander?

Once Mother had completed relaying her sorry tale of infidelity, lies, and betrayal, we both took a deep breath. This changed everything. Despite my mother's readiness to accept that I was Jacob's son, I was still not convinced. There was no guarantee that she had conceived from her pre-marriage romp with her future husband's brother. What was beyond doubt and beyond any refuting was the fact she was not a virgin. When God claimed to have inserted his seed into her through Immaculate Conception, a method, I hasten to add that I was still none the wiser as to its workings or mechanics, she had already lost her virginity.

No matter what, the news was good; no, scratch that, the news was fantastic. It surely meant that the whole thing was null and void. There was no way I could represent God in the final conflict, and with no opponent where did Lucifer and God go from here? For one of the few times in my life, I felt like hugging and kissing my mother. However, I refrained from doing so, not entirely undue to the fact she looked like a dripping multi-colored candle.

"What must you think of me?" said Mother as she rose from the sofa and moved toward the window. It didn't matter what I thought of her. I was elated, and I was more concerned as to her future sleeping arrangements as once again I glanced at her suitcase sitting ominously at the door.

"I think you need to be alone," I said, not thinking that at all, "or at least with a friend, someone out of the family. Denise, for instance." Mother agreed, and I called her a cab to take her to Newark. I needed time to think, and I needed to consult my disciples. The news I had received was monumental. There was just one thing: how was I going to tell God?

CHAPTER 29

AS SOON AS MOTHER LEFT, I called both Bob and Maggie and told them to meet me at my place immediately. I did not elaborate but told them it was a matter of the utmost urgency. I released Walter from the kitchen, but before he ventured outside, he peered precariously around, checking that Mother had left. I looked at where she had set her suitcase to confirm that it had indeed departed with her. Despite her revelation, I was more concerned that she had even suggested she stay with me. I needed to brief Harvey on the need to alert me quicker should an event like an unannounced Mother visit occur again.

I toyed with the idea of calling Ely to let him know where to find Mother and to ensure that he kept the fact that I knew about him and Marla quiet, but considering I now knew about Mother and Jacob, I supposed it was all irrelevant. I decided the one thing I would do was visit Jacob's grave at the cemetery in Brooklyn where he was interned. I would buy him some flowers and place them at his tombstone. If he was my father, I owed him that much, but it didn't change anything. No matter who my father was, Ely would always be Dad.

Bob arrived first, and I told him everything. Just as I was finishing the sordid tale, Maggie arrived, so I repeated it all over again for her benefit.

"So are you or are you not the Son of God?" asked Bob once he had heard the story twice.

"Good question," I replied, "but I do not know the answer."

Bob puffed out his cheeks and blew out breath. "But the possibility still exists that you are the Messiah?" he said again. I got the feeling that Bob was disappointed.

"The possibility still exists," I said hoping to lift his disappointment.

"Well, at least that's something," Bob said, smiling. Unfortunately, I was going to deflate him again.

"But the fact that my Mother was not a virgin, from the way I see things, makes me a false prophet," I said. Bob's shoulders slumped dejectedly.

It was Maggie who spoke next.

"So this whole thing has been a complete waste of time?" Her words hurt me slightly. I wouldn't have described our relationship as a waste of time.

"Not completely," I said, hoping she would realize I was hinting at our blossoming relationship.

"Please explain, because as far as I can see, it has been," said Maggie, a little too abruptly for my liking. I pointed at myself then back to her quickly, indicating that "we" were not a waste of time.

"Oh yes, of course." Maggie flashed me a smile, and I felt a wave of relief engulf me.

Bob was still pouting. "But there is no guarantee that you are a false prophet?" asked Bob. Maggie and I looked to where he sat. "What I mean is, you are assuming God will say that; you don't know, not for sure, anyway." Bob was correct, because I hadn't yet spoken to God since Mother's announcement, I had no idea where I stood. I was indeed presuming.

"This may be a minor technicality, and therefore you could still be the Messiah," said Bob triumphantly.

"Bob" I began, "I don't think you get it. I do not want to be the Messiah. Don't you see? Haven't you been following the plot? I am going to be condemned to the pit. I have no chance of winning the final conflict. Lucifer is going to take over the earth." I took a breath, "So, please, tell me, if you can, why you would be so disappointed if it turns out I am not the Messiah?"

"Well, I kind of like being a disciple," he said, "and the miracles could come in handy, especially during baseball season." As it was already baseball season, I felt his excuse was lame. I hoped Bob wasn't going to be my Judas.

"Oh, ok," he said eventually, "I see what you are saying. I don't want you in the pit. Who would I go drinking with?" Bob smiled, and I felt relieved that he wasn't my Judas. He was selfish and self-centered, but so was I, or I used to be, but he was no Judas. It was Oscar Wilde who said a true friend stabs you in the front and not the back. I knew that if Bob was going to stab me, he would do it smiling and in the missionary position. Maggie interjected with an extremely valid point.

"But how about the miracles?" she said. "How do you explain being able to perform miracles if you are not the Son of God?" Indicating to Bob, she continued, "We both saw you walk on water, and what about the scouts?" It was a good point, but I reminded her that I was only the vessel. If God was channeling his power through me, then it was actually God performing the miracles, not me.

"But didn't God say he could only channel his power through his Son?" added Bob. Maggie nodded, confirming that she was under the same impression.

"I really don't know," I said. "I won't know until I speak to him." I looked at Walter, hoping he was going to speak and save me the effort of repeating Mother's story a third time, but he continued to snooze on Maggie's lap as she stroked the top of his head.

"I have a question," said Maggie. "Did Uncle Jacob have any kids other than you if indeed you are his?" I shook my head. To the best of my knowledge, he did not, but of course, he was a sailor.

"You know what we need?" she asked. Bob and I looked at her blankly. "DNA testing."

"DNA testing?" repeated Bob, questioningly. "You know, you might have something there."

"DNA testing?" I said, joining in the debate.

"Yes," said Maggie, "a DNA test to validate your mother's claim so we can be sure before you tell God."

"Great idea," agreed Bob, his enthusiasm lifting. I gave him a stare, and he added, "Only if it proves you are not God's Son."

"It's a stupid idea." I said as I looked at both my disciples with pure disbelief. "I can't believe that you are even considering for one minute that it will work." Bob and Maggie looked at each other and shrugged, indicating that they did not agree with my previous statement. I felt I needed to clarify my last words.

"For a start, Uncle Jacob is dead, has been for nearly fifteen years. Somehow I do not think we are going to get any DNA from him, especially as he was cremated. Secondly, I think it highly unlikely that God is going to readily hand over a swab of his DNA, if he even has any, and I am not even sure he even exists in bodily form."

My two disciples slumped into their seats. Their dejection and disappointed was a total contrast to my feelings of elation and relief. I was happy to accept the fact I was not God's son. Their attempts to somehow prove it beyond a doubt didn't wash with me. For a start, there was the possibility that a DNA test would confirm I was God's son. That would mean God could disregard the virgin issue as a technicality, and the pit would therefore still be looming, with Lucy and Desi waiting for me to join them in eternity.

"Hey, guys, I'm as disappointed as you," I lied, trying to unify us. "One minute I am the Son of God, the next, I am the bastard child of a horny sailor." This didn't fool either of them. They knew that deep down I was elated that there was a possibility I would not be facing Bill in the Space Invader arena of doom. I made coffee and left Walter on Maggie's lap. Bob flicked through the copy of *Bytes,* which I now had delivered each week.

I returned with coffee, and we all sat in silence, alone with our thoughts. The only sound was Walter purring as Maggie stroked his head and under his chin. We had exhausted every possible scenario, and all we could do was to wait for God to call and for me to tell him the truth. We didn't have to wait long. I noticed the buzzing of Walter's purring had ceased. I looked up to check if he was still in the room. He still sat on Maggie's lap, and I knew that God had arrived.

"Well, this is nice and cozy," said God. Startled by Walter's abrupt speech, Maggie jumped up, sending Walter flying in the air.

"Sorry," she said as Walter twisted in the air but landed on all fours. Walter jumped onto the coffee table so he was in the center of the room. He licked himself before God spoke.

"That's fine, dear," he said to Maggie, "no harm done." Maggie smiled at Walter; I shook my head.

"Would it not have been easier to call?" I asked, a little surprised by God's dramatic entrance.

"Well, it's nice to see you too," said God sarcastically.

"Sorry, hi, how are you?" I said, feeling a little guilty for not welcoming God as I would any other guest. However, other guests did usually knock, and they did not use my cat as a voice box. Bob stood up straight as if he were a school kid and the principal had just walked in the room.

"Relax, Bob," said God. Bob didn't. He remained bolt upright. "I am glad you are all here," said God, ignoring the fact that Bob stood as rigid as a board. "I thought it was about time we all got together for a little chat, maybe throw some ideas around. A little informal tabletop discussion, maybe even a brain storming session. We have them all the time up here. Maybe we should start with you, Maggie. Any thoughts?" While I appreciated that God was trying to help, it didn't seem right that we all knew something he didn't. It also didn't seem right that what I was about to tell him should be told to him in public. We needed privacy.

"Maggie and Bob were just leaving," I said as I urged them to stand.

"Were they?" said God disappointedly.

"Were we?" said Maggie, looking at Bob.

"Yes, you were." I said behind clenched teeth, ushering Maggie and Bob to the door.

"Oh yes, of course, we were," laughed Maggie, "silly me."

"Goodbye your Lordship, sir," gushed Bob, his words directed at Walter, who remained perched on the coffee table. I pushed Maggie and Bob out of the door and turned to face Walter.

"Lovely touch," said God.

"I beg your pardon?" I asked as I collected the empty coffee cups discarded by my friends.

"She has a lovely touch, Maggie. While she was stroking me, it felt very relaxing. I must do that more often," said God as Walter rose, stretched, and returned to his sitting position.

"How long were you there?" I asked, unsure if God already knew what I was about to tell him.

"Oh, only a few minutes," he replied. God, it would seem, had only been in the room as we sat saying nothing. No doubt

Maggie's gentle touch had delayed his arrival announcement. I wasn't sure if I should have been jealous that my woman was stroking God, not Walter, and I was a little perturbed that he had let her carry on without informing her it was the Creator's chin she was rubbing and not Walter's.

On a scale from one to ten, one being mild, and ten being severe, I would say I had a temper rated at a number two. I hardly ever lost it, and when I did, I would remain calm, coherent, and rational. It seems I did not inherit that from God, for he was a ten, maybe even a ten plus. We all know somebody with a fiery bad temper who loses it completely; they shout, they shake, they curse, they sometimes go purple. We have all seen people flip their lids and blow a fuse. Some people fly off the handle and become violent, scream, shout, and throw things. I have seen it many times with friends of mine and of course, on Jerry Springer. Imagine then, if you will, the worst temper tantrum you have ever witnessed, and multiply it by a thousand. No, multiply it by ten thousand and then some, because that's how bad God reacted when I told him about Jacob and Mother.

"Hey," I said as I returned into the living room. Walter still sat on the coffee table. "Hey," said God cheerfully, "how are you? Getting ready for the big showdown?" He seemed extremely relaxed considering the closeness of Armageddon. I decided the best course of action would be to come out and say it, not to dilly-dally, and get it over and done with. I hoped he hadn't been selling tickets for the big showdown, because if he had, he had better get some refunds ready.

"Well, there has been a development." I said nervously.

"What sort of development?" asked God.

"A development that kind of makes me think you ought to consider finding somebody else," I said. God sighed.

"Not this again," he said, "we have been over this a thousand times. There is no one else; you are doing it."

"That's not what I mean. I would love to do it." That was a lie.

"That's good," said God cheerfully.

"But I don't think I can," I said pensively, once again God sighed.

"Of course you can do it," he said encouragingly, "I have total faith in you; you know faith goes a long way."

"It isn't that I can't do it, what I mean is I can't do it. I am not qualified; you see, my mother visited today."

"How is she?" said God. "Charming woman," he added.

"Not so good, actually," I said. "It turns out Ely told her about Marla."

"He didn't tell her I said it was ok, did he?" said God, who, it seemed, was just afraid of Mother as the rest of us.

"No, he didn't," God gave a sigh of relief. "What a fool," he said, referring to Ely. "He should have kept that quiet." I agreed, but this wasn't the forum for that discussion.

"Anyway, she came here and had her own little confession to make," I continued. "It seems that Jesus didn't do such a good job watching over her as you had thought. I think you call it a 'Code Dave.'"

"A 'Code Dave'? You mean a virgin snatch?" God sounded panicked.

"Yes, that's exactly what I mean. It seems that Mother and my uncle Jacob had sexual relations prior to your, erm, well, visitation." To be honest, I didn't know what to call my conception; I felt visitation was a good enough description.

"You mean the army guy?" said God.

"Navy guy," I said.

"Good looking, looked a bit like Moses?"

"Charlton Heston," I corrected.

"Same thing," said God.

"Well, regardless, he beat you to the punch, popped her cherry, reaped the wild wind, went boldly where no man had gone before; get the picture? She wasn't a virgin!" I felt I needed to be descriptive, especially as it seemed he was about to go off on one of his tangents.

"Rubbish," said God. "That's impossible. Your Mother was a virgin. We had it well documented. I had my best man on the job. The chances of two 'Code Dave's' occurring in the same millennium is virtually impossible."

"Not according to her," I said, "and really, she should know." There was silence. For at least fifteen seconds, there was complete silence as Walter stared at me. I noticed there was a glare in Walter's eyes that perturbed me immensely. I could feel the tension in the apartment rising. I suddenly felt afraid, very afraid.

"Jesus H Christ!" boomed God. I thought my eardrum would explode; it was as if a jet plane had landed next to me. It was the loudest sound I had ever heard, and I felt the walls tremble. They would have heard that shout several blocks away. I expected that Harvey was going to barge in at any moment to find out what the commotion was. God wasn't talking to me, he was shouting at some unknown third party. "Get me Jesus Christ, and get him now!" he shouted.

"Who are you talking to?" I asked.

"What? Oh, didn't I explain. Even though my voice is coming from Walter, I am actually still up here. It's like talking on the phone, really. Sorry, was that loud?"

I didn't reply to God's question. I had a question of my own. "What's going on?" I asked, wondering why he needed to speak to Jesus. More importantly, I had always wondered what the "H" stood for.

"I'll tell you what's going on, or has gone on. Your brother, that's what has gone on. It was his job to watch that weasel, Jacob. I knew there was something about him. I knew he was sniffing around your Mother. That's why I had Jesus on the case. This is sabotage! It is Jesus's doing." I didn't see it as clearly as God did, but I was getting the overall picture.

"Oh yes, ever since we first discussed this whole second coming and returning to earth business, he wanted the job. He wanted another chance. He said he was the one with experience. I knew something was afoot." God was talking to himself, not me. "The crafty cad has had me, pulled one over on me; I knew there was more to it, why he didn't like you."

And then God explained. It seemed that Jesus was dead set against me from the moment I was conceived. He felt it was *his* second coming. Ever since they had tabled the idea thirty-two years ago, Jesus had been against it. He felt it should be him returning to fight the anti-Christ and prepare the world for Armageddon. According to Jesus, it was what the people wanted, and it now seemed he had sabotaged God's plan out of jealousy and spite. It was his responsibility to watch over Mother, to ensure she was and remained a virgin, and that another 'Code Dave' did not occur. It appeared that Jesus had turned a blind eye to Jacob's advances. Call it dereliction of duty or deliberate sabotage, one thing was certain and there was no getting away from it: Mother and Jacob had been intimate, and it had happened on Jesus's watch.

"So what now?" I asked, but God did not reply. Walter simply meowed.

CHAPTER

30

WE HAVE ALL HEARD OF the wrath of God. Not to be confused, as Bill pointed out to me much later, with the *Wrath of Khan*, which again, according to Bill, was a damn fine Star Trek movie. The first thing I noticed, once God had vacated Walter's body, was the sky.

It had suddenly become very dark outside, despite it being 3:30 in the afternoon. It looked like the middle of the night. Dark clouds had appeared from nowhere, totally eclipsing whatever light the sun tried to radiate. It was an unnerving sight, and I shuddered as the city fell into darkness. The wind picked up, and I could see from my window (with difficulty due to the fading light) newspapers and litter swirled by the wind that made the paper dance a macabre waltz before being catapulted by an invisible bow into the sky, where it fluttered some more.

I could just make out my fellow New Yorkers scurrying below me, looking for shelter from the wind and sheeting rain that now fell hard and heavy. I could hear the sound of car horns as confused drivers dodged pedestrians, rain, and wind. Coupled with the poor visibility, it made driving near impossible. Sirens sounded as police and fire crews rushed to the minor fender benders that were occurring almost in unison throughout Manhattan. I found it difficult to draw myself away from the metamorphosing weather. I had never seen such sudden and abrupt changes in the climate. However, there was a metamorphosis occurring much closer that needed my immediate attention.

Walter, who I have explained is an extremely low-maintenance pet and had never previously so much as shed a hair in the apartment, was acting most peculiar. I don't mean that he was speaking—that I no longer considered strange—rather, he clawed at my sofa. He wasn't just clawing at it; he was destroying it. Already he had torn the cloth completely and was busy ripping out foam from inside the sofa with his teeth. I could also hear him growling. I shooed him away from the damaged sofa, and he promptly sprayed me with urine. I tried to grab him, but he flashed his teeth and swiped at me with his claws on full show. He then jumped onto my coffee table and promptly defecated.

It was not however normal cat poo that emanated from Walter's behind; it was the liquid version, cat diarrhea. As Walter jumped from the coffee table, a trail of shit traced his movements as diarrhea continued to pump uncontrollably from his rear. I tried to grab him and at least throw him into the bathroom where I could contain the damage, but as I chased after him, I slipped in his excrement and went skating along my carpet. As this was all going on, my telephone rang non-stop. Unable to catch Walter, who had now run into the kitchen to cause more damage, I grabbed the receiver.

"Hello," I said, out of breath and completely perplexed by the Walter situation. "Seth? Is that you? You sound strange." It was Maggie.

"Yes, it's me, just having some cat trouble. Have you seen this weather?" I asked turning my head in the direction of the window. Nothing had changed; the black clouds still loomed, the wind continued to howl, and the rain fell.

"Yes I have seen it. The TV is saying it is happening all over the country. The meteorologists can't explain it, freak weather all over; looks like Europe and other parts of the world are getting it too." I had a feeling that maybe I knew what was behind it and probably also behind Walter's sudden anti-Seth's apartment behavior also.

"Listen," said Maggie, "I didn't call you about the weather." Maggie sounded a little stressed, slightly agitated, and maybe a little panicky. "I have something to tell you."

I turned my attention from the events outside my window to Maggie's voice. "Yes, what is it?" I asked nervously.

"I'm pregnant," said Maggie. Her words seem to hang in the air. It was as if time stood still. Everything seemed to occur in slow motion. I could hear a beeping noise coming from my pocket and could feel a slight vibration. It was my cell phone, and for some inexplicable reason, with Maggie on the other line obviously needing to talk and awaiting my response, I answered it. With Maggie's words still reverberating in my head, my house phone in one hand held to my right ear, and my cell phone held in the other hand held to my left, the house covered in cat urine and excrement, Walter growling as he continued to rip up my apartment, and with the apocalyptic weather worsening, the last person I needed to speak to was Henry Peel, my boss.

"Hello," I said.

"Seth it's me, Henry. Sorry to call your cell, your house phone was busy."

I remembered Maggie on the other line. "Henry, hold the line."

"Maggie? Are you still there?" She wasn't. She had hung up. I was sure I heard the word "jerk" just before the line went dead.

"Seth?" It was Henry on the other line. "Seth, are you there?" I was too busy worrying about Maggie and impending fatherhood that I didn't register that I still had Henry on the other phone. I broke off from my thoughts.

"Sorry, Henry, there must be a problem with the phones," I said as I replaced the house phone receiver.

"Probably to do with this crazy weather," said Henry. "Anyway I didn't call to discuss the weather. Unfortunately, I have some rather bad news." I steadied myself, still shocked from the news I had just received from Maggie. "The thing is, Seth, I am going to have to let you go." Henry's words hung in the air; at first I thought I had misheard him.

"Sorry, Henry, for a minute there I thought you said you had to let me go," I said, with a nervous laugh.

"My hands are tied. It's the church contract; they just called, they want you off the project, and said they had confused you with someone else," said Henry hesitantly.

"Why do you need to let me go? Just hand it over to someone else, and I'll go back to the Hyomoko contract," I said, confused as to why Henry needed to fire me.

"Well, I would like to, but they stated quite categorically that if you remained with the firm, they would cancel the whole contract, and before you ask, Seth, no, they did not give a reason." What the hell was this? Why would the bishop of a church suddenly have a downer on me?

Before I had chance to even think about arguing with Henry, the house phone rang again. Thinking it was probably Maggie calling back, I needed to end my call with Henry.

"Henry, I got to go," and before he could speak, I hung up on my boss and my job. I grabbed the house phone again. "Maggie?" I said, nearly out of breath with the continual phone answering.

"No," said the voice I did not recognize; "Mr. Seth Miller?" said the voice again.

"Yes, who is this?" I asked, annoyed that the caller was blocking the line and preventing Maggie from calling back.

"I'm from the IRS. The name is Mackay, David Mackay. I am an inspector, and I need to talk to you about your last tax return so I can prepare your audit,"...and that's when I fainted.

I guess it was combination of finding out I was going to be a father, losing my job, and discovering the IRS would be auditing me all in the space of less than five minutes that did it. The fact that I had an incontinent and rabid cat in my home also didn't help. I don't make a habit of fainting; in fact, in the history of my life, it was a first.

I must have been out for thirty minutes. When I awoke, I laid spread-eagled where I fell, the cell phone clutched in my hand, and the house phone off the hook on the floor next to me. It was dark; the freak weather had not abated, and I could still hear Walter growling. As I gradually came to, I saw Walter had destroyed every piece of furniture I owned. Not only that, but he had also managed to pull open every CD and DVD case and scratch them beyond any kind of repair. My carpet looked like a stable floor occupied by a horse that had eaten Indian food mixed with laxatives the night before. I stood up and saw that Walter was now foaming at the mouth, and I was sure he was preparing to pounce on me, no doubt going for my neck. I saw I had messages on my machine. The red light flickered a number nine.

I pressed the button. The first message was Maggie. It was quick and to the point: "Asshole."

I played it back before erasing it. I shook my head. The second message was from the chair of my building's residents association, Mr. Walden, a man I had met a few times in the lobby and once at the interview before I got the apartment. The basic gist of his message was that there had recently been some complaints about the way I spoke to Harvey the doorman. Residents had overheard our conversations and alleged that I had used a racist term whilst conversing with him. That, coupled with the foul language I used and my constant references to rap music, meant the committee felt I was in violation of the agreement I signed where I promised I was a person of good character and moral standing. They were drawing up eviction papers immediately.

The third message was from Harvey. "Yo, check out the crazy-ass weather. You can bet your honky white ass that them white folks is gonna get all jacked up. Yo, let me know if you need anything." The fourth message was from Mother announcing she could not spend another minute with Denise Malphrass. She was getting a cab from Newark straight back to the city, and she asked if I could make sure I had a good supply of her favorite tea so she could have some in the morning.

The fifth message was from my bank. "Mr. Miller, there seems to be a problem with your account. It is considerably overdrawn. Quite possibly it is a mistake, but do you recall purchasing items, to the value of sixty thousand dollars, from a company called Anal Probes for Men, LLC? Please call Mrs. Bloomfield, your account manager. Thank you." Message number six was from my general practitioner. I needed to call the office urgently; they had discovered some mislaid test results, and it was imperative I saw him. His message also recommended I check my life insurance policy. The seventh message was my life insurance company informing me that my coverage had expired, and before renewing, I would be required to sit a full medical examination.

Message number eight was Maggie again, reminding me what an "asshole" I was, and message number nine was from God, asking me if I liked his wrath.

"This could be just the tip of the iceberg," his message said.

I did not like God's wrath one bit. But I knew I deserved it. I had been flippant; I had shown him no respect; I had been messing with the superior being, the creator of the Universe, God, our Father who art in Heaven, the Lord of more than just the Rings, and I had pushed things too far. God was angry, and he was angry with me.

As I sat amongst my tattered apartment with Walter clinging to the curtains as they fell and crashed among the other debris he had created, I realized that in one fell swoop, God had the power to change everything. God had the power to change my destiny, he had the power to destroy me—he had ultimate power. I had been blasé, condescending, and I had answered him back on more than one occasion. Had I not realized who I had been dealing with? This was the being who told Noah to build an ark and then flooded the earth because he could. This was the being who sent plagues of locusts to infest the Egyptians; this was the being who created postal workers. He could be a fair and good God, but he could also be cruel and ruthless. This was payback for my attitude and maybe extra for being overly pleased that another "Code Dave" had occurred. This was his wrath.

I realized I had been an asshole, and that maybe I could have handled things differently. Maybe with the gift God had bestowed on me, I could have made a difference. Just as I realized that maybe being the Messiah was not that bad after all, and if a man could suffer and die on a cross for me, then could I not at least attempt to locate and practice a stupid computer game?

Who had I thought I was? How dare I take the Lord's name in vain? I was repenting, and I felt ashamed. I was not fit to be called his son. I could only hope to walk in Jesus's shoes, or sandals. It was just as I realized all this and more that from behind a black cloud, the sun appeared again. As the clouds melted into the blueness behind them and the sun beamed down onto the city, once more a shaft of sunlight engulfed my apartment, and the reflection from the wet, glistening windows created a chasm of light that illuminated me. It was if the light shone directly on to me. I raised my hands and knelt in the dripping rays of the sun.

"Praise the Lord," I cried, "praise the Lord!"

As the last cloud seemed to evaporate, cheers rang out in the streets below. Walter, who had been hanging on to a light fitting the last time I saw him, was curled in a ball, sleeping away, his diarrhea abated and his mouth foamless. My telephone rang several times in quick succession, and for some reason I knew to let my machine grab the messages.

Message one was Henry apologizing for his earlier call. He had been the unwitting victim of an office prank. The church had made no such demands, and all contracts were fine. Henry was going to get to the bottom of it and find out who had impersonated the bishop. He suspected it could have been one of the mailroom boys, and he asked if I could I forgive him.

Message two was from Mr. Walden. He had confused me with another tenant, a former postal worker, and after speaking with Harvey, who confirmed I had never once uttered such vile and disgusting filth, he had realized his mistake. According to Harvey, I was a gentleman, and if anyone knew a gentleman, it was Harvey. There would be no eviction papers, and the residents' association would love me to be their guest of honor at their next monthly bingo evening.

Message three was my doctor's secretary apologizing for her blunder. She had misread my records and another patient's test results had fallen into my file. I was fine, no need to worry. Unfortunately, another patient, a postal worker, was about to get some rather bad news. Message four was Mrs. Bloomfield from the bank. There had been a computer error entirely due to an electrical shortage brought about by the inclement and sudden rain. I was not overdrawn; in fact, my account was extremely healthy, especially as a Mr. Alan Robes, not a withdrawal by Anal Probes, had recently made a deposit for several hundred thousand dollars. Who Alan Robes was, I did not know, but I was very grateful to God for making him up.

Message five was the IRS. There were two Seth Millers, and the Seth Miller who lived in California would be audited. Mr. Mackay apologized for his error and was happy to report that my taxes were fine; I could actually expect a rebate. Message six was Mother. Unable to find a cab in the torrential rain, she had been forced to return to Denise Malphrass's door for shelter. Denise Malphrass then apologized for also sleeping with Jacob several years ago, and now it appeared the two old ladies were laughing, joking, and comparing notes about Jacob's lovemaking style, which Mother assured me, were many and varied.

THE RELUCTANT JESUS

I thought the final message would obviously be Maggie. Before pressing play, I guessed what she would say. She would say the pregnancy testing kit was a dud, that it had been a mistake, that I wasn't an asshole, and ask whether she could come over and have a lot of sex with me immediately. Unfortunately, the final message was from Harvey, informing me that a team of industrial cleaners had arrived laden with high-velocity vacuum cleaners and other hi-tech equipment, and they were on their way up. They would deliver my new furniture at the same time.

I wondered where Maggie's message was. A bit odd, I thought. Just when I thought that maybe God had forgotten to rectify that little problem, the phone rang again and this time, rather than let the machine answer it, I answered it myself.

"Maggie?" I said, and once again, I was to be disappointed.

"I am afraid not," said God.

"Sorry, I was expecting someone else," I said.

"Pretty impressive, eh?" said God, "The weather, I mean. Haven't done that in years."

"Look, I owe you an apology," I began, but God cut me short.

"I know. I know what you are thinking. I know what you are feeling. That's why I stopped it. Well, the weather I had to stop; I couldn't destroy the world. It was the same size flood that I did for Noah's generation. Another forty days and nights and you could forget the World Series," said God.

"Well, at least now you see it," he continued. "The cat was Gandhi's idea, by the way." I nodded as if I expected Gandhi to be involved in something like that, though I had no idea why.

"I mean it," I said, "I want to be your son, not because of all this, but because I feel I should do it. I realize you put a lot of effort into creating the Universe, and I realize all the good you have done; you created life, gave us all a shot at things." I was being genuine. I was ready and willing to fight Lucifer and Bill, albeit at Space Invaders. I would practice, and somehow I would overcome the four-time world champion.

"Listen," said God, "don't worry about it. To be honest, all hell has broken out in Heaven, so I can't stay long. Anyway, the cleaners and your furniture will be there soon, so I will make this as brief as possible." God paused for a second before speaking again, "Everything has gone wrong. Jesus admitted that he let Jacob sleep with your mother on his watch, and he deliberately did not attempt to stop him, nor did he inform me. Therefore, many have raised questions as to your parentage. The legitimacy of your birth has been brought into question. A lot of traditionalists are claiming that if your Mother was not a virgin, regardless of whether I am your Father or not, then you can't fight the anti-Christ."

"I can't believe Jesus let that happen! How could he have let another 'Code Dave' occur? What was he thinking?" I asked, disappointed, after all, that I might not be the legitimate Son of God.

"Don't blame Jesus, blame me. I should have listened to him from the beginning. He was right; the people were expecting him again, not a new version. I thought I was doing him a favor by not sending him back. He went through a lot the first time. I didn't realize it meant so much to him. I thought by having another son, it would relieve some of the pressure. I should have listened. It wasn't personal; he didn't do any of this to hurt you. It was me he was trying to hurt, and I guess I deserved it." I understood what God was saying, but I felt he was being too hard on himself.

"Can he play Space Invaders though?" I asked. This had the desired effect, and God laughed.

"No. He can't. He wouldn't know a joystick from a gear stick." We both laughed at God's joke.

I felt terrible for God. He sounded dejected, and maybe if I had just got on with things, none of this would have happened. The guy was an icon, and I had the privilege of conversing with him on a daily basis. I had a hotline to the most revered figure in the history of mankind. I thought about the churches, the mosques, and synagogues devoted to him. I considered the billions worldwide who relied on his mere presence to get them through the day. I wondered at all he had created, including anchovies and cockroaches, and the responsibilities it all entailed. He may have been an absent father to me, and maybe even at times an absent father to the world that he had created, but he was back and was trying his best to put things right.

"That sure was some show you put on," I said, trying to raise God's humor.

"I didn't think you would faint; that was a surprise," said God. I could hear a chuckle in his voice, which pleased me. I looked at my watch; I had been talking to God for at least five minutes, and Maggie still hadn't called. I guessed she would have at least tried my cell phone.

"That's odd," I said. "Maggie hasn't called to tell me about her false alarm."

"Maggie?" said God.

"Yes, I was expecting her to call and tell me not to worry," I said.

"Worry about what?" said God, seemingly confused as to what I was talking about.

"About not being pregnant," I confirmed.

"I didn't know she was," said God.

"She isn't now, not since you reversed everything," I said, encouraging God to follow my drift.

"What?" said God, sounding even more confused. "I didn't involve Maggie in any of this. I have no idea what you are talking about."

"You mean you didn't make Maggie believe she was pregnant?" I asked, the reality slowly dawning on me.

"Not at all," replied God.

"Then she is really pregnant," I said. I needed to call her and tell her everything was fine. I needed to call her and tell her I loved her, and that I wanted to spend the rest of my life with her. I needed to tell her I was the happiest man alive.

"You need to call her," said God, "but in a minute; first I need to tell you what the plan is. We planned Armageddon for next week. I was going to tell you officially, but I didn't want to worry you. But to be honest, there is chaos both up here and down there." I imagined God pointing up and down where ever he spoke from. "Lucifer is still furious with his son for his attempted coercion, and I understand the anti-Christ has turned into quite the party animal. Lucifer is having trouble keeping an eye on him. Apparently he is out all night, sleeping all day, and has different women for different days. He has done no training, not so much as pressed a fire button or twiddled a joystick in days. I suspect right now he's in as much trouble as you just were." I shuddered to think what Satan would be doing to ruin poor Bill's day.

"Anyway, the plan is we all meet up here in two hours."

"Up here?"

"Yes, up here. HQ, as we call it. I have got everything organized for you both. It is highly irregular, but an emergency meeting has been called, and we felt your presence would be essential," said God.

"Me and who else?" I asked.

"Bill. The general consensus is that he needs to be here also, considering he is just as much a victim of circumstance as you. Lucifer is also going to be here, and it's been a long time, I tell you. We are having the heating adjusted so he feels comfortable. We are convening a tabletop, sit-down emergency meeting with some of the committee. It's not often we do this; in fact, it's unprecedented that we are having outsiders present, but the situation warrants it. Lucifer has agreed to attend, so it is all settled. And Bill, well, he will be doing what he is told to do."

"So I am coming up there?" I said pointing upward, unsure whether God could see me. "It's not permanent, is it?" I added, perturbed that the only way into Heaven, or so I had always presumed, was by dying.

"No," laughed God, "don't worry about it; leave that to me." I felt better knowing I wasn't going to be seeing my maker on a permanent basis. "It's so we can talk this thing through, put faces to names, that sort of thing," reassured God.

So I was finally going to meet him. I was going to meet God. I was also going to meet Jesus, Lucifer, Gandhi, and the rest of them; I was about to, like Jacob had with Mother, boldly go where no man had gone before. It was surreal, it was like a dream. I was two hours away from seeing what no other living human being on the planet had ever seen before; I was going to visit Heaven! In the meantime, I had other pressing matters to attend to, of which God reminded me.

"Now, Seth, hadn't you better call Maggie?" said God.

"Yes," I said "but before you go, how do I get to the meeting? How do I get to Heaven?"

"Take a cab," said God.

"A cab?" I queried.

"Yes, a cab." And he hung up.

CHAPTER
31

AS SOON AS I HUNG up with God, I dialed Maggie's number, but not before letting in the cleaners God had organized to clean up Walter's mess into the apartment. I told the furniture guy to just hold on five minutes and to make himself some coffee as I took the handheld receiver into the privacy of my bedroom.

"It's me," I said when Maggie eventually answered her phone. It had seemed to ring for an age.

"I know," she said, "I recognize the number." I sensed not only a little hostility in her voice, but apprehension; she sounded just as worried and nervous as I did.

"Look, I'm sorry about before, but you have to believe me, this has been a crazy afternoon. I thought that God...well, I will explain later. The important thing is that I am sorry I got caught up in things."

"Things? What is more important than me being pregnant with your child? What things?" She was annoyed, and rightly so, so I told her about the wrath of God and the events of the last hour. When I had finished explaining, I gave her a couple of minutes to digest the information.

"It wasn't the best timing on your behalf," I said. The moment the words left my mouth, I knew she would blow up.

"Not a good time?" she screamed. "None of this is 'a good time.' I'm pregnant, Seth, with your baby; we've only known each other a few weeks. On top of that, you have to take part in the final conflict, which, let's face it; you are likely to lose, so my child will be fatherless! I should be happy, but this is just awful." She cried uncontrollably.

"I know, listen, I think we should get married," I said. It wasn't the greatest proposal, but I meant it. Maggie stopped crying, but I could hear that she was sniffing back tears.

"Do you?" asked Maggie. "You really want to marry me?" Of course I did; three weeks ago I would have ran a mile, but now I wanted a wife, a family, and I wanted... commitment!

"I thought you wouldn't be interested. Oh, Seth, this is fantastic!" Maggie was crying again, this time tears of joy.

And you know what? It *was* fantastic. I felt elated. I was going to be a father. Despite everything, the impending Armageddon, not knowing who my father actually was, the guilt I felt for my part in the debacle occurring in Heaven and Hell......despite all of it, I was the happiest man on Earth.

"Look, I need to go," I said, "I have cleaners all over the apartment and a furniture delivery guy helping himself to the contents of my fridge. On top of that, I need to catch a cab to Heaven. Maggie, I love you, and I am the happiest man alive. I will call you when I get back." Maggie urged me to be take care and told me to take a camera to get some shots of God so we could show the baby its grandfather.

Once I completed my call to Maggie, I ventured into my living room. The cleaners had done an excellent job in record time, and there was no trace of Walter's torrent of destruction. They had placed the furniture where the original furniture had stood, and the delivery guy was just leaving when I returned.

"I'll take this old stuff away for you," he shouted as he struggled with the wrecked sofa. I tipped him fifty bucks and the cleaners the same amount. I had no idea who had paid them, but I could guess. My apartment was back to normal; it was as if nothing had occurred. Walter was back to his usual self, curled up in a ball on his new sofa. I was going to be a father, and I was going to marry the only woman I had ever loved; all was right with the world. Apart from, of course, the pending apocalypse, and my cab ride to Heaven. The phone then rang for the umpteenth time that afternoon, and I wearily answered.

"Your cab's here," said Harvey.

"I didn't order a cab," I said.

"No, I did," said Harvey.
"You did?" I asked.
"Yes, I did," he replied.
"Why?" I asked.
"Because I work for The Man, and he told me I should. And when the man says 'do,' you do," answered Harvey.
"You work for the man?" I asked.
"Yep," said Harvey.
"What man?" I asked.
"*The* man," said Harvey.
"In what capacity do you work for *the* man?" I asked.
"Guardian angel, class A, the best there is. Your guardian angel," answered Harvey.
"I will be right down," I answered.

I was greeted in the lobby by a smiling Harvey. Suddenly his curiosity and his interest in my life made sense; he watched after me, and he was here for one reason only. Harvey was my guardian angel. He was one of the one in four! I was lost for words; I would have never have guessed that the "gansta rapping" doorman would have been anyone's guardian angel, let alone mine.

"Yo, brother, now don't be getting all emotional on me," said Harvey as I approached, "don't you be hugging me or nothing like that. Don't want them folks around here thinking ol' Harvey is a softy, even if you is Lil' Jesus. That's what we call you, us angels: Lil' Jesus." I had no intention of hugging Harvey; I did, however, want to shake his hand.

"How long have you known," I asked, "about who I was?" Harvey smiled, and sucked on his pearly white teeth.

"Before you, I have known since the day we both arrived. I have been watching you." Harvey pointed his little finger at me which wore a gold ring. He smiled. "Hey, man, you made it easy for me; I should be the one thanking you. This was a plum assignment, watching over the boss's kid. Man, they're gonna build statues and do paintings of me and everything," Harvey whistled. "But hey, man, we can rap and jive later. You need to get this cab. It's outside waiting on your honky ass." Harvey ushered me out of the lobby and into the street. "Good luck, man," said Harvey as he blew his whistle. I looked at Harvey and shook my head.

"Wow, Harvey, I never knew," I said, "I just never knew."

"That's the idea, bro," smiled Harvey, "now you'd better hurry, you don't want to keep these guys waiting. These cats don't like to be kept waiting, and a word of advice," Harvey looked around, checking that no one was in earshot, "don't be jiving and fooling like you do, not there, man, especially with that Gandhi cat. Man, he ain't smiled in fifty years." Harvey patted me on the back as I ventured into the street.

A yellow cab pulled up to the curb, its hazard lights blinking, indicating it had been waiting. I waved at Harvey, who hurried me into the cab. As I entered and took my seat in the rear of the cab, I realized I was not the only passenger.

"Hi," said Bill as I climbed into the cab. Bill was dressed in the same style as he was the last time I saw him: dapper. He wore an Armani suit, Italian leather shoes, and he had his hair slicked back. He was a cross between Woody Allen and Al Pacino.

"I see you're keeping with your new look," I said shaking Bill's hand, "you know, it kind of suits you." I said. Bill looked pleased.

"A lot of people are comparing me to Al Pacino," said Bill proudly. I nodded.

"Pretty freaky, hey?" said Bill indicating around the taxi.

"It sure is," I answered. "Any idea what the plan is?" I asked.

"I'm not sure," answered Bill. "This guy isn't saying much." He indicated towards the driver, who eyed me in the mirror.

"Hi," I said. Our driver didn't reply. Instead, he shifted the cab into gear and proceeded into the city traffic. I was sure I recognized the cab driver, and after a moment, I realized he was the same cab driver who had rescued Maggie, Bob, and me from the pier after the walking on water miracle. He must have been some sort of angel also.

"How did it go for you?" I asked Bill, referring to his confrontation with Lucifer. "Not pleasant," said Bill, "not pleasant at all. First of all, the apartment became infested with rats, and next I was covered in boils; then he set fire to my collection of Star Wars figures. That was followed by the return of all my allergies, but he saved the worst for the last," Bill shuddered. "It was hideous, the worst thing he could have done," Bill turned to face me. "He crashed my hard drive, deleted everything, and he screwed up my broadband connection."

The cab seemed to be heading toward Queens, but then diverted left, which led me to think we were going in a big circle. Our driver seemed to be double backing, and the route didn't make any sense. I banged on the screen separating driver from passenger.

"Do you know where you are going?" I asked, looking at Bill and shaking my head.

"Oh yeah, I know where I am going," said the driver. He turned to face me. He wasn't watching the road at all.

"Whoa!" I screamed, "Keep your eyes on the road. You are going to get us all killed."

"That's the idea," said our driver who still faced me

"Get your hand on the wheel," screamed Bill. I hadn't even realized he had let go of the steering wheel. The cab driver faced us and waved his hands in the air, laughing. We seemed to be going faster. He hadn't noticed the traffic stopped ahead.

"Slow down!" both Bill and I shouted together. The man was a maniac. How had this guy ever gotten a cab license? Stupid question, forget that; a better question would have been why had God chosen this lunatic to chauffeur us? The driver smiled a toothy grin and winked. I noticed Bill had closed his eyes, which was good for him, because he didn't see the parked truck we were heading directly for.

"Oh, my God!" I screamed, "We are going to crash!" I closed my eyes and braced myself for the impact.

CHAPTER

32

HEAVEN, OR HQ AS GOD had affectionately nicknamed it, was not at all how I had expected. We certainly were not standing on a cloud, nor did I see any pearly gates. There were no angels playing harps, nor was Saint Peter checking off names from a scroll.

The first thing I noticed was the sound, or lack of it. There was no background noise, not even the sound of a bird or the rustling of a tree dancing with the wind. Bill and I seemed to be standing in a meadow, and the greenness seemed to span for miles. There was the odd rise in the ground that appeared to be small hills. To our left, I would estimate about four miles away, there was a wooded area, most probably an orchard. The sky above was blue, not a cloud filled it, and though we were drenched in sunlight, neither Bill nor I could spot the sun. The temperature was warm, not hot; in fact, if we were on Earth, it would have been the perfect day.

A gentle breeze cooled the air; it felt like we were completely alone. I looked around again, as did Bill. I scanned every horizon, and there seemed to be no structures or sign of any life apart from the grass beneath our feet and the trees to our left.

"Can you see anything?" I asked Bill as we continued to optically explore our new surroundings.

"Nothing. Where are we anyway? Weren't we approaching Broadway a second ago?" Bill was right. A few seconds ago we were about to crash into the back of either a parked truck or dumpster on Broadway and 45th Street in the back of a crazed cab driver's taxi. Somehow, and I didn't know how, it seemed we had been transported to how I always imagined England would have looked in the Middle Ages. As I continued to scan the horizon, I spotted something far away in the distance.

"Over there," I said and pointed toward what I had seen for Bill's benefit, "do you see it?" Bill followed my finger in the direction where I pointed. He squinted and moved his head.

"Yeah, I see it. What do you think it is?" he asked. I wasn't sure; it looked like some sort of structure, possibly a building.

"I don't know, but I think we should head toward it. There might be a telephone or something," I suggested. Bill agreed and we headed in that direction, toward the lone structure and the only blot on the landscape.

"Do you think this is Heaven?" asked Bill as we walked toward the unidentified structure far on the horizon.

"I guess so," I said. "It is a little different than I had imagined it would be though," I answered. "This ground, it feels like Earth." Bill agreed. We were both a little surprised that there hadn't been anyone to meet us, and we hoped our cab driver had brought us to the right place.

"Hey," said Bill, "I've just had a thought. You don't think we are dead, do you?"

I explained that God had told me this would be a short visit, and I didn't think we were dead. The thought had crossed my mind; everything had happened extremely quickly. I assured myself that God wouldn't be so cruel as to take me away from Maggie and my unborn child, not after everything we had been through together. We continued walking for what seemed like miles.

"What time you got?" I asked Bill.

Bill checked his wristwatch. He tapped the face, and then held it to his ear. "That's odd," he said, "this is a brand new Rolex, but it's stopped." It didn't surprise me that Bill had bought such an ostentatious watch; however, what did surprise me, was that, like my watch, his had also stopped.

"It seems time stands still up here," I said as Bill continued to shake his wrist in a futile attempt to get his watch ticking again.

"It's kind of weird, don't you think?" said Bill. "Us about to meet God and Lucifer—it's the sort of thing people dream about." I supposed he was right. "If you could ask one question, just one question of God, and he had to tell you the truth, what would it be?" asked my diminutive friend, the anti-Christ. It was a good question, and not something I had ever thought about before. As we continued on a path toward the structure, I mulled over Bill's question.

"I am not sure. Probably something like 'will the life that exists on other planets ever make contact with us?' or something like that. Why, what would you ask him?" Bill, who had obviously put thought into the subject, hence his initial question, rubbed his hand on his chin before he spoke.

"Well, I have actually thought about this a lot. There are several questions I have, but to narrow it down to just one, well, that was not easy. I would love to know if there are going to be androids in the future, and if so, would there be pleasure drones."

I looked at Bill and screwed up my face. "What on earth is a pleasure drone?" I asked.

"An android, or robot, that is built, designed, and programmed for a human's sexual pleasure," said Bill, as if I were mad for not knowing what a pleasure drone was. I nodded, indicating I understood what he meant, even though I didn't. "But then again, I am pretty sure there will be, so it would be a wasted question." Bill scratched his head, still thinking. "Another thing I have always wanted to know is why was the air on the planet Vulcan the same as it was on Earth? Why could Kirk breathe on Vulcan? I never understood that."

"Bill, that's a wasted question too. It's not real, it's science fiction. You could ask any geek freak that." I realized that Bill was a geek freak, or had been. He no longer looked like a geek freak, but he still thought like one.

"Yeah, you're right, one of the nerds would know. 'Trekkies' they call them. I'll ask one of them next time I am at a costume convention." I wasn't sure if Bill understood the irony of his last statement, but I let it pass. "I've got it," said Bill after several more minutes of deep thought, "I have the perfect question for God."

"Which is?" I asked, intrigued as to what had come to Bill's brain.

"I would ask him what we are meant to call male lady bugs." Bill smiled triumphantly. I supposed it was a good question, in a way. I certainly did not know the answer, and I supposed male lady bugs often got offended when people referred to them as ladies. It wouldn't have been my choice if God gave me the opportunity to ask just one question. Maybe Bill's brain had been exposed to too much champagne, and maybe the late nights and partying had fried his brain. Who knew?

Luckily, my conversation with Bill was cut short, as the object that we were heading toward began to form a shape, and we could just about make out what it was.

"Is that what I think is?" asked Bill.

"If you think that it is a castle, then yes, I do believe it is what you think," I replied as I stopped in my tracks.

I could clearly make out four turrets that seemed to join each of the four walls, and there also appeared to be, though we were still some distance away, a larger building with a spire or other tall turret-like object protruding from its middle, which was located within the castle walls.

"If my memory serves me well," said Bill "I would say that is definitely a twelfth-century castle, typical of the kind found in medieval Europe. From what I can make out, it seems to be a Motte and Bailey type, commonly found in England." I was glad Bill was a geek. "If you look closely, you will see the building in the center is actually a manor house or a great hall, which often housed the chapel, and is probably the reason for the spire." I was very impressed with Bill's knowledge of castles and their construction techniques. Though it meant nothing to me; it was just a big castle with a moat and a drawbridge. As we got closer and the castle grew larger, I could see Bill was getting more excited. "I stand corrected," said Bill as we reached the edge of the water-filled moat. "It's actually of concentric design, which means there is no keep; they relied on the main wall for defense, with towers along the length of the walls." Bill pointed at the towers which I could see quite clearly. "Most Edwardian castles had three concentric rings of walls and towers. This seems to only have one," continued Bill. "The central space was kept as an open courtyard, but some, like this one, would house the owner's home, the manor house." Bill's knowledge, though fascinating, did not tell me the one thing I needed to know.

"You see that," Bill pointed at the moat, "that's a moat." I looked at Bill and smiled widely, indicating I already knew that. "Sorry, just getting a bit carried a way," apologized Bill.

"How do you know so much about castles anyway?" I asked Bill as we stood on the wrong side of the moat.

"Dungeons and Dragons. I play it all the time. There is a whole game plan devoted to building your castle defenses."

"Well, it looks like that this castle has no one defending it. Look, it seems deserted," I said. The castle did seem deserted; I could see no knights guarding the walls and there seemed to be no activity in any of the four towers.

"How do we get across?" I asked Bill, indicating the moat, which was at least twenty feet wide.

"The drawbridge, usually," said Bill, "which seems to be raised." We walked around the castle. The moat did indeed surround all four walls, and there were no signs of life on any of the other three walls or rear towers. Beyond the castle, in all directions, was green meadow. The orchard we had seen when we had first arrived was no more than a blip on the horizon.

"I doubt they will have a phone," said Bill. He had a point; there were no telegraph poles, electricity pylons, or any other modern structures in view. "What now?" asked Bill.

We didn't have to wait long to find out. The sound of chain on wood broke the silence around us as the drawbridge began to lower. As it hit the ground with a thud, the gate, which was behind where the drawbridge had stood when raised, opened outward. I looked at Bill, and Bill looked at me. As the gate slowly opened, the sound of the creaking amplified due to the acoustical nature of our surroundings, a figure emerged from the darkness. The darkness was caused by shadows, which seemed to cloak the entrance of the castle. We both took a step back at the same time. It was eerie, almost ghostly, and I have to admit, I was afraid, nervous, excited, and spellbound all at the same time. So was Bill. I felt him shaking as he grabbed my hand.

Normally, I would have rebuked the hand of another man, but in this case I made an exception. At that moment, I needed Bill as much as he needed me. The figure slowly emerged from the darkness. He wore a cloak that shrouded his face. He slowly and deliberately removed the hood that hid his face, and he moved into the light from the sun that did not shine above us. The man at the other of end of drawbridge beckoned us with his finger and then spoke.

"You're early."

Bill and I did as the outstretched finger instructed and made our way across the drawbridge and over the moat.

"Did he just say we were early?" I whispered to Bill. Bill nodded.

"He sure did."

As we approached the beckoning finger and passed through the gate, which now meant we stood within the castle walls, I managed to get a better look at the man who had greeted us. He wore a brown cloak with a hood, which he removed, revealing a rather unremarkable face. I estimated he was in his late fifties, maybe early sixties, and he was balding. What hair he had was grey, and he possessed a rather glum-looking face, which I would describe as dour. There was a small gap at the nape of his cloak that revealed a shirt and tie.

"You do know that you are early, don't you?" said our new, unidentified friend. "I suppose it doesn't matter, as I think everyone on my list has arrived anyway," he said before either I or Bill could reply. If he looked dour, then he certainly sounded dour as well. His voice was monotone, and if I had met him anywhere else other than a remote castle in the middle of nowhere, I would have called him boring. I guessed his accent was Midwestern, probably from Ohio, but I wasn't sure. Before we got too close, Bill whispered to me that he believed it was Saint Peter who kept Heaven's gate. I found it hard to believe that the glum man was *the* Saint Peter. When I finally got within conversation distance, I spoke.

"Saint Peter?" I asked.

"No, Bernard," replied Bernard.

"Saint Bernard?" suggested Bill.

"No. That's a type of dog," said Bernard in his droning voice, "usually found in Switzerland, if memory serves. Renowned, I am led to believe, for their long history of life-saving with the small barrel of brandy that is attached to their collars, which they offer people in need. I am not sure how they offer it, but I understand that they do. To felled skiers and lost persons disoriented, I am sure, by snow. That is my understanding of whom, or in this case, what, a Saint Bernard is. I am merely Bernard." I had never heard of Bernard, and I could not recall any character named Bernard in any Bible, Koran, or any other religious publication or manual.

He seemed to be very knowledgeable about dogs though, especially large breeds. Bernard beckoned us into the castle, and we entered a courtyard. Bill was correct; the courtyard separated the gate from a large single building. It looked like a large house, and it did, as Bill had predicted, have some sort of chapel attached to the rear of it. I looked around and sized up my surroundings. It seemed, apart from Bernard, Bill, and I, that the place was deserted.

"It's a bit quiet," I said to no one in particular. Bernard ignored me, but Bill joined in.

"It's like an old western town after the gold rush when everyone left. Buildings remained but no people."

"Apart from Bernard," I said.

"Apart from Bernard," confirmed Bill. Bernard ignored our comments and instead pointed toward what Bill had called the great hall.

"They are in there, waiting for you," said Bernard, in his monotone voice. It seemed Bernard would not be joining us further. He turned and headed back to the gate where he raised the drawbridge courtesy of a wooden pulley lever. Once he raised the drawbridge, he closed the gate. He turned and saw Bill and I had not moved.

"Go on," he shouted, "what are you waiting for?" He gestured and pointed with his arm, motioning for us to move forward. Bill and I complied with Bernard's zealous and enthusiastic pointing and gesturing, and walked forward, albeit slowly and pensively, toward the great hall.

"Who was he?" asked Bill as we both spun around to see Bernard removing his cloak and heading toward a small plastic chair that sat beside the drawbridge's pulley lever.

"I have absolutely no idea," I said and shrugged at the same time, "pretty strange character, though," I added. Bill agreed that Bernard had indeed been an unlikely gatekeeper.

We were about ten feet away from what we assumed was the main entrance to the great hall when the bulky, large, double oak doors flung open widely. I immediately recognized the voice.

"You're here, welcome, welcome," said God as he stood at the entrance of the impressive building. "Found us ok, did you? Good. Bernard let you in all right? Fantastic. You are a little early, but that's not a problem. Just glad you got here in one piece; well, two pieces, seeing as there is two of you." God laughed at his observation.

So here at last was God. He stood with his arms outstretched as if about to hug both Bill and I at the same time with a big, beaming smile spread across his face. I liked the look of him immediately. Sometimes when you see a person for the first time, you get the feeling if you are going to like them or not. I definitely had a good feeling from God.

We all have our own personal images of God in our minds, though no one, apart from Bill and I, that was, has ever seen him. Most people have an idea what God looks like. Whether that image resembles the painting by Michelangelo of God atop a cloud with his white hair and beard, or maybe they imagine a more personable appearance, I am not going to spoil anyone's surprise, because sooner or later, you'll find out what he looks like yourself. I will simply say he looked friendly and exactly how *I* thought he would look.

As Bill and I entered the great hall, God embraced me. He hugged me like an old friend I hadn't seen in years or, as was the case here, as a father would hug a son. He grabbed my shoulders and pulled back as if to inspect me.

"Let me look at you," he said, and then turned to face Bill, "and you must be young Bill," he said as he grabbed Bill's hand and shook it vigorously. I supposed everyone was young to God: young Lincoln, young Churchill, and young Moses. I guess that when you were the one to get the ball rolling, and when you were however thousands of years old God was, everyone was younger than you.

"Welcome, welcome," he said again ushering Bill and I into the great hall. He looked around him and widened his arms, gesturing with his hands. "Welcome to HQ. Well, sort of HQ; this is more of a retreat from the hustle and bustle of our main office. We sometimes use it as a getaway, for weekends, and for senior staff." I was curious no more.

"So, this is Heaven? I mean, outside the castle, the meadows, and the orchard?" I asked God as he led Bill and me into the great hall.

"Part of it," said God, "you must realize that Heaven is more than a million times the size of Earth. It houses many, many residents from different time periods. This small area, and I mean the area outside the castle walls, is pretty much undeveloped." Undeveloped was right. As an architect based in Manhattan, to have that much open space to work with would be, well, Heaven.

God explained that time and other concepts, such as movement, were different in Heaven than on Earth; while he had duplicated a lot of man's structures and buildings in Heaven, he had done so to acclimatize new residents. The castle, he explained to Bill and I, was originally intended as a transitional resting place for knights killed during the crusades before they were transported to Heaven proper. The idea was to gently make them realize they would soon be meeting their recent foes, and when they discovered they all had been fighting for the same God, they wouldn't be too traumatized. God beckoned Bill and I to follow him further into the hall.

"Everyone's here," he said, "everyone that needs to be, that is. A couple couldn't make it, but not to worry," he confirmed. "It's a bit warm; we had to adjust the heat for your father," he said motioning toward Bill, "but we have plenty of iced tea, wine, and water. The caterers have done a fantastic job; I got Saint Lawrence to head up that. Considering he is the patron saint of cooks, I thought he'd do a good job. I like to do that, allocate tasks and projects to the right Saint; kind of keeps their hand in, if you know what I mean." God nudged me and flashed another one of his wide and beaming smiles.

He was not exaggerating about the heat. It must have been at least ninety degrees in the great hall, and a waft of warm air hit us as soon as we left the vicinity of the door. The great hall was just how Bill had described it to me during our journey; it was a massive room with a high ceiling, and I would say at least three hundred feet in length and about two hundred feet wide. The feeling I got was definitely medieval; I had seen movies on TV about

Robin Hood and Ivanhoe, and I had to admit, it seemed Hollywood had got it right. There were doors to the rear of the room which I presumed led to the chapel, as Bill had explained. Hung on all four walls were shields and banners. If they were duplicates created by God or the real thing brought by the fallen knights who had once passed through, I could not tell. About halfway along and in the center of every wall were large, beautifully crafted stained glass windows, which emitted light into the hall. I noticed there were though a few additions that the knights of old would have not seen during their time on Earth. Vector heaters sat at various locations, turned high to accommodate Lucifer. On a table, situated alongside the lefthand wall, sat a table laden with food and drink containers. It reminded me of a franchised hotel's complimentary breakfast buffet, with a microwave on standby, and pots that I presumed contained coffee and tea. I guessed this was the result of Saint Lawrence's efforts.

In the middle of the room, taking center stage was a large, round table. I had never seen such a table before; it was approximately eighty feet in diameter and took up much of the floor space. It seemed to be made of oak or some other sturdy wood. It looked antique, as if it had seen a lot of debate. As conference tables went, it had to be the most impressive I had ever seen. Spread around the table were ten chairs, evenly distanced from each other, which I guessed would have been from the same time period and designed by the same man who built the table. I noted three of the chairs were empty, but seven were occupied. God placed his hand on my shoulder.

"Admiring the table, eh, son?" he asked. "It's not a copy, it is actually the original. I managed to get it up here just before Camelot disappeared forever and just after Arthur arrived. He was delighted to see it again."

"You mean that this is *the* round table?" I asked, "The one from the Arthurian legend?"

God smiled and nodded his head. "Yes, but that was no legend; well, some of it was exaggerated. Merlin was no wizard, but the rest of it is true." I was tempted to ask about the Holy Grail but didn't. I would let someone else tell that tale. God led Bill and I to the table, and though nobody seated needed an introduction,

God, being the congenial host that he was, introduced Bill and I to some of the most recognizable faces in the history of mankind.

"Ok," said God, taking a deep breath and still smiling widely, "I'll go around the table quickly and introduce everybody." Bill and I stood open mouthed. Were we dreaming? It had to be the most surreal moment of my life to date, and I was the guy who walked on water!

"This is Mahatma," Gandhi rose and shook my hand first, then Bill's. "He doesn't say much," said God, "but when he does, we listen. Very resourceful, and he has great stamina. He was a little disappointed when he got here originally; expected to be reincarnated, didn't you?" God playfully rubbed Gandhi's bald head. Gandhi nodded, smiling. "But he soon got over it." God led Bill and I to the next seat.

"Mother Teresa of Calcutta," announced God.

"Please don't stand," said Bill as Mother Teresa began to rise. Mother Teresa gave a stern look and then smiled. She took my hand and shook it warmly even though her grip was not strong. She then took Bill's hand at the same time.

"Now, you two boys," she said in perfect English, "you be careful. You do know it can make you go blind?" Bill looked at her and tilted his head as if confused, and I felt myself blush.

"Next," said God as Mother Teresa returned to her seat from half rising, "Saint Peter." Saint Peter did not rise but nodded at both Bill and I.

"Hi," we both said together and waved at the bearded gentleman who was dressed in a flowing white robe and sandals.

He dabbed his forehead with a tissue. "Phew, it's hot," he said, smiling, as he waved the tissue in the air in a mock attempt to fan himself.

Next up was Joan of Arc, clad in full body armor and sporting, as I had always envisaged, a 'bowl haircut'. She too felt the effects of the heat, which surprised me. I would have thought she would have been used to the heat.

"Hello," she said, smiling as she bobbed about in her seat. "Hot in this armor," she said and gestured with her hand across her brow to emphasize the heat. "You'd think I'd be used to it by now!" She laughed loudly at her own joke. It wasn't a normal laugh but instead sounded like a pig snorting. She bobbed even more in her chair. Bill and I smiled at her weakly and proceeded to the next seat.

"Over here we have my old friend and sparring partner, Moses," exclaimed God. Moses was downing an ice tea when we reached his seat.

"Excuse me," he said as he wiped his hand across his mouth and then offered it to be shook. "Just grabbing a quick refresher before we start." I nodded my understanding. I was amazed at how much he resembled Kirk Douglas.

"I know what you're thinking," he said as he circled his face with his finger. He smiled and winked, "They cast that movie all wrong. The funny thing is that Spartacus, the real one who lives on the same block as me, is a dead ringer for Heston!" Moses threw his hands up in air as if the whole thing was an unbelievable oversight by Hollywood.

The next two attendees seated at the table certainly didn't need any introduction. The one with the red skin, horns, and little goatee beard was obviously Bill's Father. Lucifer rose as we approached, hugged Bill, and nodded at me.

"Good to see you, son," he said in an accent that Bill had already placed as Texan.

"Hi, Dad," said Bill, sounding like a schoolboy who had been kissed and hugged by his Mother in front of his friends. Lucifer looked pleased.

"Look at my boy," he boasted to the seated ensemble, "a chip off the old block, if I do say myself." He playfully ruffled Bill's slicked back hair, which, due to the amount of gel on it, made it stand up like porcupines.

I personally could see no family resemblance whatsoever, and I doubted the others in the room could either, but out of politeness, everyone implied they could see Bill was exactly like his father. Lucifer, or Satan as he liked to be called, gave me a nod and offered his hand.

"Lucifer," he announced, "but I prefer Satan," he said as we shook hands. "So what do you think of my boy?" he asked, still holding onto Bill's shoulder with the hand I didn't shake. "Ain't he something?" I agreed that Bill was indeed something. "We'll chat later, son," said Satan as he finally released his grip on Bill's shoulder and returned to his seat; he flashed me a smile and raised his hand "Good to meet you." God led Bill and I to the final occupied chair.

"I think it is about time you met your brother," said God.

"Half-brother," I reminded.

"To be decided," said Jesus as he rose from his seat.

CHAPTER

33

JESUS WAS AS I HAD always imagined; well, facially anyway. He had long hair and a beard. His complexion was swarthy, and I could see that in his day, many would have considered him an attractive man. He was dressed as though he had just flown in from the beach. He wore flared jeans and a white, baggy T-shirt; on his feet he wore flip-flops. He was, in all intents and purposes, the original hippy, and would not have looked out of place at Woodstock. He, unlike the other occupants of the great hall, was not smiling. I took his reluctantly outstretched hand.

"No holes," I said jokingly.

"What?" said Jesus, a stern look on his face.

"Your hands, you know, the crucifixion, the nails…there's no holes in them," I said gesturing to his palms, prodding my finger into the center of his hand. It was a silly joke, and considering the tension that already existed between us, in retrospect it was probably not apt. I remembered Harvey's warning of not "jiving" up here.

"Oh, goody gumdrops," exclaimed God cheerfully, "glad to see you two are getting along." He put one arm around my shoulder and the other around Jesus's. Jesus didn't say anything, just looked me up and down with a look that I would describe as contempt, and took his seat. He gave a quick nod of his head in the direction of Bill as a halfhearted greeting. It was obvious he didn't like me. Lucifer, meanwhile, had risen from his seat and was going around the table, like any proud father, showing off Bill to the rest of the group. I took my allotted seat as indicated by God, which was in between Gandhi and Saint Peter and directly opposite Jesus. Jesus eyed me suspiciously as he fiddled with his pen. I smiled at him, but he did not return my smile.

Once Lucifer had stopped showing off Bill and they had taken their respective seats, God took his chair which was bigger than the rest. With his big smile spread across his mouth, he tapped a pencil on a glass in front of him to indicate he had opened the proceedings. All heads turned toward God and any chatter immediately ceased. He stood to address the table.

"Well, as you all know, the last few weeks, especially the last few days, have been very trying indeed." He had both hands on the table, and he leaned forward, his head going around the table as if addressing everyone individually. "You have all met Bill and Seth." He looked first at Bill, then me, "and I am honored to have them here." There were murmurs of "here, here" from various places around the table. I noticed that Jesus was not one of those agreeing with God. "Of course, there is a reason for their presence at HQ today, and indeed, the presence of our old friend and dare I say 'nemesis,' Lucifer, who...." God drew his finger toward his chin and tapped it as if thinking, "now when it was it...." God pondered, "ah yes, who hasn't been here for over fifty thousand years, isn't it?" Satan smiled. It seemed he didn't mind God calling him Lucifer, but I doubted he would allow anyone else to call him it.

"Fifty-two," he corrected, raising his hand.

"Fifty-two!" shouted God, "It seems like yesterday." A few around the table, including Lucifer, laughed at God's words. Lucifer hadn't been back to HQ since he fell from grace and started up his own "franchise."

"Well, welcome back!" said God to Lucifer. "It's good to have you here."

As I had already gathered, God and Lucifer did spend time together but always on neutral ground. They seemed very friendly, and God was obviously delighted to have his old angel back in Heaven, if only for this extraordinary meeting. It was obvious to anyone that Lucifer still held God in high regard, and it seemed they had put their differences behind them regarding Bill's abandonment and God's extended travel plans thirty-two years before.

THE RELUCTANT JESUS

"I will now bring you all up to date on the full events leading up to today's 'pow-wow.'" God shuffled some papers laid on the table in front him and consulted what I assumed were prepared notes. I hoped whoever had prepared his notes was competent; I had heard so many horror stories about the admin department in Heaven, I feared that some inexperienced flunky might have passed God the wrong paper work. I imagined he had plans for the building of an ark or how to slay a giant with a stone laid out in front of him. He produced from nowhere a pair of reading glasses, which he perched on his nose. Luckily, the notes were the correct ones. God cleared his throat before speaking.

"Originally, when the chapter Revelation had been written and included in the Bible, it seems I approved the final draft for publication without reading the whole thing through thoroughly." God raised both his hands, admitting it was his mistake. "I hold my hands up to that! It was my fault and my responsibility to double check its contents, and I apologize for my tardiness."

There were murmurs of "no, no," and "not at all," from his forgiving audience. But God waved them away. "No, it was down to me; I should have read it." He dropped his hands and continued to speak; as he spoke, he occasionally referred to his notes. "So, it appears that for nearly two thousand years, man has been expecting some sort of final conflict and ultimate battle to determine the end of world. This battle is to be fought between our good friend Lucifer and his agent on Earth, and the 'lamb.'" He pointed toward me, toward Bill, and then Lucifer.

"This final battle was scheduled around the year two thousand, as not to disappoint the millions of souls who were expecting this final battle and end of days. Lucifer and I agreed we would both delegate two champions to fight on our behalf. In 1966, we found suitable mothers for these humans, and our two sons were born." Again he gestured to Bill and me. "Some of you may recall that back then, there was some discussion as to why I had not chosen Jesus to return to Earth, as many were expecting a second coming and the return of Jesus."

I glanced across at Jesus, who nodded to himself as if to say "yes, why not?" He saw me looking and once again, he gave me a look of utter contempt. I smiled weakly at him, but he shook his head and turned his attention back to God.

"I did consider this option," continued God "and, in fact, it was my first option and for a long time my favored option." Jesus looked at God as if surprised by the announcement. It appeared that this was news to him. "After much deliberation, however, I felt there were a number of reasons I should not send Jesus back to Earth. My first reasoning was that we would have an unfair advantage in the battle against Lucifer and his son, commonly known as the 'Beast.'" Lucifer shuddered at the mention of the word. God, I saw, noticed this, and improvised, "or the anti-Christ." Lucifer smiled and acknowledged God's words with a friendly nod. God returned to his prepared speech.

"Seeing as Jesus already had a large fan base and would have had vastly more experience than Lucifer's son, who I shall refer to now as the anti-Christ, I felt that by returning Jesus to Earth, it would have been a little unfair and not quite cricket." There were murmurings around the table. It seemed the rest of the committee was not aware of God's reasons for not returning Jesus to Earth. I was a little confused as to what "cricket" was. Later, Bob advised me it was a game that the English based on baseball, though I wasn't sure where he had gotten that fact.

"I know, I know," said God, once more raising his hands. "I should have made my reasoning clearer at the time, but that was not the only reason I felt a new face was needed down on Earth." God turned toward Jesus and looked at him with love and affection in his eyes. "Son, you had been through so much the first time. I didn't want you to go through it again. It was tough on you, and I thought it would be even tougher this time around. Things changed down there, and you had already done so much for the cause; it hardly seemed right sending you back. I felt you deserved your rest and your retirement." I looked across at Jesus, and I could see he was touched by what God had said.

"I know you were bitterly disappointed at the time, son, and rightly so," he said directly to Jesus, "but I felt I was doing the right thing by not just you, but by everyone. I was killing two birds with one stone, and I was hopefully ensuring your retirement remained peaceful and uneventful. I was trying to make it a fair fight for the souls on Earth."

Lucifer too was becoming emotional; he wiped a tear from his eye. I wondered if he had known that God had done the most honorable thing he could as to ensure that Lucifer's son would not be too heavily outnumbered. There were more murmurings from the table, but I got the feeling they were murmurings of understanding. It also seemed that Jesus understood his Father's reasoning, as his features softened and there was a new glow about him. He glanced at me and saw I watched him. He smiled gently at me and nodded. It seemed my brother had made peace with me. God continued to speak.

"However," he announced, "after finally reading Revelation once it had hit the streets, so to speak, I realized it was not what I had intended for neither the earth nor mankind. So I took it upon myself to contact my old friend, Lucifer." God indicated Lucifer, "I suggested that Revelation was more dramatic than it needed to be. I found all the violence and destruction rather too much. Lucifer agreed with me that the pain and suffering that would entail would be, above all things, a major drain on both our resources. The destruction of the planet and the melting of eyes from sockets was really, well, unnecessary. The last thing I wanted was a barren wasteland to have to rebuild on. We therefore agreed upon a far more civilized way of settling the prophecy outlined in Revelation. In 1976, when we discussed this subject, a new craze was emerging on Earth: video games." God looked around the table as if he were a professor passing on important and previously unheard of information to a class full of pupils.

"These things seemed liked an ideal way of settling differences. No one got hurt, and no damage was done to the environment or planet as a result. We agreed that this was an ideal way to execute the final conflict. It would take the form of a video game contest." God paused and took a sip of water from the glass on the table in front of him.

"As it was written and prophesized, the Messiah, or Seth, as he is known, would prevail, the battle was meant to be a token gesture, as not to disappoint the 'fans' or the traditionalists down on Earth." Lucifer nodded his agreement, as if acknowledging he recalled the agreement and that what God said was indeed a true recollection of the facts.

"As I knew I had upset and disappointed Jesus, I gave him the important task of ensuring that the mother of my second child was a virgin and stayed a virgin until conception. Unfortunately, and again, I am as much to blame as anyone for this; it seems there is doubt to the parentage of the Christ. Seth over there," God pointed to me. "There occurred, as you are all well aware, an unreported 'Code Dave.'" God sighed slightly when he mentioned the dreaded 'Code Dave.' He flicked over the paper he was reading from and continued.

"Now, somewhere along the track, my old friend Lucifer and I lost sight of things on Earth for a while. I encouraged him to join me on a trip around the Universe to help me develop other planets for possible future projects. Well, as the committee well knows, this trip became longer than expected. We found a lovely little spot that we simply could not tear ourselves away from. Or should I say, I couldn't tear myself away from. Lucifer, the old softy, kept on at me about our parenting responsibilities and how we should return to Earth. He badgered me every day; of course, rule number 123.3AV states that poor old Lucifer cannot be left to his own devices on Earth in my absence. Therefore, he had no choice but to stay with me. I suppose I could be described as being self-centered and self-absorbed with the whole traveling the Universe thing. I was having a great time, and being able to relax after thousands of years of creating made me complacent." God once again raised his hands in his way of admitting responsibility. I looked around the table for any reaction to this admission of guilt, but it seemed his confession was enough to appease the committee, as there were no murmurings.

"I can understand your resentment toward me," said God as he turned to face me. "I was indeed an absentee father; I should have been there for you and should have guided you, taught you, and helped you prepare for what I expected you to do." God shifted his gaze to Bill.

"Also I apologize to you too, Bill." Bill shifted uneasily in his chair. "It was my fault you father wasn't around for you. You shouldn't blame him one bit; I assure you he wanted nothing more than to be with you and watch you grow." Bill nodded that he accepted God's apology. God then turned to Lucifer.

"I also understand why my old sparring partner, Lucifer decided he would not adhere to the rules and the prophecy by attempting to win the final conflict and claiming, by default, the rights to the earth and all souls contained therein. Any loving father would have done the same, and I admit, I did feel uneasy about condemning the loser of the final conflict to the pit." Lucifer looked a little sheepish, and I thought he might have been blushing. He raised his left hand as if admitting his underhandedness. God turned over another sheet of paper and again coughed to clear his throat.

"This brings us to today," he looked around the table, "first of all, there is the immediate question of Seth's paternity and whether I am his real father." I shifted in my chair. "Well, unfortunately, we have no way of determining whether I am his real father or not." This surprised me. I listened as God explained.

"Due to the fact I made man in my own image, any DNA test would match. My DNA matches everyone's on Earth; it's a flaw, but something we are working on for the future." Unfortunately, it seemed I would never know for sure if my father was my Uncle Jacob or God. I hoped it was God. "I have come up with a proposal and solution to this whole business, which has been a cock up from the start." I glanced at Bill, who glanced back at me. Was this a way out for us?

"I propose that we postpone the battle for Earth and Armageddon for a period of one hundred years." There were murmurings again, and God raised his hands, asking for calm. "I know this is bit of a letdown for some of you, but hear me out, please," said God to the assembled table. "I propose we delay the battle for one hundred years, and my representative in this postponed battle be none other than Jesus Christ. He will be resurrected and shall descend onto the earth as expected by his followers." Jesus beamed with pride. Saint Peter, who sat next to Jesus, patted him on the back in a gesture of congratulations. God turned to directly face Lucifer.

"To compensate you for this change of plan and for all my other mistakes, I will allow you to have your own representative in this delayed battle at liberty without infringement on Earth, which, if you think about it, means you have one hundred years of unchallenged and unmonitored evil-doing. What do you say, old pal?" Lucifer turned to Bill and then turned back to God.

"Before I agree or disagree, could I be permitted to speak with my son in private for a moment?" requested Lucifer in his Texan drawl.

"Of course," said God. Lucifer rose from his seat and motioned for Bill to join him. Out of earshot from the rest of the table, Lucifer and Bill conversed. Lucifer did most of the talking, and Bill did most of the listening. After five minutes, Lucifer patted Bill on the back and hugged him. They then both returned to the table.

"Okay," said Lucifer as he retook his seat, "I have spoken to Bill, and he is in agreement with this. I have another candidate, currently on Earth, who though not actually a blood relative, is doing a fine impersonation of the anti-Christ. I propose that this individual be my new representative on Earth and, when the time comes, he shall represent me in the battle of Armageddon." Once again, there were murmurings from the table. God raised his arms to quell the chatter.

"Who is this person?" asked God. Lucifer leaned over to God's notes and, with a pencil, scribbled onto the paper. God raised his eyebrows as if he knew the name Lucifer had penned. "Oh, *him*," said God and he passed the paper with the scribbled name along the table. Each committee member nodded their agreement. But before the paper reached either Bill or I, God snatched it back.

"Sorry," he said, "but I don't think you need to know this information just yet. But I am sure you will figure it out eventually," I agreed, as did Bill, that we didn't want to know who the new anti-Christ was going to be. God once again turned to face Lucifer.

"Ok, it is agreed. I must say, I thought he was already working for you. It's a good choice, as he is naturally evil and even looks the part. I suppose you are going to give him a helping hand?"

The Devil laughed and nodded. "Well, maybe I have already been whispering in his ear, but for what I have planned, he will need more help!"

God chuckled. "I thought so." He poked a friendly finger towards Lucifer. I turned to Bill and shrugged; neither of us had a clue who they were talking about.

"As for Bill," said Lucifer, "I think he has been through a lot, and he has agreed to step down as the anti-Christ, should this be agreed." I nodded at Bill and smiled. He was off the hook and was no longer the anti-Christ.

"So," continued God, "a vote is in order." The committee would have the final say on the proposal. "I think the best way to do this would be a show of hands," said God "all those who agree we should delay Armageddon for one hundred years, please raise your right hand."

The vote was unanimous. It was settled. Jesus was especially pleased. He sat with a beaming smile spread across his face as Moses leaned over and shook his hand.

"That's settled, then," said God. Everyone stood, and Lucifer and God shook hands on the deal as Joan of Arc congratulated Jesus.

Gandhi made his excuses and left immediately whilst Joan of Arc said she needed some air. I turned to Bill. "What now, do you think?" I asked him. Bill was as confused as I was.

"I have no idea," he replied. We were interrupted by Jesus, who appeared at my shoulder. He gently tapped it.

"Excuse me," said my possible half-brother. He held out his hand. "Look," he began, "I think maybe I gave you a hard time."

"Well, I did sense a little animosity," I replied as I shook his hand.

"I was upset that Dad didn't want me to be back down there," he said, motioning to the ground. I presumed he meant Earth. "I deliberately used you to get back at him, and for that, I sincerely apologize." Jesus did sound sincere. As a Jew, I didn't know too much about the guy, but he seemed pleasant enough, and I found myself liking him.

"It's been hard," he continued. "The last two thousand years I've been twiddling my thumbs and kicking my heels, doing the odd job now and then, but I have missed it." Jesus gazed into the distance. "The dinners, the crowds, the miracles, yes, and even the attention. It was like being a celebrity," he broke his gaze, "but of course, that's not just it. I like those people." I presumed he was referring to the human race. Jesus broke off from his thoughts. "Well, all's well that ends well," he said and with that, he left the hall. That was the last I ever saw of Jesus "H" Christ.

"He seems happy enough," said Bill.

"Well, he got what he wanted; he was the right man for the job from the start," I said. "I would have been like Roger Moore as James Bond. I could never fill the shoes of Sean Connery." Bill looked confused, and I told him to forget it.

"Is he here?' asked Bill.

"Who?" I asked.

"Sean Connery," said Bill. Luckily, God interrupted our conversation before Bill got even more confused.

"A satisfactory conclusion, don't you think?" said God as he joined Bill and I.

"It seems that way. It went very well I thought," I said. "What about us? What happens now?" I added, concerned that I had a wedding to plan and my own child to prepare for. God ignored my question.

"It all came to me in a flash, a bit like South America did, I thought, 'now God, you're a bright enough fellow, surely if anyone can sort this out, you can.' I sat down and hey presto, it came to me. Send Jesus back and postpone everything." He smiled, seemingly extremely pleased with himself.

"Yes," I said, "but what's next for Bill and me?"

"Ah yes," said God, "you must both return to Earth immediately. But as for everything else, it is all over. You are both hereby officially relieved of your duties."

"Are you going to wipe our memories?" asked Bill, "like in *Men in Black?*"

"Not at all, my dear boy," said God. "Let's face it, who would believe such a ridiculous story anyway?" God was right, of course. Who in their right mind would believe any of this? It was downright bizarre. If Bill, Maggie, Bob, or I dared to tell this story, we would be laughed out of town. I had no intention of ever repeating the events of the last few weeks to anyone, and I felt pretty sure that Bill felt the same way. As Ely and Irma had their own problems, I doubted they would breathe a word also. As I pondered this, Bill went to bid a final farewell to his Father, which left me alone with God. "Well, it has certainly been interesting." I said. "I am sorry if I came across as somewhat reluctant or uncooperative."

God waved his hands. "No, son. It was my fault. I was insensitive, and it was stupid of me to put this all onto you." He put his arm around me. "Listen, I know there is doubt in your mind as to who your real father is," he looked around to check that no one was listening, "but I am going to let you in on a little secret," again he shifted his eyes to check that no one could hear, "you are my son. I checked the logs. It seems that Jacob was firing blanks! He was infertile! He knew it himself. I sent someone around to see him; he is up here, and he confirmed it. Something to do with standing too close to radars or something like that."

Despite Jesus's attempts at sabotaging my virgin birth, I was indeed God's son. Of course, God had used the questionability of my paternity to his advantage, allowing him to rebuild his relationship with Jesus and ensuring a probable victory in the final conflict to come.

"Ok," he said as he beckoned Bill. "You two need to take that door," he said, pointing to a wooden door located at the far end of the great hall. "When you go through it, take the left. Do not, and I must reiterate this, do not go toward the light. Go left and keep walking. Any questions?"

I didn't have any, but Bill had one final question. I guessed it was his opportunity to ask about the ladybugs. "Yes," said Bill, "I have a question. Who is Bernard?"

God pulled his head back. "Ah, Bernard, good question. Poor Bernard arrived here about an hour ago. Died rather suddenly, I am afraid. Turns out, his doctor confused his chart with somebody else's. Poor chap had been walking around with an incurable and fatal illness for months without even knowing it. Dropped dead on his round. He was a postal worker, I think; I kind of felt sorry for him, so I gave him something to do until I could speak to him. Awfully nice chap, extremely knowledgeable, especially about dogs. Odd thing is, and one heck of a coincidence, he has the same doctor as you, Seth." God winked at me. Bill and I made our way toward the door indicated by God as the one we should take.

"She was hot, wasn't she?" said Bill

"Who?" I asked.

"Joan of Arc," said Bill.

"Well, it was over ninety degrees in there," I replied.

"No. I mean hot as in hot in her costume; my type of chick," said Bill.

"Somehow, Bill, I get the feeling you are going to be meeting a lot of your type of chicks in the future." We both turned and gave one final wave to God and Lucifer, who stood, together waving. I opened the door, and we both walked through it.

CHAPTER

34

THE ROOM WAS NOT FAMILIAR, but the smell was. It was the sterile, clean smell of a hospital. I stared at the ceiling, confused as to how I had arrived here. I lifted my head and sat up. I saw there was another bed in the hospital room and Bill, who was also just waking, occupied it.

"Are you alright?" I asked Bill quietly.

"Yes," replied Bill "and you?"

"Yeah, I think so; a little groggy, but mostly confused," I replied scratching my head. I was dressed, as was Bill, in the standard hospital smock, and though there were monitors and drips besides both our beds, neither of us appeared to be connected to any sort of life-supporting system.

"Was that all a dream?" I asked, referring to our trip to Heaven and our visit to the castle.

"I don't think so," said Bill, sitting upright, "if you remember it and I remember it, then it can't have been a dream." Bill was right. Just to double check, we ran through the events that seemed to have just occurred, right up until we entered the long corridor through the oak door at the end of the great hall. We had done as God instructed and gone left, or was it right? I couldn't remember. I do know we did not go toward any light.

"Where are we?" asked Bill looking around the room.

"My first guess would be is that we are in a hospital," I said. I often wondered how this supposed computer genius got by in life. "Wouldn't you agree?" I said, pointing to our bed smocks and the equipment by our beds. I even tapped the bed. "Hospital bed," I said, "usually found in hospitals." Bill ignored my sarcasm.

"But how?" queried Bill, "How did we get here? In fact, how did we get to Heaven?" They were good questions, and I didn't have the answer to either one. Luckily, Bob, Maggie, and Nancy did.

Maggie, Bob, and Nancy entered our room just as Bill posed his questions. Maggie rushed over to where I lay, hugged my shoulders, and gave me a kiss on the forehead.

"Thank God you are ok," she cried. She looked over at Bill, "both of you." I kissed Maggie on the lips and smiled.

"Hey, don't cry," I said. I could see she had red blotches under her eyes. "I am fine, we both are. To be honest, we were just discussing how we got here." It was Nancy who told us. Bob introduced his wife to Bill, and I, in turn introduced Bill to Bob and Maggie. We all listened as Nancy explained the events leading up to our arrival in hospital.

Apparently, according to Nancy, who had been the first on the scene of the accident, Bill and I were rear seat passengers in a yellow cab that, probably due to the slippery surface of the roads, was unable to stop when it suddenly found itself against a line of stationery vehicles all stopped due to the torrential rain which caused flooding and unbelievable traffic congestion throughout Manhattan. Our cab ploughed into the rear of a non-moving dumpster truck. Bill and I were thrown about the back of the cab and knocked unconscious. Eyewitness saw our cab driver fleeing the scene, and they found it remarkable that he had not been injured, considering the front of the vehicle was completely crushed. Nancy had been the first to arrive on the scene and had performed emergency CPR on both Bill and I. After someone called an ambulance, we were both rushed to the New York Downtown Hospital, where doctors immediately placed Bill and I into intensive care. Apparently we were both on the verge of death, and at one point, the last rites were administered over Bill, and a Rabbi was called to my side. This had been a week ago.

"A week ago!" exclaimed Bill. "You are kidding, right?" he asked. I was in just as much shock as he was. It seemed the life support equipment by our respective beds had been attached to our bodies for the last five days; we had both been in comas.

Nancy had called Bob, who had called Maggie, and both she and Bob had been at the hospital waiting for Bill and me to come out of our comas. Two hours ago, amazed doctors had informed them that we were out of our comas and we were both sleeping. They had removed the life support machines and thought it wise to let us sleep. They were dumfounded because we had both shown exactly the same symptoms throughout the week and had both recovered from our comas at exactly the same time.

A doctor arrived just as Nancy had finished explaining the events of the week. He stuck a light in my eyes and asked me a few simple questions; he did the same to Bill. He removed his stethoscope from his ears and shook his head.

"I don't get it," he said, "you're both fine. Everything is normal; no cuts, no scratches, and all tests have come back normal. I have never seen anyone recover like this before, let alone two people. It is quite remarkable, miraculous even." Bill and I thanked the doctor, who signed some paperwork and said we could leave whenever we wanted. I looked at Nancy, and I wondered how much she knew.

"Thanks, Nancy," I said, "for saving my life."

"Me too," joined in Bill. Nancy didn't say anything at first. She stood, stony-faced, and then she did something I did not expect. She flashed me a smile and came over to my bed and hugged me. As she leant over, she whispered in my ear.

"I know. Don't worry; I think it's great, and congratulations," I looked at her "about Maggie and the baby." It seemed Bob had confided in his wife after all and told her everything. At first she was skeptical, but after she had met Maggie at the hospital and had heard the story from her, she began to believe. It seemed her newfound attitude toward me had nothing to do with the fact that I was fleetingly the Messiah; it was due to the fact that, at last, I had taken on some responsibility, and as I was about to become a father and a husband, I was no longer a threat to her.

We all agreed that Milligan's was probably the best place for us to regroup and rather than take a cab, Bill, Maggie, and I took the subway whilst Nancy and Bob took a ride in Nancy's squad car. We arrived just as Nancy and Bob pulled up to the curb. I bought a round of drinks from Sean, who called me Seth, and when I returned with them to our table, Bill and I told them what had occurred in Heaven.

After we had finished relaying our story, we all sat in silence. God was right about time having no meaning in Heaven. What had felt like a few hours in Heaven was a week on Earth. It was mind boggling. It was Maggie who spoke first.

"So, it's over?" she asked.

"Yes, it's over, I am not the Christ, and Bill is not the anti-Christ. It also seems that none of us at least will be around for Armageddon either," I raised my pint of Guinness to my lips, "and I can drink to that."

"What now?" asked Bob. "We carry on as normal, as if none of this ever happened? Boy, that's a tough call. I enjoyed being your disciple," he smiled and patted me on the back.

Bill was the next to speak. "Well, one good thing, at least. I have found four new friends." Bill raised his glass of Cristal champagne to his lips, and his Rolex caught the light, glistening on his wrist.

All our lives had changed dramatically; I was to be a father and husband. Bill had found a new confidence and friends. His whole persona had changed, and it was impossible to imagine him as his former self. Maggie was soon to embrace motherhood and her life had found a new purpose and meaning.

"I propose a toast," I said and we all five raised our glasses.

"To friends," I said.

"To friends," we all said together.

CHAPTER 35

FOURTEEN YEARS HAVE PASSED SINCE that night in Milligan's when we all toasted and drank to friends. Much has happened since then, and the world has changed; some might say not for the better. My life has changed beyond all recognition from what it was in 1999. Maggie gave birth to our third child, Luke, just three weeks ago; he joins Matthew, who is now seven, and our eldest, Molly, my little princess, who is nearly thirteen.

I became a partner as promised in Henry's company. The church deal fell through; apparently the bishop had suffered some sort of memory loss and had no recollection of the deal. It didn't matter, as Hyomoko gave us just as much work. In fact, we couldn't have coped with both contracts, so Henry let the church off and did not sue for breach of contract. I told him God would reward him in Heaven, but he just laughed.

Maggie retired from law and has become the happy homemaker. She is doing a great job with our kids, and I have promised to take her skiing on our anniversary this August. I am happy to say that she has returned to the Catholic Church and re-found her once lost religion. Though we do not see eye-to-eye on some aspects of the philosophy, we agree to disagree.

I moved out of my apartment, and we got a great house over the water in Jersey where Walter, who remarkably is still going strong and doesn't seemed to have aged, loves to play with the children in the orchard we have at the bottom of our garden. I often ask Molly and Matthew if Walter ever speaks to them, but they think Daddy is being silly.

Ely and Irma, on my advice, sought counseling for both their marriage and sex. On one hand, I am happy to report that they forgave each other for each other's infidelities with their respective siblings, and their marriage is stronger than it ever was. I am not as happy to report that Molly caught them making love again last week in our greenhouse. That is the third time in so many months. They are thrilled at being grandparents; the only problem is revolving visiting the family and me with their twice-daily lovemaking schedule.

Harvey, my gansta-rapping guardian angel, is a regular visitor to the house. The kids love his visits, especially as he has become somewhat of a celebrity. We still call him Harvey, but he is now known to his legions of fans as "Ice Cross, the Gansta Rappin' Soul Saver" his first single "Bitchin wid da God Pimp" became a worldwide hit. However, he does not call me "Lil' Jesus" in front of strangers.

Bob and Nancy Nancy separated and divorced six months after our celebration in Milligan's, only to get back together six months after that and re-marry. Nancy could not take the ribbing from her colleagues and friends when she reverted to her maiden name of Mucus. They now have two great kids, and after what Nancy called a "miracle diet plan," she was voted Miss NYPD two years running. I have to say, she does look great, but her diet was no miracle, and I should know. Bob keeps threatening to write a book one day based on a fictional character who claims to be the Son of God and the new Messiah. He wants to make it a comedy, but I told him not to bother; it would not be that funny, and who would be interested anyway? In the meantime, the school promoted him to principal, and though the kids call him "Mr. Ferret Face" behind his back, it doesn't seem to bother him. We see the Nancys often, and my son Mathew and Bob Junior are good pals.

Uncle Bill, as Molly calls him, we don't see as often, but that isn't surprising, seeing as though he lives in Japan with his bride, Omi. Omi is the current World Cosplaying Champion and a former Miss Japan. Bill made a spectacular comeback onto the world Space Invader scene when he re-won the title he had last held over twenty years before, setting, in the process, a new high scoring record, surpassing the old one by five thousand points. Only last week *Bytes*, which I still have delivered, did a four-page spread on the "pin-up boy" of video gaming. We hope to see Bill and Omi this coming Christmas, when he is over here, launching his new game, *Return to Castle Hell*. I have read in reviews that the game will sell millions, and the main character is an all-action postal worker on a mission from God called Bernard.

As for everything else and the state of the world, I see God was true to his word, and he is indeed letting Lucifer have a free reign, sort of. Neither my children nor I will be around when my brother returns to Earth to sort out this mess once and for all, but my grandchildren will be, and so will their children, and I hope their Great Uncle looks them up before he saves the world from evil.

Every third Monday of the month at around eight in the evening, I get a phone call. I gently shove Walter out of the chair where he sits by the phone so I can talk to my regular caller. He asks about his grandkids, and sometimes he speaks to Maggie if she is not too busy with the children. We pass the time of the day and talk about father and son things. No longer an absentee dad, he regularly watches over my family, and he assures me day and night, despite his busy schedule, that he will never miss a call. Everyone 'up there' who knows me always sends their best. He has a new administrative system, Windows-based, he tells me, and though there still is red tape, overall things seem to be working a lot better in Heaven. They are prospecting another planet later on in the year, but he hopes to be back for Christmas. Jesus would be disappointed if he missed yet another birthday, and he assures me he will still call me to keep in touch.

So life goes on, at least for another eighty years at least, and though tempted, I haven't tried any miracles of late. I have to admit, I did do a sneaky one back in 2000. My beloved Yankees won the World Series for the third time straight, beating our great rivals, the Mets, in a five game series, four to one. What? Oh, come on, please. You didn't think they managed that without a little help, did you? It was courtesy of me, my final miracle, as The Reluctant Jesus.